TRAIN
to
HELL'S
GATE

TRAIN
to
HELL'S
GATE

R D Rettew

XULON PRESS

Xulon Press
2301 Lucien Way #415
Maitland, FL 32751
407.339.4217
www.xulonpress.com

Printed in the United States of America.

ISBN-13: 9781545623367

PART ONE
THE LETTER

CHAPTER 1

Vancouver. British Columbia, Canada

*"Oh what a tangled web we weave when first
we practice to deceive."*
– Sir Walter Scott - 1808

It was a beautiful morning, until the letter arrived.

Fouad, who always enjoyed his paper with breakfast, was sitting out in their garden patio, reading the latest issue of Al Ahram, Cairo's Arabic paper. Then, after scanning the headlines of the local Vancouver Sun, he put down his paper and looked off through the beautiful area surrounding their home by the university's campus.

He was thinking that Vancouver was such a hospitable city for them to come to as foreigners. It was more than a beautiful city with an excellent climate. They had discovered that it was also a great multicultural city. About fifty percent of Vancouver's population consisted in people like themselves, people for whom English was not their first language.

Our life here is certainly quite a contrast to what it was back in Egypt. We are sheltered from the spreading conflict and war in the Middle East that is destroying families and creating a world filled with millions of homeless. Here we are protected from that epidemic of hatred spread by men justifying their evil by calling themselves jihadists.

It is so satisfying to be teaching here. I can address major issues of the day. The three years since joining the faculty here in Vancouver have gone by quickly. My courses in Middle East Studies deal with the real issues. Best of all, here I can really prepare my students to confront the realities of our world today.

Fouad lowered the paper to watch his wife, Vashti, setting out their breakfast on the patio table. What a wonderful woman. In that lovely Egyptian robe, with her long dark hair falling loosely over her shoulders, she's really beautiful.

Fouad was feeling good about the life they were experiencing as a couple in Canada. Our life together here is so enjoyable. We have so many friends. And real friends! God has been good to us. He has deepened our life together. What a wonderful marriage we enjoy.

It was one of those mornings when Fouad had no early class. Vashti had promised a special breakfast, one like they might have had back in Cairo. It took perseverance to find all the ingredients but she had persisted.

As they shared the result of her efforts Vashti asked, "Well, how did I do?"

"It's delicious. I need another serving." With a laugh, Fouad repeated his verdict in Coptic Arabic, "*Dah lazeez aawee.*"

Vashti felt like exercising her prerogative to check out her husband's clothing. "Fouad, you really are a three piece suit man. I like the gold watch chain across your vest. You're a professor and you look like a professor. With your distinctive white hair and beard, with those bushy white eyebrows, everyone on campus knows you. The tortoiseshell glasses complete the picture." She paused to focus her eyes on him. "And I love you."

"Thank you. The feeling is mutual."

They sat there silently enjoying each other.

Vashti laughed. "Don't let your Turkish kahvesi put coffee stains on that handsome mustache." She loved the way his tan face set off his white hair and beard.

Vashti enjoyed just looking at her husband across the table. "Fouad, I enjoy being your wife. I enjoy our life here. I really feel quite westernized. The Creator knew what he was doing when, as our Christian friends say, he established and blessed the marriage of a man and a women for the welfare of mankind."

Fouad said, "Our life here is certainly a contrast to the things I read in Al Ahram.

Vashti glanced at the Cairo headlines. "Yes, we enjoy a very different life here."

Fouad nodded. "It's not only the freedom from all the political turmoil. It's the fullness of our life here." He reached out and held her hand.

Suddenly their mailman surprised them by coming around to the back patio. With a big grin he said, "I have what looks like a very special letter for you. I thought I'd come around and deliver this one personally."

Fouad greeted him. "Mr. Werner, we have a special treat for you. Join us for some Egyptian coffee."

Vashti moved quickly to serve him. "This is the real stuff, Mr. Werner. We won't take no for an answer. No one will ever know you took this coffee break."

Vashti took the small copper coffee pot, her *cezve,* and poured out the mixture of fine coffee grounds with hot water and sugar into a small porcelain cup. "Here, Mr. Werner, and with your coffee enjoy some Egyptian flat bread" She laughed, "Your increased efficiency will make up for any time lost."

Their mailman sipped his coffee and smiled. "This is quite an experience. I have to tell you why I brought your mail back here. I have what looks like a very special letter for you. It's from Egypt and since you're from Egypt, I decided I should deliver it to you personally."

Fouad took the letter. "Many thanks, Mr. Werner. Yes, the envelope is wall papered with Egyptian stamps. Look at all these images of the Great Sphinx of Giza. Thanks, Mr. Werner. We appreciate the special delivery."

After their friend was gone Fouad just stood there with the envelope in his hand. As their eyes met Fouad and Vashti reinforced each other's fear.

Fouad expressed what they were both thinking. "This letter looks just like that special letter we got from Nile University three years ago. Yes, it's from the same department there in Cairo.

As Fouad held the letter they looked at each other with a great apprehension. They both saw that the envelope looked exactly like a very disturbing letter they had received from the university back in Egypt three years earlier. It stirred up for both of them some very unpleasant memories. Fouad looked at the letter. "I'm not sure I want to even open it."

When they received that very similar looking letter three years earlier, Fouad was in the process of accepting a new and challenging job, the faculty position he now enjoyed at the university in Vancouver. He had been in the process of forwarding his credentials to Vancouver. Then, in the midst of the process, he had received a similar official looking letter from the same office.

That letter had notified Fouad that there were some questions regarding his credentials. Confirmation of his credentials for the position in Vancouver would not be issued until he came in and cleared up these issues in Cairo.

When Fouad met with the his department heads he learned that his credentials would not be forwarded to Vancouver until he agreed that, while living in Canada, he would serve as recruiter and regional director for the Two Vipers Brotherhood in Canada.

The department made it very clear that his academic credentials would be provided only if he agreed to maintain a private office in Toronto to further the interests of Two Vipers. It was clear that he had no choice but to submit to their demands.

Now, Fouad found himself holding a very similar looking letter from the very same officers of the university. As they looked at each other, the eyes of Fouad and Vashti reflected their shared fear over what demands this letter might contain.

Three years ago, Fouad had no choice but to accept the conditions set forth. During his first year in Canada he worked to recruit new Canadian immigrants from the Middle East for the Two Vipers Brotherhood. However, as he and Vashti began to enjoy their Canadian life, Fouad found increasing difficulty in having anything to do with Two Vipers and their anti-west agenda. During the past year, Fouad had been merely going through the motions of recruiting new Middle East immigrants for Two Vipers.

Now, as they looked at this very similar looking letter from the same office of the university, they both were wondering what new demands might be contained in this letter.

Finally, Fouad opened the letter, He spread it out on the table and read it aloud for them, "Professor Fouad: The scheduled lecturer for this year's Pyramid lectures has suddenly become seriously ill. Yesterday, with no advance notice, he informed us that he would be unable to deliver the planned lectures. These widely promoted lectures are scheduled to begin in a little more than three weeks. Many plan to attend these lectures. We have a problem. We need someone who can step in and present lectures close to the announced subject, The Arab Spring as Seen Today.

"Since you are on our list for a future invitation we are asking you, as a highly esteemed alumnus of Nile University, to help us meet this crisis. We believe that if you accept this invitation you will continue the Pyramid lectures tradition with distinction.

"We are suggesting an appropriate shift in topic as follows, The Arab Spring as viewed from the West.

"We are confident that you, a scholar with a doctorate from the Middle East, now lecturing on Middle East Studies in Vancouver, would fill this position with distinction.

"We recognize that this is extremely short notice. The lectures begin in a little over three weeks. We believe that you could adapt some of your recent lectures in Vancouver and fill this assignment to address Middle East student and others with distinction.

"We hope that, with your help, we will not have to cancel the Pyramid Lectures. We send this official invitation to you in writing by express mail. Arrangements are described on the adjacent pages. Upon receipt of this official invitation, please reply immediately by phone."

Fouad and Vashti looked at each other in amazement. They were overwhelmed that Fouad was being honored with an invitation to return to his university in Cairo as a special guest lecturer.

"Quite an honor and a major recognition of you as a scholar," Vashti said.

"Vashti, this subject is right at the heart of my interests. It would be very appropriate for me, an Egyptian teaching in the west, to return to my university for presentations on the Arab Spring as seen in the West. Growing deadly turmoil and war is spreading over the Middle East, since the Arab Spring broke forth in Tahir Square in January of 2011. This invitation is an opportunity to address real world issues. I am a product of the Middle East. I specialize in Middle East Studies. My current lectures deal weekly with issues that threaten greater world turmoil. They came to the right man more than they realize for this assignment. If I am granted leave by my faculty here in Canada I will go to Cairo. I will exploit this opportunity. I will meet their schedule. Vashti, I'm loaded on this subject."

Vashti's eyes sparkled as she laughed. "Yes, and now you've been given the opportunity to lighten that load in Cairo."

Fouad studied the letter again. "This is astonishing. Vashti, this opportunity is really an answer to our daily prayer for peace in the Middle East. Just because we've moved to British Columbia doesn't mean we have stopped praying for our homeland. We have been praying that the Arab Spring would lead to more than political change. Our Arab brothers and sisters, and the whole Middle East need an alternative mind set, a spiritual change. The Middle East world needs, as that brilliant Somali woman urges, a reformation, a turn around. Our own discoveries of new life here have shown us how, throughout history, God's way to bring real change in this world has been through changed persons."

Vashti nodded, "Yes, Fouad. Egypt and the Middle East need far more than simply political change, more than freedom from rulers like Mubarak or Morsi. Egypt needs escape from all the manipulations of men to gain power."

Fouad agreed. "All across North Africa and the Middle East the Arab Spring has degenerated into chaos. Throughout the Arab world, millions of helpless people are being driven from areas in the Middle East where they have lived in for centuries. Homeless families living in tents or less, along with migrants, number in the millions. People are being exploited and destroyed by so-called militants and self-promoting terrorists who call themselves jihadists. The world changing power of religion has been seized by politicians to gain power for themselves."

"You are being given an opportunity to speak to the heart of a world crisis."

"Vashti, we want real freedom for Egypt and the greater Arab world. That calls for more than changes in political leadership. It calls for changed people. Our lives have been changed here in Canada. Now, I am suddenly invited to return to Cairo to speak on the future of Egypt and the Arab world. Amazing."

Vashti was quite for a few moments. She was wondering whether what was running through her mind was also disturbing Fouad.

Finally, Vashti expressed her fears. "Fouad, are you thinking, what I am thinking? With all its flattery, this letter somehow puts me on my guard. I think my fears come from more than a woman's intuition. This letter seems suspiciously almost too good to be true. Could there be something else behind this invitation? This letter comes from the very same men and the same department that sent us that threatening letter three years ago. This letter comes from men with a world view totally different from ours. I still don't trust them. Do you experience something of the same feelings, Fouad?"

Their eyes met. "Yes, Vashti, we share the same questions."

Vashti said, "Both of us have the same basic questions. Yes, you can deliver these lectures with distinction. What I want to know is how this invitation came to us. Your one remaining friend and advocate on the faculty, your old adviser, is no longer with the university. Whose idea was it to invite you? Who was your advocate? Could there be some further reason behind this letter of invitation?"

"Vashti, the subject of the lectures is at the heart of my concerns. Yes, this invitation raises many questions. Yes, the opportunity sounds almost too good. However, as an Egyptian in the West, I am well positioned to lecture on this world changing subject."

"Fouad, they know of your slowdown in recruiting immigrants for the Two Viper Brotherhood. They must be very dissatisfied with your service to them in Canada. Once they learn you are coming to Cairo, the leaders will want you to meet with them in Gaza City. They will insist that you travel from Cairo to Gaza City to meet with them."

"Yes, they must realize that I have been merely going through the motions."

Vashti said, "They would be even more upset, Fouad, if they had any idea of the real turn around in our lives since coming here. We have simply no sympathy for the anti-west objectives of the Two Vipers brotherhood."

Fouad agreed, "We have become Canadians. We love this country. Our friends are here. Meeting with the Two Vipers in Gaza City will be difficult but I think I can handle it."

Vashti poured out her concerns. "Fouad, this invitation is an honor. It recognizes you as a scholar. It's a feather in your cap as a professor." She paused. Then with tears in her eyes she said. "My woman's intuition says that there is more to this letter. This letter is not telling us everything. Coming from these men, there is something dishonest with this letter."

Fouad put his arms around Vashti and they held each other close.

Vashti continued, "If you go to Cairo, Two Vipers will insist that you visit them in Gaza City. Since the uprising against Mubarak and the overthrow of President Morsi, both Cairo and Gaza City are dangerous places for people like you. Gaza City spells trouble. It is a very dangerous place for people like ourselves."

Fouad said, "Yes, knowing the present makeup of the faculty over there, I am wondering who pushed to have me invited. Still, I believe that I have something to say to the Egyptians. Also, there are more than Egyptians enrolled in Cairo's Nile University. There are students in Cairo from the entire Middle East and parts of Africa. With the spread of war across the Middle East and Africa, since the Arab Spring, I have something that needs to be heard by future leaders. Despite the questions, I believe that I should go."

"Fouad, if that is your decision, I will support your going. We will pray about this. We will sleep on it. Tomorrow, you will call them."

The next morning Fouad and Vashti came to a decision. They agreed that, despite their concerns and the hostility Fouad might encounter, the opportunity to give the lectures was too great an opportunity to reject. His department head in Vancouver was enthusiastic about Fouad's going. Fouad phoned Cairo with his acceptance. He spoke with the official in Cairo who had sent the invitation and indicated that he would accept the invitation.

After he hung up, Fouad began intense preparations. His task was primarily one of organizing lectures he had already written on the subject. As he was packing he told Vashti, "Make sure I take my e-book reader. I've got three long flights, first to Toronto, then to London and finally to Cairo. I want to continue reading Chuck Colson's book, How Now Shall We Live."

Three weeks later, at the airport, their goodbye kiss was filled with mixed feelings. Vashti told Fouad, "I wish you were not going. But you are going. I am grateful that through our Canadian friends we have come to know God as the personal God He is. He really holds our lives in his hands. I will pray for you daily. I will ask Jesus to hold you in the hollow of his hand. I will pray that you do not fall into a trap in Gaza City. And if you do land in a trap, I will pray for a servant of God to spring you out of the trap."

ii

Gaza City in the Gaza Strip

In the outskirts of Gaza City and within sight of the Mediterranean Sea, in an area where very few buildings remained free from the destructive ruin of the endless war between Hamas and the Israelis, alongside one of the battered buildings, in the shade of a trellis and its spreading grape vines, a man was sitting by himself, sipping Turkish coffee. Beside him, leaning against the wall was his AK-47 rifle. He was waiting for the arrival of the men he had ordered to meet him here today. They called him Hamu.

As he watched the constant flow of people, mostly of them quite young, they seemed to confirm the report that the Gaza strip really was one of the world's most densely populated areas.

Ever since the six day war won in 1967 by Israel, many born in this region shared a special anger and hatred for Israel and the supportive nations of the West. The man, Hamu, sitting there shared that same anger intensely.

When he was just a boy, Hamu had learned that, during that 1987 battle, called the first intifada against the Israel's occupancy of the West Bank, his grandfather had died. Each of the wars that followed increased Hamu's hatred for Israel and Israel's western allies. His wife, who was killed in another battle fought against Israel, supplied with weapons from the West. Hamu's anger deepened as he suffered the loss of his left foot in the ongoing intifada against Israel. Hamu wore a prosthetic devise that took the place of his left foot.

There was good reasons for keeping today's meeting in this half demolished building very secretive. Hamu had some deadly rivals in Arab circles to avoid. Another reason for keeping a low profile was the fact that Hamu was a fugitive, constantly on the run from international police. This meeting would have been of great interest to Interpol and the Jewish intelligence agency, Mossad.

But there was a more pressing need to keep the meeting today very private. When you are working on a plan to murder someone you need to keep things very private. You want to avoid attention.

The four men coming to this meeting were looking forward to seeing Hamu's copy of the letter that had been sent as bait to draw this Egyptian professor back over the seven thousand miles from Vancouver to Cairo to deliver the Pyramid Lectures. To eliminate the man, first they had to draw him back to Egypt and Gaza City.

Hamu laughed. The men will be encouraged to learn that the professor has taken the bait and that he will be arriving in Cairo in about three weeks.

As Hamu waited for the men, he was reviewing how even the idea for carrying out this murder had come into being. The germinal idea for this death plan had been planted when two of his men returned from Canada with an amazing photo of Professor Fouad. No one had seen their agent in Toronto for over three years.

The men told how amazed they had been when they met the professor. One said, "The man looked exactly like you, Hamu. Over the years both you and the professor developed white hair. The professor was sporting a white beard and mustache just like yours."

The other man laughed. "When I first saw the professor I thought I was seeing you. I was thinking that they would need a fingerprint test, to distinguish between the two of you. His white mustache and beard are exactly like yours. Those eyes, looking out from under his bushy white eyebrows, could have been yours. You both have bushy eyebrows and, what I'll call, the same strong nose features"

That day his men led Hamu to a mirror and held up the professor's photo by Hamu's face. They were amazed and laughed that two unrelated men could share such an amazing likeness.

The striking similarity was not just amusing for Hamu. In the days following, the idea that Professor Fouad was his exact double, that each of them could pass for the other, continued to incubate in Hamu's mind. Finally, this fact that each was a double for the other gave birth to a plan. Hamu saw that the existence of such a look alike could provide the way for a fugitive like himself to end the pursuit of the Interpol and Israel's Mossad international police for good. "We'll kill the man and make it look like I died."

Gradually the plan took shape. The first step was drawing the professor back to Cairo. The letter inviting the professor to come back to Cairo as a guest lecturer was the bait. Once the professor returned to Cairo, they would persuade him to visit in Gaza City and spend the night in the Two Vipers' guest house. That day, while their guest was on his way to Gaza City, a barrage of rockets would be fired from the Gaza City into Israel. The plan was for the rockets to provoke an Israeli retaliatory air bombing in Gaza City that night. The antic-ipated Israeli retaliatory air raid would give cover to the next step. That night, during the expected retaliatory air raid, while bombs were falling, Hamu's agents would detonate the explosive devise hidden in the guest house and kill the sleeping look alike professor. His death was planned to look like the result of the Israeli air raid.

Hamu's men would identify the look alike body as the body of Hamu. Authorities, believing that Hamu was dead, would end their pursuit of Hamu. He would vanish, take on Fouad's identity and using the professor's passport take off for Canada.

Suddenly Hamu saw the men appearing. He turned off his mental review of the plan and invited the men to enjoy some good Turkish coffee.

Once they were inside, the men enjoyed seeing the copy of letter sent to the professor in Vancouver. They were excited to learn that the professor had accepted the invitation. One of the men looked up from the letter. He tightened his lips in a grin. "The letter is excellent, Hamu. The death letter has done its job. The bait is drawing the victim to the death trap. Good work. But one question. How in the world did you get the faculty's committee to send such a letter?"

Hamu smiled. "All you need to know is this. The scheduled speaker received a phone call. Following that phone call the sched-uled speaker called and informed the University that he had suddenly become very ill."

Hamu smiled. "Yes, very ill. The scheduled scholar informed the faculty that he could not fulfill his commitment to deliver this year's Pyramid lectures. In the midst of the confusion at the univer-sity someone strongly recommended Professor Fouad as a possible replacement."

There was a moment of silence. The men got the message.

Hamu continued his briefing. "The professor's phone call of acceptance was received yesterday. The professor's return to Cairo and Gaza City has begun."

Hamu clenched his fist and spoke to his men with a commanding voice. "To carry out this plan, men, each of you must stay focused on your assigned task and why you are doing your part. If you are involved in a murder you better know why."

Hamu reviewed the significance of the letter. "The letter of invi-tation is drawing the professor back to Cairo foe the lectures. He has agreed to visit Two Vipers in Gaza City following his last lecture. While he is on his way to Gaza City, we will be launching our special rocket attack to provoke an Israeli retaliation air strike. That night he will stay in our guest house. During the anticipated Israeli air strike, we will detonate the explosive device under the Guest House. It will appear that Israeli bombs hit the guest house and killed the professor."

Hamu paused. "Now your assignments."

Hamu spelled out the two stages of the plan. "First, when the professor is killed, his remains will be recovered and displayed in a way to convince everyone, especially the media and international police, that the long sought fugitive, Hamu, has finally died. I will be finally set free from the relentless pursuit by international police and Israel's Mossad.

"Remember the importance of your assignment to damage the fingers. This is to discourage any attempt to check the fingerprints. Mine are on file. You will give further damage the left leg to simulate the area where I wear my prosthetic devise.

"Then after all have seen the body, the condition of the battered body will call for immediate cremation. This will prevent any DNA study and further inquiry."

Hamu continued, "Now, the second way we will exploit the death of this look alike professor. You will gather and collect the victim's passport and all his personal things. These will be delivered to me at the professor's apartment in Cairo where I will be waiting for these essentials to begin my impersonation of the professor. The next day, armed with his personal things, and especially his passport and ticket, I will fly to Canada."

Hamu continued, "Keep in mind the objectives of our plan to kill the professor. The first objective. We want to use the professor's look alike body to lead the police to conclude that their fugitive, Hamu, is finally dead. When a death certificate is issued by our friendly physician, the battered body will be quickly taken for cremation.

"Secondly, as I impersonate the professor in Canada, I will step into Fouad's position as Director of the Two Vipers brotherhood. I will be their Canadian Pharaoh and I will give new direction to our attack against the West."

One of the men interrupted, "Hamu, why do we need this involved plan of provoking the Israel raid? Why bother to make it look like

Israeli bombs destroyed him? Why don't we just eliminate him and send you over there to replace him?"

Another one of the men echoed the same concern. "Yes, why depend on Israeli bombs to conceal what we will do through explosives? Why not just use a bullet?"

As they waited for his answer the complete authority of their leader was evident.

Barely raising his voice Hamu continued, "I will spell it out for you again. When you plan to kill someone the first objective is to avoid investigation and prosecution. The cover of the Israeli air raid is an essential part of this murder plan. If handled correctly, it will be appear very obvious to everyone that this death was caused by another Israeli air raid. No one investigates the Israeli air force. This will be the perfect crime. There will be no investigation."

Hamu continued. "But there is more to this scheme than avoiding investigation. We have goals. First, when we eliminate the professor we must encourage the police to identify this battered body as my body. With me seen as dead, I escape forever the pursuit of international police. Secondly, equipped with my lookalike's passport, I impersonate the professor, fly to Toronto and take over leadership of the Two Vipers in Canada.

"Is everyone clear about this?"

The men nodded.

"Let me review your assigned tasks.

Hamu continued, "Immediately after the end of the Israeli air raid, Rachti will carry out his assignment to find, dig out and recovers the professor's look alike body. When Rachti signals he has found the body, gather round him immediately.

"Two of you will gathervthe professor's clothing, his briefcase and all his personal things and clothe the dummy in Rachti's car with the professor's clothing. Surround the bandaged dummy in Rachti's car with the professor's personal things. Make sure that the bandaged dummy appears to be the injured professor. Create the impression for bystanders that the injured professor is alive and waiting for transport to Cairo for medical treatment.

At the same time two of you will work quickly with the body of the victim. Gather round the body immediately. Make sure that damage to the hands prevents checking fingerprints. Damage to the body must include damage to the area of my prosthetic foot. Clothe the body in my familiar galabeya. Surround the remains with my personal things. Be sure to place by my body my prosthetic devise, loaded with my fingerprints, and my well known AK-47."

One of the men said, "We will see to it that any agents of international police, agents of Interpol or Mossad on hand, are convinced that this bomb battered corpse is your body."

Hamu was pleased. "Yes, and while all this is taking place I will have made my way to Cairo. An Egyptian national will drive the car, past Egyptian border officers with me concealed.

"I will be waiting in the professor's apartment for the arrival of his personal things to begin my impersonation of the professor. Then, the next day, posing as the injured but recovering Fouad, using his passport and return ticket, I will board British Air for the flight to London and on to Toronto. Upon arrival in Toronto, I will take over the leadership of the Two Vipers brotherhood in North America."

Hamu tapped the copy of the letter in his hand and smiled. "The death letter has done its work. He is on his way to his death."

CHAPTER 2
NAIROBI, Kenya

"You can't go home again."
– Thomas Wolfe, 1940

It was six am when Fouad's flight from Toronto landed in London's Heathrow Airport. Two legs of his journey, Vancouver to Toronto and Toronto to London, were now completed. He had an all-day wait for the ten o'clock evening British Air flight to Africa and Cairo. He decided to just stay there at Heathrow. With the reading material on his e-book reader, he could make good use of these hours between flights.

Fouad's first priority was a good breakfast. He selected a fast food restaurant that seemed popular. The place was busy but he found a table where he thought he could continue reading his e-book.

Fouad was biting into his egg sandwich when he suddenly realized someone was standing by his table. A man was speaking to him. "Sorry to interrupt your breakfast. Is it OK for me to join you at this table?"

The man who stood there holding his tray gestured toward the other tables. "Things are pretty crowded."

"No problem. Welcome. I'll be glad to have some company."

The new arrival at his table introduced himself. "The name's Roger, Roger Renoir. I'm waiting for tonight's British Air Africa flight that will leave tonight and drop me off in Nairobi tomorrow morning."

Fouad reached out and greeted the man. "The name's Fouad. You came to the right table. Looks like we are waiting for the same flight. I'll be getting off at the Cairo stop. I'm on leave from my university in Vancouver to lecture at my old university in Cairo."

Roger said, "You're on leave from your university? That's interesting. Guess what. I'm also on leave from my university in USA. I'm heading for Nairobi on a four month leave from teaching art to serve as pilot for a medical mission air team that flies out of Nairobi."

Roger smiled. "Looks like we have something in common. We're both leaving the dusty halls of our universities for the real world."

Fouad said, "Yes, and as we are leaving the academic world for Cairo and Nairobi, we're both heading for some real challenges."

"You're giving lectures in Cairo. What's the subject of your lectures?"

"I'm speaking on the Arab Spring as seen from the West."

Roger said, "Now that sounds like something I would like to hear. I'm returning to Nairobi to pilot a medical mission team flights to refugee camps. The four of us flew together in Kenya a couple years ago. We are returning, as a team, to meet the overwhelming needs caused by civil war and crime."

"A big change for you and your friends, Roger, but a very valuable service for the victims of those self-centered and hate filled men."

Roger said, "As you return to Cairo, Fouad, it sounds like you are heading into the center of a real storm in the Middle East. On my first day in Nairobi, I will be piloting our team into a really challenging situation. Our team will fly up to a huge refugee camp called Yida in South Sudan. We were told it is filled with over 70,000 and more coming every day."

Fouad said, "You're flying to Yida? What a coincidence. My wife, Vashti, and I attend one of many churches in Canada that are supporting the Samaritan's Purse operation at the Yida camp. Christians across Canada contributed to make possible the water for that camp."

"Fouad, we have a long wait for our flight. What are you reading on your e-book reader?"

"I'm reading 'How Now Shall We Live' by Charles Colson. Colson has something real for all sorts of prisoners. He helps prime my pump."

The two men found that they shared many common interests and continued to visit together as they waited for their flight. Roger explained to Fouad that artists have to keep their eyes open for subject matter for painting. "Would you mind if I made a quick sketch of you?"

When Fouad indicated that he had no problem being the subject of a sketch, Roger whipped out his sketch book and made a quick sketch of his new friend with the distinguished white hair and white beard. He explained that his sketch book was a painter's treasured resource.

ii

Cairo, Egypt

As his plane came in over Cairo, Fouad enjoyed the opportunity to look out over Cairo and spot familiar landmarks. It had been three years since he and Vashti left Cairo. Although there had been major changers politically, the basic appearance of Cairo had not changed very much.

He was excited to spot Tahir Square from the plane. He had watched on TV the crowds in Tahir Square during that great Egyptian uprising against President Mubarak. He recalled seeing the many tents and the thousands of enthusiastic young people that filled the square during the Egypt's experience of the Arab Spring. He felt a deep sorrow for the young men and women who had died on the streets of Cairo. When he made his decision to return to Cairo to give the lectures, Fouad did so with a deep desire that those young men and women who gave their lives to bring an end to the years of President Mubarak's oppression would not have died in vain.

For Fouad the turmoil of Tahir Square was only a first step in the push needed for real freedom in the Arab world. Later, he saw the nation rise up in widespread protest against their new president, Morsi, who, through a takeover by the Muslim Brotherhood, sought to make Egypt an Islamic state. Fouad saw the people seeking something more. He was wondering how, as he gave his lectures, students and others would receive the views of one of their own who was now a Canadian citizen?

Fouad had deep longings for his Egypt. He coveted for his homeland more than simply political freedom. His desire for them was real freedom, freedom to become the person their God and Maker created them to be.

As he came off his plane, Fouad was glad to see a delegation of five men from the university there to extend a warm welcome. His greeters drove him to a special apartment adjacent to the campus. They informed him of the special dinner scheduled for that evening to welcome this year's lecturer. He was pleased to learn that the next day had been kept free to give him a day to rest from his two day flight and get set for the lectures. The lectures would be presented the following five evenings in Ramses Hall.

Fouad enjoyed the opportunity to have some time to himself and relax after his trip. Once he was settled in at his apartment, he was remembering how difficult it had been for Vashti to see him make this trip. That letter of invitation had stirred up a great deal of anxiety in her. He knew that he needed to call her.

When he called Vashti in Vancouver, Fouad shared with her the cordial reception by the representatives of Nile University. Fouad sought to assure her that everyone seemed genuinely pleased that he had come to give the Pyramid lectures.

Vashti's concern was whether he had heard anything about a trip out to Gaza City.

Fouad told her that he had been invited to make an overnight trip to Gaza City the day after the lectures ended. The Two Vipers people in Gaza City were looking forward to meeting with him. He was feeling better about such a trip. It would give him, as a scholar, valuable first-hand contact with leaders in the Middle East conflict.

To reassure Vashti, Fouad added, "You will be especially pleased to know that your old friend Taka's husband, Rachti, will be driving me from Cairo to Gaza. I'm looking forward to making that trip with him."

iii

Nairobi, Kenya

After his early morning arrival in Nairobi, Roger picked up his car and set out for the Nairobi Game Park. On his way he pulled over to take in a familiar spot, the Nairobi train station. Many drivers of Nairobi's' notorious *matatu* vans were busy lining up for the flood of passengers that would soon emerge from the overnight train from Mombasa.

Roger stayed just beyond the dense collection of waiting vehicles. He watched the scene from his rather well-worn Land Rover. As

Roger sat there behind the wheel of his Rover, just beyond the swarm of Kenyan drivers, he was probably the only white man, or *muzungu*, as they say in Swahili.

Although his Rover was rather beat up, there was nothing shabby about the driver. In a way suitable for a pilot in his late twenties, Roger was well outfitted. As was his custom in this job, he was wearing a sort of military jacket with epaulets and brass buttons. It was the semi-uniform of many small plane pilots in Kenya. It helped to identify them and give them, they hoped, that bit of authority that pilots of small planes sometimes needed on flights. Another tradition for him was his aviator style polarized and tinted sun glasses.

The scene at the station brought back memories of his years growing up in Kenya. Roger had been a passenger on this overnight train coming to Nairobi from Mombasa many times. He could envision the train slowing down for the villages outside the city. Many of the travelers would be tossing candy or coins to the children who ran along the tracks.

Soon the train would be passing by the corrugated metal roof tops of the vast Kibera slum, the largest urban slum in Africa. Kibera, said to be the home of a million people, was a place where very few *muzungus*, whites like himself, risked venturing.

Roger slipped the Rover into gear and drove on to his destination, the vast Nairobi Game Park that bordered Nairobi. At the Park entrance he pulled over to look around. Although he had been away teaching art in the states for a couple years, everything here looked pretty much the same.

Now that he was back, he was reviewing what brought him back to Kenya. It was that urgent plea from Bill Williams, the Mission Air director. Williams had contacted all four of their team. He had presented the desperate need for a temporary return of their team to meet the human needs of victims of the ongoing violence and war.

The news that the other three members of their old team were able to arrange a leave of absence had made him really eager to be return. All four of them, the entire old team, would be flying together again.

There were other factors in their return for each of them. He laughed. Of course the news that their team nurse, Emily Henderson, was coming back had nothing to do with his decision to return. With their team physician, Joan, and their communications man, Hank, returning it would be like old times.

Roger was open to the idea that they would discover other reason for their return. He knew that, if you are a person of faith, you learn sooner or later that your life is not ruled by chance. This morning, he was remembering the counsel of his father. "Roger, you'll discover the real reasons why you're there, when you get there."

At the game park's entrance gate, two Kenyan park guards had been watching the slowly moving vehicle. Suddenly they saw the familiar face behind the wheel. They looked at each other and laughed. "It's Roger."

They called out in Swahili. "*Habari*. Roger! What a surprise."

He responded, "*Habari!* What a wonderful way to start my first day back in Kenya. It's great, seeing you guys!"

One called out, "How long's it been, Roger? Two years?"

Roger had known these Kenyans since his school days. He jumped out of his Rover and embraced his old friends. Harry and William. "I flew in this morning. Here, on my first day, I'm back at Nairobi Game Park to paint. I came early. I'm due at Wilson Airport this afternoon."

Harry said, "Wilson? So, you've come back to fly with Mission Air again?"

"Yes, they asked our whole old team, all four of us, to come back for a few months. All four of us managed to arrange a leave of absence from our jobs."

William said, "We know you want to get out there painting. However, before you head out, Roger, you need to know that we are having a few problems."

"What's new? We always have problems."

"Not like these, Roger. We have a new sort of two-legged wildlife in the park."

"More crowned cranes?"

Harry laughed. "No, *homo sapiens*. Kenya has always been a magnet for fugitives from Sudan and Somalia. Now, among them, we're being invaded by some brutal and violent men claiming to be agents of their god. Now, instead of stopping ships for ransom, they're seizing people for ransom. Right here in Nairobi Game Park."

Harry added, "You've heard of their bloody attacks on big shopping malls. Now, to extend their power in Kenya, they are attempting to invade our great game parks."

Roger laughed, "If they try to impose *sharia* law in the game park, female zebra and giraffe will give them a rough time."

William laughed. "Right, Roger. No one tells zebra or giraffe what to do. You are still a Kenyan at heart. But this is different. These characters are at war with us. They aim to impose their law on us and control our way of life. Their underlying mind set is hatred. Evil stalks humanity here in beautiful Africa."

"What are they up to in the game park?"

"Our game parks are, of course, a major source of income for Kenya. No tourists, no tourist schillings. These barbarians are seeking to scare off our visitors."

Roger put the Rover in gear. "Thanks for the warning. I will keep on my guard."

When Roger was a boy, Nairobi Game Park had been a sort of second home. Here he had developed skills as a watercolorist, painting landscapes and wild life. He probably knew as well as anyone those special places to find different species of wildlife.

As he rolled along the familiar dirt roads of the game park, Roger enjoyed the brilliance of the morning sun, sparkling on the tall, dew-coated grasses. He found himself singing a song that was part of him. "Morning has broken like the first morning, like the first dew fall on the first grass." Then he spotted a small herd of giraffe loping gracefully along. They confirmed his conviction that you have to see giraffe galloping to really see giraffe.

Roger had come to the park early with a special objective in mind. He wanted to paint a special water color. He was looking for a particular wildlife scene encountered only in the early morning.

Then he saw what he was hoping to discover. "Eureka!" There in the brush, under the spreading branches of a huge acacia tree, he spotted a large pride of lions stretched out and sleeping off the night's hunt. Wow! It looks like they had a good night. They must have taken down a large buffalo. Having gorged themselves on their kill the pride was sleeping off that big feed. Only two cubs were moving.

Roger worked his vehicle slowly and carefully into position to sketch and plan his painting. He wanted to be close but not too close. He didn't want to disturb the lion pride. Roger would be painting from the vehicle. He was very familiar with the rule that in the park you must stay within your vehicle. He was organized to paint from the Rover.

After he made a preliminary value sketch, he proceeded to lay out the scene on a large pad of watercolor paper. This is going to be fun. He was soon completely involved and absorbed in painting.

Then it was time to focus on the acacia tree with its branches spreading out over the lions. There on one of the large spreading limbs and partly concealed by the foliage was a beautiful surprise. Stretched out with her legs dangling down around both sides of a great branch was a large lioness. "She's fast asleep."

While he was focused on painting Roger had forgotten about the good Kenyan coffee he had brought along in the Rover's cup holder. He reached out for the cup. Cold. He laughed and drank some anyway. He had to keep working to make his meeting with his team at Wilson Airport at two.

As he was putting his cup back, Roger spotted something that disturbed him. There was a beat-up old red truck with two men approaching. Roger was holding his breath. Are those guys going to blunder in here and disturb the lions or block my line of sight? He had a lot to do if he was to get to Wilson Airport by early afternoon.

The old truck continued to approach. "Keep going! Stay away, please."

The truck kept heading toward him. Roger found the oncoming vehicle upsetting. Then the driver pulled up right alongside of him on the right side of his Rover.

That's strange. He's facing away from the lions. The truck's windows were down like his own. With Kenya's system of driving on the left side with the driver on the right side, the driver of the truck was right there next to Roger, only a foot or so away. He and the other man were clearly more focused on the painter than the pride of lions.

Roger sized them up. They were obviously not tourists. Roger had painted portraits in Africa as well as landscapes. He knew many national and tribal characteristics. With his lighter skin and the distinctly more oval shape of his head, the driver appeared to be a Somali. The other man was definitely a Kenyan.

This was not a time for small talk. Roger turned back to his work. He was concerned to make his meeting with the team in the afternoon..

The Somali looking driver greeted him "*Amni salama.*"

Roger responded with the brief Swahili greeting, "*Habari,*" and continued with his work.

The driver spoke again, this time mixing in some Swahili. "*Mzure sana*, very good, *muzungu*. How come you got out here so early to paint?"

Roger looked up and replied briefly. "The light is better in the morning. Please allow me to continue painting. I'm due at Wilson Airport this afternoon."

The Somali seemed surprised. "Wilson Airport! What takes you there, *muzungu*?"

"You're Somali. You may be interested in knowing that tomorrow morning I will be making a flight from Wilson Airport to South Sudan. I will pilot a Christian medical team to the Yida refugee camp. You have hear of Yida. Many of your Somali people are living there." Roger turned back to his watercolor.

"That's interesting, *muzungu*. So you're a pilot. You plan to fly a mission plane to Yida tomorrow morning. You know what I think, *muzungu*?"

Roger looked up. The painter found himself staring into a revolver.

The gun holder's face was covered with a big grin. "This is what I think. I think you must have money. Hand over your wallet."

Roger was dumbfounded. He just stared at the man. Somehow he was not experiencing fear as he stared at the weapon. He was simply angry. I came to do a job. This barbarian with his little gun is not going to defeat that purpose.

"The wallet, now. I don't want to waste a bullet on you, Mr. Painter."

Suddenly the driver's Kenyan companion, tapped the Somali's shoulder. He nodded toward the cloud of dust from a vehicle approaching rapidly in the distance.

The driver turned to look. Roger looked also. He saw a cloud of dust trailing behind what looked like a fast approaching green Park truck. The Kenyan was nervous and kept pointing anxiously. Roger felt an immediate sense of relief.

The Somali said, "We must get going, *muzungu*. *Kwaheri*." The driver swung the truck back on to the dirt road and headed in the opposite direction.

When the green game park truck pulled alongside the Rover, Roger called out, "Great Scott! It's William and Harry. You got here just in time, like in the movies."

"Those guys giving you trouble?"

"Not unless you call holding a gun on me trouble."

"We had been keeping our eyes on you and your Land Rover. When we saw that old truck staying so long, we decided it was time to check out the situation."

"Your timing was perfect. This guy had just pulled a gun on me. He was holding out his hand for my wallet. When they saw your truck coming they took off. Thanks to you, old friends, I still have my wallet."

William replied, "They wanted more than money, Roger. We give thanks to Jesus that you still have your life. They would have shot you, with or without the money. Their goal is to spread fear and discourage the tourist business and safaris."

Roger said, "When I saw that he was Somali, I tried to establish some good will. I told them that in the morning I would be flying from Wilson with a medical team to the Yida refugee camp where there are many Somalis refugees."

The eye brows of Roger's old friends went up. They looked at each other.

William said, "Roger, are you telling us that you told that barbarian the plans for your flight? You've been away from Kenya too long. You know that in Kenya telling men like this anything is telling them too much. Sharing your agenda was not wise."

Harry added, "Be careful. You are no ordinary visitor for us. Africa needs you."

After his friends left, as Roger finished his painting. He studied again the male lion lying there in all his imperial majesty. Even when asleep this lion says, "I am king." That man with the gun was one of many who think that with a gun they can be king in this world. My escape impresses on me the fact that the Creator is the real King of this world.

Roger closed his palette, packed up his painting materials, and headed off to meet the team at Wilson Airport.

iv

The two men who fled from Game Park guards in the red truck vanished by crossing into Nairobi's great Kibera slum. When someone disappears into Kibera, the largest urban slum in Africa, they disappear.

The men made their way to a typical Kibera shack of mud walls with concrete coating and a corrugated iron roof and dirt floor. They reported to their superior, whom they called General. They told him what the *muzungu* had said about why he was in Kenya and his planned flight to Yida the next day.

Their leader laughed. "So, this infidel is going to be flying a plane from Wilson to Yida refugee camp tomorrow. You did better than getting his wallet. This information may be very helpful. The *muzungu* made the mistake of giving too much information about himself. I think we will be seeing this pilot again."

CHAPTER 3

Nairobi, Kenya

The best laid schemes of Mice and Men gang aft agley."
— Robert Burns, 1785

Despite the day's rough start in the game park, Roger continued as planned to Wilson Airport. When he walked into the huge expansive hanger and looked around he felt immediately at home.

A familiar strong voice called out "Welcome back, Roger!"

Roger turned and there was that very special old friend, their Mission Air Director, Bill Williams. "Bill! It's great to see you."

"Roger, I was really delighted when I learned that all four of you, your whole team, would be coming back. With the thousands driven from their homes by the brutality of war, we've been desperate for experienced teams like the four of you." He smiled. "And I bet you missed flying."

"You're right, Bill. As soon as I walked in here I felt this is where I want to be. I missed flying."

Bill laughed, "Yes, and you missed more than flying. I think you missed that nurse, Emily. Come with me. I've got another beauty to show you."

Bill led Roger over to a new plane. "This is the plane you will be flying up to Yida tomorrow." He pointed out the new features in the plane. "This plane has more space for passengers and a greatly increased load capacity in its baggage pod underneath. Another plus is that this plane uses jet fuel which, as you know, is cheaper here than the aviation gas we have to use on the older planes. Also, you will be able to land and take off more easily from the short runways we use in many locations."

In his office the flight director provided Roger with more details about the plane. He gave him maps and information about the landing site at the Yida refugee camp. He described the desperate needs of the thousands in the Yida camp.

As Roger listened to his old friend and flight instructor, he was stunned with how desperately their flight the next day was needed. Then he heard some familiar voices.

Bill said, "Here they come. Here comes the rest of your team."

Emily Henderson, the team's nurse, gave Roger a welcome hug. "I heard rumors that you might be back to pilot our team. I came anyway." She laughed.

Roger replied, "Emily, I heard that you might be joining the team. Of course that had nothing to do with my decision to return."

Roger greeted the team's physician, Joan Landis, a specialist in pediatrics. Like Emily, Joan had arranged to be on leave for four months from her hospital in Toronto.

Roger was really glad to see his old friend, Hank Edison. Hank was their communications man. Roger and Hank had something special in common. Like Roger, Hank had also grown up in Kenya.

Bill led them over to the plane they would use the next day. He laughed. "Getting all four of you back together again was no small job. How did you explain to people why you had to return to Kenya?"

Hank replied, "My answer why I'm was very simple. I told them to read John Piper's little book, "Don't Waste Your Life.""

Bill said, "Well you certainly won't be wasting your life flying to the Yida refugee camp tomorrow. This is the plan for your flight tomorrow. Emily and Joan will stay at the camp for two additional days. Roger and Hank, you guys will return to Wilson tomorrow. During the following two days, you will be making two more flights to deliver additional supplies from Wilson. The third day you will all return to Wilson."

As they watched the men packing the medical supplies in the plane, Joan said, "I wish those people who dish out the dollars for these supplies could see how their gifts are bringing life and hope to these people."

ii

Roger arrived early the next morning to check out the plane and his flight plan. In the quietness of the hanger he enjoyed remembering key events in his life that took place at Wilson Airport, flight school and his first solo flight.

When the team arrived for the flight they all laughed when they realized that they were dressed pretty much the same as when they last flew together before. Roger was wearing his aviator style glasses as always. He wore his old flight jacket with the gold and blue shoulder epaulets to say that he was the captain.

Bill Willliams gave them what he called his pep talk. "Government forces are failing to protect these people. We are committed to bring healing and care until the fighting ceases. You are bringing hope to mothers with children, some of whom were born on the way to Yida. Your flight extends to these people that unconditional love God has shown us in Jesus. You fly to these people with the message they are not alone."

Bill continued to prepare them. "The Yida camp is said to be home now for seventy thousand and each day more desperate people stagger in. They are thirsty and starving. Many are refugees simply because they are christians or of another tribe. Most are the women and children left behind by war."

Joan said, "Bill, thanks for preparing us for these flights."

Bill replied, "The material you will deliver to the team at Yida has been provided by gifts across Canada. Through these gifts, Samaritan's Purse is providing life saving help to thousands in the Yida Camp. You are taking in resources to help care for thousands of children under five years."

Joan turned to face their team. "And we debated whether or not to come."

Their director said, "Gifts from generous Canadian Christians made possible the pumps that are pumping clean water to holding tanks. You will be the delivery team for the compassion of many people."

Roger said, "When we land at Yida it will be good to be reminded that we are not alone in facing the tremendous needs of these people."

Bill nodded, "When you hit Yida you will be devastated by what you see. You really need to know that behind you are the prayers and love of the many Christian people who put others above self. Your flight may not make the eight o'clock news but you will be good news to thousands where you land."

Joan spoke for the team. "Thanks Bill, for bringing the four of us back together. We needed this time of preparation. Thank you."

Together, before takeoff, the team prayed together.

The team boarded. They were out on the runway waiting for the tower signal for departure. Suddenly, Roger received a call from Bill. He asked them to delay take off.

Bill explained, "We have just received an urgent call from one of our village clinics, the Mutundu Village Clinic near Machacos. They asked if our flight to Yida camp could make a short detour with a drop off for the clinic. I don't know how they even knew about this flight. For security reasons we keep details of these flights under wraps.

"This man said that you should use their temporary landing strip, south of the village. It is marked with Kenya flags at each end. A truck from the clinic will pick up the delivery."

Roger replied " I'll find it. I know the Mutundu village area"

After their takeoff, in a short time Roger said "Looks like we're approaching Mutungu Village. Now to spot that temporary landing strip. I think I see their temporary landing strip. I see the flags. It doesn't look like much more than a dirt road."

"Prepare for landing, as they say on passenger flights," Roger announced.

Hank called out, "Looks a bit rough but we can't be too choosey."

Roger adjusted his favorite polarized sunglasses, and studied the dirt runway.

Emily laughed, "Now that your sunglasses are adjusted I feel safer."

Roger warned, "Hold on! We have a slight problem."

"Problem!" Hank shouted. "Understatement! Wow! Look at that herd of giraffe and zebra on the landing strip!" Everyone was gripping what ever there was to grip.

Emily was puzzled, "Roger, how are we going to land here with that herd of giraffe, and zebras grazing all over the place?"

Roger smiled. "No problem, Emily. First, you address them politely by their Swahili names. They are not giraffe but *twiga*. They are not zebra but *pundamilila*. You simply say *twiga* and *pundamilila* be gone."

With lips pressed tightly together, Roger banked the plane and, making a wide circle, came back to head over the landing strip again. He gunned the engine a bit, making it sound louder as the plane headed down the strip.

The giraffe scattered with their usual graceful gallop. The zebra galloped off in several directions.

"Look at them, they're really moving." Hank was amazed.

Roger smiled, "Giraffe aren't dumb. They've seem a few Jurassic Park films. When they see a flying dinosaur, they scatter. Hear the giraffe cry out, 'Pterosaurs! Pterosaurs!'"

"Great!" Hank laughed, "Our plane does look a bit like a flying dinosaur."

Roger landed their plane and taxied down the very rough improvised landing strip to a small hut.

Hank looked around, "We're here. Where's the jeep from the clinic with red cross on the roof?" Then he pointed down the runway, "Look! Look what's coming." Two vehicles were heading toward them.

The vehicles were stirring up a cloud of dust as they raced down the landing strip toward them. A jeep and a truck pulled up in front of the plane. The jeep held two men. The truck was loaded with several men, all of whom were armed with the AK 47 rifles. The jeep and truck were positioned to make sure that the plane was not going anywhere. The armed men quickly surrounded the plane.

Hank said what they were all thinking, "They do not look like clinic people."

Emily said, "This was a trap. Someone knew about our flight today and made a fake call to bring us here."

Hank said, "How could these guys have even known about this flight?"

Roger nodded. "I was the big mouth. Yesterday, I was stopped by some men in Nairobi Game Park. Since one of them appeared to be Somali I told him about this flight to Yida this morning."

Roger slid open his window, "We have an emergency shipment of medicine here. Please get your truck out of the way. We are on the wrong landing strip. This medicine is urgently needed."

Their leader laughed, "Everyone off the plane. Now."

As they stepped out of the plane, the men moved them with prods from their 47 K's into the nearby shack. One man announced, "Here they are General."

The man called General was sitting behind a table with a cigar in his mouth. With one hand he twirled a revolver on a finger. He was seated in a wooden swivel chair, rocking slightly. He had a big grin on his face as he looked at his prisoners.

Finally the leader spoke, "Which of you is the pilot?"

Roger raised his hand. "We are loaded with relief materials for the Yida refugee camp. Every hour you detain us here, more people are dying."

"Mr. Pilot, you are not going to Yida. Your Christian movement is not going anywhere in Africa." He laughed, "*Muzungu*, this is the post-Christian era." The man rambled on, "Soon all of Africa will know the true African religion."

Roger spoke softly to the team. "This guy has been brainwashed. Christians have been sharing the love of Jesus in Africa since the first century."

The General turned to his men. "If there is a computer on the plane bring it here. Take them to the old white man's stone house."

The general ground his cigar into a plate. He said, "Don't even think of escaping. We will squash you like this cigar. No one has ever escaped from this camp alive."

His men laughed. They took the team out to the pickup truck and drove them to a nearby stone house. They shoved them into the building. Someone left a bucket of water with them. The team heard a key turn in the lock and the men drove off.

The four of them looked at one another with the realization that their situation was desperate.

Hank tried to lighten up things. "Looks like we're up a tree again, Roger."

Joan said, "What are you talking about, Hank?"

"When we were kids, Roger and I sneaked into the Game Park so Roger could paint a rhino. The rhino drove us up a tree, where we spent the night. This looks like another night up a tree with Roger."

Roger nodded. "Yes, but the general, looks more threatening than that rhino. Our only hope is to get out of here. If they hold us for ransom that means a death sentence. We are going to get out of here somehow or other, alive. Let's give this building a going over. There must be some weak spot."

CHAPTER 4

Kenya Bush

*"Love is not patronizing and
charity isn't about pity, it is about love."*
– Mother Teresa

As soon as their guards left them the team went to work examining their prison for weak spots. They soon found that they were being held in an extremely strong stone building from colonial days. Efforts at wiggling loose iron window bars, looking for loose stones, and pushing against roofing panels was unproductive. They found no potential way of escape. Meanwhile the building was heating it up like an oven.

Hank said, "We would need a bulldozer to get out of this hellhole."

Suddenly they heard a key turning the lock on their door. The door was yanked open and their captor, the General, entered with several men armed with rifles.

"My men are giving you pads and pens. Each of you will write down your name and Kenya address. Give us the phone number of the person to whom you report in Nairobi.

When he had the data he needed the General said, "Enjoy your quarters." He laughed. "Get used to staying here. We will be contacting your superiors. If they want to see you alive, they will meet our demands quickly. After three days, no ransom money means the end for you." He made a chopping action with his hand.

Roger spoke up. "The Kenya Air Force will be looking for our plane. They are going to spot our plane. You will never hide it from the Air Force."

"We have taken care of the plane and the flags. They will never find you."

Roger said, "Children are dying every day in the Yida camp. Those supplies are needed now!"

"Get used to the idea. We will not allow western infidels to provide medical care for people. You are not going to buy converts with medicine."

"We're not buying converts. Our provision for the people in Yida is unconditional. God made of one flesh all people. He wants these refugees, and even you to know His unconditional love."

The general laughed. "Your God loves me? I don't think so, Mr. Pilot."

Roger replied quickly, "The Creator who made you wants you to know His love for you." Roger thought he saw one of the men with the AK 47 rifles quietly smile and just slightly nod his head.

Their captor said, "We will give your superiors our conditions for your release." He rubbed his hands together. "You are going to bring us much money.'

"The general's voice became stern. "Now, let me warn you. This place is surrounded by men with guns. They are instructed to shoot on sight any attempt to flee this camp. Don't even think about escape.

"We would hate to have our men use you for target practice. You are worth more to us alive." He stormed out with his men.

When they were alone again, Hank warned, "This old house, built years ago by white settlers, is as strong as a prison. All the windows have iron bars."

Joan said, "You know that the Kenya government does not pay ransom. They will not allow any ransom. If we are going to get out of here alive, we will need some outside help."

Roger said, "When news reaches Wilson that we failed to land at Yida things will start happening. Search planes will be out looking for us."

Hank was shaking his head, "It will be difficult to find us if our plane has been wheeled out of sight from the air."

Roger was nodding, "We will have to get out of here on our own,"

"On our own? Well not completely on our own," Emily smiled. "We need to pull a Philippian jail scene."

"A what?" Hank asked.

Emily responded. "You know, we start singing!"

"Singing?"

"Yes, Hank," Emily laughed, "Don't you ever read the Bible, Hank? Remember how Paul and Silas were in prison and in chains in Philippi. In the middle of the night they were praying and singing hymns and the other prisoners heard them. Remember what happened? Suddenly, a huge earthquake! The prison doors flew open. The chains fell off. All the prisoners were loose."

"Good try, Emily, but we can't depend on angels in the bush of East Africa."

"I wouldn't be too sure of that. Start singing, and see."

They began singing with Emily. After a couple songs, they stopped for a moment. Emily put her finger to her lips. "Listen! I hear them."

"What?" Hank replied.

Joan laughed, "The angels, of course, Hank. Listen."

They listened. Then they heard voices singing in the distance. It was the same song they had just sung but in Swahili.

Emily laughed, "Don't you hear that, Hank? Listen! Those people heard us. They are responding to our songs. They are singing the same songs in Swahili."

Joan said, "It's marvelous. We may be in prison but we are not alone. That's the best thing I've heard since we landed here. God is going to get us out of this place."

ii

The team did not do much sleeping that night. Then, suddenly, as it was getting closer to dawn they heard a soft tapping on their door. A voice whispered. "Quiet." They heard a key quietly turning in the lock. Two Kenyans stepped in quietly. A young man and an older man whose hair was growing white. .

The senior member of the team held his finger to his mouth. He spoke in a whisper. "We have come to help you."

The young man added, "We are going to lead you out of this place. We will go with you. For us there will be no return."

"Wonderful!" Roger exclaimed. "We began to realize we were not alone when we heard your people singing."

Their younger man said, "Our people will go on singing to create a distraction among the guards. They are not just singing. Bwanna Roger, Mganga Joan, Nurse Emily, Radio man Hank. They are praying. And we are praying. My father and I have come to get you out of here. We waited until just before dawn for enough light to find our way."

Roger was startled, "You know our names!"

"Of course. And you know us." The young man spoke quickly. "Bwana Roger, three years ago, we called the hospital in Kijabe. My wife was about to deliver our first child. Her life was in danger. In the middle of the night the four of you came on that plane. God used you to save my wife and our first child."

"Yes," his father continued, speaking softly. "You flew to our village. You, *Mganga* Joan, Nurse Emily. You saved my son's wife and you saved *Mtoto*, my little grandchild."

The young man said, "Emily, you were the nurse. Joan, you were the doctor. God sent you to save my wife and my beautiful child." Turning to Roger and Hank, he said, "You got them there and made it happen."

In the semi-darkness Roger's his eyes opened wide. "I remember now. Yes, you are David, *baba*, the father. And the mama was Sara. And you are David's father, Samuel."

Samuel said, "We must move quietly. These men are evil. They have been attempting to enslave our people. They told us that your plane held corrupt government workers. Then our people heard you singing. We must move quickly."

Once they were out Samuel locked the door again.

As Roger followed the two men, it began to sink for him that there was no going back for these men. He was stunned. When David and Samuel came to free them they were putting their own lives on the line.

The four of them ran along with their rescuers. They silently exchanged looks, They were sharing the same thought. Our efforts to save this man's wife and child was nothing compared to the risk that they are taking now to help us.

As she hurried along, Emily was experiencing something new. As a nurse she had always been the one helping someone else. Now, she was on the receiving end.

David urged them on. "Soon your escape will be discovered. As the guards report that you are gone, our friends will create a big fuss. To delay pursuit, our people will start a big argument. To give us more of a head start, our people will start a big argument over which way we went."

David's father added, "Some will say they heard you going one way. Some will insist you fled another way." He laughed. "They are good at making confusion."

As the team moved along they could hear men yelling and shooting off their AK47 rifles. Samuel and David urged them on. "If the guards discovered our trail and catch us there will be no mercy."

The morning light was increasing. The team kept running behind their guides. They were following a trail in a ravine. The path ran along a large a rushing stream. Now they could hear, in the distance, the sound of those in pursuit. The blood thirsty yelling seemed to be growing closer. Suddenly, to make matters worse, they heard the thunder and roar of what had to be a powerful waterfall up ahead. They were dismayed to realize that their flight in this ravine was running into a dead end at a huge waterfall. The roar of a powerful waterfall was growing louder.

When they saw the powerful waterfall they stopped cold. They were overwhelmed by the sight of a huge wall of water crashing down up ahead of them. Their guides were debating which way to go. Whatever they decided to do had to be done quickly. They could hear the cries coming closer.

Roger pulled them all together so he could be heard above the thundering falls. "I know this place," he said. "These are the *MauMau* falls."

Everyone was getting soaked by the spray. Roger put his mouth close to their ears. "I was painting here some years ago. There is a cave behind this water fall. The *MauMau* rebels hid here during their fight for Kenya's independence. We can hide there too. It's our only chance."

The eyebrows of the Kenyans went up. They were amazed that a *muzungu* like Roger knew something about Kenya than they didn't know. They laughed, "Let's be *MauMau*."

Roger first took off his prized hat. He ran quickly along the trail a bit and spun his hat up the trail to mislead their pursuers. "Maybe it will serve as a decoy!" With a beckoning gesture, under the loud roar of the waterfall, Roger mouthed the words "Follow me."

Roger grabbed Emily's hand and pulled her along with him as he beckoned everyone to follow. He and Emily disappeared as he forced their way through the edge of the powerful roaring torrent of the falls. The rest followed into the cave behind the great waterfall.

The cold water hit them hard as they pushed through the powerful torrent of water at the edge of the falls. They moved quickly back, as far as possible, into the darkness of the cave behind the falls. They were surprised at the size of the cave. Since very little light hit the canyon this early, the cave was quite dark. This encouraged their sense of security.

They stood closely together in the cold darkness of the cave. It was a tense moment. Despite the powerful thunder and roar of the falling water that shielded them in their hiding place, they could make out faintly the yells of their pursuers out on the trail. Would the mob of men press on? Would any of the pursuers know of the *MauMau* cave? In the cold darkness of the cave, as she held on to Roger, Emily put her mouth to his ear. "Will they know about this cave, Roger?"

Roger said, "Pray they're not locals."

Through the roar of the falls they could hear faintly the shouting of the gang and occasional firing of an AK 47. As the six of them, soaked and shivering, stood huddled close together, they shared a common awareness of how close they were to violent death. In the darkness of the cave, protected as they were by the powerful deluge, Emily was realizing how much it mattered to her that, Roger was holding her. She held on and pulled closer.

Through the thunder of the waterfall they continuing hearing the shouting of their pursuers along with some occasional shots. They continued to huddle together in the darkness of the cave, waiting and hoping their pursuers would move on. Then they heard a voice cry out in Swahili, "*Kofia, Kofia!*" Someone had spotted Roger's hat decoy farther up the trail beyond the falls. "*Kofia, muzungu!* White man's hat."

Roger smiled and mouthed the word, "*Kofia*. They're taking the bait."

Finally the sound of gunshots and shouts began to grow fainter. Roger moved to the edge of the falls and listened. The sound of the yelling and shooting was growing more distant. Cautiously he moved out past the edge of the powerful falls. He looked very carefully up and down the trail to make sure there were no stragglers. He motioned to the others to follow and stepped out.

David, who was leading their escape, shook his head in amazement. "I was worried all the time that one of them would know about the cave. Not one of them did."

Roger said, "Yes, I kept praying, that none of these traitors were local Kenya men. It was my prayer that if any were locals that they were too young to know how the *MauMau* hid in this cave behind the falls. That was back around 1956. The MauMau who hid in this cave were fighting the British for Kenya's independence."

Emily said, "But Roger, if even the Kenyans didn't have a clue about this cave behind the falls, how in the world did a *muzungu* like you know about it?"

Roger laughed. "Years ago, I shared in a picnic here with some very special friends, a German missionary couple, Hugo and Isolda. While I was painting a quick watercolor sketch, Hugo told me how the *MauMau* warriors hid from the British in this cave behind the waterfall."

David said, "This has given us time to cut back toward the village along the Mombasa railroad. We must move fast. Let's roll. We will have friends there."

When they finally reached the village it was market day. The place was packed. There were many people from nearby villages. Men were there with goats. Ladies were selling chickens. Crates of eggs were piled up. Bags of charcoal were on sale. In one area the ground was covered with piles of second hand clothing.

David and Samuel quickly located the village leaders and described their desperate need for help. They explained the need for some diversion to help them disappear. After talking with David and Samuel, the village chief called the market day crowd together.

When the crowd settled down the village chief spoke. He told the story of how the mercy flight was diverted from its flight to the Yida camp. He told how the mission air team was being held for ransom. "The mission team and their friends are running for their lives. This gang is hunting them down."

The crowd began to get stirred up. Their chief spoke with feeling. "These people are family. We have the same heavenly Father. They came here to bring hope to suffering people. Are we going to help these brothers?"

The crowd exploded in cries of support. As their leader spoke they could hear the whistle of the Mombasa train bound for Nairobi. He called out, "Hear that? The Mombasa train will be here passing our village in minutes. To escape their enemies these friends must board that train. We are going to stop these evil men and buy time for our friends to board the train."

Word was spreading that the *muzungus* were members of the Mission Air medical team. That was enough. Many knew someone whose life had been touched by Mission Air.

The chief spoke intensely to David. "The Mombasa train is minutes away. Quickly, take our friends across the tracks. Get across the tracks, so that the moving train will be running between you and your pursuers. Help them board the train as it slows down. You can count on our village to mix up things up with those men. Our people will enjoy frustrating the men who are after you. Here comes the train. Get across the tracks."

The six of them darted across the tracks with some village leaders.

Samuel explained, "This train is loaded with tourists and others heading back to Nairobi. As it passes this village it will slow down, as is the custom. As the train slows down the village children on the other side will be running alongside the train. They hope the tourists will throw out candy or coins. With the train moving slowly, here on this side we will be able to run alongside the train. Grab a hand railing and swing up on board."

As the train came rolling along they all managed to grab hold of the hand rails and swing up on the train. All six of them successfully boarded the train.

The team and their two rescuers looked out through the others side of the train. They saw that the gang of their pursuers was being thoroughly mobbed by the villagers.

Soon the train was resuming speed as it headed toward Nairobi. Hank said, "I have just one question. How will I explain all this someday to future grandchildren?"

Roger said, "No problem. Tell them you were saved by the Lunatic Express! We are all now Lunatic Express Loonies?"

"The Lunatic Express?"

"Yes. Back around 1900 when the British were laying the track for this train from Mombasa inland to Uganda, the cost was rising. Many workers were dying. Over a hundred workers from India were carried off by lions. Investors back in England started calling it the Lunatic Express. However, despite opposition, this train got established. So, here we are, safe and sound, thanks to the Lunatic Express."

"Tickets please." It was the conductor coming their way.

"Conductor, we have a problem." Roger gestured to the others and turned to the conductor, "We have no tickets. As a matter of fact all six of us have no money either."

"So I heard," The conductor said, "Your friends, David and Samuel, have been telling me your story. They tell me that our old Mombasa train helped save your lives."

David broke in to explain their situation more fully to the conductor in Swahili.

The conductor stared at them in amazement. Finally, the conductor spoke in English to the team. "David has told me what happened. It seems that Jesus brought our Mombasa train along at just the right moment to save you."

Roger said, "It was amazing. Your train rolled through the village at exactly the right moment. And we are very thankful." Roger was starting to say. "We will arrange for our tickets to be covered by Mission Air,"

The conductor broke in, waving his hands repeatedly. "No way, no way." He looked from one of them to the other in amazement. "No tickets for you. You were on your way to serve at Yida. No way. No tickets for you."

Hank broke in. "Mr. Conductor, we have an urgent concern. We need to recover our plane and those very valuable medical supplies as soon as possible. Once the plane is recovered, we need to resume our flight. Is there any way, here on the train that I could connect with Mission Air, at Wilson Airport? We need to alert the Kenya Air Force to this situation. Kenya Air Force needs to recover the plane and the medicines on board. The plane needs to be recovered and flown back to Wilson Airport in Nairobi as soon as possible."

"No problem." The conductor replied with a smile. "Come with me. The manager on this train will be glad to get such a call through for you."

Roger spoke up, "*Asante sana*. Many thanks. All of us are glad to meet such an understanding and helpful conductor on the old Lunatic Express."

The conductor laughed and answered with a smile, "The Lunatic Express? Good name. We have lunatic conductors too."

iii

Nairobi, Kenya

When the train arrived in Nairobi many Air force officers were at the station to meet them. The team learned that security forces had been dispatched by helicopter to find and recover the plane. The officers questioned the team to learn as much about their captors as possible.

Joan expressed the urgent need to complete their trip to Yida. She impressed on the officers the needs of the refugees. She spoke of the priceless medicine on the plane.

Roger told the officials that as soon as the plane was returned to Wilson, and was ready to go, they would complete the flight to Yida refugee camp.

An Air Force officer assured them that as soon as the plane was recovered it would be flown back to Wilson.

In an amazingly short time, the Kenya Air force located and flew the plane back to Wilson Airport. After a thorough check by the maintenance crew, the four members of the flight team boarded the plane and took off to complete their flight to the Yida refugee camp.

When the mission air team touched down at the Yida camp, the desperate circumstances of the thousands of homeless people hit them hard. The utter desperation of the people driven from their homes, the widespread health problems and the continually growing number of people was staggering. The task of meeting the basic needs of thousands of young children was overwhelming.

The team was stunned by the sheer size of the refugee camp. Yida, with its 70,000 refugees had become an instant city. Desperate and starving people, mostly women with very young children, were staggering into the camp every day. Some women came with another child born along the way. By maintaining many bore holes Samaritan's Purse was providing liters of desperately needed clean water for the camp, a major life saver.

The team's physician, Joan, was overwhelmed by the way Samaritan's Purse was meeting the needs, providing hygienic care and distributing food rations to thousands of desperate people. As she worked with the Doctors without Borders, Joan was impressed with their care for thousands of children under five years.

Although the team had been in many challenging situations they found the needs at the camp overwhelming. The team kept saying, "At Yida we were finally doing the job we came to do."

CHAPTER 5

Cairo, Egypt

*After eight months, Stanley found Livingstone on
the shore of Lake Tanzania. "Doctor Livingstone, I presume."*

When the Mission Air team returned from their
flight to Yida the four members of the team were immediately ushered into an office to meet with the lead officer of the Kenya Police

The officer expressed his deep regret for the ordeal of their capture by the terrorists. "We want you to know that we at Kenya Police regret greatly this terrible experience of your being held for ransom by these evil men. The information about them which you supplied has been of much help and we are going to find them."

The officer paused. "But right now we have an urgent and immediate concern. Your escape was a miracle that saved your lives. With or without ransom these men would have eventually killed you. People held hostage in Kenya are never seen again. Why? Such criminals want to destroy all witnesses. Since, despite your escape, you are obviously witnesses to their crime these men will make it high priority to destroy you. For this reason our primary concern right now is your safety."

"Our safety?" Roger asked.

The officer nodded. His face showed anxiety. "Our primary concern is make sure that you are well out of reach of these men. They will certainly make every effort to eliminate you."

Hank said, "You're concerned for our safety?"

"Yes, very concerned. Here's the situation. We have no idea where these men are hiding. They may be lying low in Kibera Slum.

Wherever they may be, they know that you can identify them. As long as these violent men are at large their first priority will be to find and eliminate you, their former captives. You are definitely on their hit list."

The team looked at each other in amazement. Roger said, "So?"

The officer continued, "We know that you did not come to Nairobi for a vacation. You came with Christian purpose. You came here to relieve suffering and to help people."

The officer paused. "I find what I am about to say very difficult. You are now in a very dangerous situation. It is not wise for you to remain in Kenya. Our department has decided that it is urgent that the four of you vanish from the Nairobi scene, immediately. If possible, tomorrow."

The team members simply looked at each other, stunned.

The officer looked at their faces. "You look rather baffled."

Hank said, "Yes, that's exactly how we feel, very confused."

The officer said, "We appreciate why you are here. Kenya needs people like you. However, right now you are in great danger. Your recent encounter with these very vicious men makes you very vulnerable. They have personal information about each of you. They will certainly seek to eliminate the four of you. As long as you remain in Nairobi, you are prime targets for them."

The officer continued, "In the interest of your safety, we request that you leave Kenya as soon as possible. We request that you book flights to leave Nairobi tomorrow."

The team looked at each other. It was sinking in. For their protection they were being ordered to leave Kenya.

The officer saw their reaction. He added, "We appreciate why you are here. However you are all in grave danger. We must ask you to book flights to leave as soon as possible. Tomorrow, if at all possible. Until then we will provide around the clock protection."

ii

After the police left, the team huddled. Hank said, "This is crazy. We just arrived. We've been here just four days and now they want us to get out of here."

Hank sat there with his eyes closed, shaking his head. Then he looked at the others, "We came with purpose. We'll leave with the prayer that we can soon return."

There was a long silence.

Hank said, "This calls for dinner together to night."

Joan said, "Good thinking, Hank. Are we all thinking of the same place?"

Emily said, "Yes, the Gourmet Carnivore, of course."

That evening the team enjoyed a special time in one of their favorite places. The waiters kept bringing all sorts of game meat from the huge charcoal cooking area. But it was a farewell dinner. Everyone was having a hard time forgetting that this was their last meal together before heading home.

They had all taken an extended four month leave of absence from their jobs. Now, after only four days, they were returning home. They were all concerned how they would use the considerable weeks ahead of them.

As they discussed their situation, Emily came up with the idea that, when they got back, they should do something together. "All four of us, as Roger told the conductor, were all saved by the timely arrival of the Mombasa Train, the old Lunatic Express.

"We are all Lunatic Loonies..." She paused. Then, with a big smile, Emily continued, "Since we are all Lunatic Express survivors how about all of us getting together for a special Lunatic Loonies reunion. How about a get together later in August. Let's all go some- place together."

Joan agreed, "Sounds great to me."

Hank said, "I'm sure open to doing something."

Roger replied, "Let's do it."

Emily said, "Brace yourselves. I've got a crazy idea what to do. Since we escaped by jumping on the Mombasa train, the old Lunatic Express, how about a special reunion trip on a train. We could travel across Canada from Toronto to Vancouver on Canada's great trans- continental train."

"A trip on a train?" Hank asked. "Does anyone ride trains these days?"

Emily replied, "People from half way around the world come to travel on this great transcontinental train from Toronto to Vancouver."

Roger said, "Sounds like a great idea. That train must go through Jasper in the Canadian Rockies. We could stop off in the Jasper area and do some exploring together."

Hank said, "Emily, you're a genius. I can't believe I didn't think of that first."

"It sounds great to me." Joan chimed in. "Hank and Roger will find a fisherman's paradise out there."

Roger added, "The Canadian Rockies sound like great painting country."

Emily said "And the final destination is a fantastic city, Vancouver!"

The four of them looked at each other. Hank said, "Like the four musketeers." He grabbed their hands and pulled them together, "One for all and all for one,"

After some discussion, it was agreed that to plan the trip in the latter half of August. Since Emily and Joan lived in Toronto they would work out the details."

Emily pulled out a calendar. "I recall that when some friends took that trip their train pulled out of Toronto on a Tuesday. How about the third Tuesday of August, Tuesday, August 18."

Roger said, "That sounds great. It so happens that there is a faculty symposium in Toronto the weekend just before that date. Now, I could take in the Symposium too."

Emily spoke up. "Roger, I have another great idea for you. You may remember my telling you that my family has a north woods cabin in a wilderness setting, several hours north of Toronto. If I could arrange with my parents, perhaps you could fit in a week painting up there, before your faculty symposium. It's the sort of place, that once you're there you don't want to return to what we call civilization."

"Sounds great. Let me know if I could use their cabin that week."

As the team continued talking of their flights home, Roger said, "You know, all these return flights we are booking from Nairobi to London pass through Egypt. Many flights make stops in Cairo. Over the years, in my trips back and forth to Kenya, I've always wanted to stop and see the pyramids and do some painting in Egypt. It's on our way home. We have the time. Why don't we all plan to break the trip with a stopover of a few days together in Cairo?"

As they bounced the idea around, they found that the idea of a stopover in Cairo appealed to all of them.

Hank said, "A great idea. We've got the time. Our flights from Nairobi to London pass through Cairo. It may soften our having to turn back and go home."

The next day, as the team made arrangements for their flights, they all made plans for a fstopover in Cairo.

Roger said, "My father was always fascinated with what those surprise meetings he called divine encounters. Who knows? Perhaps on this flight from Nairobi there may be some divine encounters waiting for us."

iii

When the team arrived for their stopover in Cairo, they found accommodations at a hotel near the university. They sat down over lunch at a restaurant popular with students to map out the best way to use their time in Egypt. They wanted to visit the museums of Cairo, the pyramids and the great sphinx of Giza. They were also interested, if possible, in a cruise up the Nile to the historic sites between Luxor and Aswan.

While the others examined pamphlets designed for tourists, Roger was taking in the student life around them. Suddenly he saw a poster advertising the Pyramid Lectures. The poster and the lectures were in English. To his surprise he recognized the face on the poster. Professor Fouad. That's the Egyptian professor I met at Heathrow.

Roger directed everyone to the poster. "See this notice of the Pyramid lectures by a Professor Fouad from Vancouver. I know this Professor Fouad."

Emily said, "Roger, how could you know a man giving lectures in Cairo?"

Roger said, "I met the man giving these lectures at Heathrow in London on my way to Nairobi. We were both waiting for the same flight. I was on my way to Nairobi. He was on his way to Cairo to deliver these lectures. He's from Vancouver. He's a great guy."

Emily said, "And quite impressive looking with that white beard."

Roger studied the poster again. "It looks like he will be is giving his final lecture tomorrow evening. His subject is the Arab Spring and how the West sees it. I was really impressed with this man. We could catch the last of the series tomorrow evening. I would like to go. Anyone interested?"

It was finally decided that Roger and Emily would take in the Professor's lecture.

The next evening as they took their seats for the lecture, Roger and Emily were amazed at the great crowd of Egyptian students. As the speaker came out on the platform, Emily said, "Your professor friend certainly looks like a professor. His white beard and white hair give him a very distinguished appearance. I like his tortoise shell spectacles too."

As the lecture got under way, the professor, as an Egyptian who once sat where they sat, pleaded with the students to break free from those who use religion to fuel the fires of Middle East war and gain power for themselves.

Emily turned to Roger in amazement. They could scarcely believe that they were hearing this in Cairo.

The professor continued. "In response to the failed revolution of the Arab Spring, your president, el-Sisi, has called on Egypt to promote a reading of Islamic texts in a truly enlightened manner. Many in the Islamic world are making enemies of the whole world.

"Both Egypt's leaders and other leaders in the Arab world need to consider more seriously the call of Egypt's president for a reformation in Islam. President el-Sisi has called for Islam to reform its interpretations of the faith. Fanatics have turned the Middle East into a battlefield and pitted it against the rest of the world. Millions have been driven from their homes. Many in the Arab world are saying that, just as the Christians experienced a reformation, Islam need a reformation."

Roger said softly to Emily, "Am I hearing tonight what I think I am hearing? Did I hear this man use the word reformation, here in Cairo?"

The lecturer continued, "Pakistan's Malala Yousafzai, the teenager shot in the head by the Taliban, in her call for education for women, has launched a revolution, a call for reformation. That could lead to a real Arab Spring.

"The constant urging to wage jihad, or holy war, must be rejected. There is no such thing as holy war. We must reject exploiting religion to gain power over others by war."

Roger waited to hear some outburst of protest from students. There was none. Roger was impressed by the authority with which this man spoke. He turned to Emily, "I'm amazed that this man can speak as frankly as he does to these students. I have the feeling that his strength comes from something very real within the man himself."

Emily said, "Isn't he putting himself in a dangerous position?"

At the lecture's conclusion, Roger and Emily pressed through the crowd to greet his friend from that London meeting in Heathrow.

The professor quickly recognized Roger as the American he had met in London. "Roger, what a surprise. When we each went our way, just a few days ago, you were on your way to medical mission flights in Kenya. What are you doing in Cairo?"

Roger replied, "An emergency situation forced us to exit Kenya temporarily. We happen to be making a stopover in Cairo on our way home.

Roger introduced Emily, "This is I'm Emily Henderson, the nurse on our team. On our first flight as a mission air team, four days ago, as we were headed for the great Yida refugee camp, we were taken prisoners and held for ransom. Kenyan Christians helped us escape. Kenyan officials ordered us, for our safety, to get out of Kenya. So here are on or way back home."

The professor's bushy white eyebrows went up. "You came to help Egypt's neighbors." He paused and closed his eyes for a moment.

Then, gasping Roger's and Emily's hands, the professor drew them close and spoke quietly. "There are many of God's people suffering throughout the Middle East and Africa. Like Egypt, these people need a real springtime, a God-given springtime of the heart, a springtime of discovery, a discovery of the Creator's loving purpose for all people. Thank you for being a harbinger of that spring."

Still holding their hands, he looked intently at Roger and at Emily. Leaning very close to them he spoke quietly, "The Middle East is far from hopeless. Remember how first century Christians prevailed under Rome. Remember God's promise to Hosea." Then he sang softly Hosea's words of the great Springtime of God. "And He shall come, He shall come to us like the rain, like the spring rain, watering the earth."

Continuing to speak very quietly he said, "Pray for me. I'm heading for Gaza City tomorrow. I am heading into a storm. Pray for this man Fouad, in Gaza City." Then he turned to speak to some students.

CHAPTER 6

Gaza City

The grand jihad is a stealth plan to conquer the United States, a stepping stone toward a global state.
– Mohammed Akan

Once again, in the same partially demolished Gaza City building where they had met previously, four men, with great caution, had come together again, as ordered by their leader, Hamu. As before they had concealed their cars in various places.

These men were focused on something very different from the many schemes floating around in Gaza City. Not too far away, some men, might be working on ways to improve their tunnel to smuggle arms from Iran to destroy Israel. Everywhere, other people were always working on schemes to move up the immigration ladder to Europe. Though less obvious, the various recruiters for jihad were competing with one another. These men, the small group of men sipping their Turkish *kahvesi* with Hamu, were focused on a very specific objective, murder, a very carefully planned murder, tonight.

Hamu's men were pleased to learn how well the death letter inviting Professor Fouad back to Cairo had done its job. The bait of being invited to deliver the Pyramid lectures had worked. Their prey had arrived in Cairo. He had delivered his final lecture the previous evening. Today was the crucial day of his trip from Cairo to Gaza City.

Shortly after their meeting in Gaza City, the target of the plot, the professor, would be starting his trip from Cairo to Gaza City. An old friend of the professor in years past, Rachti, had been recruited to drive the victim to the special reception for him in Gaza City. The professor's meal at the reception would be his last. Tonight was the night.

Hamu's facial expression reinforced his words. His white eyebrows drawn down intensified what he was saying. As he spoke his white mustache reinforced his words. "Be very clear about your assignment. Each man's action is essential for the total plan."

The men looked intently at Hamu, nodding.

Hamu continued. "The professor, agreed to work for our Two Vipers brotherhood, to recruit new immigrants to advance our goals in North America. He has been just going through the motions. He appears to have abandoned our war against the West. In fact, he has been becoming more like one of them."

"Tonight, this very night, we will destroy this traitor. With your help, by morning the body of my look alike will be seen as my body. I, Hamu, will be seen as dead. My years of pursuit by Interpol and Israel's Mossad will finally end. The next day, armed with the professor's passport and return ticket to Canada, I will step into his shoes. I will become the Professor."

Suddenly Hamu received a call on his phone. He answered gruffly, "Yes?" No names were spoken. He turned on the speaker phone and gestured to the men to listen. Covering the phone with his hand he said, "Our man Rachti is on his way to pick up my look alike, the professor."

Hamu continued the call. The men heard him asking, "At what time will you pick up your passenger?" After listening briefly he said, "Good."

Hamu spoke into the phone. "If you turn on your car radio, you and your passenger may hear some interesting news from Israel."

The men heard Hamu laugh and wind up the call. "Have a good trip. Everyone is looking forward to your arrival in Gaza City with the sacrificial goat." There was a pause. Then Hamu said intensely, "Remember, failure is not an option." He said it again, with added force. "Remember, failure is not an option."

Following a review of their assignments for the coming night, one by one, the men were on their way to their assigned location.

For the first few minutes after the men left, Hamu remained sitting there alone in their meeting place. He was enjoying his anticipation of success. He could almost taste the freedom from living as a fugitive that he would experience with his new identity. Hamu, your days of running are about to end tonight. The day after tomorrow you board that plane as Professor Fouad.

Hamu was experiencing again that flash back to the birth of his bitter hatred for the West, that he often experienced. He could see again that, the day of his father's death, back in 1981. Egypt was celebrating President Sadat's conclusion of the Yom Kipper war with Israel. Hamu's mother had taken him as a young boy to see his father's military unit participate in the celebration.

President Anwar al-Sadat, standing there all his regalia, was in the reviewing stand, saluting the military parade. The band was playing. Everyone was celebrating Sadat's success in making peace with Israel and regaining the Sinai Peninsula for Egypt. Many, including his father saw it as a sell out to the west.

Hamu could still see that event. Suddenly a military vehicle stopped abruptly. A team of five soldiers, later labelled as members of a terrorist group, jumped out. Firing machine guns and throwing grenades, they ran toward the reviewing stand. Egypt's President Sadat and six others were killed. Hamu's father was part of that band of men who killed Sadat. His father was taken prisoner. That day, when he last saw his father, Hamu's hatred of the West was born.

Tonight, as those Israeli retaliatory bombs fall, our explosive device planted in the guest house will explode like a falling bomb. We will destroy the professor in the guest house. With the help of my men, Interpol will see the professor's body as my body, as the body of their fugitive, Hamu. The day following a new and different person, the impostor of the professor, will board that British Air flight for London. I will board that plane as Professor Fouad.

ii

Rachti, the man at the other end of Hamu's phone call, was burning with resentment over Hamu's final words, "Remember, failure is not an option."

As he drove on to pick up the professor at his apartment in Cairo, Rachti was boiling with anger. Those words, failure is not an option, were a threat. Hamu was repeating that threat. He was reminding Rachti that any failure to carry out his assignments would result not only in Rachti's death but also the death of his wife, Tala. That threat had forced Rachti to participate in this plot. Now, once again, he was being warned that there was no escape. He had to participate.

Rachti's assignment was to drive the victim to Gaza City. Hamu had needed someone the professor would trust, someone like Rachti, to carry out the plan. Rachti and his wife, Tala, had been old friends of Fouad and Vashti when they lived in Cairo. They had all gone to school together. Rachti had no choice. He had been drafted to carry out this assignments in the plot with the warning that his failure to participate would be fatal for him and his wife, Tala. Full compliance with the duties assigned to him was the only course of action open to him.

As Rachti arrived at the professor's apartment on the university campus, he was feeling like a Judas. What do I do? Give him a kiss and say your old friend has come to chauffeur you to your death?

From the window of the Cairo apartment the university had provided, Fouad, was watching for Rachti. He was reflecting on his last phone call with Vashti. She had been reassured when she learned that their old friend Rachti would be driving Fouad to the meeting in Gaza City.

Vashti had been churning with anxiety about her husband's relationship with the Two Vipers brotherhood. She reminded him, "Fouad, you and I have changed during these years in Vancouver. We don't even think like those men."

Vashti had continued to express her fears, "Fouad, you and I share a completely different world view from those hate filled men of the Two Vipers brotherhood. We have become new and different people. Our lives are no longer ruled by the hatred that fuels them. Some of our closest friends are the people they call infidels. If they knew where we are in our walk with God they would treat us infidels. Be on your guard."

Fouad saw the car coming for the trip to Gaza. He swung open the door. He was delighted to see his old friend. For a moment the two men just looked at each other.

"Greetings Professor!" Rachti smiled. "I still like calling you Professor."

When Fouad saw that Rachti's hair showed no signs of white, he said, "Rachti, I think that my white hair makes me your older brother."

As they loaded up the car, Fouad said, "Looks like a good day for our drive to Gaza City."

"Yes, I plan to go by way of the new bridge across the Nile and head out of Cairo on Sharia Ramses. The bridge across the Suez Canal may give us the opportunity to see really big ships passing under the bridge. Then we head north to the coast and East across Sinai. We will be in Gaza City for supper. They are planning a big feast for your arrival."

The two men were practically the same age. Although they had grown up together, their appearances were very different. Fouad with his white hair and white beard looked considerably older than his driver. Their clothing was also very different. Rachti wore the traditional Egyptian loose fitting white galabia. Fouad was dressed in the western style three piece suit he wore on campus back in Vancouver.

Fouad had a number of things in mind when he accepted the invitation to Gaza City. As a professor of Middle East studies he wanted to sharpen his insight in what was really going on in Gaza and neighboring Israel and Egypt. His other concern was to get out from under the demand of Two Vipers leadership that he continue recruiting Middle East men for the brotherhood. Fouad was very aware that the brotherhood was far from satisfied with him.

Rachti glanced at his friend and observed, "Besides your looks, Fouad, I have the feeling that in many ways you are a very different man from the Fouad who left here three years ago for Vancouver."

"To be truthful, Rachti, we have enjoyed becoming part of our community at the university in Vancouver. People have been very gracious to us. I am no longer comfortable recruiting young immigrants for Two Vipers. I would rather help them become a part of the Canadian people. I gather that the men in Gaza are very dissatisfied with me."

Rachti was silent for a few moments. "Fouad, you have many old friends within the brotherhood but there is a great dissatisfaction with your direction in Canada.

Fouad was thinking of Vashti's anxiety about his visit to Gaza. Vashti is right. We're no longer a part of their world."

As they drove along, Rachti turned on the car radio. He smiled, "Let's see if we can pick up any news."

Suddenly the program being aired was interrupted. A loud alert buzzer sounded. "We interrupt this broadcast to bring a special report." The news continued in Arabic. "Officials in Israel are reporting intense rocket attacks launched from the Gaza City. Observers in Israel report that the rockets are new and more powerful. They are reaching farther into Israel. Israelis are claiming that the rockets are a new type supplied by Iran."

The commentator stated, "Israeli officials say that rockets fired from Gaza City have landed near Ashdod. Israeli media report that several blasts had been heard in Yavneh, about 25 km south of Tel Aviv. The extent of the damage is not yet known."

The commentator went on: "It is expected that the attacks will prompt an Israeli response by air strikes tonight. Israel has promised immediate reprisals to any attacks. Israel's defense minister has warned that Israel will not tolerate these terrorist attacks."

Rachti turned off the radio.

Fouad asked, "As Gaza City launches these attacks they must expect some response. What sort of retaliation does Gaza expect from the Israelis?"

Rachti said, "On the basis of our past experiences we in Gaza City must be braced for a strong aerial bombing attack. Sorry, this may happen the night of your visit."

For the next few minutes they drove on in silence. Rachti was feeling the burden of knowing that the Israeli air attack was being deliberately provoked for one reason, and one reason only. Those rockets were being launched to provoke a bombing raid tonight so that the explosive device planted in the guest house to kill this man sitting beside me will appear to be the work of Israeli bombs. Here I am, under threat of death myself, forced to be a part of this plan, forced to drive this old friend into the hot spot of this deadly attack.

Rachti had seen the men plant Israeli type explosives in the guest house where Fouad was to spend the night. At the proper time, as the Israeli bombs began to fall, the men assigned to the task would detonate the explosives concealed in the guest house where Fouad would be sleeping.

Rachti was sickened as he reviewed his assigned tasks. When the bombs stopped falling, he was to hurry to the ruins of guest house. He was to search for and retrieve, as quickly as possible, the body of this look alike professor. When he retrieved the body he was to signal men to come and do what was needed to make the look alike body appear to be the body of Hamu.

Then most repulsive part came next. With the help of the other men he was to remove the western clothes from the body and re-clothe the battered corpse with torn and bloodied clothing of Hamu. They were to make sure that the body would be seen by agents of Interpol and Mossad, or MI5, as a confirmation of the death of Hamu.

Since it was known that Interpol had fingerprints of Hamu, they had to make sure that forensic agents could not take finger prints from the corpse. The body had to be damaged in such a way as to eliminate any possibility of taking prints.

The team had an even more difficult assignment. Hamu wore a left foot prosthetic devise. This team would have to quickly simulate damage to the lower left leg to conform to this difference. They were prepared to place near the body a prosthetic devise Hamu had worn and that carried his fingerprints. Another prop would be Hamu's AK 47. He was known to be inseparable from this weapon.

While the men were working to re-clothe and make the battered look alike body appear to be Hamu's body, Rachti had another crucial task. Rachti was to gather the professor's clothing and personal things and pack them in his car alongside a special dummy that was dressed to look like an injured Fouad. The dummy was to be dressed in the professor's clothing and covered with bandages and wrapped in blankets. Rachti had the job of gathering and putting alongside the dummy all of the professor's personal things. This would include things like Fouad's distinctive ostrich leather briefcase, his well know heavy tortoise shell glasses. He was to gather personal items from the body, things like the professor's wedding and university rings. All of Fouad's papers and personal things like his wallet and especially his passport and air ticket home. All was to be loaded in Rachti's car.

Word would be spread that Rachti was driving the injured Fouad back to his apartment in Cairo for medical care before his flight back to Canada the next day.

Meanwhile Hamu would have travelled to Cairo. He would be waiting in the professor's apartment for Rachti's arrival with the dummy and the professor's personal things. With access to the professor's western clothing and some bandages to represent injuries from the Israeli attack, Hamu would be set to step out as the professor. The following day, with Fouad's passport and return ticket, the impersonator would head for the Cairo International Airport.

As Rachti drove along, it was difficult to hold back his feelings as he glanced at his old friend riding beside him. With his white hair and beard, yes, Fouad really looked like Hamu. He could see how the plan had developed to exploit this unusual resemblance.

Finally they were there at the Two Vipers headquarters. A crowd of men quickly surrounded the professor and ushered him into the reception hall. Rachti observed the warm greetings and the enthusiastic expressions of pleasure by many at the arrival of their old friend. Who would think that a plot to exterminate this man was under way? Only a select few knew that the celebration was planned to disarm the professor for what was coming. Hamu had slipped away, several hours earlier, to begin his drive to Fouad's apartment in Cairo.

Fouad was pleased with the warm reception. He was enjoying their hospitality. He laughed, "With the spread of food put out for this crowd, one would hardly believe the stories of food shortages in Gaza due to the Israeli blockade."

Rachti watched the scene for a while. Then, as soon as he could, Rachti hurried off to his home. It was time for him to level with Tala and tell her exactly what was going on and the assignment forced upon him with death threats.

CHAPTER 7

Gaza City, Gaza Strip

"O what a tangled web we weave,
when first we practice to deceive"
– Sir Walter Scott - 1771 - 1832

After a very emotional visit with his wife, Tala, and making sure that she understood what was going on, Rachti jumped in his car and drove off.

At the given time, as instructed, Rachti parked under a particular car port near the brotherhood's guest house. He turned off his motor and slid down out of sight to await the anticipated Israeli bomb raid. His hideout, a little over 150 feet from the guest house, was dangerously close but it was essential for his assignment. His orders were to be the first person to reach the demolished guest house after the bomb was exploded. The plan called for him to dig through the devastation and find the body before anyone else arrived. As he waited for the certain Israeli attack to begin, Rachti turned on the car radio to monitor any information that might be broadcast concerning the anticipated Israeli raid.

Four men assigned to work with Rachti were waiting nearby in another building. They were to wait while Rachti searched through debris for the body. Once he found and extracted the body from the ruins, these men were to join him and work quickly to make sure that the body would be seen by everyone as the body of Hamu. When he waved his shovel, indicating he had found the body, they were to join him.

They were all well prepared. One man wore a small backpack that held some of Hamu's clothing and a duplicate prosthesis for his left foot. Another waited with Hamu's personally modified AK 47 rifle.

Suddenly the air raid sirens began their terrifying wail. Radio stations began to notify the people of an imminent Israeli air attack. People were urged to take cover in the secure parts of their buildings. Spokesmen warned that the Israeli airstrike was expected to hit the areas of Gaza City from which the rocket attack was launched.

Radio reports soon indicated that the barrage of guided smart bombs from the Israel planes was tremendous. Israeli forces were directing a powerful airstrike on Gaza City in response to the rocket attacks. Commentators reported hits on various buildings. Tense voices described the attack. Rachti was worried. Perhaps they provoked the Israelis too much.

Suddenly, while bombs were still falling on nearby parts of the city, Rachti saw the planned powerful explosion blow the guest house apart. As planned, it appeared as though the guest house where Professor Fouad was staying had received a direct hit by an Israeli bomb. The tremendous explosion brought down much of the building. No one could have lived through what appeared to be a direct hit.

Since his assignment was to be the first person to reach the demolished guest house, Rachti did not wait for the wail of the all clear sirens. He pulled on his work gloves, picked up the crow bar and shovel he had planted nearby and headed for the ruins.

Rachti had been coerced and forced into this assignment by threats against the lives of both himself and his wife. He went to work, as ordered, prying and digging through the shattered and smoldering ruins to find the remains of the victim. Searching for a body in such a demolished building was no easy task. He concentrated his effort in the area of the professor's room. It took considerable muscle to lever aside some of the heavier pieces of the debris with his crowbar. His heavy gloves helped him to push aside timbers and lift broken pieces of concrete. The considerable broken glass made the work quite hazardous.

He found it a very difficult and challenging task to search for the body of a man in these ruins. The search involved moving quite a bit of fallen building debris.

Finally Rachti spotted the body. He saw the western clothing. He pried building materials away carefully. Although he had made an effort to prepare himself, Rachti found it very difficult even to look down at what he had uncovered. There lying in the building rubble was the broken and misshaped remains with a piece of rebar protruding from the body. He gritted his teeth, extracted the mangled body and waved his shovel signaling the team to join him.

When the men arrived, they were stunned to see the battered condition of the body. Only a few hours earlier at the reception they had enjoyed dinner with the professor. Although they were part of the conspiracy to kill the man, they were not prepared to for what they saw lying before them. Rachti had to push the nauseated men into action.

The men got to work removing the western style clothing from the battered body. The professor's university ring and his wedding band had to be removed. They gathered up things such as the professor's well known tortoise shell glasses and his gold watch and chain. In one of the pockets they found a letter Fouad had received from his wife along with a picture of her. They put all the professor's personal things in his ostrich leather briefcase.

Two men took the personal things of the professor, along with his briefcase and personal papers, to Rachti's car. These things were packed in alongside the bandaged dummy that people were told was the injured professor. This dummy dressed in western clothing and was well wrapped in bandages in preparation for a trip to Cairo, supposedly for medical attention.

Demonstrating careful care for what was supposed to be the injured professor was a vital part of the plan. They had to convince everyone that the professor, though injured, was alive and would soon be returning to Canada. This was necessary to set the stage for the appearance of Hamu, the impersonator of the professor, at the airport the next day.

The men working on the body tackled the unpleasant task of making it appear that the bomb had so damaged the hands that it would be impossible for the police to run a check of finger prints..

They got to work on the other major challenge, the task of working on the lower left leg. They had to make it appear that the bomb had blown away that part of the lower left leg where Hamu would have worn his prosthesis. When they were satisfied with their efforts, they placed the prosthesis, covered with Hamu's finger prints, alongside the body.

The men clothed the body representing Hamu in a bloodied and torn white cotton galabia. A key prop, Hamu's AK 47, was placed by the body on the stretcher. Everyone would recognize Hamu's personal weapon.

News of a direct hit on the guest house was soon spreading. People were telling others, "Hamu was killed while visiting the professor. The professor was injured."

The news that Hamu had been killed spread quickly. Surrounded by the growing crowd of mourners, the men brought out the body on a stretcher for all to see. Soon the police were there in force. Reports that Hamu had been killed brought in plain clothes agents of the international police.

This was a key moment. It was essential that the body found in the guest house ruins would be quickly seen by everyone as the body of Hamu.

Things moved along as the planners had hoped. No one questioned the identity of the body. There was widespread mourning for Hamu. That the severely damaged body in the familiar clothing was Hamu's body was confirmed by the growing anger of the crowd. The sight of his AK 47 by his side intensified the grief.

Rachti spotted some men known to be international police agents. He and the other men involved in the plot made it a point to help the officials examine the body. Seeing the damaged hands, one of agents lifted fingerprints from the prosthetic devise and Hamu's AK 47. The wide spread grief of the people was very convincing.

Suddenly another action planned to convince the police took place. Hamu's weeping physician appeared and identified the body. The physician, as planned, made much display of his sorrow for the death of Hamu. He quickly signed a death certificate indicating that the dead person was none other than the Two Vipers leader, Hamu. For the plotters this step was regarded as very essential.

To prevent any further examination of the battered body the plan called for a mortician to come quickly on the scene. When he arrived the mortician immediately wrapped the body in a *kadan* or shroud, according to local custom. With the help of men involved in the plot he quickly moved the body to his vehicle. The mortician explained that due to the terrible condition of the remains immediate cremation was necessary and drove off with the body.

A local physician had been lined up to look after the injured Fouad. This physician went to Rachti's car to examine the supposedly injured Fouad. The dummy representing the professor, dressed in western clothing and wrapped in bandages, was to be driven to Cairo for treatment. The university was informed that the injured professors needed rest in his apartment without visitors. This was planned to give Hamu privacy as he prepared to take on his new identity as the professor's impostor.

One of the men held up out some of Hamu's personal affects. "Look here is Hamu's wallet with the picture of his dear wife, who, as we all know, was also killed by weapons from the West."

To distract the journalists from any question about the identity of the body several these men began cursing the Israelis. Shouting and shooting off their weapons the men shouted, "Israel will pay for the death of Hamu." The news stations were soon broadcasting how Arab leaders were promising to avenge the death of Hamu Adullah.

The final task for Rachti was to make the trip to Cairo with the dummy dressed to appear as the injured professor. The final objectives of the murder plot made this trip necessary. The purpose of this trip to Cairo was to give the impression that Fouad, the professor from Canada, had survived the bombing. Rachti had to be seen driving to Cairo with this well dressed and heavily bandaged dummy, to confirm that the professor had survived. At the Egyptian border Rachti flashed the professor's passport,

Rachti was also taking to Hamu in Cairo those very important personal things that Fouad needed for his impersonation of the professor. He was bringing such things as the professor's personal papers, his briefcase and wallet. This collection included personal things like Fouad's rings and personal photos. Perhaps they would find among his thing keys and checks that might lead to bank accounts in Toronto. Most important of all, Rachti was delivering Fouad's priceless Canadian passport and plane tickets. Equipped with those essential items the impersonator would be ready to fly to London and on to Toronto and impersonate Fouad.

Rachti was bringing quite a collection of the professor's personal things in Fouad's beautiful ostrich leather briefcase. Along with Fouad's rings, pens, and personal note book he would be delivering a special pair of tortoise shell glass frames that duplicated the professor's familiar glass frames. These had been made in advance, with lenses suitable for Hamu. Fouad's passport and plane tickets were the key items.

Before leaving Gaza City for Cairo with the dummy representing Fouad, Rachti, as instructed, made a special phone call to Hamu in Cairo. He then slipped into his car with the disguised and bandaged dummy and headed for Cairo.

CHAPTER 8

CAIRO, Egypt

"What dreams may come,
when we have shifted off this mortal coil."
– Macbeth, Shakespeare, 1606

Hamu was waiting in Fouad's Cairo apartment for Rachti's call from Gaza City. He was getting the feeling that this could be a very long night. The call for which he was waiting was planned to confirm that everything in Gaza City had gone as planned. Shortly before morning Rachti was to arrive and walk the bandaged dummy representing the injured professor into the apartment.

Once the dummy was delivered and destroyed and Hamu held Fouad's passport in his hand, he would cease to be Hamu and his impersonation of the professor would begin.

As he paced back and forth in the apartment, Hamu was amused with the questions running through his mind. Yes, the man Hamu will be ruled dead by the police but this man Hamu, the man who planned all this, will remain very much alive. I will be impersonating Fouad. Men will be calling me professor. But who will I be? I've heard of the man without a country. Who will I be? The man without an identity?

Hamu was realizing that he had not taken much time to consider the impact of this murder scheme on himself. The focus had been on eliminating the professor in what he believed would be the perfect crime. The goal was that everyone, people, press and police, would see the body dragged from the ruins, as Hamu's body. He had not thought too much about what it was going to be impersonating the man he caused to be dead.

As he waited there in Fouad's apartment, Hamu he looked in the mirror. Who am I looking at? That is no longer going to be Hamu. That's not the real Fouad.

Hamu looked at the clock again. When is he going to call?

The call would deliver, hopefully, the word yes, spoken three times. The first, "Yes" would signal that the Israeli air attacks had provided cover for the destruction of the Gaza guest house and the recovery of the body in the ruins. The second "Yes" would confirm that the body recovered from rubble was being seen by everyone, and especially by the international police as his, Hamu's body. The third "Yes" would verify that everyone was viewing the bandaged dummy in Rachti's car as the injured professor, awaiting transport to Cairo for treatment.

Hamu was thinking that waiting must be one of the most difficult things life asks of a man. With the curtains drawn in Fouad's Cairo apartment, he continued to alternate between pacing back and forth and sitting there waiting for the call.

That one phone call was needed to confirm the fact that, as far as the police were concerned, the look a like's body was regarded as Hamu's body. Rachti's call would mean that right then and there the fugitive Hamu officially ceased to exist. He would be taking on a new identity. With that call, while sitting there in the professor's apartment, he would begin a new life as an impostor of the man whose death he had arranged.

Suddenly the silence of the apartment was shattered with the ringing of the phone. Hamu held the phone to his ear but remained silent.

A voice grumbled, "Yes." The voice mumbled again, "Yes." Again the third time, the voice mumbled, "Yes." Then the caller hung up.

Hamu pounded his fist. All three objectives had gone according to plan. Yes, the destruction of the guest house to kill the professor was seen as a hit by the Israeli retaliatory air strike. The perfect crime. Yes, the look alike body, clothed with the clothes of Hamu was seen by everyone as the body of Hamu. The body taken from the ruins had been accepted as the body of Hamu, not only by the media but by international police. As planned, a death certificate for Hamu had been issued by his physician. The bomb battered body had been taken for cremation. Yes, the professor was seen as injured but alive and on his way to Cairo for treatment. Hamu pounded his fist again.

As he sat there, alone, in the professor's Cairo apartment, the architect of what seemed to be the perfect crime, Hamu was suddenly talking to himself, "No more looking over my shoulder for agents of Interpol, wherever I go. Their fugitive has died. Officially I no longer exist."

Hamu was suddenly experiencing some totally new feelings. I'm officially dead, but physically I am very much alive. From now on the man Hamu does not exist. I am no longer Hamu. I look like Fouad and will pass as Fouad, but I'm not really Professor Fouad. It seems like a life after death. Who am I?

He sat there letting the reality of it all sink in.

Rachti should be here soon. When he arrives with the professor's personal things that will help me step into this new identity. Wearing his gold watch and chain, wearing his rings, will help me step into this new identity. Glasses fitted to heavy frames matching his will help. When I finally hold his Canadian passport and his British Air return ticket in my hands, then the new life of this impersonator will really begin. The moment Rachti walks in that door with the professor's personal things, I will begin to be Fouad.

Hamu heard a car pull up. That has to be Rachti. Hamu watched from the darkened apartment as Fouad very carefully and gently went through the routine of assisting the clothed and bandaged dummy figure from the car. For the benefit of anyone who might be observing, Rachti carefully assisted the well clothed dummy to the door. White bandages were very much in evidence.

At the door Rachti reached out with Fouad's key in hand. He opened the door and continued to help the supposedly seriously wounded scholar. Then leaving the lights still off, Rachti returned to his car and brought in the Professor's suitcase and briefcase.

Hamu was ready to turn on the lights.

Rachti's first words were, "No lights yet. First, I must deflate and pack away the dummy. I was instructed to first to make sure you were properly dressed and outfitted with the bandages and provided by your physician friend.

"First, let me deflate the dummy and stuff it in a bag. I will take it with me."

After he had deflated the dummy, Rachti proceeded to provided things to reinforce the idea that this man, preparing to pose as the professor, appeared to be a man with some injuries. Rachti slipped on Hamu a sling for his left arm. Then, as he pulled out another item, he said, "Here is that very special item you requested." He provided a walking caste to cover Hamu's prosthesis for his left foot.

Rachti stepped back, took a look, and said, "You are now Professor Fouad. Now we turn on the lights.

"As directed, your physician informed the university officials that, due to injuries, you were to have no visitors. The university was also notified that, despite your injuries, you will be taking your scheduled flight for London tomorrow morning."

Hamu exclaimed, "Wonderful! Free at last. Free from British MI5 agents. Free from Interpol. Free from those Israeli Mossad blood hounds. Canada, here I come."

Rachti said, "As directed, I have brought you the professor's ostrich leather brief case. There are still some blood stains we were unable to remove. All his papers and personal effects are now yours. Here is his wallet.

"Here is that most important item." Rachti handed Hamu the professor's passport. "And here are his return tickets for tomorrow's flight to London and on to Toronto."

Hamu grasped the passport and waved it. "At last I have you in my hands." He moved quickly to a mirror and help up the passport photograph by his image. "Yes. Now, I am Fouad."

When Hamu turned around Rachti was already out the door and on his way. Hamu watched the vanishing car. Rachti did what was required. What lies ahead is up to me.

Hamu went back to checking out the personal things of the man he would be impersonating. There was much to examine jammed into the professor's briefcase.

He started going through the man's wallet. I didn't anticipate this. I feel like I'm snooping in someone's personal possessions. Reluctantly he continued pulling out things.

And then he saw it. There was a photo of the professor and a strikingly beautiful woman in an Egyptian dress. It was obviously a photo of Fouad and his wife. He was looking at something that in all his preparation he had never considered.

Hamu was stunned. There's a wife. In all the plans to lure the professor back to the Middle East, to eliminate the man and impersonate him, somehow he had never considered the fact that the man would have a wife. How could I have been so stupid? Could this stupid thoughtlessness be related to the fact that I've been living alone, without my wife, since she was killed in combat with western backed forces three years ago?

Hamu was realizing the complexity of his problem. I can't go about claiming to be the professor with his widow out there in Vancouver telling people I am not Fouad?

As soon as possible, I have meet this woman. She must be getting all sorts of reports about her husband. She must not know whether her husband is dead or alive. I need to clear up the confusion. I have to inform her that her husband was killed in that Israeli air raid. Then I have to explain to her the reason for the confusion as to what happened to her husband.

She needs to be told that, after his death, we encouraged the international police to identify her husband's body as my body. She has to understand that the reason for exploiting his similarity to my appearance was to help me end my days as a fugitive. To help me vanish from their radar the police were encouraged to conclude that it was not Fouad, but Hamu, who was killed by those Israeli bombs that night.

This woman deserves to know why everyone was led to believe that her husband, Fouad, though injured was alive and heading back to Toronto. She needs to be told that it was not her husband who was returning but a man who closely resembles her husband. I have to explain that we are exploiting the remarkably similarity between her husband and myself.

I've got a job to do. If I am to vanish as a fugitive by impersonating her husband, this woman has to be persuaded to back up my impersonation of her husband.

"I will catch the Cairo to London flight tomorrow. I'll deal with the wife situation after I pass through customs in Toronto.

He studied the picture. An unusually beautiful woman. Perhaps equally intelligent. I hope that she will be wise enough to realize that she has no alternative but to go along with the impersonation. She will not want to be removed from the scene, also."

ii

The mission team's brief stopover in Cairo was coming to a close. The visit to the pyramids of ancient Egypt had helped soften their being forced to leave Nairobi. Reluctantly, they were resuming the trip home, as directed.

Roger and Emily were booked on the same flight from Cairo to London. Due to the short notice of their arrangements they had not been able to get adjacent seats.

As they boarded and were moving to their assigned seats, Roger spotted a familiar looking Egyptian boarding. That looks like the man I met at Heathrow on my way to Kenya. He pointed him out to Emily. "Look! There's our professor friend."

"This is amazing. I met Professor Fouad in Heathrow, on my way here. Then we heard his lecture here in Cairo. Now, we find him on our plane to London."

Emily smiled. "It's your professor, alright. Where else would you see such a handsome white beard topped with tortoise shell glasses?"

To Roger's delight, the man moved along the aisle and took the seat just across the aisle in the row ahead of Roger. After stashing his beautiful overloaded ostrich leather briefcase in the storage area above, the man dropped into his seat.

Roger laughed. He saw their third meeting as something akin to the famous Stanley and Livingston encounter in Africa. He called out a modified version of the famous greeting, "Dr. Fouad, I presume."

The man, now seated, turned and just looked at him with a rather blank stare.

Roger repeated his greeting. The man, after a forced smile, nodded and turned back to his Cairo paper.

Is this the man the man I met at Heathrow? He shows no sign of recognition at all. With all he's been through this week, perhaps his mind is on other things. He doesn't seem to recognize me at all. He might as well be the man in the iron mask.

Roger was really perplexed. He isn't acting like the man who spoke so warmly to Emily and myself after the lecture. Could it be his twin brother?

Roger sat back in his seat and opened his International Herald Tribune. He held the paper in a way that permitted him to study the face. The striking features of the man conformed to the details Roger remembered from the sketch of the man he had made at Heathrow. All the same features were there, the strong nose, the white beard and mustache.

Roger slid out his pocket sketchbook. Once more, he made a quick sketch of the man. He smiled. We painters can do pretty well without smart phone cameras.

After the flight was airborne Roger noted that the unresponsive man was wearing a walking cast on his left foot. That's the answer. He's been injured. He may be experiencing pain. He may be heavily medicated. That might explain his lack of sociability.

Roger studied the face of his subject across the aisle while the man was absorbed in reading something. Those strong facial features were excellent material for a watercolor portrait. Still something seemed different. The face had a certain harshness he had not seen at the lecture. The warmth that he had seen at the lecture was lacking. It is hard to believe it is the same man.

Finally Roger called over to the man, "What takes you to London?"

There was no reply. Roger tried again, "Is London your final destination?" The man turned, looked at him briefly, nodded and turned away. He said nothing.

Roger was baffled. Is he pretending he knows no English? Unless he's a twin brother, he's certainly is the man we heard giving that lecture that called for a Muslim reformation. Could he be in danger? Roger gave up and turned to an e-book.

After a while Roger tried again. He threw across the aisle the expression used in many African cultures, "Peace be with you." No response. Maybe he's flying incognito.

Once it was evident that there was going to be no conversation, Roger returned to his sketch book. He laughed. Perhaps I should call this sketch Pharaoh in disguise.

When the plane touched down at Heathrow in London, the Egyptian rose and left with no comment. Roger and Emily left the plane to for their connecting flights.

While they were waiting for their flights Roger pulled out the sketch book and worked to touch up his sketch of the man on the plane.

Emily who was waiting for her flight to Toronto, watched. She commented, "There is one key detail your sketch doesn't show, Roger. The professor, or whoever he is, was wearing gloves."

"What's so important about gloves?"

"Gloves? Roger, don't you read any mysteries or suspense stories? The bad guy always wears gloves to avoid leaving a trail of incriminating finger prints."

PART TWO
THE IMPOSTOR

CHAPTER 9

Toronto

"But evil men and impostors will
proceed from bad to worse, deceiving and being deceived."
– Paul - First Century

In the stream of passengers moving down the ramp at Toronto's Airport, one man was moving rather deliberately. He was slowed down by a walking cast on his left foot. The left arm was in a sling. It was all what Hamu called his camouflage. The injury props were designed as a distraction in case he met someone who had known the professor previously.

The impostor sailed through customs. To match the photo on Fouad's passport Hamu was wearing a duplicate of the professor's tortoise shell glasses. He had allowed his white beard to grown fuller. The agent held up the passport, glanced at him, and waved him through. As he expected, no problem.

Toronto at last. No more dodging international police. I am now Professor Fouad. But his celebration was tempered with caution. The impostor was being very careful.

At the baggage carousel, as he was reaching out for his bag, another passenger said, "You need some help, aye?" The man pulled off the bag for him. Then the stranger pulled off his other bag too.

When an attendant offered to take his baggage, Hamu nodded. "Taxi line, please." He gave the taxi driver the only Toronto address he had. It was an address he had found on a tag attached to a key among the professor's things. He hoped that it might be the key to an apartment the professor used for his Toronto recruitment operations.

Hamu was enjoying the ride through the streets of Toronto. I'm really here. Except for that awkward encounter with the American on the Cairo-London flight, the trip has gone well. That meeting was a disaster. On the other hand, that encounter confirmed the effectiveness of his appearance in this impersonation of the professor.

When the taxi arrived at the address on the key tab, Hamu found himself looking at a small town house. Could this have been Fouad's base in Toronto while recruiting new immigrants from the Middle East for Two Vipers?

He asked the driver to wait while he went to the door. Not knowing what to expect he rang the doorbell. After waiting a reasonable time he tried the key tagged with this address. It worked. When he entered he was relieved to find on the floor some mail addressed to Fouad.

He gestured for the driver to bring in his bags. He told the driver to wait. He was going to need wheels.

As Hamu went about exploring the place he remembered something. He pulled on his gloves. Professor Fouad can't go spreading Hamu finger prints.

As he explored the place he was encouraged to find a rent notice addressed to Fouad. He found a photo of the professor meeting with some men. It was taken in this place. Yes, Fouad had met with his recruits and leaders here.

Hamu was thinking that it would be good to hold his first meeting with some key leaders at the house. The familiar setting could help their acceptance of me. He recalled that Fouad's papers mentioned a meeting place called the warehouse. I'll get the leaders to take me there to meet the recruits.

Among the professor's things Hamu had found references to a particular Toronto bank and what was obviously a bank safety deposit box key. He decided that his first real impersonation as Fouad would be a visit to that bank.

For the bank trip Hamu left behind the walking cast and the sling. He decided to be seen moving slowly with a cane. He was quite confident he could pull off a successful impersonation at the bank. Using his considerable skill in forging signatures, with much practice, he had perfected the professor's signature.

Hamu told his driver. "Take me to the nearest sporting goods store, and wait." Hamu came out of the store with a good sized day pack. He gave the driver the name of the bank indicated in the professor's papers. As they approached the bank he slipped on his driving gloves, hung the day pack over his shoulder and told the cab to wait for him. He was eager to get access to that bank box. He was hoping it held some cash. He was in urgent need of Canadian money.

Once in the lobby he looked for the area of the vault and the safety deposit box attendant. He identified himself and presented the bank box key. The attendant pulled his card from her file.

Hamu smiled as he signed below the professor's previous signatures. He was very satisfied with how well his forgery matched the previous signature by Fouad.

After using both his key and the bank's key, the lady handed a large bank box to him along with his key.

Still wearing his gloves, Hamu took the box into one of the privacy booths. When he opened the box he just stared. The bank box was loaded with packets of Canadian cash. He thumbed through one packet of Canadian hundred dollar bills. Since he had arrived with very little cash he was greatly relieved to see all this Canadian money. The box appeared to contain thousands in Canadian dollars.

With the day pack, he was prepared to take with him everything in the box. He planned to take the cash to another bank and open a new account with his own signature as Fouad.

As he moved the cash to his day pack, in the bottom of the bank box, he discovered a notebook. He flipped through the pages. He was amazed. He found himself saying, "This is incredible." He held in his hands Fouad's personal notebook with pictures and personal information for all Fouad's Canadian recruits for Two Vipers. "This is priceless. This is just what I need."

Hamu returned the box to the attendant and terminated the box rental. For his own information, he jokingly asked the attendant which bank was their primary competitor?

Outside the bank, with the back pack loaded with the cash on his back, Hamu directed his driver to take him to the bank referred to by the attendant. Using the professor's passport for identification, Hamu opened a new account. With a confident smile he signed the necessary forms. He rented a bank box to hold the cash in his back pack. In the privacy of the bank booth, he enjoyed transferring the bundles of cash in the pack to the bank box. He was pleased to have this nest egg to begin his life in Canada.

After he pocketed a couple bundles of cash, Hamu leaned back in his chair and said softly, "That should get me started!" He had never actually possessed much money. The cash in the bank box gave him a new feeling of security. He smiled as he spoke softly to himself, "This is interesting. I have taken steps to wipe out the only person who knew of the contents of this box. Everything in this box is mine and I am accountable to no one."

Back at the townhouse, Hamu paged through the notebook he had retrieved from the bank box. It contained personal information for all the agents recruited for Two Vipers in Canada. As he studied the photo and the personal information about each man, Hamu was particularly interested in where the individuals worked and where each one might be of special use. This is great. When I hold conferences with men, as the professor, I will be able to greet them by name. I will have some knowledge of what they have been doing.

Two key leaders in the notebook caught his attention. One man named Nibal worked as at a nuclear power generating plant. Hamu smiled. He was immediately thinking of the potential of having a man working within a power station. A possible source for radioactive material for dirty bombs.

Hamu discovered that another special agent, a man named Daoud. This man was a dining car manager on a great Canadian transcontinental train. A dining car manager on a transcontinental train might prove to be very useful.

Hamu phoned each of the two men. He let them known that their Two Vipers leader was back in Toronto. The men had heard of the Israeli bombing of Gaza City and reports he had been injured. They were excited to hear that he had survived and was back in Toronto. He asked them to come to the town house in the evening for a special conference.

Hamu was still feeling new in his impersonation. He attempted, on the phone, to prepare the men for the meeting. He told them about his injuries during the Israeli air attack. "I'm doing OK. However, be prepared. The man you greet tonight may seem not fully himself and a bit absent minded. I am moving more slowly. You may have to remind me of things. Be prepared for some new directives from Two Vipers bothers in Gaza."

That evening, before the two men arrived, Hamu slipped on again the bandage around his head. He snapped on the walking cast to cover his left foot prosthesis and put his arm in the sling. He hoped that these props would divert attention from any differences in his personal mannerisms.

When they arrived, Nibal and Daoud had no trouble accepting of him. The two men, Nibal, the nuclear plant worker and Daoud the dining car manager, were delighted that he had survived the bombing attack and had returned. They seemed to accept him as Professor Fouad without question.

Nibal said, "When we heard of the attack in Gaza City, we were quite concerned about you. We are glad to see you all in one piece."

His stage props, the bandage and the arm in a sling, all seemed to be doing what he intended. He coughed now and then and stopped to take a pain pill to distract from slightly different mannerisms of speech. He explained his wearing gloves as due to an allergy.

Hamu was feeling reassured. If these men accept me, the others, who spent even less time with Fouad will have no problem. They will take my mannerisms for granted.

Hamu put a serious questions to Nibal, the man working in the nuclear power station, "The men in Gaza want us to get the attention of folks here in the West with some dirty bombs. Do you see any way that we could obtain some suitable radioactive material from the power station?"

"Radioactive material for a dirty bomb?" Nibal was stunned for a moment. Then he shared some ways that, despite strong security measures, the power station was vulnerable. He had some encouraging information. "I am not the only one of our men working there. Three of us work there now. We are all on the night shift."

Hamu asked Daoud for suggestions on how his position on a great transcontinental train could be useful in promoting the operations of Two Vipers across Canada.

The dining car manager described his great streamlined stainless steel train with enthusiasm. "The consist of our great train usually includes as many as thirty cars. When the train pulls out of Union Station in Toronto and heads west it goes through some principals cities of Canada, West of Toronto. Major stops include Sudbury, Winnipeg, Edmonton, and Vancouver. In the mountains the train stops at Jasper and Kamloops. There is one characteristic of the train that could be very useful for us. Many of the passengers are internationals.

Our agents would not be conspicuous. And one thing more. There is much less presence of security."

"You've got my wheels turning, Daoud. This is very useful information. I have much to say to our men. I am anxious to hold a meeting with all our recruits."

Nibal said, "The men will be pleased to meet with you, as usual, at the warehouse."

"I have some major challenges to share with all our recruit at the warehouse. I would like you, Nibal, along with you, Daoud, to escort me there. I want the men to see that I have survived the Israeli attack and that I am ready for action.

"There is one further need with which you can help me. My phone was destroyed during that Israeli attack in Gaza City. I want you to take me to a location where I can acquire a new smart phone."

On the evening scheduled for local agents to gather, Nibal and Daoud chauffeured their leader to the meeting at the warehouse. When they arrived at the old brick warehouse out on the docks Hamu was impressed to see that more than twenty agents had gathered.

Nibal opened the meeting. "Tonight we welcome back our leader, our Canadian Pharaoh, the Professor. As you have heard, while he was visiting our brothers in Gaza City, our Pharaoh suffered some major injuries during a vicious Israeli bombing attack. We are all here to welcome you back, Professor."

The men responded with applause.

One by one, each man stepped forward to greet their leader. Each man took the leader's hand, while putting his left hand on the other's shoulder. Then each kissed the other on each cheek. It was a ritual of greeting and a renewal of unquestioning obeisance.

Finally, Hamu addressed the men. " Keep in mind our name, Two Vipers. Our symbol contains Puff adders, one of the most dangerous and venomous vipers in all of Africa. Our special tattoo, two puff adders encircling the left wrist, is a symbol of our strategy. We attack the West at two levels. First, through a hard war, the exhibition of our power. Then through the soft war in which we quietly undermine their way of life."

CHAPTER 10

Toronto Union Station

All the world's a stage,
and all the men and women merely players . . .
and one man in his time plays many parts.
– Shakespeare, 1591

In the early morning bedlam and pandemonium
surrounding Toronto's Union Station, a clever cabbie finally captured
a spot to unload his passenger and baggage. There, in the turmoil and
traffic filling First Street between Bay and York, while the cabby was
struggling to unload some rather large pieces of baggage, the passenger beckoned a porter, a tall black Canadian, to load his baggage
on the cart.

The porter piled the large pieces of baggage on his cart and headed,
as directed, for the first class pre-boarding lounge for the day's great
cross transcontinental train. The passenger, trying to keep up with the
porter, kept calling, "Fragile! Handle with care!"

As he hurried along after the porter Hamu kept muttering, half
aloud, to himself, "Yes, with very much care. Don't bring down the
whole station."

Hamu was thinking, I would never have gotten near a plane with
this load. By using this train, he laughed, no one will have a clue.

As they pushed on, it was not just the magnitude of Union Station
that astonished Hamu. It was the great constantly moving crowd.
The terminal was like a bee hive. Thousands of people were constantly moving. All were intently focused on one objective, getting
to their destination. Hamu followed close behind his tall porter. He

appreciated having this rather large black man running interference for him. When Hamu finally saw the sign, First Class Boarding Lounge, he said, "Mission accomplished."

Hamu expressed his appreciation to his baggage man. He extended his hand. He said, "You are African-Canadian? I am Egyptian-Canadian."

With a smile, the tall man drew himself up and replied, "Pleased to meet you, sir. No, sir. I am Caribbean Canadian." The man explained that the majority of black Canadians in Toronto were of Caribbean origin.

Hamu studied the faces of the First Class Boarding Lounge crowd. He was impressed that such a diverse collection of people could afford the luxury of first class tickets on this great train. It was very definitely, as Daoud had said, a train packed with internationals. He found himself scrutinizing the faces around him. Being on guard for the notorious Israeli intelligence agents of Mossad had been a way of life for him.

He laughed at himself. Still looking for Mossad agents? You are Professor Fouad, now. Yes, but you still need to keep on guard.

Suddenly a loud gong sounded and a strong voice addressed everyone. "Time to board the train. Passengers, be warned that this train, with its consist of thirty cars, is longer than the boarding platform."

Hamu followed his baggage handler, looking for his car, number 3032. Finally they found it.

The attendant, stationed at the steps under a small Canadian flag, greeted him and examined his ticket. "Welcome aboard Manor Car number 3032, Mr. Fouad." Turning to the bagged handler he directed him, "Compartment F."

As the baggage handler placed the large pieces of baggage in the special space provided he grunted, "Really hefty bags." Hamu replied with a generous tip. "Yes, thank you."

The attendant came by to say, "Welcome aboard, sir. My name is Bruce. I'm here to make sure that you have a comfortable trip on the this great train. Let me know if there is anything I can do for you?"

"Everything looks very comfortable. I could use a small table."

"No problem, sir. I'll have it for you shortly."

In a little while, as Hamu looked out his window, he was surprised to discover that the train was moving. He was impressed. This huge train was starting out of Toronto so smoothly that it was only as he saw things moving outside his window that his eye brows lifted and he said, "We're moving!"

Just then his attendant, Bruce, appeared at his doorway. He smiled, "Yes, very smooth." Quiet something to move so many cars so smoothly."

"How many cars?"

"Our consignment today includes 30 cars in addition to the two loco-motives and the baggage car. The first call for lunch should come about 12:15. Here is your card for the first lunch setting," As he extended his hand with a yellow card, the attendant's sleeve got pushed back a bit and exposed the tattoo of Two Vipers on his wrist. "Good to have you on board sir."

Hamu reached out and to receive the card. He did so in a way that made visible on his wrist the identical tattoo. Their eyes met silently.

Looking around compartment F, Hamu saw that it was, as Daoud promised, a spacious compartment. He had been told me to ask for compartment F. It was a bit larger than the others. The front wall had an attractive and well lighted wash basin and mirror. To one side was the door to a small toilet compartment and to the other a closest of about the same size.

As he brushed his white hair and beard, Hamu held up his passport by the mirror to compare it with what he saw in the mirror. "Excellent! Welcome aboard, Professor Fouad."

After first turning the lock on his compartment door, Hamu rolled out the large pieces of baggage he had brought to his compartment. He moved aside the protective top layer of clothing and examined, in each piece of baggage, the powerful explosive devise he had designed and assembled at the warehouse. He was especially concerned to check the coded detonation settings on each devise. He carefully compared this information with the address for detonation on his smart phone. These three beauties goes to Winnipeg, Edmonton and Vancouver. People in each of these cities are in for a big surprise.

ii

The next morning, the second day out of Toronto, Hamu stepped out into the corridor of his car and headed for break-fast. Anyone who looked up from their breakfast saw a tall and rather distinguished looking man standing there, waiting to be seated. There was nothing at all threatening in this well-dressed white haired man who sported a white mustache and beard. The contrast between the white facial hair and his tan complexion was striking. His beak-like nose and his heavy bushy eye brows gave the face a rather strong and commanding presence. He had an expression on his face that suggested he was accustomed to getting what he wanted when he wanted it.

Now, on the second day of its journey out of Toronto, the great train was several hours past Sudbury. They were rolling out across the great mind-boggling grain fields of the vast Canadian midlands

Most passengers were focused on the panorama of the spacious open country through which the train was passing. Hamu was preoccupied with a very different concern. He was focused on the passengers enjoying breakfast at their tables. The dining car was obviously at the heart of life on the train. This was the place to be scanning faces for any possible plain clothes officer.

As Hamu waited to be seated he listened to the conversation of the people at two nearby tables. One man, apparently a German wheat farmer, was looking out through the large windows and pointing to the endless wheat fields. Hamu heard the man exclaim in English, "I have seen a lot of fields in my life but I have never seen fields like this. They are unending. They go as far as the eye can see! Wunderbar!"

The German awakened Hamu's interest in the passing panorama of wheat fields. He was amazed with the vastness of the Canadian wheat fields. However, as an Egyptian, Hamu was fascinated by the wheat fields for a very different reason. In Egypt, wheat was a very sensitive issue. During the Arab Spring of 2011, when eighteen days of mass protests forced President Hosni Mubarak to resign, a key issue was the shortage and the rising price of wheat. Similar problems had provoked riots against former President Anwar Sadat and his assassination back in 1982. As a teenager, Hamu had actually witnessed that assassination being carried out by Muslim fundamentalists, His father had been one of them.

Hamu heard one of the German tourists say that Canada was the seventh largest producer of wheat in the world. It reminded Hamu that his homeland, Egypt, was the world's largest importer of wheat. Yes, and why, after the Arab Spring, was the new President, Morsi deposed in 2013? In addition to his efforts to make Egypt an Islamic state, the new president was stopping wheat imports. Hamu continued to take in the unbelievably great panorama of the endless wheat fields. He found himself laughing at the irony of his position. And I've come from Egypt to bring to bring revolution to this land?

Hamu continued observing the passengers and catching bits of their general conversation. The impersonator was becoming very conscious that, by stepping into the professor's shoes, he was moving among people whose whole way of life and world view was very different from his own.

As he took in the gulf between himself and these western travelers he was suddenly feeling very much alone.

Hamu looked back on what he proudly called his perfect crime. Wiping out the professor and assuming his identity was a brilliant achievement. It had made it possible for him to escape the radar of international police. However, taking on the late professor's ID to escape from his old identity had also cost him something.

I am neither Fouad nor Hamu. Now, I am neither an Egyptian nor a Canadian. I feel like the man without a country. That man had to spend the rest of his life on a ship that sailed all over the world. He was never allowed to set foot on his country's soil. There is a certain isolation and loneliness that goes along with this life of an impersonator.

As Hamu stood there at the entrance to the dining car, waiting to be seated, he watched Daoud, the dining car manager, extending special courtesies to a couple. The manager was giving much attention to this young couple. Hamu knew, of course, who they were. They were special agents recruited to board the train for a special assignment.

He watched the dining car manager seating the couple. The manager now directed his attention to the man with the white beard waiting to be seated. The manager held up his finger, gesturing to wait. Hamu gave the dining room manager a wave of his hand as if to say, "OK, I'm in no rush."

Finally, the dining car manager beckoned the waiting man to the table he had selected for him. He was seating the man with the white beard across table from the couple just seated. Hamu made his way down the aisle, consciously making an effort as he did so, to walk in the manner of Fouad. This took some effort due to his prosthesis.

The new arrival at the table eased himself into his chair and exchanged greetings with the couple. As people do on train dining cars, they talked about where they were from. The woman identified her husband as a Lebanese and herself as Egyptian. She spoke of how excited they were to be making this trip across Canada. Hamu indicated that he was returning to Vancouver.

The young woman did most of the talking for the two of them. She did not hesitate to ask the question on her mind. "Gloves? Aren't they a bit unusual in August? Why the gloves?"

The new arrival at their table grunted. "Allergy."

"Oh," the woman said somewhat apologetically. "So sorry." Both she and her husband noted the tattoo on his wrist and turned slightly to look at each other. Later as he reached to extend his coffee cup to the waiter, the young man turned his wrist so that his small tattoo of the two vipers would be seen.

Before the couple left the table, Hamu invited them to visit him in car 3032 in compartment F.

When the couple left the table Hamu remained at the table. Then the manager seated another couple across table from him. After getting acquainted, this couple was also invited to join him in Manor car number 3032 at Compartment F later in the morning.

In preparation for his visitors, Hamu brought out two special pieces of baggage. When the two couples came to compartment F, Hamu proceeded to prepare the couples for their special assignments. He showed each of the couples their particular piece of baggage. On arrival at their assigned city, each couple was to pick up from him their assigned piece of baggage for delivery to special workers in their city, Winnipeg or Edmonton. Hamu took special care to show each couple the special procedures for setting up their devise. The actual detonation could be activated only by Hamu using the secret addresses on his smart phone. Hamu would be delivering the third devise to the Vancouver agents.

He explained to the two couples that the explosive devises were to be set up and concealed in special key locations in each city. Once planted in these locations the devises would remain in place until the time came to detonate them. When the time came, each explosive device would be activated from his smart phone.

Hamu rehearsed each couple in a special procedure to pick up their special baggage upon departure from the train. As they exited the train in Winnipeg or Edmonton the man in each team was to come by his compartment door and switch his own look alike rolling baggage for that of their leader. The woman would make a similar maneuver to pick up a special briefcase.

iii

The plan for agents to switch bags was first imple-mented at Winnipeg. As passengers were preparing to exit the train Hamu stood by his open compartment door with his own large rolling duffle in the door way. People were rolling their suitcases toward the end of the car to exit.

The procedure was activated as planned. As the young man was coming on his way to exit the train he paused to rest with his rolling duffle by the door of compartment F. He stopped there as though to rest for a moment. Then his gloved hand reached down to continue rolling his suitcase. His hand, however, grabbed hold on the handle of the other large duffle sitting in the open doorway. He gave his own rolling duffle a shove with his foot into the doorway and moved on.

The switching of bags at the Winnipeg station went very smoothly. The man rolling the large duffle declined the first taxi to respond and pointed to the one waiting for him. It was a prearranged pickup. He now allowed this driver to assist him in lifting the baggage into the trunk of the taxi. This heavy baggage was being handled carefully. They were very aware that this baggage contained the essential components of a powerful bomb. The bomb was ready for placement. At a later date other substances for the bomb would be delivered in order to make the bomb a dirty bomb.

Hamu continued the procedure at his compartment doorway. Now, with a large briefcase hung over her shoulder, the young woman of the team approached. As she moved along the corridor with the other pas-sengers, she nodded and spoke some pleasantry to the man by the door. She paused there for a moment, as if waiting for the line to move on. The man in compartment remained standing there with his back against the door with a similar briefcase hanging over his shoulder. Suddenly the young woman moved forward. She quickly helped the strap slide off on her shoulder. As she did so, her arm had slipped thru the strap of the brief case of the man at the door. It was a well-practiced maneuver and well done.

Like the young man before her, this young woman declined any assistance from the baggage agents and taxi drivers. She also was par-ticular about her taxi. She beckoned to the driver whose taxi had the right number.

Two days later when the train arrived in Edmonton, a similar scene took place. The procedure carried out in Winnipeg was repeated. Once again a gloved hand reached down to continue rolling a seemingly identical piece of baggage as this man with his foot shoved his suitcase into the doorway.

A few moments later Hamu stood at his doorway with the strap of the large brief case over his shoulder. Once again a passing woman paused, slipped her arm thru the other pack strap and marched on with it without missing a step.

Hamu pounded his fist. Delivery accomplished. No one is going to stops us now. He would deliver the special baggage for Vancouver.

iv

When Hamu arrived in Jasper it felt good to step off the train and mingle with other passengers exiting at the Jasper station. He took time to check out the Japer famous icon, the historic steam locomotive parked by the station and took a few moments to study it. Then he signaled a cab to take him to the hotel where he had a reservation.

The impersonator was glad for a stopover in Jasper. Impersonating Professor Fouad could be turned off. He needed a brief change in pace. His next challenge was visiting Fouad's wife in Vancouver. As he faced the prospect of meeting this woman it burdened him that he had made this woman a widow by his scheme to eliminate her husband?

Hamu needed time to prepare for the challenge of talking, faced to face with Professor's wife. What could be a more difficult assignment? He was facing the task of informing this woman that her husband had died from the injuries caused by Israeli bombs. That was one challenge.

Then would come a greater challenge. After informing her that, despite what she may have heard, she was a widow, he had to go one step farther. He had the task of persuading her to support his impersonation of her late husband. He could continue his impersonation of the professor only if this grieving woman, his widow, could be persuaded to pretend her husband was alive.

CHAPTER 11
Vancouver, British Columbia

And the Lord God said, "It is not good that man should be alone.
I will make him a helper comparable to him."
– Genesis

With the additional locomotive added in Edmonton, the great train, powered now with three locomotives, pulled out of Jasper and began the climb through the Canadian Rockies. Almost no roads cut through these mountains. The train alone provided the opportunity for breathtaking views of the majesty of creation encountered in this portion of the Canadian Rockies. The passage through the awe-inspiring mountain landscapes was one of the principal reasons why many travelers booked passage on this train.

The mirror in compartment F, of car 3032, there was an indicator of how this mountain grandeur had moved one passenger. One inspired traveler had taped to the mirror a portion of Psalm 121. "I will lift up my eyes to the hills, from whence comes my help. My help comes from the Lord who made heaven and earth."

Hamu, the present passenger in compartment F, was little affected by the scenic panorama unrolling outside his window. Hamu was focused on a small picture in his hand. It was a photo of a very attractive woman, Vashti, the wife of the professor whose death he had plotted. He studied the picture he had found in the personal things of Fouad, which Rachti had collected from the demolished Gaza guest house and brought to him in Cairo.

As Hamu studied the small photograph he continued turning over in his mind the task ahead of him. Upon his arrival in Vancouver, he had to tell this woman that, despite various reports that her husband had been only injured, her husband had been killed during that Israeli air attack on Gaza City.

Hamu felt the irony that he, the man who developed the scheme to kill her husband, faced the task of informing this woman that her husband, reported as only injured, was killed during that Israeli air raid. After provoking the Israeli attack, I have to inform this lovely woman that her husband was killed by those Israeli bombs.

To tell this woman that she is a widow will be difficult. But that will be only half the task. This woman will want to know why the media, along with everyone else, has been reporting that her husband was only injured during the air raid. That will not be easy.

I will have to explain the situation. When the body was recovered the men were amazed at how much Fouad resembled me, Hamu. They saw that if the three piece western suit were replaced with an Egyptian gallaiya, this body could pass for the body of Hamu. They were overwhelmed with the idea that this Professor Fouad's body could pass as the body of Hamu.

I will have to explain to her that the men knew that I, as a leader of Two Vipers, had been running from Interpol and Mossad for years. Suddenly, these men saw in this tragedy as an opportunity for me, Hamas, to escape forever from the pursuit of the international police. They saw that this body could easily pass as the body of Hamu.

I will tell her how these men decided to identify the look-a-like dead body recovered from the ruins as my body, as Hamu's body. They would use the body recovered from the ruins, the professor's body, to convince everyone, the media and the international police, that Hamu had been killed by those Israeli bomb.

A woman like this is going to have questions. She will ask why was she was told that her husband, the professor, was alive and only injured? I will have to tell her that the word was spread that the professor was only injured so that I could step into his shoes and impersonate the man.

Then will come the real challenge. I am going to have to tell her that she must suppport my impersonation of her husband. She must continue promoting the fiction that her husband is alive and recovering from injuries. I will have to ask this woman to tell the world her husband is alive. That's going to be a big order.

As Hamu continued to focus on the photo he came to the heart of the matter. It boils down to this. She will have to support my impersonation of Professor Fouad by pretending her husband is recovering. She has to realize that she has no other choice. Vashti will have to realize that she has no alternative.

Hamu looked out his window for a moment with a tight smile. Mountains. I've got my own mountain waiting for me in Vancouver

I have to meet her privately somewhere. When I call her I will have to prepare her for the fact that I so closely resemble her husband. Our meeting will have to take place at a location where there is little chance of our being observed by her associates in Vancouver.

ii

Vashti had been sitting out on the terrace of their home under the sheltering canvas. She was reflecting on that day when she and her husband had received the letter of invitation for him to lecture in Cairo. She had such strong feeling then that he should not have gone.

She had been getting mixed reports from Cairo. She had received reports that Fouad was injured during an Israeli air attack. Still no word from Fouad.

She looked at the picture of her husband on the table. Christian friends who had been spending time with her had just left. She was having a cup of her favorite Egyptian licorice tea.

Suddenly the phone rang. She lifted the receiver

"Hello. Vashti?"

Vashti was startled.

The caller introduced himself. "I am Hamu, from Cairo. I am a friend of your husband. I have just arrived in Vancouver from Cairo. I have come with a special message for you."

She immediately caught the significance of what the caller said. He said I am a friend of your husband. He didn't say I was a friend of your husband. Her eyes widened. She answered. "Who is calling? Please say that again." She pleaded. Yes, please say that again."

He repeated everything in Arabic.

She had been in prayer for some good news. Vashti could scarcely believe she was hearing what she was hearing. Vashti said, "You say you have a special message for me. That's exciting. I have been going crazy because I keep hearing such conflicting reports from Cairo.

"I have been told he was recovering from injuries caused by Israeli bombs in Gaza. City. Is he well? Please, tell me, what is going on."

Vashti's mind was racing. She kept reminding herself that he says I am a friend of your husband. He clearly did not say I was a friend of husband.

The caller said, "Vashti, my message for you needs to be delivered in person."

"That sounds serious."

"I have just come from Cairo. This is my first trip to Vancouver. I would like to meet with you and share with you some things. Could I meet with you somewhere?"

"Yes, Hamu, it would be good to meet you."

"I have to tell you that I have some very important news to share with you. As I said, this concerns your husband."

"Has something happened to him? Tell me."

"I cannot deal with these things on the phone. Vashti, can you suggest a public but still rather private place to meet? I need to talk with you privately."

Vashti was thinking that he was going about this very carefully. He asks for a private place where we can meet and talk. She replied, "Well, I am certainly eager for news about my husband. I will be pleased to meet you about 2 o'clock this afternoon. May I suggest that we meet in one of Vancouver's big tourist spots? There is a place called Grand Totem Restaurant. It has some outside tables. You can get directions from where you are."

Vashsti saw Grand Totem as a good place. It is not likely that I will run into any local Vancouver people who know me or, most importantly, who knew my husband.

The caller replied, "Great. Can you describe what you will be wearing, so I can find you quickly?"

"Yes, of course. I will wear, a yellow traditional woman's costume such as you would see in Cairo, and a blue scarf, I will hold a newspaper across my knees."

"Thank you. Let me give you a picture of myself. I will be wearing a dark suit and a hat of a light woven material hat. "

"OK."

"Also I need to inform you in advance of something else. I need to tell you that your husband and I have very similar features. In fact some people call me his double. So do not be upset if, when you see me with my white hair. It will looks like Fouad is approaching you. You will see a difference in my walk."

"You resemble Fouad that closely?"

"Yes, some might think I was his twin brother. I even have a white mustache and beard. So don't be too startled. It may look somewhat like your husband coming. It is I, Hamu."

iii

As Vashti waited for her caller she felt tense and very anxious. She was preparing herself to respond to whatever news this man would share. I've got a challenge before me.

Then she saw the man approaching. She kept staring. She was stunned. Is this some prank? Is it Fouad, himself? No, Fouad would never play such trick on me. Then as she watched she saw that, as he said, the man's walk was different. There was a slight limp. She recalled how the caller had tried to prepare her for this. He had said, "I will look very much like Fouad."

As Hamu approached the woman in yellow he was thinking that the picture in his wallet did not do her justice. This is a very attractive woman. Very! She is poised. Beautiful."

She stood. "I am Vashti. When I saw you approaching, it was quite a challenge to keep my composure. Thank you for the warning of your similarity. It is some time since I have heard from Fouad. I have been wondering if he is dead or alive. And then I saw you coming. Thank you for warning me. You told me that you resemble Fouad. What an understatement. Yes, it is like you said on the phone. You and my husband could be identical twin brothers."

"I regret causing you any strain."

"I was not prepared to be confronted so suddenly by someone who could have used my husband's passport."

"As a matter of fact you need to know, for starter, that I actually did use your husband's passport in coming here."

"You used his passport. What do you mean?

"It was the only way I could come to Canada. It was necessary. I am here to inform you of something you need to hear personally."

Here was the moment for which Vashti had been preparing herself.

"I have a serious message for you. While your husband was in Cairo he made a trip across the border to Gaza City. During that visit, as you have heard, an air strike of Israeli bombs hit the guest house where Fouad was staying. You may have heard that he was injured. I regret to inform you that the injuries were fatal. Your husband was killed during that Israeli air attack on Gaza City."

Vashti looked up and stared at this man. Holding her scarf across her face she bowed her head and covered her face with her scarf for a few moments. She lifted her head and stared off in the distance. Finally she spoke. "Friends had warned that there might be some bad news. When you called, I was fearful that this would be your message. I was not completely unprepared."

"Vashti, I express my sorrow for your husbands' death. Bringing this news to you has been the most difficult thing I can remember doing. It was a tragic moment for all who knew him."

Vashti finally spoke, "Can you tell me more fully what happened?"

"Well, let me say simply this. The injuries were severe. The Israeli bombs had done their work. Under the circumstances it was necessary for his body to be cremated."

"And his ashes?"

"They have been disposed of."

Vashti looked away and covered her face. She spoke softly through her scarf, "Excuse me." She got up and went into the restaurant.

Vashti sat at an empty table for a few moments. Since they had come to Vancouver and made close relationships with new Canadian friends, some major change had taken place in their lives. Through their new friendships they had come to discover and share together the great love of God in Jesus. They no longer thought in the same way as their old friends in Cairo. She and Fouad had come to share a common faith.

With their discovery of the love of God their marriage had grown and their love for each other had deepened. Together they had found the assurance of eternal life through faith in Jesus Christ. Now, with this tragic news, she was discovering the meaning of that assurance. I will see him again. She looked off in the distance. I will see him again. After a few minute she returned to the table outside and sat there for a few moments.

Her visitor spoke, "Here is a special cash gift for you from your friends in Cairo. They have sent these funds with me as a means of helping you with your needs at this time." He placed the envelope on the table.

Finally, Vashti wiped her tears and spoke to him. "It is most kind of you to come here to personally bring me the news of Fouad's death. Please convey to our friends in Cairo and Gaza City my thanks for their special gift. It will be most helpful, especially now that I will be without the income from my husband's teaching."

"Vashti, I have a special feeling for this time in your life! I myself lost my wife in our ongoing war with the West."

"You have had a wife taken from you by war? I am so sorry to hear that you lost your wife in these troubled times."

Hamu pulled out his wallet and showed her a picture of himself and his wife. "This was taken shortly before she too was killed by bombs provided by the West."

Vashti took the picture in her hands. "We have a common sorrow."

"Yes, Vashti, it is, a shared sorrow. My wife was killed in a way similar to the way your husband was killed. She was killed by weapons supplied by the West."

"How long have you been alone?

"I have been alone for three years now."

After a few moments of silence, Hamu said, "Vashti, we regret that you received such confusing reports about your husband, whether he was injured or whether he was even alive. There is more that you need to know about that Israeli air raid that caused your husband's death."

"Oh, what is that?" She looked at him feeling puzzled..

"Immediately after that powerful and destructive Israeli air raid, our men immediately went digging through the ruins for any survivors. They were hoping that your husband might have miraculously survived the bomb that hit the guest house.

"Then they found his body.

"As our men held in their hands the broken body of this look alike guest they were struck with how thoroughly the victim resembled me. They were thinking that if it were not for the professor's western three piece suit, it would be hard to determine whether it was Fouad or me, Hamu. The victim so well resembled me

"As they were preparing to take out your husband's body on a stretcher, someone said, "If the clothes were changed this body could pass as the body of Hamu.

"Suddenly an idea was born. They decided, among themselves, to use the tragedy of the professor's death in a positive way. They came up with a simple plan to use this tragic death to help me, Hamu, escape my life as a fugitive hiding from Interpol and Mossad.

"They quickly took steps to remove everything that identified this battered body as that of the visiting professor from Canada. They removed the western three piece suit and all personal items, rings, wallet, notebooks.

"They then worked rapidly to identify the corpse, as my body, as the body of Hamu. They quickly pulled a gallabiya and other Egyptian clothing on the body. Someone knew where to find my well known personalized AK47 rifle. They placed it on the stretcher.

"They took steps to extend the damage of the bomb to prevent finger print checks and further injury to the foot, since I wear a prosthesis. They put one of my left foot prosthetics on the stretcher. While doing these things, the news was spread that our visitor, the professor, had survived the bombing with some injurie but Hamu had been killed..

Then they brought out a stretcher with what everyone saw as the body of Hamu. Soon Al Jazeera was broadcasting that I, Hamu, had been killed in the Israeli bombing. Fouad's personal things and his passport the tickets were made available to me. Now, I am here in Canada as Professor Fouad.

"In other words, you took up my husband's passport and plane ticket, just stepped into his shoes and began impersonating my husband to escape Interpol."

"Exactly. Vashti, I can see how cruel this seems. Your husband was deceased. I needed a sure way to leave Egypt and to get past Canadian customs. I took his passport and became Professor Fouad.

"But there is more involved. I need to continue to appear as Professor Fouad. First, to evade Interpol. And one thing more, to take up Fouad's position directing Two Vipers here in Canada."

Vashti spoke up angrily. "You presumed to use his passport. How do you plan to go on impersonating my lost husband while people are consoling his widow?"

"Vashti, that is the problem. For me to continue presenting myself as the professor, I need your help. I need you to continue telling others that your husband is alive and recovering from his injuries."

"So, it is not enough that you tell me my husband is dead. Now you want me, his widow, to live a lie and pretend he is alive. You are living a lie. Now you have the nerve to demand that I share in the same deception.

"You are demanding that I pretend that my dear husband, whose ashes were scattered in Gaza City, is still alive. You expect me to explain to friends and associates that Fouad is recovering in Toronto. It is all one lie after another."

Vashti paused and looked sharply at her visitor. "Does another lie waiting down the road? Are you going to be suggesting that we carry this impersonation further, that we pretend to be husband and wife? It is not only you who will be posing as someone you are not. You are asking that I also pose as someone I am not. I was the wife of Fouad, a wonderful and brilliant man. And now I am his widow."

"Vashti, listen. This is a matter of life or death for me. It is necessary for me to be seen as Fouad. It is absolutely necessary that you cooperate."

"And if I do not participate in this grand deception?"

Hamu was silent.

There was a long silence. Vashti's mind was racing. Would they really eliminate me?

Finally she spoke: "What is the alternative? There is only one. If the professor's wife will not go along with charade then the professor's wife will also have to disappear."

Hamu said, "I would not put it all so bluntly. The simple fact is that only you can provide for me the cover I need."

"How do you expect me to carry out such a masquerade?"

"In an obvious way. Announce your husband's was seriously injured in the Israeli air attack, as reported. Explain that he is still recovering. You will go on living as though he were still alive. You will tell friends that your husband is continuing his recovery in Toronto."

"How can you even suggest such a thing? You mean that you want me, now a widow, to present myself as though I were still married?"

"Vashti, I am not asking you. I am telling you that it is necessary for you to continue, for the time being, to go on with your life, as though your husband were still living."

Valhi looked at the man silently. She was wondering why God set this situation before her. First, he tells me that I have lost my dear husband. Now he is demanding that I support this impersonation. He is deadly serious. Perhaps I need to play the same game."

"Any questions, Vashti? Anything further that I need to explain? Do you need some time to ponder this? Shall I come back another day?"

As Vashti looked at the man she was realizing the enormity of the situation. This man is demanding cooperation from me. His new identity can be maintained only by my cooperation, or by my being silenced."

Finally she spoke, "My answer to your request is yes. Do not expect to take the place of my husband in any other way. You will board the train taking you back East and I will return to my home. Is that clear?"

"Perfectly clear."

"I think that you had best leave here now lest you run into any of my friends. I will tell folks that Fouad suffered serious injury but that he is recovering."

They stood to leave and looked intently at each other. Vashti said, "In case someone is watching, don't you think you should embrace me?"

He embraced her and got into his rented car. Hamu sat in his car watching Vashti walking away. This is a very attractive woman. Our relationship might improve.

iv

When Vashti returned home she picked up her phone and called a special friend. In phone talk they did not use names. "It was as you suggested it would be. This man confirmed what you had suggested might be the case. This man brought me news that my dear Fouad is indeed gone."

"I am sorry to hear that you have had this news confirmed."

Vashti said, "When I heard this blunt confirmation of rumors that Israeli bombs had destroyed my husband, I closed my eyes and I rejoiced that we had received God's great gift of life, that our lives had not only been changed but that we had received the gift of eternal life!"

"You knew immediately that you, Vashti, will see him again!"

"Yes, I will see him again, but there is something more?"

"Yes."

"This man has a shocking resemblance to my husband. He appeared as Fouad back from the dead. It was shocking."

"And what did he say of his looking like Fouad?"

Vashti said, "He explained to me, that since they shared many characteristics, he took advantage of the opportunity to make use of my husband's passport. He not only looks like Fouad's twin. He has taken on Fouad's ID and is impersonating Fouad."

Vashti's friend asked, "How is that going to be possible?"

"He came using Fouad's passport to enter Canada. It was unbearable. He is using Fouad's ID to escape the international police. He is impersonating Fouad to take over Fouad's leadership of the Two Vipers brotherhood here in Canada."

"And how is that going to be possible?"

"This man expects me, Fouad's widow, to give him cover as though he were Fouad."

"This man is going to continue to present himself as Fouad?"

Vashti said, "Yes, and to make this possible, he expects me to pretend that I have had no loss. He expects me to support his impersonation of Fouad. He expects me to simply go on as though my husband were still in recovery. He is insisting that I tell people that my husband is still healing from the injuries. He wants me to help maintain this act so that he can he can continue going about as Fouad."

"How did you respond?"

"It was really an order. This man implied that there was really no alternative."

"No alternative?"

"I realized that if I refused someone might have to eliminate me."

"What will you do?"

"Thanks to the confidence that I am not alone I was able to focus on this evil proposal with surprising steadiness. I believe that through the faith Fouad and I share, God gave me a surprising strength. When this man indicated that he would stop at nothing to maintain this fiction, I realized I really had no alternative. I told him that, for now, I would tell people my husband had been seriously wounded by bombs from Israel but was recovering."

"How did you feel telling him this?"

"I discovered that God was helping me cope with this. I remembered how you shared with me that God sent His Sons to die for us because he holds a higher purposes for our lives. As I faced this man I discovered that 'the man for others' is alive. I was surprised at my inner peace. I am not alone."

CHAPTER 12

Aboard the TransCanada train.

A Fifth Column is a group within a state that attempts
to subvert and weaken the state in order to assist an enemy
World War II, 1939 - 1943

Hamu boarded the train and settled down in compartment F for his return trip to Toronto. He could see that the white bearded face he saw in the mirror showed the strain of his visit with Vashti. Hamu could still see in his mind that lovely lady in yellow in the park. What an attractive and vital woman. She handled what I had to tell her better than expected.

All that I am doing in my impersonation of her husband depends on whether this woman, Vashti, will be able to do what, under pressure, she agreed to do. Will she really do what she reluctantly agreed to do? Will it come across to her friends as genuine? Will she be able to conceal her grief over her husband's death? How convincingly will she speak of his ongoing recovery? As she talks with women who really know her, will she be able to mask her underlying grief?

That personal encounter with my victim's wife was no picnic. Telling her that her husband was dead was difficult but only the start. The real challenge was telling her of the decision to use that broken body as evidence to convince everyone that it was I, Hamu, who had been killed by the Israeli bomb. She handled well my telling her how her husband's broken body was stripped of personal things and given a change of clothes to make it appear to be my body. She handled well the explanation that the body found in the ruins was used to convince everyone that I, Hamu, was the one killed by the bombs.

She understood rather quickly why she had been hearing that Fouad was only injured. She got the point that I could impersonate her husband, only if, despite his injuries, he was reported being alive.

Then came the real challenge. On top of learning that her husband was dead she was told that she had to pretend he was still alive.

This woman was sharp. She was not only beautiful. She was very intelligent. She went right to the real issue. When she learned that I was concealing that I was alive by my impersonation of her husband, she saw right away that her cooperation was not just an option. Even in her grief she saw that my impersonation was a vital issue and required her support. She saw immediately the unspoken alternative. She recognized the implied threat. She realized immediately that refusal to cooperate was not an option.

What will I do if she breaks down and cannot continue providing support for my impersonation? If, to protect my impersonation, it became necessary to silence her could I do it? Could I really carry out the implied threat? He looked at the picture of the woman. Maybe there's a more pleasant alternative.

Hamu looked out on the constantly changing scene of the Canadian Rockies. It was time for him to focus on another concern.

Before the start of his trip west, Hamu had brought together a small group of men to investigate the agenda of some prominent civic agencies and organizations across Canada. He had the idea that the objectives of some existing civic bodies might unknowingly be, in some respect, parallel to some Two Viper's goals.

If this special team discovered any such organizations, they were to make contact and express the interest of an anonymous individual to meet with representatives. They were to hint at possible financial support.

He directed this special team to invite representatives of selected organizations to confidential conferences with him on the train. These private conferences were to take place on his train as he travelled east. His agents were to arrange the needed bookings on the train for those interested. Those who accepted would be his guests on the train. His identity as the host was to remain confidential.

The team had been surprisingly successful. They found quite a few civic bodies with objectives that might prove useful to Two Vipers. His men lined up quite a few individuals to share in such meetings on board the great train. Depending on location some invitations were scheduled for only a few hours. Some would share lunch in the dining car. Some might be scheduled to come on board for dinner on the train. The generous invitations included arrangements for the return of individuals to the point where they boarded the train.

The response was quite positive. The invitation to meet on the train was seen as a creative and practical idea. It would save time for those who came as well as for their host.

Hamu wanted to explore the possibility of supporting organizations whose agenda, without their knowing it, might parallel some of his objectives in working to undermine the west's vitality. Some groups might unknowingly serve like a World War II fifth column.

As these meetings took place, Hamu could scarcely believe what he was hearing. He was quite surprised. The agenda of some organizations really paralleled his own goals for tearing down underlying and traditional foundations of North American life. He found that there were some very aggressive and powerful forces already at work to change the way of life in both Canada and the USA.

He was amused to hear some boast of a strange virtue, being inclusive. In effect, many were saying that it really doesn't matter what you believe.

Hamu kept his mouth shut and listened. Some agents of what they called civic liberties were really focused on imposing their own agenda on the public. A major weapon of some well-funded organizations appeared to be the threat of law suit to intimidate and impose their viewpoint on people. While some paid lip service to a western religion, Darwin seemed more their real prophet.

As he listened Hamu found that many seemed more like aliens than Canadians. As an impostor, and himself a man without a country, he was surprised how many prominent people he met sounded like men and women without a country and without God.

Many he interviewed would pass as infidels in almost any culture. They seemed to lack any thing they really believed. Many made it clear that they had no moral absolutes. Few had any underlying religious faith that shaped their goals. Many seemed to simply hold Hamu's own view that when you're dead you're dead.

Hamu was especially surprised to see the extent to which the family was under attack on both sides of the border in North America. Many who talked of an inclusive society were in effect launching attacks on marriage and the family. Some seemed ready to accept almost any situation as marriage and family. He was staggered not only by the number of children born outside of marriage but the casual acceptance of such a way of life. The only cure for most basic problems across the nation seemed to be more money.

As he listened, Hamu was thinking that many of these people are not leaving us much to do. They lack direction. They seem like people without a compass.

After one person left, Hamu leaned back in his chair amazed. These self-appointed judges of society are working to impose their ideology on this nation. The people seem so vulnerable. Yes, they have no compass.

Hamu was amazed. The people, even leaders in schools and churches and government, seem so blind to what is happening to their way of life?

It made him think of the vulnerability of Germany, at the start of the World War II. The Germans were being destroyed by the British air raids because the Germans couldn't see them coming. They lacked effective radar. That appears to be the problem in large parts of North America today. There is a war going on for the hearts and minds of the next generation and the people don't seem to realize what is happening. It is as though they had no radar!

Canada is already under attack. Where are their fighter pilots?

There were exceptions. Hamu hosted for dinner one night a representative of a mission agency working in Africa. This man had taken training to prepare him to live in a village with the people of a rural Africa. The man surprised him with his strong conviction that went beyond the view that when you're dead you're dead. This man was different. He was very definite. Jesus Christ is God. Jesus came back from the grave to show us that he has overcome the last enemy. This was the first time, in his train interviews, that Hamu encountered anyone who strongly believed in the alternatives of hell or eternal life.

The man caused Hamu to think of his own life. He had arranged a murder and took on the victim's ID so that he could come to Canada. Hamu reviewed what he had done to reach Canada. If there was a hell he was certainly headed in that direction.

ii

When he arrived back in Toronto, Hamu called a special meeting of all recruits at the old warehouse on the waterfront. That night Hamu set out objectives for Two Vipers.

"We fight our war with the deadly power of two vipers. In our war against the west we wage this war with two strategies, a hard war and a soft war.

"First, we attack our targets with the power to destroy. We strike the people with the demoralizing power of the hard war.

Hamu continued. "Meanwhile, another sort of warfare, the soft war is going on. We work to weaken and undermine our opponent's ability to do battle. We attack the very foundations of their life as a nation. We help them forget their principles. We bury the things they believe in. We help them forget their foundations. We undermine and pull out from under them the very way of life for which they are fighting.

"In the soft war we destroy their inner strength. They will discover that the very things for which they thought they were fighting are gone. The things they thought they believed in will have evaporated."

Hamu paused and asked, "What will their strengths have become?"

The men shouted, "Forgotten foundations

"And by what strategy will this come about?"

"The Soft War."

After a pause, Hamu said, "Now let's get down to the business of the hard war.

"Our first campaign is Yellow Pig. Yellow Pig is a campaign to attack the Brown Valley nuclear power station and obtain quantities of radioactive material to build dirty bombs.

"Across this nation we have powerful explosive devises in place in highly secretive places in key cities and The terrorizing impact of these explosive devises will be made even more damaging by making them dirty bombs. The main purpose of a dirty bomb is to terrify people.

"This highly dangerous radioactive material is stored in special yellow lead lined protective containers called yellow pigs. That is why we call this operation Yellow Pig.

"The attack team will find that these lead pigs stored on dollies. You will roll one of these loaded dollies, as directed by your leaders, to our special vehicles. The getaway vehicles will be two especially modified ambulances. The drivers and their crews will be prepared to race away with the material and all team members in these two ambulances. They will take off with their sirens sounding. The ambulance crew will wear special ambulance uniforms.

"Police, responding to the special alarm of the power station, may be approaching the power station as you are leaving. The ambulance drivers will have their emergency lights flashing. They will be seen to be taking injured people to the hospitals. We expect that the police will wave you on your way. Once you get past the incoming police you will head for a special remote locations to unload and conceal this dangerous material."

For a few moments their Pharaoh stood there silently, looking from one face to another. Then he spoke slowly and very deliberately. "I want to speak to you now about a second project. We call it Operation Toronto.

"This project will take place during the rush hour in downtown Toronto. This work is crucial to establishing a cash base for Two Viper across this continent."

Hamu continued. "The date and time of this operation is determined by special information from insider contacts. We have learned that on this particular day a special bank money truck will be delivering very large amounts of previously circulated cash to several Toronto banks.

Hamu paused for a moment and then continued. "What is noteworthy about this shipment? Simply this. This truck will be delivering cash to some large down town banks, cash that comes from various parts of the country. This currency has not been registered.

"Why are we interested in hitting this bank money truck in a busy public location in the midst of the morning rush hour? Why attempt such a very dangerous daylight robbery at this hour? The unregistered cash being delivered by this truck will be especially useful for us. Officials will not be able to trace it.

"This action must take place while the cash is on its way to the banks. You must be at your assigned points at five am. This cash is will enable us to extend our efforts in North America. During the morning rush hour official response will be very difficult. We will make it more difficult. They can't fight what they can't get to."

CHAPTER 13

Ontario Northwoods, Canada

"Be still and know that I am God."
– Psalm 46

Roger arrived in Toronto about two weeks before the team's planned train trip across Canada to Vancouver. He had originally planned to come a week early to take in the Toronto Faculty Symposium before their big trip. Then, back in Nairobi, Emily had come up with the idea his heading north to paint at her family's north woods cabin. She said, "If you're coming earlier for the Symposium, come a week earlier and use our family's north woods cabin for a week of painting."

Emily's description of the cabin had been hard to resist. "My family's wilderness retreat is just a day's drive north of Toronto. The cabin is on a lovely lake called Bobcat Lake. It is surrounded by unspoiled wilderness country. It's a real painter's paradise. Once you're there you will not want to return to civilization. You will have the beautiful setting to yourself for a week of painting. You will not see a single person."

It was an offer Roger could not refuse. So, here he was, in his old Land Rover, rolling north out of Toronto, with great expectations. Emily had assured him. "The only voices you hear will be the loons. The only spectators will be the herons."

Roger was well dressed for the trip. He wore a favorite long sleeved faded sap green shirt. He liked the deep pockets and way it blended with the aspen. He wore a special tan safari vest from Africa. Emily had modified it for him back in Kenya with special slots for brushes. He wore a special wide brimmed hat which not only shielded his eyes when sketching in the sun but also served as a mini-umbrella when needed.

He enjoyed sporting a well-trimmed mustache and his special polarized, tinted prescription glasses. When flying in Kenya he insisted that these were not flight glasses. They were painting glasses. The Polaroid feature helped especially when painting cloud scenes.

Om his roof rack rode his very special cedar strip canoe. Roger had been very particular about the color for the canoe. He had mixed up a special color he called "sunlit sand," a special tan that he used in his paintings, a careful blend of lemon yellow and light cobalt violet. Roger wanted his canoe to blend with the sandy beaches and rocks and the sunlit drift wood. On one occasion a fellow painter had a hard time finding him because Roger's canoe had become so much a part of the scene.

As he rolled along farther north, Roger enjoyed seeing the spruce and pines becoming more numerous and taller. He was soon seeing more vehicles with a canoe on the roof. The sky was filled with tremendous high white thunderhead clouds. Roger found himself signing a song with which he grew up, "Ye clouds that sail in heaven along, Oh, praise Him, Oh praise Him."

Suddenly, traffic was slowing. Roger saw flashing lights ahead. He spotted several Ontario Provincial Police cars. There was a road block on both sides of the divided highway. The Police were stopping vehicles going both north and south. Officers were running some scanning devise under the vehicles. Two officers were directing the work of specially trained dogs.

Finally it was Roger's turn.

"Your ID, please," the officer requested. "Pop the bonnet please." Another officer was inspecting every inch of the Rover and opening suitcases. "From USA, eh? Please step out of your vehicle. The officer looked from the US Passport picture he was holding to Roger. "What is your height and age, please?"

"Six foot one. Age 30."

"What is your address in USA? And what is your destination?"

Roger gave his US address and said, "I am heading north to a wilderness cabin to do some watercolor painting." He felt like saying that he was heading north to artist paradise. But these men were very serious.

The officer smiled and commented, "I see a slight change from this passport photo. The blue-grey eyes are about the same. It's that growth on your face. That mustache changes things a bit. I think you're still the same guy. OK, have a nice day." The officer waved him on.

Roger spoke up, "Could I ask the reason for the road block?"

The officer shook his head and said, "We have to keep traffic moving. This circular will explain the reason for the road block."

Roger looked at the hand out sheet quickly. There had been a break-in the previous night at a nearby nuclear power generating station. The leaflet was asking citizens to be on the lookout for any signs of stolen radioactive material.

After the police road stop Roger found he was getting hungry. Finally he saw a hamburger place on other side of the divided highway. It looked like a possibility because there was a pedestrian bridge built over the divided highway. He pulled into the parking lot for northbound customers and walked over the bridge to the other side.

On the southbound side, Roger spotted a large ambulance in the parking lot for southbound traffic. With all its antennas and other features the ambulance appeared to be a sophisticated piece of rolling technology. Roger had to laugh over one detail. Like all ambulances this one carried a big front sign lettered boldly in reverse so drivers ahead of the ambulance could read it in their rear view mirror "AMBULANCE." What seemed so funny was that the sign on this high tech ambulance was misspelled. It read not "AMBULANCE" but "AMBALANCE."

In the restaurant he spotted the uniformed crew of the ambulance. He was surprised to see that the entire crew, surprisingly, looked like South Asian or Middle East immigrants. Their apparent leader sported a beard.

Roger sat down with his burger..

As the crew walked away Roger was surprised to observe that their uniforms seemed to be just pulled over other work clothes. He focused on the leader. There was something on his hip that looked like a gun. It was a gun. That's strange, I never thought of an ambulance crew being armed. I guess they need to be prepared.

Roger was soon on his way again. He wanted to arrive at the cabin as early as possible. Since the last part of the trip involved quite a few miles on dirt road through wilderness country he wanted to keep moving and get there before dark.

Roger was really eager to see this cabin. Emily's parents, the Hendersons, had told him that the property had been in their family for generations. From Emily's description of the wilderness area around the lake Roger had great expectations.

From the map they had given him Roger saw that he would be passing through two places where he had to unlock a gates or move a locked obstruction. They were barriers to protect the cabin's isolation.

The cabin was situated on a large privately owned property of several hundred acres. For a watercolorist the opportunity to paint in such an isolated wilderness area was a rare privilege. The Hendersons told Roger that he would see few foot prints of man. He had laughed. He told them that he would be looking for the Creator's footprints. Now, as he drove along he remembered that conversation. He found himself singing, "This is my Father's world. He shines in all that's fair. In the rustling grass I hear him pass. He speaks to me everywhere."

On the topographical map Emily had provided, he had spotted an indication of the ruins of an old cabin from the nineteenth century lumbering days. The old ruin was at the far end of Bobcat Lake. He was planning to check out that area once he was on the water.

Roger was thinking that August was an ideal time for a landscape painter. The insects would be slowing down. A few maples might be showing color this far north. He was eager to explore the possibilities for landscape painting. And to think that he would be alone and have the place to himself.

ii

While Roger was driving north on highway 400, some distance to the East another vehicle was moving along a parallel country road toward the same destination. In a jeep with four wheel drive, two men were heading for the ruins of an old lumbering cabin on Bobcat Lake. They had been instructed how to reach Bobcat Lake by means of an old overgrown forestry road that had not been used for years.

The two men were an advance party that had been sent ahead to blaze their way and open up this long forgotten way to the lumbering cabin ruins on Bobcat Lake. This old forestry firefighter's back road had been blocked off for years by a long unused and rusted shut cattle gate and lock. Their first obstacle would be the old gate. The greater challenge would be the old forestry road. They were told that no vehicle had driven up this road for years.

When they arrived they were concerned to make their entrance quickly and without being seen by locals. The men went to work on the gate with their crowbar. As they had expected the gate and lock were rusted solid. When they finally broke the gate open they drove their jeep through, closed the gate with all its brush and put on a new, but old looking, lock.

Once past the gate they went to work making their way up the old long unused forestry road. They had to work their way through the brush and growth of many years. The team was prepared to use their chain saw to remove any saplings or fallen trees. They had to make this old forestry road passable for the ambulance that was lying low and would be coming early the next day.

They expected the ambulance and another jeep with their leader. The driver would have keys for the new lock. They would be able pop open the gate and drive right up the forestry road to the ruins of the old lumbering cabin.

The ambulance was keeping out of sight on back roads roughly parallel to Highway 400 on which most northbound traffic was moving. The ambulance was an authentic well equipped ambulance. It had the flashing lights and medical equipment. The men on board wore uniforms. Authentic ambulance equipment was visible from the back window. The vehicle carried the familiar identity of a local ambulance organization. After leaving hiding places and taking some back roads, it would head to the gate of this largely forgotten old forestry road and up to an old lumbering ruin on Bobcat Lake.

iii

Roger, pulled off the highway at a local gas-station grocery. He reviewed again his directions. "About five kilometers above Rockhaven look for a Northlands Grocery. Our road is a small dirt road just past the Grocery. You won't see any arrow sign pointing to Bobcat Lake. We keep our location as private as possible."

Roger went in to check out the grocery. It was what they call "a general store." He picked up some milk and eggs. Then he saw what he was looking for. "Great, you've got it! Pea meal bacon, real Canadian bacon." He added a pack of it to his collection on the counter. He picked up the paper to add to his items.

"Some headline, eh?" The proprietor pointed to the headline.

Roger glanced at the headlines. "Nuclear Generator Security Breached! Wow!"

"Yeah! Some guys ripped off material from the Power Station. The police are everywhere."

Roger stashed his purchases in the Rover. According to his map he had about fifteen kilometers on this dirt road till he would come to the turn off for the cabin. Finally he came to the gated side road. There was no sign or any indicator of what lay beyond the gate. It was secured with two padlocks. He used the keys given to him, pulled past the gate and, as directed, locked the gate after passing through.

He had to stop a couple times to lift fallen branches from the roadway. After proceeding a short distance he came to the next turn off shown on his map. This barrier was really different. This time it was not a gate but a huge log suspended on chains that had to be swung out of the way when the two additional locks were opened. Again he locked the log gate behind him. Finally after several kilometers, he began to see the lake through the trees. And then, there it was, the cabin.

"What a trip." Roger stepped out of the Rover. "A long journey but great to be here." He walked around taking in the place. A cabin? More than a cabin! He walked around it taking in the building. The first and most impressive feature was the size of the tremendous logs with which it had been built. The logs appeared to be huge lodge pole pines. Some parts of the building used logs more than about two feet in diameter.

He walked around to the lakeside deck to take in the quietness of the lake. As he looked out over the perfectly still mirror of the lake, a heron glided by on the other side of the lake. Glad someone was here to greet me. The beauty and quietness of the scene was spectacular.

Although Emily had described the cabin's wilderness setting, nothing she had told him prepared him for the sight of the cabin on this wilderness lake.

Roger looked around the cabin. They call this a cabin! What an understatement! What a masterpiece of construction. Some of the logs must be about forty feet in length.. The cabin looks as though it had simply been pasted into the setting. It sat so snuggly here among these great century old pines and oaks.. If I were flying over this area, this cabin would be almost invisible from the air.

The steeply sloping roof was well designed to shed the heavy snow this far north. Heavy planks boarding the windows kept the cabin protected during the long winter. As he used his key to open the heavy oak door, he saw the deep scratches of bears. The heavy door had been doing its job to protect the place. He was glad to see the good a supply of split firewood under the protecting firewood shelter.

Roger walked down from the deck to check out the lake. Beautiful! What a painter's paradise! Everywhere he looked there were scenes that seemed to dramatize the Creator's purpose that all creation should reflect His glory.

Roger got to work unloading his gear. In addition to his clothing and supplies he unloaded his carefully selected painting materials. His painting equipment was compact and designed for painting outdoors.

Then came the job of carefully removing his prized light weight cedar strip canoe from the roof of the Rover. He settled its yoke on his shoulders and walked it down to the lake. He turned it over, placed his paddles under it. All set for early morning.

As he looked across the lake, where the darkness of evening was falling, Roger spotted a slightly spreading wake out on the surface. It appeared to be a loon. Suddenly he heard the screeching call that confirmed that it was a loon. He called out, "Thank you for that wonderful welcome. Good to be reminded that I am not alone here."

Roger's eyes followed a large heron, gracefully winging his way across the lake. Roger stood silently taking in the golden sunlit sky, "Beautiful." It triggered in his memory the famous words of Keats, "A thing of beauty is a joy forever.'"

The privilege of just being there struck him. He was thinking what a difference it is when you are not preoccupied with your agenda. We grow up hearing those words of the psalm, "Be still and know that I am God" but most of the time we are filled with our own agenda. There's good cause for being still here.

Roger was impressed with the large stone fireplace designed to warm the entire cabin. He soon had a fire going and then prepared his supper on an LP gas stove.

He observed that one of the features of this wilderness setting was the absence of any electrical appliances. No phone! Great! He read a card on the wall. "In an emergency, there is one spot where your cell phone might get through, to the South near the far end of the lake. There, near the old lumbering cabin, it might be possible to make cell phone contact. Your cell phone has to be charged, on your vehicle."

It had been a long day. After a simple supper, Roger enjoyed just looking out over the lake. He watched the quickly changing spectacular sunset.

Roger lighted the lanterns. As he checked out the books on the shelves on each sides of the fireplace, he observed the great variety of interests indicated by the Henderson's books. Books on the trees and wild life of Ontario. Mystery stories. Some volumes of C. S. Lewis including his Chronicles of Narnia.

Roger unfolded the topographical map provided to help him become familiar with the area. Bobcat Lake appeared to be well named. Two streams feed the lake through small bays to the North that appeared on the map like the ears of the Bobcat. The cabin appeared to be situated on a point of land under the chin of the Bobcat. To the Southeast the outlet flow of lake appears at the end of a bay that could represent the tail.

Roger was glad he had picked up the newspaper. Reading his paper by the light of an LP lantern was something he hadn't done for a long time.

He was interested in reading about the security breach at the Nuclear Power Generating Plant. "An undetermined amount radio-active material appears to have been taken from the generating station. Authorities stated that considering the remoteness and security of the facility, this crime appears to have been carried out by knowledgeable Canadians."

Roger was a map person. As he studied the map he noted with interest the location of the ruins of an old lumbering day's cabin near the South end of the Lake.

Roger read further in the "Cabin Info" sheet given him. "Since the cabin enjoys such isolation we have employed a local man to give continuing oversight to this property. His name is Sam Macintosh. Most people just call him Mac. He lives a bit farther north. Mac serves as our special care taker and guardian of the property. We employ him to keep his eye on the property at regular intervals. Mac checks on the cabin twice a week. He operates on horseback."

The information booklet continued, "To preserve the unspoiled and natural beauty of this wilderness we strive to keep the existence of this property unknown as far as possible. We ask Mac to keep his employment with us confidential. You may see him appearing out of nowhere on his horse.

"If any problems occur or any special needs arise, such as need for medical help contact Mac. To reach him drive North on 400 about five kilometers and ask directions to his home from anyone."

Roger settled down to enjoy the fire. What a privilege to be on this lake alone. He liked the idea that he would have this cabin and this wonderful wilderness setting on Bobcat Lake all to himself. He was enjoying his isolation in this beautiful setting.

iv

Roger was not as much alone as he assumed. While he was enjoying the fireplace, in his wilderness hideaway, at the other end of Bobcat Lake, unknown to him, Roger's sphere of isolation had been invaded by the two exhausted men who had opened up the old forestry road.

Slowly and with a good deal effort and hard work, the two men had worked their way up the old road. Six hours after breaking open the gate, the two men finally reached their target, the cabin at the southeast end of Bobcat Lake. They had been told to look for the ruins of a century old lumbering era log cabin. By the end of the day two exhausted men had reached their goal, leaving them just enough time to get set for the night

"Bobcat Lake, we're here," the leader exclaimed with relief. "And it looks like we've got this place to ourselves."

At their end of the lake, the two men who had blazed their way up to the lake were resting from their work, huddled over a small fire. They had prepared the way for the arrival of the ambulance with the radioactive materials seized from the power station. Their job would be to help unload the seized yellow pigs and get them stashed in the ruins of the old cabin.

The younger member of the team spoke up, "We're in the middle of nowhere? Why are we bringing the hot stuff here, of all places?"

The other man, the leader, nodded. "A logical question. This is supposed to be a great place to conceal the loot from the power station. Our local contact, this guy called Mac, told us that this old cabin still has below it the ice chamber from the old days. It's a space below the cabin where they once stored ice cut from the river. Let's check it out."

He inserted their crowbar and pried up an old floor board. "There it is. That must be the ice chamber. In the old days they cut blocks of ice from the lake and stashed them under saw dust down there."

"So we're going to cool the hot stuff here."

"Right on the nose. No one is going to find the hot stuff here."

CHAPTER 14
Bobcat Lake, Ontario Northwoods

"Take everything as it comes, the wave passes,
deal with the next one."
– Canadian Northwoods painter – Tom Thompson, 1877- 1917

After an early breakfast that included pea meal bacon, Roger got his canoe packed and ready to go with the painting materials he would need for the day. He packed a brown bag lunch, and stuck in his pocket the digital camera for reference shots for future paintings. He had found, when out painting, the less stuff the better. He left things like his cell phone behind. He left his bulky wallet filled with cards and other things at the cabin. "I don't think I'll need my credit card on Bobcat Lake."

After having stashed the things he would need in the canoe, Roger gently moved the canoe further out on the water. Making sure there was enough depth to float the canoe he stepped in and with the other foot and gently shoved off. The canoe glided silently across the mirror surface of the lake. As he moved his canoe along he spotted a heron that seemed to be effortlessly propelling himself on his great wings, looking for his breakfast. The heron was keeping just ahead of him, as he noticed heron seem to do.

Following the rain that fell during the night, a delicate mist was risings from the surface of the water. Soon the sun began to break through. The morning rays were soon highlighting the tips of the tall surrounding pines. He gave a few gentle under water pushes with his paddle. The canoe continued to glide across the surface.

Morning has broken. Yes, and what a magnificent morning. Roger found himself softly singing the song, "Morning has broken, like the first morning. Blackbird has spoken like the first bird." Half aloud he said, "All I need now is Mr. Blackbird." Then, to his amazement, almost immediately that is exactly what he saw and heard. Several red-winged black birds flew by perching on some tall cattails by the shore, squawking with their typical gruff call. "Great. Black bird has spoken."

Roger was in awe as he took in the quiet beauty of the lake. He followed with his eyes Mr. Heron winging his way down the lake. Silently, he took in the clear sunlit sky, the privilege of just being here struck Roger. What a privilege to be in a setting like this. With the canoe you can glide along as part of the scene. Roger was completely absorbed in the unspoiled beauty of this lake. Just being here is awesome. I've come here to paint but something else seems to have a priority. Worship!

The canoe glided along with scarcely a ripple. Roger was thinking what a difference it is to draw near to God when you are not coming with your own agenda. What a time to simply enjoy being alive.

"Be still and know that I am God." The words of the familiar verse filled his thoughts. There's a lot of opportunity for being still here. Maybe it will give God a chance to get through to Roger.

In the face of all the terrible things going on in the world, is it escapism to simply enjoy moments like this? Be still and know. I wonder what he wants me to know.

I'm here to paint, but the gift of a morning like this can help you search for the deeper purpose in your life. If you don't have the real presence of God in your life you lack something for which you were created. While I'm here God must have something he wants me to discover.

As Roger continued to explore the lake, he was recalling something he had spotted on the topo. The map showed an old lumbering cabin at the far end of the lake, about two miles farther down the lake. Maybe I could include that old relic of lumbering days in my landscape today.

Finally he was there at the other end of the lake. Back in the forest he could see what appeared to be the old lumbering cabin hidden by trees and undergrowth.

Roger paddled along the shore, moving gently through the tall grasses. He let the canoe glide in the shallow water until it was stopped among the Indian Arrowhead plants. It occurred to him that his canoe and the muted colors of his clothes just blended with the plants. Nearby stood the large intricate fan display of the roots of a great toppled forest giant. Everything he saw looked like good material for a painting. He was thinking that if he continued sitting here motionless no one would notice him or the canoe. I feel like I'm part of the scene.

Roger moved his canoe snugly in place against an old log. He saw the scene that he wanted for his first painting. He decided to include a bit of the old cabin. Anyone who has ever been on Bobcat Lake, upon seeing this painting, will know exactly where this painting was made.

Nestled in the canoe, Roger organized his gear to begin painting. He scooped up water from the lake for painting and was soon at work. He was really enjoying himself. In painting mode time rolled along for him.

After working on the scene for a while, Roger said to himself, "It's time to take a break and give this a rest for a bit. When I come back to it I may see some things that need changing."

He stood up in the canoe to take his lunch break. Located as he was in the shallow water he was able to step out and go ashore. It was good to stretch his legs. He pulled out the sandwich he had packed. He took a sip of his beverage and walked around a bit exploring the area.

Then he stopped. He stood still listening, very intently. I hear something I didn't hear while busy painting. It sounds like voices, but that's impossible here. No one could be here. "By gum, I do hear voices!" he exclaimed half aloud. How could anyone get in here? The access roads are all gated. There's no way to get here by canoe.

He moved quietly through the tall grasses and silently made this way toward the voices. He could see more of the old forestry cabin now. Suddenly he saw men moving about. They were hauling boxes to the old lumbering cabin.

What could these men be doing here? How could they have gotten here? This does not look good? I wonder if they realize they are on private land.

How could anyone get into this lake? He was thinking of the obstacles of gates and the locks on the road in to the lake. There is only one road into this place, unless you include that old overgrown forestry road on the topo. The Hendersons said that old road has been closed for years. Only a tank could come through there.

As a boy growing up with in Africa Roger had developed skills in moving quietly to observe wildlife with African friends. Now he moved into what he used to call his stealth mode. He pushed quietly through the tall grasses, as he used to do in Africa. Then he saw what some men were doing. He froze.

Roger watched silently. Some men were moving heavy boxes to the old forestry cabin. Then he saw the ambulance. The front sign for motorists was misspelled as ambalnce. It had to be the ambulance he had seen at that hamburger place. Roger whipped out his little digital camera. He snapped a few shots and moved a few steps closer.

He observed with amazement that the boxes the men were carrying were stenciled with the international trefoil symbol for radioactive material.

Don't they know that stuff is dangerous. Then it hit Roger! I'm looking at the haul of those men who broke into the nuclear power station.

Roger edged closer through the brush.

Suddenly, something else hit Roger and it was not another idea. Roger was knocked out cold.

When Roger regained consciousness he found himself all tied up. He was a prisoner. To keep him from seeing too much some sort of a hood had been thrown over his head. His hands were fastened to his waist with nylon ties and his ankles were tied together. Grey tape and wire had been used freely. He was propped up against a tree. With the hood over his head he could hear someone yelling orders in another language.

Some orders were repeated in English. "Everything, back on the truck. Fast. This prisoner must be an RCMP agent. Like rats, where there's one there must be more. Out of here, fast. We're switching to plan B."

Roger heard a man, apparently their leader, talking about him. "We can't take him with us. We can't leave him here to tell people what he has seen. We have to take care of him."

Propped up as he was against a tree Roger found that by rubbing his head against the tree, despite the hood, he could see a bit of what was going on around him. He saw the men loading the boxes back on the ambulance. He got glimpses only of the back of the man who seemed to be in charge.

Roger heard the apparent leader yelling into his cell hone, "There is no question about it! This must be a RCMP agent. I can't see how they spotted us. Someone must have talked too much. There's only one way this agent could have found us. We may have a mole among us. We're out of here."

Roger got a partial glimpses, from the back only of their leader, using his smart phone. Roger could not see his face. The man was busy conferring with someone on his phone.

The apparent leader talked about having captured a plain clothes RCMP scout. Then he heard him yell, "Somehow they must know we are in this area. We've got to get out of here, fast." The man was very angry. He slammed down his cell phone on a fallen tree and yelled, "Let's get moving."

Roger worked his hood up a bit and saw that leader's smart phone was still lying on a fallen tree.

Roger heard the leader yell, "Everything back on the ambulance. Fortunately, we have not hid all our eggs in one basket. We have yet the other cache near Sudbury."

Roger heard someone call out, "Mac, about time you showed up." It sounded like a late arrival had joined the gang. Someone said, "Yeah Mac, what took you so long?"

Roger heard the voice of the man who seemed to be their leader. He was talking to this man called Mac, "We have caught an RCMP agent. They must know we are in this area. Mac, you found a great place for us but we have to abandon it."

"You have to do what you have to do," the new comer replied. The leader continued, "We have a problem. This RCMP man. We can't leave him here and we can't take him with us." He yelled, "Roll him over flat on the ground." We need to put some lead in him. He knows too much."

The leader called out, "Who's our best shot?"

Several voices said, "Mac. He never misses."

"OK, Mac. When we are loaded up, take care of him."

Soon the vehicles were loaded and back on the forestry road. The engines were running. The leader yelled, "Take good care of him, Mac." He laughed, "Don't waste more than one bullet. Let's go."

The man called Mac laughed, "Yes sir! He'll be, as they say, dead as a door nail."

CHAPTER 15
Northwoods, Ontario, Canada

"The rumors about by demise have been grossly exaggerated."
– Bob Hope, 1998

Lying there, Roger heard the order, "Don't waste more than one bullet." Then the laughing reply, "He'll be, as dead as a doornail." Roger braced himself. "God, help!" Then the shot came.

Roger felt the impact. Am I dead or alive? I still hear the trucks. My ear is buzzing. I must be alive. The lead seems to have pounded into the earth against my ear. He must have missed. The shot hit the dirt right up against my ear. That guy Mac missed. But if he missed he may not realize it. Lie still Roger. Wow! I'm still here! "What an answer to prayer! I'm alive. Thank You, Jesus!"

Roger continued lying on the ground with his hands and feet tied. He wanted to keep from moving. I don't want someone to fire off a second shot. He continued listening.

Finally, he could no longer hear the departing vehicles. He felt sure they were gone. He tried to understand his situation. What happened? I heard the order. I heard the shot. I felt the powerful impact of the shot. But I'm alive. I'm alive.

Roger rolled over on his side. Lying there on the ground he opened his eyes. There, lying flat on the ground, all bound up, with ropes and wires, like a mummy, he found himself staring at some small blue objects waving slightly in front of his face . Lying there flat on the ground he could see nothing except this clump of delicate wild Ontario blue berries. "Great Scott! They're wild blue berries. They look delicious. Roger wiggled around so that, even with his arms bound, he could draw a bunch of blue berries into his mouth. "Wow. I'm not dead. I'm eating. What a way to be told that you're alive and God is going to provide for you! I'm eating wild Ontario blue berries. I'm really alive."

Roger blinked his eyes. Left for dead, the first thing I see are wild blue berries. Wow! Instead saying consider the lilies, Jesus saying consider the blue berries. Roger. You're alive! Northwoods wild blue berries confirm the fact that you're alive."

Roger attempted to say, against the grey tape that partially covered his mouth, "I'm alive. I'm still here."

I was ordered shot. I heard the shot. I felt the bullet pound into the earth against my ear. And here I am. Wow! God knows I'm here. He's alive. He's not just someone in a book. The God who gave me this life is right here. He's given me my life again."

Some people may try to tell me that I was lucky. No one's going to sell me that lie. You can't tell me this was luck.

Roger began asking himself what to do? Roger, get your grey matter working. You're alive but you're totally immobilized with rope, wire and grey tape. No one knows I am here. No one is going to see me here all wired and tied up like a mummy. No one is going to spot my canoe tucked away among those arrow head plants. Even if I could wiggle my way to the canoe there's no way I could get into it.

It was good that I left my wallet and smart phone at the cabin. They had no way to identify me. I could sure use that cell phone now. Roger began to stretch and roll about seeking something against which he could work to pry loose the grey tape and loosen the ropes. The tie up job was done very thoroughly. The best he could do was to get one arm partly free. Now what?

Roger tried to move his legs. Then he realized that someone had used wire to fasten his ankles together. I've got a problem. Somehow or other I've got to let someone know that I'm here. In this condition I have no way to start a fire and send up smoke. People these days don't read smoke signals. How am I going to let anyone know I am here? Everything is by smart phone.

A smart phone. That's what I need. Wait a minute. The man who ordered me shot, the leader of those crooks, was using a smart phone. He was yelling over it to someone one about plan B. I got a glimpse of him banging his phone down on a fallen tree and yelling at his men. What if, in his anger and the rush to get out of here, he left his smart phone behind! It's worth a try. Get wiggling, Roger. Roger started rolling his body across the open area.

After rolling and twisting his tied up body, Roger made his way to the area where he had seen the head man put down his phone. Then he saw it. Eureka. That man's phone is still there on that fallen tree!

The challenge was to swing his legs up there and draw the smart phone to the ground. After many attempts Roger finally managed to knock the smart phone to the ground. Roger rolled over until he had the smart phone in his one free hand.

Rodger realized that he had another problem. His mouth was partly overed with grey tape. This will have to be a text message. With his one free hand Roger sent a concise emergency text message. "SOS SE Bobcat Old Cabin. Helpless. Urgent."

Roger kept working away at his message until the battery died. What do you do when the battery dies? You use Christian ingenuity. You pray. With the battery dead, Roger continued to work on his ropes and tapes.

Then, after a while, he heard something. A motor. It was the unmistakable thunder of a helicopter. That's the most wonderful sound I've ever heard.

The helicopter came in low and kept swinging over that end of the lake. They were obviously looking for the person who sent the message. Roger was thinking hallelujah. He could be singing the hallelujah chorus of Handel's Messiah, except for the tape. The helicopter kept circling. I've got a problem. They can't see me or my canoe.

On board the helicopter the officers kept searching for some sign of the person who sent the SOS. Nothing caught their attention. As they circled over the lake again and again they saw no one. They saw no canoe or any sign of someone in trouble. Roger's canoe was still tucked in among the grasses where he had been painting.

The RCMP officer got on his radio. "Officer Mackenzie here. There doesn't seem to be anyone around here. The text message mentioned the old logging cabin. We'll take her down and put her on the water." As they brought the helicopter down, it created a great circle of whipped up water. They edged closer to shore in the shallow water along Bobcat Lake's sandy beach. The two men, Officer Mackenzie and Officer Brown, searched the area intently. MacKenzie reported, "There is no canoe or tent insight. No one gets into a place like this without a canoe."

Officer Brown spoke up, "Maybe it was a false alarm."

Officer Mackenzie cautioned, "The caller's didn't say 'Help.' He said, 'Helpless.' Maybe the caller is injured and unable to make himself known. He sent a text message. It's possible he cannot speak. Let's go exploring. Let's go in to shore."

As Roger heard the helicopter come in he was feeling as helpless as an Egyptian mummy. He could hear the two officers calling to one another but he was unable to do much more than wiggle. With his mouth partly taped shut with grey tape, he had no way to help them find him.

After quite a time searching the two men returned to the helicopter. Roger could hear the helicopter turning around and moving slowly along the beach for a clear area for takeoff. They're taking off. They've given up. Within his whole being he called for help.

In the helicopter, suddenly Officer Brown called out. "Hold everything!" He pointed. "Is that drift wood or a canoe. Look! There among the Arrowhead plants. I think it's a canoe."

Makenzie said, "Let's go see. That's why we're here." He moved the helicopter closer. "Yes, it is a canoe, an empty canoe! Its color that just blends in down there. It's a canoe. In this country an empty canoe means trouble. There's someone down here. Let's find him."

The two men waded ashore again and starting with the canoe worked their way through the area toward the cabin ruins. Finally, they came to the clearing. Then they saw him. They saw a man, flat on the ground, beating a log, with a stick held in his one free arm.

The men greeted Roger and quickly went to work freeing him. They cut away the ropes and wires. Very carefully they removed Roger's grey tape. They cut off the wires that were holding his legs. They helped him stand and held him upright until he could get his bearings. Then they led him over to a fallen tree to sit down for recovery.

Roger just looked at his rescuers. For a few moments he just stared at them in silence. He closed his eyes for a few moments shaking his head. Then, when he could speak, looking at his rescuers with tears in his eyes, he said, "You came back. You came back. You didn't give up. You didn't give up. You came back. Thank you. Thank you."

The officers introduced themselves. "I'm Officer Mackenzie and this is Officer Brown. Whoever tied you up really didn't expect you to leave here alive. You must have quite a story for us. How in the world did you get here and in this condition?"

Roger introduced himself and explained how he got into this situation. "I came here to spend a week at that beautiful cabin at the other end of the Lake.

"The Henderson Cabin?"

"Yes, the Hendersons were kind enough to offer me the use of their cabin on Bobcat for a week painting."

When did you arrive here?

Yesterday evening. You may have spotted my Rover by the Cabin."

"Yes, we saw the Rover."

"Well, early this morning, I had paddled down here to do some painting. I was surprised to hear voices. I stepped out of the canoe to find out what was going on. I saw a group of men at work. They were unloading containers marked with the international trefoil symbol for radioactive material. You may find some of their containers. Then someone must have knocked me out. When I came to I found that I had been wrapped up like a mummy."

The officers were amazed to learn that this situation was tied in to the Nuclear Power Station break in. Officer Mackenzie said, "This is our first sign of them. "

Roger explained what had happened. "They decided that I was one of your men, a plain clothes agent for the RCMP. When they saw me, their leader decided to change their plans and get out of here. They packed up everything. Before they left their leader decided that I had to be eliminated."

Mackenzie asked, "Then, how come you're still alive?"

"Their boss ordered someone called Mac, to put a bullet in me. I heard the man tell him not to waste more than one bullet. They said Mac never misses. But he did miss."

Roger showed them where he was lying when the shot pounded into the ground. "The shot came as close to my head as possible without killing me. "They must have thought I was dead. I lay still as they drove off. When I opened my eyes this is what I saw." Roger showed them the wild blue berries. He couldn't continue. He found himself in tears.

Officer Mackenzie said, "So, since they did not know who you were they decided that you were one of our officers. They took action to kill you. When they drove off these men were under the impression that they killed you.

"This puts your situation in a new light. We have to keep them thinking that they killed you. We need to contact headquarters before we do anything further." He waded out to the helicopter to use their radio.

When MacKenzie returned he said. "Here's what headquarters told us. Roger, you are still in great danger. They acted to kill you. If they learn that they failed and that you are still alive, they will certainly try again. They will want to find and eliminate the man who might identify them. Although you survived, Roger, you are in great danger."

"What do they suggest I do?"

"Let me talk to headquarters again." Mackenzie went out to the copter.

MacKenzie returned to shore. "Headquarters sees two key facts. First, of primary importance is the fact that, fortunately, these men found no identification on you. That is very significant. Secondly, they do not know that you are alive. We must keep it that way."

"I guess the best thing I did was leave my wallet at the cabin."

"Exactly. They have no idea who you really are and that you are alive. The number one task is to keep it that way."

Roger said, "What does that mean for me?"

"It means that as you return to your normal activities you must keep what happened here on Bobcat Lake today completely to yourself. It must be a life and death secret."

"In other words, I must go on as though this never happened to me."

"Exactly, Roger. No one, not even your closest friends, must know you went through this ordeal."

"That will be difficult."

"Yes, but this is a matter of life or death. Our chief officers says there is another key fact that may prove helpful. These men were convinced that you were a RCMP agent. They believe they killed an agent. Alright, we will help them go on thinking they killed an agent. As of now, they have no idea that the man they ordered short was Roger Renoir. For your safety we must keep it that way."

"And how will we do that?"

"Since they tied you up and partly hooded you they don't have much of an idea what their victim looked like. So, this is what our office will do. For your protection we will take steps to confirm the idea that the man they shot was indeed one of our officers."

"And how will you go about doing that?"

"Just in case someone is observing us, we will fashion right now, some sort of a dummy. We will put this dummy on a stretcher, take it to headquarters in the helicopter. We will go through the motions of recovering the body of one of our officers. Headquarters will come up with a name and report that this officer was killed in the line of duty on Bobcat Lake."

Roger said, "Great, but how do I get out of this mess?"

"Headquarters instructs you to stay concealed after we leave. Stay concealed until about dusk. Then just before dark quietly paddle back along the shore to the Henderson's cabin. When you get there go back to being Roger Renoir the painter. Tell no one, not even your mother, that you left the Henderson's cabin today. Tell no one about this experience. This never happened. Even your closest friends must not know that you were here and escaped this shot."

"Will do."

"If anyone, anyone at all, asks you if you know anything about some action on Bobcat Lake, you must play dumb. Plead total ignorance."

Officer Brown chimed in. "Do you remember that character, Sergeant Schultz, in that old TV series, Hogan's heroes? What was Sergeant Schultz's favorite expression?"

"Roger laughed, "I know nothing. I know nothing."

Officer MacKenzie agreed. "Exactly. Make him your model. That's what you must say, I know nothing. If someone brings up the death on Bobcat, you must say that you know nothing. You must tell no one, absolutely no one, what happened here. No one. Not even your best friend."

"You want me to be a kind of dead man walking?"

"Exactly. Chief Inspector will announce the tragic death of one of our agents. He will give the media a false press release. When you drive back to Toronto, stop and confer with the officers in the RCMP headquarters."

Officer Brown went digging for the bullet. "Eureka! I found it." He held in his the lead bullet mushroomed by impact with the earth. "This will confirm your story. We will also take the bindings with which you were held. They will confirm the story that we flew the murdered agent out of here."

The officers made a stretcher from poles. They improvised a dummy, wrapped it in a blanket and carried it out to the helicopter.

Roger watched the helicopter take off until it was out of sight and laughed. Who says there are no such things as angels? Mine even had a helicopter. Trouble is I can't tell anyone. Roger snuggled down to stay out of sight by his canoe till dusk.

As the shadows started to stretch across the lake Roger got into his canoe and pushed out from the tall grasses. He stayed close to the shore and quietly paddled back to Henderson's cabin.

Sitting there on a fallen log, rubbing his ankles and the ear missed so closely by the bullet, Roger sat there, reviewing his day and his rescue. My rescuers tell me to be glad I'm alive and live as though this never happened. The man who ordered me killed and the man who says he never misses, the man who fired shot, are real people. They out there. Whoever they are they must never know who I am.

CHAPTER 16

Bobcat Lake, Northern Ontario

"We are always paid for our suspicion by finding what we suspect."
– Henry David Thoreau, 1917 - 1862

Roger took seriously the words of the officers who had rescued him. "Leave this day on Bobcat Lake completely behind you. Go about your life as though that shot was fired at someone else." He decided that was exactly what he was going to do. He told himself, "I came here to paint." He decided to stay clear of that end of the lake.

The next morning, as he was loading up his canoe, the painter studied his half-finished watercolor from the day before. He was thinking that the unfinished painting had some potential. He had been painting it as a possible gift for the Hendersons..

Roger told himself, "I can't just throw this away. I've got to finish this one." He decided to paddle down to that end of Bobcat and complete the painting. The Hendersons would enjoy this one."

Roger returned to the very same spot. Once again he let the canoe glide into the shallow water until it was snuggled in among the Indian Arrowhead plants.

After a while, as he took a break from painting, he gave in to his curiosity to check out the spot that was almost the last scene of his life. Then he saw something shiny in the grass, his polarized painting glasses. This must be near where I was attacked.

As he retraced his steps he spotted his small pocket sized camera. This camera may have pictures useful to the police. They could say that the pictures were on the camera of the officer who was shot.

Then he remembered something else. As long as I'm here, I would really like to find the smart phone their leader left behind, the phone with which I texted my SOS. Without that phone there would have been no helicopter rescue. After a few minutes Roger found it. He held the phone in his hand reliving again his survival. Here's the phone that God used to save my life!

At the end of the day, Roger paddled slowly up the lake. Once again a heron was there flying ahead of the canoe. As he propelled his canoe on the still water he was enjoying that special feeling experience shared by canoeists. There is nothing quite like the experience of canoeing in the evening and sending a widening soft V across the surface of the water. He was wondering if such a moment inspired that century old hymn his father enjoyed singing. "God who touchest earth with beauty, make my heart anew. With Thy Spirit recreate me, pure and strong and true."

As his canoe glided silently through the lily pads and the lilies along the shore he was realizing that the canoe doesn't drown out what the Creator may be saying. Here in the midst of the water lilies I'm hearing it again. Your life has been handed back to you, a second time. Despite voices to the contrary, someone really is in charge of human events. That same Person that gave me this life is directing my life with loving purpose. What is He saying to me through this gift of giving me my life a second time?

As Roger continued paddling toward the beach below the Henderson's cabin he was thinking of that haunting title of John Piper's book that Hank liked to refer to, "Don't Waste Your Life." OK, I've literally received my life a second time. If I'm not going to waste this life given to me again, what's going to be my focus and goal in life?

After he turned over his canoe, Roger took in the reflection of the sky on the lake. I should be focused on something more than just seeing the guy who ordered me shot arrested. I should tackle something challenging. Something like seeing that even such a dark heart as ordered me shot become a new and different person.

Roger enjoyed his supper out on the deck with the evening cries of the loons for dinner music. He was listening to their calls when suddenly, as he looked along the road to the cabin, he saw a man approaching on horseback. Hendersons told me to expect a visit from their caretaker. This must be the man.

When the rider got to the cabin, he introduced himself, "Hi. My name's Mac, short for Macintosh. I'm Henderson's caretaker for the cabin. They must have told you about me. They told me to keep an eye on you."

Roger responded, "Glad to meet you, Mac. Yes, the Hendersons told me about you."

"I hope you are enjoying the cabin. Anything you need?"

Roger said, "I've been really enjoying this place. This lake holds some great possibilities for painting." Remembering the counsel of the officers, Roger said, "I've just spent yesterday and today here around the cabin, sort of settling in."

His visitor smiled. "Emily told me to make sure you didn't spend too much of your time fishing. She said that she wants to see some more paintings. Thought I'd come by and see how you're doing."

His visitor, Mac, told Roger many interesting things about the cabin and the lake. . He was plainly a local. He impressed Roger as that jack of all trades you have to be when you live this far north. He explained that he found he could get around better on horseback, what with all the barriers on private roads like those to this cabin.

Roger was striving to be polite but his head was spinning. As he rather mechanically shook hands with this man who called himself Mac, Roger was really startled. When he heard the name Mac, a big question started bouncing around in his brain. "Mac? Could this be the local named Mac who was there with those men yesterday? Could this be the Mac who never missed, but missed me?

Roger was remembering that while he was lying there tied up with a hood partly over his head he had heard the men greeting someone who arrived a bit late. That man was apparently a local recruited to help them. They called him Mac. The man who was ordered to shoot me was called Mac. Now here comes Henderson's caretaker and his name is Mac.

Sitting there in the cabin, talking with a man who might very well be the man assigned to kill him was really upsetting for Roger. On the other hand, how could anyone who had worked for the Hendersons for years be involved with a criminal gang?

As he talked with the man Roger remembered that much of the time his head was partly covered with the hood. The man who was ordered to shoot me could not possibly have seen much of my face. I was lying down when the bullet grazed my ear. This man, if he is one who fired that shot, would have no way of knowing that I am the man he shot.

Mac told Roger he wanted him to know he was around, and how to reach him. "You could drive out to the Country Store, they will know how to find me."

Suddenly Roger's visitor asked a question that really rattled him. "By the way, did you see that RCMP helicopter that came down over the lake yesterday?"

Roger was startled by the question. How do I answer this one? Then he remembered that strong word of advice the officers had given him, "Remember, like Sergeant Schultz, you know nothing."

Roger smiled as he came up with an answer. "Yes, I was here in the cabin when I heard whatever it was that flew over. It scared the daylights out of me. I went out on the deck to see it, but by the time I got out it was gone. You say it was an RCMP helicopter?"

His visitor smiled. "Let me know if there is any way I can be of help to you." His visitor swung up on his horse and as he smiled, Roger noticed that the man had quite a scar on one side of his face."

Roger sat there a while wondering how well he had handled the visit. I actually never saw the man they called Mac. I was lying on the ground. I believe the shooter never fully saw my face, since I was lying down. If this was the shooter he would have no way of knowing that this man sitting here in the cabin was the same man. Whoever fired that shot must be quite certain he had killed his target.

CHAPTER 17
Toronto

"People come into your life for a reason.
You may not know the reason why,
but there has to be a reason."
– Joyce Carol Oates

After those life and death encounters of the first day, Roger was determined to focus on painting and enjoying the unspoiled wilderness setting of Bobcat Lake. Day by day he explored the area around the lake and produced what he considered some excellent watercolor paintings. He hated to leave. Finally, at end of his week he regretfully loaded up the Rover, tied down his canoe, and headed back to Toronto.

He was looking forward to seeing the Mission Air team again but that raised a problem. The four of them were accustomed to being very straightforward with each other. How was he going to keep to himself his life threatening encounter on Bobcat Lake?

Those officers were deadly serious. "Tell no one anything about this experience. Absolutely no one. You have to go on as if that shot had never been fired." The four of them on the team, however, were used to being very honest with each other. Not sharing the events on Bobcat Lake with his close friends seemed dishonest to Roger.

On his way back to Toronto, Roger stopped, as requested, at the Toronto RCMP headquarters. The Chief Inspector gave him a warm reception. "I can't tell you, Mr. Renoir, how sorry we were to learn of your ordeal at Bobcat Lake."

Roger had the highest praise for the men who rescued him. "I'm here today because Officers MacKenzie and Brown didn't give up in their search for me. Through their determination to find me, I am here today. They persisted until they prevailed and here I am."

Roger handed over his mini-camera to the Chief Inspector. "There should be some pictures taken before the gang attacked me. Let's just call it the camera of that officer that was reported shot and killed."

During their conference Roger expressed the question that continued to bother him. "I am concerned about the identity of this man who was ordered to shoot me. They treated this man called Mac like a local. The caretaker of the Henderson's cabin, the man who came to visit me at the cabin, was called Mac. Could they be one and the same person?

"I was tied up and partly under a hood. I never saw the man who was ordered to shoot me, but they called him Mac. I was lying there on the ground. I feel quite sure that the man ordered to shoot me never saw completely my face either. The next day the Henderson's caretaker for their cabin stopped to see me. His name was also Mac."

The Chief Inspector replied, "You can put your mind at rest, Mr. Renoir. We have checked out the Henderson's man, Macintosh. He is well known by locals. They seem to think very highly of him. In fact they have a local name for him, "Scarface Macintosh." He got the name from a scar he picked up protecting a young boy from a black bear. Our background check and inquiries give us no reason to suspect that Mac, the caretaker, is the man called Mac who was ordered to shoot you."

Roger thanked the Chief Inspector but he was wondering how much they really knew about that man, Macintosh.

After leaving police headquarters, Roger headed for Great Lakes Castle, the large hotel in down town Toronto that was the meeting place for this year's Faculty Symposium. As he entered the hotel Roger found himself saying, "They sure knew what they were doing when they called this place a castle." Roger enjoyed these Symposium meetings because these events usually brought together faculty from his and other disciplines. He was very pleased that he could fit this year's Symposium in before the team's planned train trip.

The receptionist who handed Roger the electronic key card for his room said. "Sir, you will be in Room 2510, on the twenty-fifth floor. Roger looked at his room number, "Wow, floor twenty-five! I should be able to see a lot of Toronto and perhaps see across the Lake Ontario to New York State."

Roger was impressed with his room. The view of the Lake Ontario waterfront was great. He plopped himself down on the bed. "After a week in a canoe I can use a little of luxury!"

When Roger picked up the Toronto paper he found himself looking at a front page picture of five rather sorry looking young men. They were labeled, "The Toronto Five." The article described them as young men involved in the recent nuclear power station break in.

Roger learned that all of the men arrested were young Canadian immigrants from the Middle East. They were apprehended in a road block. While no radioactive materials were recovered in their vehicle, a modified ambulance, the inspectors did find enough traces of radioactive material to confirm that the ambulance had been used to moves the stolen material.

As Roger kept looking at the pictures he realized that these men were part of the ambulance crew he had seen during his stop at that restaurant on highway 400. The young men pictured were described as all recent immigrants and new Canadian citizens."

The paper said, "Canadians are struggling to understand this home grown crime. The paper referred to these young men as recent immigrants. The article said, "To Toronto's 2.5 million, who pride themselves on their acceptance of a great diversity of people, the arrests of such radicalized young men came as a shock."

The Toronto paper said, "Whatever the recruiters promised these young men, money or fame or some sort of paradise, the recruiters exploited their naiveté and ignorance. The recruiters of these men brought disaster to their families. The 'Toronto Five' were recruited to destroy the very people who had extended hope and opportunities to them."

Roger put down the paper. As he looked out across Lake Ontario he reviewed the previous week's experience. I went north to highlight the beauty of the Creator's work, to paint rainbows for a fallen world, scenes with a message of hope. In my landscapes I wanted to make folks curious to discover the purpose of the Creator for their lives. Then, even in the unspoiled wilderness of Bobcat Lake, when I stepped out of my canoe, I stepped into the quick sand of evil and hateful purpose.

Now, back in the city this newspaper confronts me with the faces of men who have never heard the Creator's wonderful plan for their lives. In Kenya the four of us were confronted by the depth of human evil. I come to this land of opportunity in North America and I am sill confronted with darkness.

He looked out over Lake Ontario. Why was I there on Bobcat Lake that day? Why did You intervene? You were doing much more than saving my life.

CHAPTER 18

Toronto

"The world is a dangerous place to live;
not because of the people who are evil,
but because of the people who don't do anything about it."
– Albert Einstein - 1945

A real conglomeration of faculty types was milling around in the spacious Great Lakes Castle reception hall. Those attending this year's Faculty Symposium included faculty from many disciplines. Folks were pleased to meet their professional counterparts and scholars they had known only through their published articles. In the midst of this beehive of scholars, suddenly many heads many turned in the direction of two new arrivals.

An older couple, who had just arrived, were making their way through the crowd. Many knew Albert and Sara Weiss from previous years. Sarah Weis was greeted by fellow scholars in her field, German Literature. She was an attractive and very pleasant lady and definitely a people person. She was well dressed. Her grey hair was neatly styled. As she smiled and acknowledged the greetings of familiar faces it was evident that she was not only respected but well liked.

Her husband, Albert, drew enthusiastic greetings from scholars who knew him. Friends responded to the intelligent but warm and friendly eyes that looked out under bushy eyebrows. He was not a great deal taller than his wife. A coffee stained mustache was part of his identity. The real attention getter for Albert Weiss was his bushy hair. It formed a scraggly halo around his smiling and friendly face.

Old friends enjoyed his obvious resemblance to a famous German personality.

As the couple moved through the crowd, people could be seen commenting on Albert's striking similarity to the well-known historic genius. Many had to be thinking, "It can't be Albert Einstein! He came to the USA, in the thirties, to escape Hitler before World War II."

Someone was saying, "He reminds me of those days in the forties, when we often saw Einstein walking down Mercer Street in Princeton."

Another voice was heard saying, "But Einstein died shortly after World War II"

Someone laughed and said, "Yes, Einstein died in the fifties, but like Disney they froze him, and then revived him to jazz up this year's Symposium."

Finally the word got around. "That's Albert and Sarah Weiss." Former attenders at the Symposium knew Dr. Weiss as a scholar of international stature. He was a member of the Association of Christian Geophysicists. This scholar's knowledge of the universe was enriched by his Biblical world view. Many had read his writings on Creation.

The Weiss couple had come to Canada from Germany quite recently. They were well known for their pride in having recently become Canadian citizens. Soon the conversation around Albert and Sarah focused on the news of the Toronto Five. People were really bothered that the men captured in connection with the break in at the Power Station were recent immigrants. Someone was asking, "As a new Canadian, what's your reaction, Dr. Weiss?"

Professor Weiss roared, "Send them back to where they came from." The Professor went on, "When Sarah and I became Canadians we swore, "I pledge my loyalty and allegiance to Canada." We swore, "I promise to respect our country's rights and freedoms, to defend our democratic values, to observe our laws, and fulfill my duties and obligations as a Canadian citizen." And we added, "So help me God."

Those standing around broke into applause.

Weiss added, "When these young men spoke that oath of loyalty to Canada they lied. If they ever sang, O Canada, they lied! *Gross Lugen!*" He stopped. His eyes were squinting. He was holding back his tears. Then he spoke up again, "But we…" There was an emphatic pause. "But we didn't lie!" He pounded his fist. "We are Canadians! When we sing, O Canada, we mean every word!"

The circle of friends broke into singing O Canada. Sarah led the refrain again, "God keep our land glorious and free. O Canada, we stand on guard for thee. O Canada we stand on guard for thee."

When Albert and Sara arrived at their room they laughed. "The Twentieth floor. We may need oxygen." Their room enabled them to look down on Toronto traffic.

Sarah was quite impressed. "The four lanes of cars are like a river!"

Albert said, "Looking between the buildings is like a visit to the Grand Canyon. Looking at that traffic, I'm glad we didn't rent a car."

As Sarah turned on the large screen TV, the news was reporting on the nuclear power plant r break in. "The five men captured were driving an ambulance as a getaway vehicle. The men taken prisoner are all recent immigrants from the Middle East and Egypt. Officers believe this crime was carried out to gain radioactive material for dirty bombs."

Sarah turned off the TV. "Albert, what a contrast between these men, who came here from the Middle East to hate and kill, and the medical team our church here in Canada sent to the Middle East refugee camps. They went there with love to save lives."

Albert said, "Yes, it confirms what God's Word tells us. There's a basic war going on in this world. The real war is not fought with guns. We are fighting to preserve the very foundations of life we received from our loving God and Father in Jesus Christ. And, if we persist, we will prevail. God says so."

Sarah was unpacking and hanging up a few things for Albert when she spotted an unusual leather case among his clothes. "Albert, what in the world is this?"

Weiss turned quickly. "Careful, careful Sarah! Just leave that where it is. It's a test model of a new and very sophisticate devise for detecting and measuring radiation. It's the newest thing. It is very sensitive."

"Albert, we are on vacation. Next you will be telling me you brought this along to track down thieves who might seize radioactive material at a power station."

"Sarah, my friend who teaches in Vancouver was very interested in seeing this devise. So, since it is a bit delicate to ship, I brought it along for him."

"Albert, what else did you bring with you? Your class notes for Fall?"

ii

───────────

When Roger came down from his room at the Symposium for dinner, he found himself standing in line behind a couple having a rather energetic discussion. They were both speaking forcefully and with a very evident German accent. He was standing behind Albert and Sarah Weiss.

At one point, in response to something his wife was saying, Albert turned, around to face the person nearest him, who happened to be Roger. "What do you think about that, my friend?"

Roger was surprised to be invited to join the discussion.

"We were discussing these immigrants who engaged in crime against their new homeland. I say send them back to wherever they came from. What do you say, my friend?"

Roger smiled. "It appears that we have all been reading today's paper. Another strategy might be, before they are recruited by hate filled men, give them an alternative, something better to live for."

Albert laughed. "I knew you were a wise man."

Sarah said, "Anyone who agrees with him is a wise man. It looks like you are here at the Symposium by yourself. Please do us the honor of joining us at our table."

"Of course, I would be very happy to join the two of you."

Once they were seated Sarah took care of the introductions. "Our name is Weiss. Sarah and Albert."

"I am Roger Renoir. I teach art."

Sarah said, "Do you just lecture on art or are you yourself an artist too?"

Roger pulled out his pocket sketchbook and thumbed through it, showing her some sketches. "This is my sketch book. Does that answer your question?"

Albert said, "I am impressed. What have you been sketching lately?"

Roger opened the sketchbook. "On my flight from Cairo to London, I sat across the aisle from this distinguished looking Egyptian with his white beard and mustache."

Albert said, "And this sketch book? This is something you keep with you?"

"Constantly. My sketch book is priceless. I give away or sell paintings, but no one gets my sketch book. I'm looking forward to doing some painting when a few of us travel to the Canadian Rockies."

Sarah said, "That's interesting. We're doing the same thing. Shortly after the Symposium closes, we are taking the train west. In our new Canadian homeland we have never crossed to the Pacific coast. After the Symposium ends we will take the train to Vancouver. We go August eighteenth."

Roger was amazed. "Did you say the August eighteenth train? Some friends and I are taking that very same train. We are booked for the same date, August eighteenth. Our trip is a celebration. We call it the reunion of the Lunatic Loonies.'

Albert asked. "A celebration of what?"

"The Lunatic Loonies. It's a reunion. We will be celebrating our deliverance from some terrorists who held us hostage in Kenya." Roger told them how, when his mission flight team had been taken prisoners, they had finally escaped by jumping on the Mombasa train to Nairobi. the train once called the Lunatic line.

Weiss nodded thoughtfully. "Lunatic Loonies. Not a bad label. People who trust in God are often regarded as lunatics. The Bible speaks of believers as fools for Christ's sake."

Sarah smiled, "Roger, we'll be delighted to be on the same train with you and the Lunatic Loonies."

iii

The next morning Roger and Albert met to have breakfast together. Roger nudged his new friend and nodded toward a man entering the dining room. "There he is. See that white beard. There's that Egyptian whose sketch I shared with you last night. He is a Middle East Studies scholar whom I heard lecture in Cairo and met again on the plane."

Roger pulled out his sketch book and showed Albert the sketch again.

"See, here is the sketch I made on the plane. After his lecture we had a pleasant talk with him in Cairo. Then a few days later when he boarded my flight from Cairo to London he seemed a different person.

It was strange. He didn't seem to remember me. He showed no interest in even talking with me."

Suddenly the man in Roger's sketch book was about to pass their table, Roger called out a greeting, "Good morning, Professor. Would you like to join us?

The man paused a moment. Then without any hint of having seen Roger before the man said, "Good morning," and continued on his way.

Roger continued to follow the man with his eyes. "I am sure he's the man I saw again on the flight from Cairo. On that flight he wore a walking cast on his left foot and this man is walking with one today. On the plane, like today, he didn't want to talk."

Weiss said, "He's certainly is not in a hurry to let people get to know him."

They continued to watch the man as he seated himself at another table. Another participant in the symposium walked over to the table where the Egyptian professor was seated and greeted him enthusiastically. The Egyptian stood up and greeted the man. They talked for a few moments and then the other professor went on his way.

Weiss said, "He's not very outgoing in his contacts with others. Strange."

iv

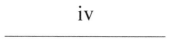

As Hamu continued to have awkward encounters with scholars who obviously knew Professor Fouad from previous meetings at the symposium, the new Professor Fouad was wondering if he had made a mistake to come to the Symposium. Hamu had found in the Professor's briefcase a letter confirming that his university had registered him for the Toronto Symposium. The impostor had seen the Symposium as a great opportunity to practice his new identity. He thought the Symposium would help him get used to meeting individuals who obviously had known the real Fouad. The gathering could provide opportunities to practice passing as Professor Fouad in other situations..

The impostor looked down at the hotel table ware. He gave himself a silent scolding, Leave no finger prints. If you can't wear gloves make sure that you use only one implement and wipe it off well. No touching any water glass."

Just then a participant at the Symposium stopped by his table and extended his hand. "Good to see you here, Fouad. We had heard that you suffered some injury through a deadly Israeli bombing in Gaza City. We are glad to see you are recovering and that you are well enough to be here."

The impostor smiled, "Thank you." He focused quickly on the participant's name tag which identified his university. "Thank you Professor Witherspoon. How are things in Winnipeg?"

Another participant stopped by with greetings. Hamu realized that this was apparently someone who had known the late Professor Fouad quite well.

This man who wore no name tag pointed to Hamu's sling. "So you survived an actual Israeli bombing in Gaza. That sling indicates that you take your Middle East studies seriously." The man laughed, "Maybe a bit too seriously? We're glad you're back safe and sound, and able to share in the Symposium again this year. How are you doing?"

"Bear with me. I am not quite myself as yet."

The other professor said, "My wife's parents lived through the Nazi bombing of London. They survived and it looks like you have survived your boombing. Glad you're able to be here." The man moved on.

Hamu was thinking that his appearance was passing the test. If I can pass myself off in conversation with old friends of the Professor in this crowd I've made it.

Another individual stopped and greeted him. This man was wearing a name tag with the name of his University. Hamu could respond, "How are things at Illinois?"

After that man had moved along Hamu smiled. I'm almost enjoying this. Being greeted as "professor" is quite satisfying. I'm actually stepping into his shoes.

Suddenly, along came another acquaintance. He was obviously a colleague at the university in Vancouver. This man spoke about internal affairs back at their university in Vancouver. The impostor was feeling on the spot. Hamu made use of a mannerism of Fouad's. As the man rambled on Hamu adopted the tactic of just nodding.

Then the situation became difficult. This man spoke of the church in Vancouver where apparently Fouad and Vashti had worshiped with him.

As the man chattered away he suggested that the professor meet him in the lobby about ten o'clock, Sunday morning and go to church with him.

Hamu did some fast thinking. To be the man I am impersonating, here in Canada, I need two faces. Those young Middle East immigrants need to see me as a leader of the Two Vipers. This colleague from Vancouver has to sees me as someone with whom he would enjoy going to a Christian Church. I have to wear two faces.

Hamu replied "OK. Sunday morning, I will meet you for church in the lobby."

V

Since the Symposium came to a close Saturday

evening, Roger had arranged to meet with the members of the team on Sunday morning, for worship together at a down town church known for excellent Biblical expository preaching. He invited the Weiss couple to go with them.

Sunday morning, while they were waiting for the service of worship to begin, Weiss nudged Roger and nodded toward the balcony. He said softly, "Look up in the balcony. Isn't that the man from Cairo, the man who greeted you so abruptly in at the Symposium? He looks like the man in your sketchbook."

Roger said, "I am really confused. After his lecture in Cairo the professor even quoted Scripture. The professor I saw on the plane seemed to treat me as an infidel. Now I see the man in church."

Weiss said, "Confusing?"

"Yes, very.

Weiss said, "Roger, there is, of course another possibility. It may be that the man with whom you had such a cordial visit after his lecture and the man you met on the plane are not one and the same. The professor whose lecture you attended and the man who was so cool on the plane, and at the symposium, may be simply two different persons who resemble each other."

Weiss continued his analysis. "My friend, it is plain to me that you have met two different men. The man lecturing in Cairo was one personality. He opened up to you as a person easy to talk to. He allowed you to know him. That was one distinct personality. The man you encountered on the plane, the man we saw in the dining room, and whom we see in the balcony is an entirely different individual."

Roger said, "I'm having a hard time accepting that."

"From what you have told me, Roger, the only explanation is that you have been seeing two men who look remarkably similar in appearance."

"Perhaps you are right, Albert."

Weiss replied, "What do you mean, perhaps? Roger, human beings do not have the qualities of chameleons to change color to fit the environment. You've encountered two different individuals."

CHAPTER 19
Toronto waterfront

*"It pleased God to make rainbows...and...to give
certain people gifts of drawing...and art is to keep
its holy rainbow character..."*
– Calvin Seerveld -1980

On Monday morning, with the Symposium over, Roger set out to look for some possible scenes for painting on the Toronto waterfront. He loaded up the Rover with his painting gear and set out looking for a possible dock scene.

As he drove along the docks and wharfs, Roger was fascinated with the all the activity. He was impressed with the huge cranes and big plumes of smoke and steam rising from industrial complexes. There was a great diversity of activity. He enjoyed seeing the great display of power manifest in the great ocean going ships. It was quite an awesome experience to stand so close to the giant ships moving by.

Then while investigating things, out on one of the piers he discovered an old brick warehouse. It had to be more than a hundred years old. He saw great possibilities in contrasting this weathered old building with the great ships that were moving by, so majestic in their power.

"This is it!" Roger unpacked his gear and set up his field easel.

The texture of the old worn bricks in this old two story building was very appealing. The detailed brick work was surprisingly ornate. The details were a work of beauty that spoke of the skilled bricklayers of the past. He was trying to visualize what it was like for the workers in this building to see the changing types of ships that passed this pier over the years.

Roger checked his watch and decided to get to work. He was to meet Emily at the Graf Zeppelin Diner at one. After taking in the scene from different angles he settled on his perspective for the painting. His first step was to make a preliminary drawing in his sketch book. He worked on designing the painting by first making a value sketch of the warehouse with one of the huge vessels passing behind it.

He enjoyed the challenge of painting the texture and the pattern of the bricks in the old warehouse. There was a barely legible sign that once announced someone's fish market. On the second level of the building, there were panels nailed across some of the windows He was interested in the old rusted fire escape attached to the building on the second floor level.

Absorbed in his work, as he was, Roger didn't pay much attention to any activity around him. When he was painting Roger wasn't thinking about anything else, not even food. This total absorption was for him a major part of the joy of painting.

Then, as he stopped to take a midmorning break, he Roger realized that two vans had pulled in behind the warehouse. He was surprised to see signs that someone was still using the building.

As Roger went on painting he became aware that a man standing behind him was watching him. Roger assumed he had come from the warehouses to observe. Onlookers were not something Roger, like most painters, particularly desired. Painting required concentration.

Finally, Roger turned to look at the man. He wore work clothes, and a heavy well-worn jacket? A hat with a wide brim covered his head. The lower part of his face was covered with some sort of scarf. The little Roger could see of his tanned face suggested that he was from some part of the Middle East.

As Roger continued painting the stranger asked, "What you doing here?"

Peter said, "I think it should be obvious that I am painting."

Roger stopped to let his paper dry a bit. Then, without looking up, he said. "I'll tell you what I'm doing? I'm painting some special aspect of the beauty of this world as God created it, to encourage hope. As someone put it, I'm painting rainbows for a fallen world."

Roger's visitor said, "A fallen world!" I've heard talk of a warming world. Are you telling me that the world is not only getting warmer but that it is also falling out of orbit?"

Roger answered, "The fallen world I'm talking is not the natural world but the people. The darkness and hatred in this world, man's inhumanity to man. Those are signs that show it is a fallen world."

"Fallen from where?"

"Fallen away from what the Creator intended when he made mankind, male and female, in His own mage."

"And you're painting rainbows?"

"The rain bow was given to show us that there is hope. Rainbows remind you of that there is hope in this troubled world because our Creator God is in control. Actual natural rainbows are not so frequent. I'm painting scenes that show that the beauty of purpose and hope in this world."

"Are you telling me that the world is not only getting hotter but that planet earth is falling out of the solar system?"

"No it's not the planet. It's the people that have fallen. They've fallen away from the Creator."

The man turned and walked away.

After the man was gone Roger speeded up the painting in order to keep his lunch date with Emily. He got up from his folding stool to stretch and walk around a bit. He stepped back to critique and evaluate his work. He was startled to see so much activity at the old warehouse. I was so busy that I never saw those men drive up. He smiled. I was working with meeting Emily for lunch on my mind.

Roger decided it was time to stop. He tossed the rest of his equipment into his Rover and headed out.

As he passed the men gathered near the warehouse, he gave his horn a slight beep and waved. The men kept looking intently but they didn't wave back.

Roger looked in his rear view mirror. Great Scott! One of those guys is actually taking a picture of my Rover. Now why in the world would he be doing that?

ii

As the Land Rover drove off in its dust cloud, one of the men at the warehouse spoke to the man using his smart phone camera to snap a picture of the departing vehicle, "Send that to the Professor."

The man taking the picture turned to another member of his crew, "That wasn't any artist. Artists don't come and paint old beat up warehouses. That guy was pretending to be painting. He was obviously sent here by somebody to snoop and see who we are and what we are doing. That means someone is interested in us. If he shows up around here again we should grab him and hold him for the Professor."

CHAPTER 20
Toronto

"Something is rotten in the state of Denmark."
– Hamlet (Shakespeare)

The Graf Zeppelin diner, where Roger was meeting Emily for lunch, was located along the entrance road to the Graf Zeppelin private airport. It was one of Roger's favorite places in the Toronto area. He was very familiar with this airport and knew the manager, Wilbur Linnberg, quite well. On several occasions he had rented a small plane from Wilbur. Another reason for setting up the lunch date here was that he had made arrangements with Wilbur to rent a plane that afternoon. He was planning to surprise Emily after lunch with an air borne date.

He saw that Emily's red BMW was already pulled up in front of the dinner's impressive building. In addition to its excellent food, the diner was known for its unusual appearance. The front of the building was covered with large aluminum panels that been designed as a miniature representation of the historic German dirigible, the Graf Zeppelin. Inside the diner the front walls were decorated with representations of the aluminum girders of the famous dirigible. On one wall hung a large sheet of damaged aluminum. It was labeled as relic from the Graf Zeppelin's fiery 1937crash in Lakehurst, New Jersey. Enlarged photos of the Graf Zeppelin added to the atmosphere of the diner.

Roger greeted Emily and slipped into a chair across from her. He took her hands with a smile. "You're looking special. It's great to have lunch with you today."

Emily laughed, "Don't you think it's about time. The last time that just the two of us sat down together was in Nairobi."

"How could I forget? It was on our last day in Kenya."

Emily said, "Yes, it was a special time. Perhaps we will return to Nairobi someday."

Roger looked around the place. "The Graf Zeppelin isn't as fancy as Nairobi's Carnivore Gourmet. No charcoal grill or spicy African samosas. But it's great to be together again."

"You were looking for an interesting scene to paint on this morning. Did you find something that you really wanted to paint? Were you able to change gears from painting North wood scenes at Bobcat Lake to painting docks and passing ships on Lake Ontario?"

The waitress arrived. "Hi, I'm, Barbara. Here's the menu with our specials,"

After they had selected something from the menu, Emily asked, "What did you find that you wanted to paint?"

"I found a century old brick warehouse. It showed the weathering of the years and was full of interesting brick work details. Beyond this old building you could see great cargo ships passing by. I think I have a painting that says something."

"Sounds like a subject with potential. Did you complete the painting this morning?"

"Yes, but I want to go back tomorrow. Want to come along?"

Emily laughed, "I'd like to go with you, but I know from our days in Kenya that when you're painting there's not much conversation."

"Emily, I need to warn you that a friend of mine may stop by our table. His name is Wilbur. He's the manager of this place, the Graf Zeppelin Airport."

Emily smiled, "Wilbur? Good name for someone running an airport. Is he someone unusual like Wilbur of the famous Wright Brothers?"

"Unusual is an understatement. His last name is also unique. His name is Linnberg, Wilbur Linnberg. It's spelled differently, with two n's, but it sounds the same."

They were waiting for their lunch to be served when a strong voice called out, "Hi Roger!" The friend Roger had warned Emily to be braced for had arrived.

Wilbur pulled a chair over to their table. He was a somewhat heavy man, around fifty. He was very obviously absorbed with flying. His outfit underscored his business. Wilbur wore an old World War II Canadian Royal Air Force leather flight jacket. What was really peculiar was that he also wore an old World War II leather helmet.

"Good to see you again, Roger." Beaming toward Emily, Wilbur raised his eyebrows and asked, "And who is this?"

"Wilbur, meet Emily Henderson."

"Welcome to the Graf Zeppelin, Emily." Turning to Roger, Wilbur demanded,. "Roger, the girls you bring in here keep getting prettier. Where in the world did you find this one, Roger?"

"Actually, Wilbur, half way around the world. I had to go all the way to East Africa, to Kenya. Meeting Emily was one of my fringe benefits in flying with Mission Air in Kenya. She was the nurse in our medical mission flight team."

"Emily, you'll have to give Roger a course in journalism. His descriptions of you were completely inadequate."

"I've been trying to help him, Wilbur."

Roger called attention to Wilbur's jacket. "There's a reason why he wears his old air force jacket with all those various pins from the Royal Canadian Air force. He hopes people will ask, "How many Nazi Messerschmitt planes did you shoot down?"

Wilbur laughed, "Did you actually fly with this guy in Africa, Emily? You must be a trusting person. Some of the planes I've rented him have never come back."

Emily replied, "Wilbur, I think I have a pretty good idea of his ability as a pilot."

"What brings you back to Toronto, Roger?"

Roger explained, "Four of us who flew together in Kenya are meeting here in Toronto for a special get-together. We plan to take a transcontinental train trip across Canada to Vancouver together."

"Why in the world a train trip. Why not a flight? Why not get a plane from me?"

"We thought we would enjoy taking the train together. We plan to spend some time camping in the Jasper area. We'll do some hiking and camping together. I'll do some painting. Then we'll continue on to Vancouver."

Emily added, "Although I'm a Canadian, I've never crossed Canada by train. It should be an interesting trip for us to share in together. Roger hopes to paint some more watercolors at Jasper. Then on across the Rockies to Vancouver."

"Wilbur pounded his fist. "Roger, the trip you are planning reminds me of a terrific opportunity you might want to consider. A plane just arrived here at the Graf Zeppelin airport. Some guys flew it here from Vancouver. They have a problem. Theiir plane has to be flown back to Vancouver as soon as possible. They're looking for a qualified pilot who would chauffeur their plane back to Vancouver. The pay offered is very generous. If you took the job, Roger, you could check out the sights ahead of your train trip together."

"Sorry, Wilbur. I'm set to just make the trip with the team."

"But think of it, Roger. You could scout out the train trip, maybe with a stop to check out Jasper. You would get well paid for doing it, Their plane is very much like those single engine planes you flew in Kenya."

"Wilbur, I'm looking forward to making the trip with the team."

"Well think about it, Roger. It would be a great opportunity to first check out that trip by air, before you make the train trip. You could get the lay of the land ahead of time and plan your time in the Jasper area better." Wilbur laughed, rubbing his hands together.

Roger replied, "Wilbur, I see you rubbing your hands together, the sign you see money coming your way. Good try, Wilbur. We're committed to our present plans."

"Well, I tried. I'll get some more of the details to you. Let me know if you change your mind. Enjoy your lunch at Graf Zeppelin. Great to meet you Emily."

After Wilbur had gone on his way, Roger and Emily continued to enjoy their lunch together. They were thanking their waitress Barbara for her service when Emily noticed a tattoo on her arm. She commented, "That's a beautiful tattoo."

'Thank you."

"What language is that in your tattoo?" Emily asked.

Barbara, pleased someone had noted her tattoo, replied, "It's a saying written in Japanese calligraphy."

"Oh, that's interesting. What does it say?"

"I don't read Japanese but it's supposed to says, "Nothing is good or true. Nothing is bad or false. Don't believe anything you read."

"It's a fancy tattoo, but do you believe that?"

"I suppose so."

Emily, smiling said, "May I ask you a question?"

"Sure."

Emily said, "Supposes you were raising a child. I'm sure there would be things you would teach your child as good or bad. Right?"

"Of course. I would certainly do that. Definitely."

"Emily laughed, "Then you are smarter than that saying in Japanese."

"In what way?"

"Well, with regard to whether there are things eternally true, and eternally false. I think you're ahead of that saying. You know that there are things which are true and good. You know there are things that are false and unquestionably bad. And it is not just a matter of opinion."

"So, you're telling me that while the tattoo in Japanese looks fancy, what it is actually saying is a really a lot of nonsense."

"Barbara, I do not want to offend you, but this is a very crucial issue in the world today. Every day people deny the existence of anything in this world that is universally true. They deny that there are statements that are objective and universally true. You hear such people say in effect, "Well, what is true for me may not be true for you and what is true for you may not be true for me. In other words they would say that what is good and true is only a matter of opinion. They would say there is nothing which is completely good and desirable in life."

Barbara replied. "You tell it like it is. I like to talk with people who are straight forward about things. Now, as I think of it, I was taught that the Bible provides us with the way our Creator God has planned for all people to live. It is not something good for some and not good for others. It doesn't go out of style. Like love for your enemies or the Bible's description of marriage. It is always the right way."

Emily laughed. "Barbara you are right on target. Are you a permanent worker here?"

"No. Actually, this is a temporary job. I work as a waitress in the dining car of one of the big transcontinental train. I am temporarily laid off because my dining car has been under repair and remodeling. They are getting my train ready for a special run later this month. I go back on the job soon. In fact we leave Toronto on August 18th."

"August 18! That's incredible. We're heading west on the great transcontinental train with some friends. Guess when we leave? We have reservations for that August 18 run." Emily laughed. "Great, Barbara! You might move from being our waitress on the Graf Zeppelin to being our waitress on our train."

"That would be fun."

"Look for four of us, Barbara."

Wonderful. I'll look for you on the August 18 run of my train."

When they left the diner, Roger told Emily, "Hop in my car, I want to show you something." He drove out to the hanger.

When they got to the hanger, Emily said, "This looks just like one of our planes at back at Wilson Airport in Nairobi. I feel like I'm back in Kenya."

"It's been quite a while since we've been flying together. So I arranged with Wilbur to use one of his planes for a flight. You will not be looking down on Kenya's Ngong hills today but you'll find that the pilot looks the same. Are you game?"

"What a neat idea. It would be great to take a flight together again, Roger."

They were soon flying along the shore line of Lake Ontario. Emily said, "Roger, this is the first time it's been just the two of us together since our dinner date in Nairobi. That was a special time."

"I can't top that dinner back in Nairobi but how about a high altitude kiss."

"That was awfully short, Roger."

Roger laughed, "Sorry. No auto pilot on this plane."

ii

After Roger and Emily toke off for their flight, two men met with Wilbur his office. They were eager to hear about his efforts to find someone to pilot their plane back to Vancouver. "What sort of a response did you get from that pilot you were telling us about?"

Wilbur was a bit apologetic as he faced the men seated in his office. Finally he said, "I had a chance to mention the possibility to him today at lunch. He has had a lot of experience with single engine planes like this. He's flown all over East Africa. There's no question that he would be the man to shuttle your plane back to Vancouver."

"And his response?"

"As of now, negative. I suggested that he take your plane to scout out a planned cross country train trip. I told him that he could make a prior survey flight and be paid for it. So far, no interest."

One of the two men spoke up, "Maybe we need to sweeten the deal. Maybe he needs some further inducement. We really need to get the plane back to Vancouver."

Wilbur replied, "I'll keep working on it."

"Fine. Keep in mind, Wilbur, there will be a percentage for you here at the Graf Zeppelin."

iii

After their flight, Emily and Roger drove down town to Toronto's Union Station. Emily wanted to confirm the team's reservations and get any further information that might help them in planning their trip.

Roger was impressed with Union Station. "I've never been here before. This station is a tourist attraction in itself. What a landmark! It's huge."

Emily said, "We Canadians take Union Station for granted. They say that 250,000 commuters and travelers pass through here every day."

When they got to the booking desk, Emily explained that she wanted to confirm their bookings. "The bookings are listed under Henderson. I'm Emily Henderson. The tickets are for four of us. One compartment for Emily Henderson and Joan Powell. One compartment for Roger Renoir, and Hank Edison."

"Yes, I see your bookings for August 18 with a seven day lay over at Jasper. Great! You are signed up for departure from Toronto on Tuesday, August 18. You have picked one of our best runs for your trip."

Emily asked, "That's good to know but what is so special about this trip?"

"This train passes through the mountains at one of the best times of the year. The aspen are starting to turn yellow and the scenery is spectacular. This train which takes about 300 people is almost sold out. It is good you made your reservations when you did. There is quite a demand for these bookings."

Roger asked, "Why the great demand?"

The railway cars on which you will travel have been remodeled and are newly decorated. There is, however, another reason why this train is booked so fully. You just happen to have scheduled your trip for a run in which arrangements for the night time stopover in Jasper and Kamloops are different."

Roger asked, "Jasper and Kamloops? The cities where we stop in the Rockies."

"Yes, on this trip, when the train reaches Jasper and Kamloops in the Rockies we stop and spend the night in both Jasper and Kamloops. This is so you are not passing through the most scenic areas of the Rockies while everyone is sleeping."

"What is different about this run?"

"On this run, when we make this stop we will not make the usual transfer passengers to local hotels. Passengers on this special run will simply retain their accommodations on the train. The train will be your hotel in Jasper and Kamloops. On your trip you will spend the night stops in Jasper and Kamloops on the train rather than a hotel. That is another reason why the August 18 run is booked so fully."

Roger was puzzled, "Why should that arrangement be so appealing to people?"

"Primarily for convenience. The baggage arrangements are different. At Jasper and Kamloops your baggage will stay with you. You will not have to unload for a hotel and load up again. Many, especially those with considerable baggage, find this quite preferable."

Emily had a further question. "I see a sign that reads, "First Class Advance Check in Baggage. What is that all about?"

The attendant explained, "Individuals can bring their baggage for advance check in some time prior to boarding. This advance check in baggage is stamped with the check in date. It is given special handling and security in handling.. It will be delivered to their compartment, or held in the special baggage car till needed."

As Roger and Emily were leaving Union Station, Emily stopped as she spotted a familiar person. "Roger that looks like Macintosh, our family's cabin care taker who visited you at the cabin. He hates cities. What in the world is Mac doing in Toronto? Emily waved and called, "Mac! Hi! What brings you to the big city, Mac?"

Mac was startled. He seemed to feel awkward about meeting them.

The encounter was more than a surprise for Roger. Seeing again that visitor at the cabin brought back his Bobcat Lake ordeal. He realized that, despite those assurances from the Chief Inspector, he was still concerned whether this Mac was the man who fired the shot that almost killed him.

While Emily was talking over old times with the man, Roger was feeling very troubled. Could this man, this old friend of the Henderson family for years, be working with that gang?

Mac turned to Roger, "It is good to see you again, Roger. I hope you had a good week up North painting. What are you guys doing here at Union Station?"

Emily explained the plan for the team's special trip together. "Our mission flight team is planning a trip together on the great transcontinental train. We're checking out arrangements."

"Guess you're wondering what brings a North woodsman down here to the big city. I'm sort of wondering that myself. Someone told me they needed a man to work the baggage car on one of these trains. They offer good pay and for the round trip west. Some years ago I had worked on one these trains. I knew the routine. So they signed me up for the job. I'll get to see the country again."

"We're booked for the August eighteenth departure from Toronto. When would you be going, Mac?"

"What a coincidence. That's the same as my train. Working baggage you don't see much of the passengers. I hope you have a great trip."

Emily said, "I hope you enjoy crossing Canada again, Mac."

As they moved along Emily checked out Roger, "You seem sort of preoccupied, Roger."

How could he tell her what was really troubling him? He said, "Our trip will have another coincidence. The couple from the Symposium that joined us at church, Albert and Sarah Weiss, will also be on our August eighteenth run."

It bothered Roger that he could not share with Emily what was really on his mind. He was still wondering how that immigrant gangs knew of that old closed off forestry road to Bobcat Lake? They had to have help from a local. Mac was certainly a local.

CHAPTER 21
Toronto Waterfront

"Miracles always come from unexpected sources."
– Rick Warren

As planned, Roger returned to the Toronto waterfront for a second day of painting a watercolor of the old brick warehouse. He set up his field easel for a different approach to the scene. He had come early again so that the early morning light would bring out the texture of the old weathered bricks.

After a while, as he worked away on his painting, Roger was aware again of someone standing behind him watching him paint. When he looked over his shoulder quickly he was rather surprised to see that the man appeared to be the visitor he saw the day before. Perhaps the warehouse workers were checking him out. He laughed. Maybe they think I'm really a plain clothes officer. Eventually the man watching vanished.

After he had been painting for a while, Roger noticed more vehicles pulling in behind the warehouse. It seemed like a lot of workers for an old warehouse.

Roger was a painter who knew when to stop. By two o'clock he was ready to wind up things. He needed time to get dressed for tonight's dinner party with the team. He folded up his field easel and carried it with everything back to his Land Rover. When he got to his vehicle, he set the field easel down in shock.

Roger just stared at his Rover. Both of the rear rims were resting flat on the ground. Both rear tires had been slashed. His first thought was that he had only one spare. This presented a problem. How was he going to pick up Emily at six o'clock for the team's dinner party tonight? For a few moments he stood there looking at those two dead tires.

Suddenly Roger remembered that he could use his AAA membership from the States in Canada. The CAA would honor his AAA card. On his smart phone he called the area number listed on his card. He was relieved when the agent told him that two men in a CAA truck would be there in about 45 minutes. He popped his keys and the cell phone under the floor mat.

As Roger waited he was getting a bit anxious. He occasionally looked at his watch. Emily was expecting him at six o'clock. Roger was walking around the Rover looking at those very flat tires. Suddenly, when he turned around he found himself facing several men. They looked like some of the men he had seen working around the warehouse. Then he saw that one man was holding a revolver. He was smiling at Roger and seemed very pleased with himself.

The man with the gun was apparently the one in charge. He gestured with a nod. "Wrap him up." Two men quickly tied Roger's hands behind him. They tied a blindfold on him.

The men laughed as they made some sarcastic remarks about the condition of his tires. It was both frightening and very humiliating to be led blindfolded back toward the warehouse by these men. Roger was feeling like a lamb being led to the slaughter.

Most of them were talking in some language he could not identify. From his days in Africa it sounded like some form of Arabic. Some of the men spoke English. Roger was realizing that his situation was quite desperate. I wonder why they felt threatened by my being here. This old warehouse must be a center for some major illegal action. There has to be some reason why they are so upset by my presence.

Then he heard one of the men speaking in English, "Remember that guy we grabbed up North. He was wearing a vest just like this man. He had painter's brushes sticking in the vest pockets, just like this guy. Could this be the same man?"

Someone said, "Impossible. Scarface really took care of the guy up there. Mac never misses. Besides, the paper reported that the police found the body of one of their men shot at Bobcat Lake? That guy's dead and buried. I read it in the paper. This can't be the same man."

Another one of the men agreed. "Yes, all those Canadian police all look alike."

Roger was growing more anxious. One of them thinks I am the man left for dead at Bobcat. That means that these men were involved in the break in at the nuclear power station. If they learn who I am they are really going to want to turn my lights out.

When they got to the warehouse, he heard someone say, "The CAA service truck is out there working on his vehicle."

Their leader replied, "Let them think the caller got a ride and took off. If we interfere they may make more trouble. Those guys have a radio. We don't want them calling the police. Let them replace the tires. We may have use for the Rover."

Roger heard quite an argument going on among the men over what to do with him. One man kept insisting, "He's been snooping out there for two days. Wire a cement block to him and drop him in the channel."

Roger heard the men finally agreed to go and get directions from someone they called the professor. Two men grabbed Roger on either side and walked him, blindfolded, up some steps to a room on the second level. He heard a door open. He was taken into a room. The two men went to work tying him up. They tightened his blindfold.

When the two men were satisfied that he was securely bound and that he wasn't going anywhere, the men fastened him to some sort of pole. Then, without a word they left him alone in the room. He heard the door close and the key turning in the door. Then he heard the slamming of doors, down below, and the sound of several vehicles leaving.

Roger was feeling very much alone and helpless. If he could get this blindfold off he might look for something to help him loosen these ropes. His effort to free himself made him realize that he wasn't going to free himself. "Lord Jesus, things look pretty impossible. I need some help."

After the men had been gone for a while, Roger was surprised to hear someone coming up the stairs. He had thought they were all gone. He heard the key turn in the lock. Someone was unlocking door. With the tape on his mouth he could say nothing. Someone entered the room. Had this man been sent to finish him off?

Roger listened intently. The silent person, whoever it was, stood behind him. Was he sent here to get rid of me? Still not a word. Nothing was said. Suddenly he felt the movement of a knife cutting some of his ropes. Then a wire cutter was cutting the wires on his feet. Roger was wondering if they were getting ready to take him somewhere.

Roger felt some of the ropes that held him to the pole being cut. Now something different. He could feel the knife cutting the nylon ties on his right wrist. He was still bound, but now his right hand was loose

Roger was wanting to say, "Whoever you are, thanks. That felt good."

Then suddenly, to his amazement, a knife was placed in his hand. Roger heard the man go out the door, and hurry down the steps.

He puts a knife in my free hand and leaves. There must be a rebel in the gang? I'm out of here.

Roger got to work with the knife. First he got rid of his blindfold. Then he went to work on the remaining ropes and nylon ties that held him. Finally. he was free.

The question was how do I get out of here? Then Roger remembered the old rusted upper floor fire escape. He quietly checked at the windows of the room. Great, the old rusty fire escape is attached to this side of the building. He got the window open. He crawled out very carefully on the fire escape. I hope this old thing does not make too much noise. He carefully edged out on the ladder designed to lower a person to the ground. There was no way this rusted fire escape was going to swing down. He worked his way out on the rusty ladder. Then hanging by his hands, having reduced the distance of the drop as much as possible, he let go. He made a successful landing.

Roger quietly discovered that there was no one in the warehouse. He made his way around a small building and hurried to his car. He was relieved that the CAA men had made the necessary repairs. The Rover now had four good tires. CAA had left an invoice on the dash board. He found his keys and his smart phone under the floor pad where he had left them. Roger swung into the vehicle. He started the engine up and just drove off. "Wow that was a close one."

Moments after Roger made his escape, two vans drove up to the warehouse. The men had brought back their leader to decide what to do with their catch. They went up to get their prisoner. They unlocked the door and stared at the cut ropes and nylon ties in amazement. Their leader was furious. "Next time you better leave men behind to guard your prisoner. Obviously he cut himself free. Have you ever heard of a search? What did you do, hand him a knife?"

One of the men replied, "We searched him and checked him out thoroughly."

Another man said, "We double checked this guy. He had no knife."

The professor said, "Then it points to a more serious problem. "Only our own men have access here. The cut wires and ropes mean that one of our men is a mole, a traitor. I am putting you all on notice. Whoever set this man free will be discovered. He will wish he had never been born."

CHAPTER 22
Toronto

"For from within, out of the heart of men
proceed the evil thoughts…"
– Jesus

Roger drove away from the waterfront as fast as possible. His mind was racing. He couldn't believe the things that had hit him in the last two hours.

What an afternoon. Two of his Rover's tires had been trashed. He had been taken prisoner at gun point and held blindfolded. Then, to make matters worse, someone in the gang had identified their prisoner as the man they had left for dead up north on Bobcat Lake. This had hit like a death sentence.

The men had been talking about dumping him in the harbor. Fortunately, they had set out first to confer with their leader, this man they called the professor.

It was a fast moving day. Then, shortly after that gang left, there in the darkness of his blindfold, he had heard someone silently enter his prison. That silent liberator ad quickly cut away some of his ropes and nylon ties, put a knife in his hand and vanished.

As Roger continued driving away from the warehouse, he kept wondering who could have cut him free. It had to have been an inside job. His liberator had to be someone familiar with gang operations.

Back at his apartment, after a quick shower, Roger made an effort to change gears mentally. He was due, in a couple hours, to be sharing in a big Chinese dinner celebration. The mission air team and Emily's parents, the Hendersons, would be there. He had to leave the unbelievable events of this afternoon behind. To complicate things he had to continue total silence regarding what had happened on Bobcat Lake. At this dinner celebration tonight he would have to act as if the events at the old warehouse never happened.

He was relieved to finally arrive at Emily's apartment on time. Several hours ago he had been wondering if he would ever see her again. It was quiet a refreshing change to pull up and hear her voice as she called down through an open window, "Be right there."

When Emily arrived at the car, with a big smile she announced, "I was exercising my feminine prerogative to keep the man waiting."

Roger replied, "When you look as great as you do this evening you are entitled to arrive when you arrive. Emily, you do look wonderful this evening. You have no idea, no idea at all, how glad I am to see you. Hop in."

"And you, shining knight, must have spent the afternoon polishing your armor. Tell me about your day on the waterfront?"

"My day at the waterfront?" Roger was silent for a moment. He had planned to tell Emily nothing. He found himself wondering just how much of what happened he should unload on Emily before this special evening. He realized that with Emily he could not pretend very long that all went well. She knew him too well. Sooner or later Emily would be asking some pointed questions.

Emily asked the anticipated question, "Well, how was your day, painting?"

Roger decided he had to tell her what had happened. After a momentary pause, he said, "The painting went great but there were problems."

"Problems?"

Roger said, "Yes, people problems."

"Most problems in this world come from people. What kind of people problems? Roger, I want the whole story."

"A few hours ago, when I finally stopped painting and packed up my gear to leave I found the two rear tires of my old Rover, slashed."

Emily eyes opened wide, "Two tires slashed!"

As he had anticipated, Roger had to tell the whole story. "It looked like someone was not very happy to have me out there painting their old warehouse. With two flats and one spare. I was wondering how I was going to pick you up for our dinner. Then I remembered that great reciprocal policy between the AAA in USA and the CAA in Canada.

I called CAA for road service. I thought I might be walking around while waiting. I told them to look for my AAA card and charge card under the floor mat on the steering wheel side. I left the keys and my phone on the floor under the other floor mat and took a little walk.

"Suddenly I found myself surrounded by several men from the warehouse. One of them was pointing what looked like a Smith and Wesson magnum at me. I wasn't going to argue with him.

"They tied a blindfold on me and marched me back to the warehouse. They took me up some steps to a second floor room. There they tied me up and bound me with nylon ties, rope and lots of grey tape.

"They made me immobile and left me there fastened to a pole. They locked the door. I heard them go down the steps. Then it sounded like they drove off to check with their top man. I heard them planning to sink me in the channel where the ships passed."

Emily was stunned. "All this and you're here to go to dinner? How in the world did you get here?"

Roger continued his story. "As I sat there, in the darkness of my blindfold, wondering how I was going to get out of this mess, I heard a key turning in the lock.

"Someone entered my prison and silently went to work on some of my nylon ties and the ropes. After he cut a few more ropes, he put the knife in my right hand. Then, still without a word, he quickly vanished."

"Wonderful. Have you any idea who cut you free?

"No, but one thing was very clear. It had to have been someone very familiar with gang operations."

Emily smiled. "He sounds like an angel. He was sent there."

Roger said, "With my right hand free, I was able to remove my blindfold and use the knife to finish the job. From my preparation to paint the warehouse, I remembered an old rusty fire escape along one side of the warehouse. I found I was on that side. I crawled through a window and went out on the fire escape. From there I dropped to the ground. "When I reached the Rover, I was happy to find that the CAA had been there and done their job. The two destroyed tires had been replaced and the keys and phone were still there under the floor mat. I got out of there fast. Here I am."

Roger and Emily looked at each other for a moment. Emily was overwhelmed with the enormity of the danger Roger had survived. Miraculously, someone had come to Roger's rescue. Soon they had their arms around each other. For a few moments they stayed as they were, enjoying that closeness.

Finally, Roger said, "Emily, let's just keep quiet about this at our dinner tonight. I don't want to be talking about this at our reunion dinner tonight. OK?"

Emily smiled, "OK, my lips are closed. But you could make sure they are sealed."

When they arrived at The Happy Mandarin Chinese restaurant they were greeted by the other members of their flight team, Hank and Joan. Soon Emily's parents, the Hendersons arrived. They were seated at a round table for six.

"The Lunatic Loonies are all here," Hank announced to the head waiter. Bring on the feed."

They started off with a fantastic array of special Chinese appetizers. They had all been busy since leaving Nairobi and their stopover in Egypt. They had a lot of catching up to do. They enjoyed sharing what they had been doing.

As they shared their experiences Roger felt a bit dishonest in not leveling with them about Bobcat Lake and his ordeal at the waterfront. He remembered the stern counsel of the officers. He knew his continued silence about those events up north was essential.

Mrs. Henderson said, "You would have to go pretty far to find four people who have been through as many things together as the four of you. Your planned train trip together sounds great."

"Yes, we've made a few forced landings together," Hank replied. "However, when we return to Kenya I think we will keep the same pilot."

Their team physician, Joan, commented, "We are continuing to receive firsthand information on the efforts to track down the gang that held us hostage. When things clear up in Nairobi we hope to return and resume our flights together."

The Hendersons, were interested in hearing about Roger's time up at the cabin.

Roger told the Hendersons how much he enjoyed the cabin and its unspoiled wilderness setting. "Bobcat Lake is, as you promised, a painter's paradise. There are few places like that without the human footprint. It was a special time, being alone in that North woods wilderness retreat."

"We hope you were able to produce some great paintings." Mrs. Henderson said.

Roger said, "You're going to do more than hope. I have brought along some evidence of a very productive week. In appreciation for your making the cabin available to me, I have a set aside a special painting for the Hendersons. Since the painting is large, I left it in a portfolio out in the Land Rover. However, I have right here in my sketch book the preliminary sketch for your painting."

Roger pulled out his sketch book and showed the Hendersons the preliminary sketch for their painting. "On our way out this evening I will transfer this painting to your car?"

Emily's dad was thrilled to see the sketch. "Great. A real Bobcat Lake scene. It includes the ruins of that old cabin built by the lumberjacks."

The team discussed various aspects of their cross country train trip. They were each researching various aspects of the areas they would pass through. They were especially looking forward to the time in the mountains at Jasper.

Hank said, "The more I think of it, the greater this trip sounds. It also sounds a bit more luxurious than Kenya's Lunatic Line."

Roger said, "Emily and I heard a crazy suggestion this week. My friend, Wilbur Linnberg, the manager of Graf Zeppelin Private Airfield, was trying to talk me into making an advance flight along the path of the train, before our trip.. Someone is looking for a pilot to fly a plane back to Vancouver and then take a commercial flight back to Toronto. Wilbur is pushing me to fly out over the route in an advance of our train trip. I told him that we're looking forward to making our trip together."

ii

As they left the Happy Mandarin on their way to the parking lot Roger was looking forward to getting his Bobcat Lake painting out of the Rover for the Hendersons.

Suddenly, as they came around to the parking area they were stunned by the sight of the Roger's Rover. The car had been broken into and trashed. Windows were smashed. The doors stood open. The car was smoldering from an attempt to torch it. The rear tail gate hung open and the contents of the back section had been pulled out and scattered.

For a moment they stood there stunned. Mr. Henderson was the first to speak, "Its utter destruction. Who could carry out such vandalism?"

Roger rushed to examine the interior to see what the thieves might have taken. He was anxiously looking for the portfolio of the paintings he had left locked in the vehicle.

Roger said, "Oh, no! The portfolio with the paintings! It's gone. The portfolio held four of my paintings, two from the Lake and two from here on the Toronto waterfront. All four are gone."

Roger turned to the Hendersons. "I told you, I had a special scene painted for you. It was waiting for you. I'm sorry but these van-dals have taken it. It really hurts to have lost that painting. I enjoyed painting it and I anticipated surprising you with it. It's gone along with another Bobcat Lake painting. Also, my two paintings on the Toronto waterfront are gone."

As Roger looked over his trashed Land Rover he said, "I doubt if I will ever see those paintings again. I'm sure glad I took my sketch book into The Happy Mandarin. In my sketch book I have the prelim-inary sketches and data from which the stolen paintings were made. Not all is lost." He just stood there silently holding his chin in his hand taking in the mess.

Hank and Joan, saddened by what had happened, began picking up things and tossing them in the Rover.

Emily was looking at Roger. As she saw him standing there taking in the senseless destruction and the theft of his work, she was sharing his feeling of loss. Then it hit her. How surprisingly well he seems to be taking the ruin of his Rover. He is concerned about something else.

She got to thinking of the day's earlier encounter that he had shared with her. There may be some connection between all this and the ordeal he suffered this afternoon.

Emily put her arm around him and said quietly to Roger, "There's something else involved here, isn't there?"

"Yes, Emily," Roger replied. "There is something more involved here than wrecking a car and stealing paintings."

Roger turned to include Hank and Joan "All this is related to another concern, that up to now I have not been able to share with you. Now it is urgent that I share the whole situation with you. It is very urgent. I want the four of us to go quickly to some place where we can talk. Perhaps your place, Hank. The four of us need to go someplace to talk."

"What about contacting the police," Mr. Henderson suggested. Roger said, "Thank you. I do not want to involve the police just yet. There are some things I need to share with the team. There's more involved than this wrecked car."

Roger spoke to the Hendersons. "I'd like to ask you folks to head home. The four of us need to go to a more private place where we can talk."

After seeing the Hendersons on their way, the four piled into Hank's car.

Roger said, "We are not playing cops and robbers, but it might be wise, Hank, if you dove in a way that would throw off any car that might be following us."

Hank turned and looked at Roger for a moment, "You're serious aren't you."

Roger nodded. "Yes, Hank very serious. I'll explain when we get to your place."

Hank made some quick turns and watching in his mirror said, "I believe one of those cars back there may have been following us. Don't worry. I know how to do this."

Hank pulled into a major street with much traffic. He suddenly swerved into a large mall's parking garage and then left by a different exit. "I think we're clear. No one's following now."

Roger said, "Where did you learn that maneuver, Hank?"

"Roger, don't you ever watch TV detective shows."

CHAPTER 23
Toronto

"Evil scheming distorts the schemer."
– Solomon

When the men returned to the old warehouse with the professor, they were eager to lead him up the stairs to see their prisoner. They were still feeling his anger. The professor was furious over their attention drawing blunder of taking prisoner this man who was simply painting at the warehouse. He called it as stupid an act as possible.

One of the men unlocked the door of the upstairs prison. When he swung open the door and they stepped through the doorway, they all stood there looking at a room that was completely empty except for cut ropes and nylon ties.

There was a moment of silent shock. Then, boiling with anger, the professor said, "First, you blunder in calling attention to yourselves by taking a man prisoner. Then you let him escape? To check out a man painting by the warehouse you take him prisoner? Then, after making yourselves known to this man, you compound things. You let him escape?"

The men cringed at his rebuke.

Their leader continued. "First stupidity. Then carelessness! Did he escape because one of you failed to check his pockets for a knife? Or, did he escape with the help of some deceiver among us?

"And now, to complicate the situation, you come up with the story that this man looks like the man we captured and left dead, up north on Bobcat Lake. Are you trying to tell me that Scarface Macintosh, who never misses, missed that time? What' a mess."

Hamu was really upset. "I've ordered two men to find that car with those brand new tires. They are to bring me anything they find in it, strip it and trash it. They are to make it look like another act of street vandalism and set it on fire. They were to bring me everything they find. Everything. And here they come."

The professor asked, "How did it go?"

One of the men who had found and trashed the painter's Rover said, "You told us to make it look like a vandalism job. That's what we did. We stripped that guy's Rover and set it on fire."

"What did you find?"

"Only this portfolio, professor." The man laid the portfolio on the table.

Hamu opened the portfolio and spread four paintings on the table. He bent over them and examined each painting, one by one. He was soon nodding his head and smiling.

"Look what we have here. There are two rather interesting paintings of our old warehouse here on the Toronto waterfront. But there ae two more paintings. These paintings are obviously scenes from that Bobcat Lake, up north. In one of these paintings I see the old lumbering cabin where we were starting to stash radioactive material in those Yellow Pigs. Two paintings at Bobcat Lake and two paintings of the warehouse. All four are obviously the work of the same man. Yes, one of you was right. It's the same man."

Hamu bent over to look more closely. "Let's see who he is. Most painters like to sign their work. Yes, here is his signature. Roger Renoir. His name is Roger Renoir. Look. See the signature on all four paintings. Roger Renoir. The paintings from up North on Bobcat Lake and this week's paintings of our warehouse on the Toronto waterfront all have the same signature, Roger Renoir."

Hamu turned to the men. "Who was the man who noticed the special painting vest on your prisoner? Was it you, Ahmed? You knew what you were talking about. The paintings confirm the fact that this man working on a painting of our old warehouse here on the waterfront is indeed the man I ordered shot at Bobcat Lake. Thank you, Ahmed."

"One of the men cautiously said, "And that means?"

Hamu laughed. "It means that what Ahmed suspected is correct. The man who saw our operation up north, that man I ordered Mac to shoot is alive. For the first time in his life, Mac missed. The witness to our operations up north is alive. Somehow, he stumbled on us again, here at the warehouse.

Their leader, the professor was emphatic. "It is very clear that the prisoner we held up north and this painter snooping around the warehouse are one and the same man. The man who escaped here from this old warehouse is the man we thought Mac had silenced at the Bobcat Lake. Mac missed. The man is alive and he knows too much"

One of the men asked, "What do we do now?'

"We have a problem. The man knows too much."

"Say the word, Professor, and we will track him down and take care of him."

Hamu said, "It is clear that we need to put him out of business. However, I keep thinking that I have heard this name, Roger Renoir, before. I'm trying to think where I've heard that name."

One of the men asked, "You've heard of this man?"

"Yes. And now, I remember where. Wilbur, manager of the Graf Zeppelin Airport, told us of a pilot by this name. This painter, this Roger Renoir, just happens to be the pilot that Wilbur has been trying to recruit to pilot our special plane to Vancouver.

"Wilbur has been working hard to recruit a man named Roger Renoir to pilot our special flight to Vancouver. Wilbur says that this man, Renoir, would be the perfect man for the job. This man, Roger Renoir, flew single engine planes like ours all over East Africa."

Ahmed asked, "So what has that to do with the way we take care of this man?"

"Well, if this painter and Wilbur's pilot friend are the same man, perhaps we can make use of this man to fly our plane with its special bomb package and get rid of the painter and the pilot at the same time." Hamu laughed, "We may be able to kill two birds with one stone."

One of the men said, "You mean that instead of taking care of Renoir here, we need to push Wilbur to recruit the painter to unknowingly fly our plane."

Their leader continued. "Wilbur's last report was that Roger Renoir turned down the job. But Wilbur is still working on it. He thinks that he might persuade this man to take the job if the deal we offer is too good to refuse.

"Perhaps I can sweeten the deal for both the pilot and Wilbur. I will call Wilbur tonight. If there is something in it for him Wilbur may work a little harder.

"Wilbur suggested that this man, Roger Renoir, might be interested if the offer included an opportunity to stop a few days and paint near Jasper. In addition I can instruct our man Wilbur to offer this man a generous bonus for delivering a special pack of high tech material from another company. Wilbur, of course, has no idea about the special contents of the package.

"If this man, Renoir, accepts the job, we will insist that he delivers the plane and the package on a specific date. The special package will be set to explode on that day. This devise will be rigged with an additional new feature, a special small altimeter. This devise will detonate the bomb on that date when the plane flies in from the mountain elevations and descends over Vancouver at an altitude under one thousand feet."

"Quite a plan, Professor."

"It will be two birds with one stone. We will achieve the delivery of a special dirty bomb over Vancouver. At the same time we will be getting rid of this man who knows too much. Two birds with one stone." Hamu laughed. "Or two with one bomb."

Hamu quickly got on the phone with Wilbur. He told Wilbur that he was in urgent need of a pilot to return this plane to Vancouver. He gave Wilber an increase in the amount he would pay for the flight.

Hamu instructed Wilbur, "Make him an offer he can't refuse. Inform the pilot that another company will be sending some very hi-tech baggage on this flight. This will mean an additional very generous bonus for the pilot."

Then Hamu reminded Wilbur, "There will be, of course, a corresponding increase in your finder's commission. Don't take no for an answer."

CHAPTER 24

Toronto

"Be anxious in nothing, but in everything,
by prayer and supplication with thanksgiving,
let your requests be made known to God."
– Paul *(Letter to the Philippians)*

As they arrived at Hanks's place with Roger, the team was anxious to hear what Roger had to tell them. Hank welcomed everyone and got things started. "OK! Roger, your friends, these three musketeers are here. One for all and all for one. Fire away. Let us have it. What's going on?"

Joan said, "Yes, Roger. We all want to know how we can help."

Hank laughed. "Roger, in what kind of a tricky situation have you landed us this time? First, you said we have to go someplace to talk. You suggested a car might be following us. A car was following us. With my expert driving we lost the car following us. OK. Roger, what did you do? Rob a bank?"

Joan laughed, "Roger Renoir, did you forge the signature of your famous impressionist predecessor, Pierre-Aguste Renoir, on one of your paintings?"

Roger smiled. "Thanks for the suggestion, Joan."

Hank said, "We're with you Roger. Fire away,"

"Your problem is our problem," Emily added.

Roger began his story. "During my week up north at the Henderson's cabin, something happened that, up to now, I could not share with you. The officers involved ordered me, for my own safety, to tell absolutely no one what happened on Bobcat Lake."

"This is sounding pretty mysterious. Roger." Joan said.

"It all began at your family's cabin, Emily. On my very first day, while painting at the far end of Bobcat Lake, near the old lumbering cabin, I was surprised to hear voices. Voices on this isolated wilderness lake? I had to go ashore to explore."

Emily laughed, "Sounds like you, Roger."

"Suddenly, I found myself watching men unloading stuff from an ambulance. They were hauling yellow pigs labelled with the international symbol of radioactive material.

"I was shocked. Then it hit me. These must be the characters that the Police were looking for when they stopped me on highway 400. They're stashing here the radioactive stuff stolen from the power plant. Their activity reminded me how early Canadians cut ice from the lakes and stored it in ice chambers below their cabins. These men were stuffing hot stuff below this old cabin where old timers stored the ice from the lake."

"What did you do?" Hank asked.

"Not much. Suddenly my lights went out. When I came to, I was lying on the ground, all tied up with ropes and wires and lots of grey tape. I was their prisoner. They threw a hood over my head to keep me from seeing too much."

Hank said, "How could such a gang have even known of such a hiding place?"

"I had the same question. I figured that they must have recruited some local who told them of this old cabin and how to get in there by an old closed off forestry road."

Emily asked, "So what happened?"

"Their leader, whose face I never really got to see, immediately assumed that I was an agent of the Royal Canadian Mounted Police. Fortunately I had no ID on me. He was very upset. He decided they had to get out of there. Despite the hood I managed to get partial glimpses of him from the back. He was yelling on his phone about having to switch to plan B. They were soon packing the nuclear material back in the ambulances.

Hank asked, "What were they going to do with you?"

"Their leader felt that they had to get rid of a witness like myself. He ordered their best shot, a man who supposedly never missed, some local guy called Mac, to take care of me.

"As I was lying there on the ground, I heard them starting up their vehicles. Suddenly I heard the shot and felt the impact of the bullet. But it had not hit me. It had pounded into the earth right up against my ear. As you can see, he missed."

Hank was stunned, "When they drove away and left you as dead you were lying there all tied up like a dummy. What did you do?"

Roger said, "Not much. Tied up like I was with ropes and wires, I realized that, although that shot had missed, to get out of there alive I would need outside help."

"But how were you going to get help?" Joan asked.

"What did you do?" Emily kept asking.

Roger went on to brief his friends. "Despite the hood I had a partial glimpse of their leader from the rear. He was yelling into his smart phone. I remembered that in anger he had slammed his phone down on a fallen tree. I got the idea that his phone might still be there. I managed to wiggle and roll over to that area. Wonder of wonders, the phone was there.

"Since they had left me plastered with grey tape, some of which ran part way across my mouth, I could not speak. With a lot of effort the best I could do was to get one hand partially free. I managed to get the phone and with my free hand I texted an SOS.

"Finally, after a long period of waiting, I heard the wonderful sound of a helicopter. The RCMP got my SOS, They kept flying over that end of the lake. Those men were persistent. They kept searching until they found me."

Roger paused, moved by the wonder of his own story. Shaking his head he continued, "They found me."

Joan asked, "Why are you telling us this now?"

Roger said, "Up to now these men had no way of knowing for sure that I was the man they thought they had left dead at Bobcat. They had no idea that their man Mac, the man who never misses, missed me. They did not know that I had survived my execution. But now that has all changed. Their trashing the Rover and seizing my portfolio will have changed the situation."

Hank said, "How in the world does that change things?"

Roger explained the new situation facing him. "They now hold my portfolio with four of my paintings, two from Bobcat Lake and two from the Toronto warehouse. With the theft of those four paintings, two from Bobcat Lake and two from the Toronto waterfront, everything has changed? They will now see that the man painting at their warehouse was the same man thy held captive and presumably left for dead by the old lumbering cabin on Bobcat Lake.

"As their leader holds in his hands my paintings, he will see that the two paintings from Bobcat Lake and the two Toronto waterfront paintings are from the same man. It will be obvious that the shot fired up at Bobcat Lake missed. He will see my signature, Roger Renoir and the dates on all four paintings. He will not only know that the man he ordered shot at Bobcat is alive. He will know that the same man was painting the warehouse here on Toronto's waterfront. Now he knows even my name."

Hank asked, "What are you going to do, Roger?"

For a moment Roger held out his empty hands. "It's an impossible situation. This man who ordered me killed once now knows all about me. Now, he can track me down. On the other hand, I know absolutely nothing about him. I never got to fully see his face at Bobcat. I know neither his name nor what he looks like. I have no idea from whom I would be running. He has my number. I haven't a clue about him. I don't know his name or what he looks like."

Hank said, "It sounds like you have to become invisible and fast, Roger."

Roger nodded. "That's what I'm thinking, Hank. This character now knows who I am and I know nothing about him. Roger Renoir needs to disappear, and fast. I need to vanish immediately from this Toronto scene. Those officers assured me that if this man learned that the witness at Bobcat was alive that witness would not be alive very long. Somehow I have to disappear."

Emily interrupted. "We happen to be a different sort of people. We not only believe in prayer, we pray. Knowing Jesus, we know to whom we are praying. We are going to ask for a way to get Roger off this man's radar."

Hank said, "Right on!" Hank led them in prayer.

As they considered ways for Roger to get out of sight, quickly. Emily suggested that Roger might return to her parent's cabin on Bobcat Lake.

Hank didn't think that was the best solution. "The guys that took Roger prisoner up there must have some contacts in that region. They would soon learn he was up there."

"What about simply returning to the USA where you teach?" Joan suggested

Hank objected, "Those characters now know Roger's full name. They know who he is. They would have little problem tracing him."

Suddenly, Roger's smart phone rang. He accepted the call. "Hi Wilbur." He laughed, "Yes, I remember that crazy idea of my flying West, the plan you unloaded on Emily and me at Graf Zeppelin. Yes, I received your message with their increased offer of payment for the flight."

Roger turned to his friends, "It's Wilbur Linnberg, from the Graf Zeppelin airport."

"Wilbur, you're talking too fast. Start over and please repeat what you just said." Roger turned on the speaker phone so everyone could hear.

Wilbur continued giving all sorts of reasons for Roger to accept this job of flying this plane back to Vancouver. "It's really a great deal for you Roger. Fly out there, scout out the Canadian Rockies before that train trip you and your friends are planning."

"Wilbur. I told you it was a crazy idea."

"Roger! This beautiful plane is sitting here at Graf Zeppelin. These people are very anxious to find someone familiar with this sort of plane, someone who could fly the plane back to Vancouver. Since my last message, these guys are willing to increase their offer. They like your East Africa experience. They really want you to make this flight.,

"Wait a minute, Wilbur. You're throwing things at me too fast." Roger put his hand over phone and looked at his friends and whispered, "Did you hear that?"

He spoke to Wilbur again, "Well, it still sounds sort of crazy, but I'll listen. Tell me more about the arrangements."

"Roger, you would find this plane very similar to those planes in Africa. The plane is also a high wing plane, an excellent plane for aerial photo work. It has good instrumentation." Wilbur laughed, "And even a parachute."

"Sounds interesting. Any other inducements for me to do this?"

"They really need to get the plane back to Vancouver as soon as possible. Thinking of you, Roger, I suggested that they think in terms of ten percent above their previous offer. They agreed. And of course, cash for the commercial return flight back. Are you at all interested?"

"What about a layover of six days for painting in Jasper?"

"I told them that you wouldn't consider the job without a layover in Jasper to paint."

"And what did they say, Wilbur?"

"They are ready to meet your conditions, just so the plane is back in Vancouver on the scheduled date and time. Are you at all interested?"

Roger covered the phone again and whispered to the team, "Talk about needing a quick way to disappear from the Toronto scene?" Then speaking into the phone, Roger said, "I might be interested."

Wilbur said, "There's also an additional possibility for added pay. Another company wants to ship a special pack of very delicate electronic equipment on the plane. You will be paid generously for handling this special shipment."

"OK, Wilbur. I am willing to consider the flight. There's one problem. I would have to take off tomorrow. Wilbur, there's only one way I could make this flight. I would have to check out the plane, load up and take off by midday tomorrow."

Wilbur replied, "Tomorrow? No problem. Great. The plane will be ready."

Roger covered the phone and looked at his friends. "Amazing!"

Roger resumed the call. "OK, Wilbur! I will plan for takeoff in the afternoon. I'm going to need a lot of help with the flight plan. Can you help me with this?"

"I'll be glad to help you with the flight plan, Roger? I have everything you will need."

"Great. Wilbur, I will need to borrow some of your maps and a GPS for the flight. One other thing, Wilbur. This flight must be kept private, very private."

"No problem, Roger."

"I will be there for a check out with your mechanic, first thing tomorrow."

Wilbur replied, "I will do some homework tonight to gather the maps and information you will need for the flight plan. I will arrange for that the additional baggage pack to be delivered in the morning."

Roger hung up and turned to his friends. "Well, it sounds like I've been handed a great way to get out of sight. I'll need everyone's help to get loaded up tomorrow. I'll try to find a way to keep in touch with you without telling the world where I am."

Hank said, "If this character who has your paintings is determined to find you he may keep all of us under surveillance too. We may have to be careful about the way we keep in touch with you.

Roger said, "A good point. Hank, since you and I are both licensed ham radio operators we should be able to use our two way handheld rigs to keep in contact."

Emily said, "Roger, how well do you know this man Wilbur? He's an old friend but how much can you depend on this old friend Wilbur to keep things to himself?"

"Good question. Yes, he's quite a character. I'll have to hope for the best."

PART THREE
THE FLIGHT

CHAPTER 25

Graf Zeppelin Airport, Toronto

"The most difficult thing is the decision to act."
– Amelia Earhart

Very early the next morning, when Roger arrived at the Graf Zeppelin Airfield he found Wilbur waiting for him. "This is great, Wilbur. Thanks for helping me with this flight planning. There is much preparation for a trip like this. I was quite surprised when you called last night, Wilbur. What made these guys so anxious to offer this job to me?"

"All I know, Roger, is that they are under pressure to get this this plane back to Vancouver. They liked your credentials. They were impressed with your African experience with similar single engine planes. They are quite aware that flying a single engine plane across the nation and over the Rockies calls for an experienced pilot. They definitely wanted you. When I shared with them your reluctance to make such a trip, they improved their offer.

"Let's head out to the hanger. My mechanic has gone over this plane from prop to tail.. He's completed a comprehensive checkout of the plane. We'll go out and hear what he has to say as he goes over things with you."

After discussing various features of the plane with the mechanic, Roger and Wilbur returned to the office to work on the flight plan. Wilbur had contacted the Canadian Flight Informational Centers for the areas involved in the trip for advance flight information. Together, Roger and Wilbur worked on the flight plan for the trip. They considered the range of the plane and its special performance features.

Since the flight would cross the Canadian Rockies, they gave special attention to recommended flight altitudes for a single engine plane.

Together, they went over various items such as the terrain he would be flying over and regions of unpredictable weather, where conditions could change quickly. They developed a tentative flight plan with special consideration for the pilot's endurance. Various aspects of high mountain flying for this single engine plane were reviewed.

In his flight plan Roger was planning to follow, as far as possible, the route of the transcontinental train through the mountains. He planned for fuel stops with at least an hour's reserve.

Roger planned, once he reached Jasper airport on the east side of the Rockies, to take time for special briefing from locals on crossing the mountains at this time of year. From his experience in East Africa, Roger had learned, when possible, to fly when the temps were cooler, because the aircraft's performance would be better. He was also planning for days when he might land to miss the afternoon storms.

When Roger returned to the plane he found Emily had arrived.

"What's in the package, Emily?"

"Guess."

Roger opened the bag. "Cookies, Great!"

"Something to remind you of me and the team when you are way up there."

"I'm just about to take the plane up for a get acquainted flight, Emily. Hop in. We'll check her out together."

Roger and Emily took off for his preliminary test flight. Roger was pleased with the way the plane handled. "I think this will be a good plane. It will be quite a flight."

Emily said, "Roger, the timing of that call from Wilbur last night still seems strange to me."

"It was quite a coincidence. I still do not really know for whom I am flying. Right now I'm just concentrating on putting space between me that man who now holds my stolen portfolio of paintings. When I return I hope we can all follow through with our plans for the train trip together."

"Roger, our team is going to make that reunion train trip, no matter what."

When they returned to the airfield they saw a delivery truck heading out to the hanger. The truck pulled up by the plane. Two delivery men in uniforms hopped out.

"Roger Renoir?" Roger nodded. "We've got a special shipment for your plane." One of them, the driver, handed Roger the inventory form. They got to work unloading a large and heavy black pack. It took both of them to handle the pack.

The driver handed Roger a form. "Mr. Linnberg insisted that he confirm the indicated weight on his scales. Here is his confirmation of the weight."

Roger looked over the manifest listing the technical items in the pack. He examined the tags on the pack indicating that the material was being shipped by a firm called, Industrial Technology. The pack was addressed, "Attention: Richard Harbison, Vancouver."

A sealed envelope was delivered to Roger. He found that it contained the cash payment for his delivery of the baggage. He signed a receipt which he handed to the driver.

The driver explained, "We've been instructed by the company to open the packs sufficiently for your personal inspection to confirm that the pack contains technical equipment as described," The man continued, "They want you to know you are hauling some very sophisticated high tech material and not any controlled substance."

"OK, let's take a look."

The driver inserted a key in each of two locks holding the pack shut. He unzipped the pack and showed Roger a maze of electronic equipment and wires. Roger made a cursory inspection. He gestured to the men to lock up the pack again.

Following his inspection, the driver said, "We will return these keys to the shipper. The party receiving the shipment has the same keys."

Roger said, "OK, let's get the stuff on board. I'll show you where to place it. There are straps to hold it in place."

The delivery men worked with Roger to strap down the load in the correct place on the plane. As they were crawling out of the plane, one of the men handed Roger's wallet to him. "Looks like that tight squeeze pushed this out of your pocket."

"Thanks," Roger replied as he put the wallet back in his pocket.

After the freight was in place Roger's friends helped load his personal things on board.

Hank said "It is good we are both ham radio men. I'm looking forward to keeping in touch with you with our ham radio equipment."

Joan added, "And here is a list of proposed times and frequencies we worked out for possible contacts."

Emily laughed. "Roger, this means you will have no excuse for not letting us know how things are going."

At their lunch together at the Graf Zeppelin diner, the team, as was their custom, held hands for prayer. Joan said, "After making so many flights together it seems strange to be sending you on your way without the rest of us. Roger, we're asking Jesus to hold you and your plane in the hollow of His hand."

As Roger started down the runway, it seemed strange to be taking off without the team. It was a special moment for him to see his friends waving.

Parked a littler distance down the road from the Graf Zeppelin, the two men in their delivery truck uniforms were watching the plane lift off. They smiled. One said, "He hasn't a clue. He is going to be very surprised when he opens his wallet and can't find his driver's license."

The other said, "Yes, and even more surprised when he reaches Vancouver."

The two men drove back to the airport's small office.

The men greeted Wilbur at his desk. "We have a special envelope we were asked to deliver to you."

Wilbur opened he envelope. There was a typed message. "The firm is very grateful." The note was folded around a bundle of large bills."

Wilbur said, "And I have something for you men to take with you. Here, as requested, is a copy of the flight plan for the plane. This will help, whoever receives this, to know where the plane is day by day."

After the men left Wilbur thumbed through the contents of the envelope. He was quite pleased. That's what I call appreciation! I can work with people like that. It was surprisingly easy this time to talk Roger into the flight. With all his earlier objections I wonder what persuaded him to go.

ii

A short time later the men drove their truck into their headquarters in the old warehouse. They quickly removed the large delivery truck signs posted on either side of the van. They went into another room where their leader was waiting.

The driver gave his report. "The big pack is on its way to Vancouver. We opened up the pack for inspection, as you told us. We urged him to inspect it, as you suggested. The more we encouraged him to check what he was hauling, the less he wanted to bother."

"Good. In about ten days the world will know that this special delivery has arrived."

The driver said, "You asked us to obtain the pilot's driver's license,"

"Yes, I asked you, if possible, to obtain his driver's license."

The driver smiled, "When he winds up at the bottom of Vancouver harbor he isn't going to need a license."

Hamu spoke to his men, "There is one further problem. We have still not recovered my smart phone. The men I sent back to Bobcat Lake came back empty handed. I need that phone."

"Can't you just buy a new one?"

Hamu laughed, "Not with the information on that phone. I need that phone. When we searched his quarters and we found nothing, absolutely nothing. It is my suspicion that, he might be carrying that little souvenir with him on this flight? We need to examine his personal things at some point on this trip, before he is blown to pieces in Vancouver?"

"How in the world will you do that? He will be flying across Canada."

"We have his flight plan. He is planning to stop in Jasper. The two of you are going to follow him to Jasper. When he lands to go painting in the mountains search the plane. If it is not in the plane, as he goes camping, search his gear. Find that phone. Do not come back without that phone."

CHAPTER 26

Jasper, Alberta

Earth's crammed with heaven,
And every common bush afire with God.
But only he who sees, takes off his shoes –
– Elizabeth Barrett Browning (1846)

As his plane lifted off from the Graf Zeppelin Airfield, Roger circled the field and, with a wiggle of his wings, sent a salute his friends. As he gained altitude Roger was really enjoying the plane. It was great to be flying this new model with its special features.

One item Roger had needed for the trip was a good GPS and Wilbur had loaned him his Garmin GPS. As they mapped out the flight plan Roger had worked with Wilbur to avoid controlled airspace as much as possible. This called for more information regarding individual airfields. Wilbur was a gold mine of information about smaller airfields like his own. He had briefed Roger about the availability of self-service fuel and airfields with nearby motels. As the flight continued, Roger appreciated the way Wilbur had provided him with valuable information about alternate airfields for fueling stops or weather delays.

Roger had been able to borrow from Wilbur the aeronautical charts so greatly needed for such a flight. The charts would be a major help in dealing with the concern such as high terrain.

Roger's plan was to follow major portions of the transcontinental train route. For much of the trip he would be able to actually see the shinning silver tracks of the transcontinental train. He expected that this would prove very helpful, when it came time to fly across the

Rocky Mountains and the Continental divide. One practical benefit in following the route of the train was that the train followed the lowest passes across the Rockies. This was of great value for his flight with a single engine plane.

Roger enjoyed wearing his favorite jump suit with its many pockets. This outfit was loaded with all sorts of equipment for emergency situations. His forced landings in Kenya had underscored the value of his old Kenyan Scout motto, *Uwe Tayari,* Swahili for "Be Prepared!" His jump suit bore an old sewed on patch of a lion. This signified that he had reached Kenya Scouting's highest rank. Growing up in Kenya he had become appropriately not an Eagle Scout but a *Simba* Scout, Swahili for lion.

Roger's pockets included the topo map of the area over which he would be flying that day. From lessons learned through emergency landings in Kenya, Roger gave high priority to having the best maps. His outfit included basic items, such as a pocket compass, a multi tool knife and several means for starting a fire. As he reached in one pocket and pulled out something new. It was a picture of herself Emily had stuffed in the pocket.

As the flight continued, Roger found the experience of flying over the Canadian prairies mind-boggling. Viewing the vastness of Canada's limitless fields from the air gave him a new appreciation of the sheer vastness of Canada.

After three days and about 1800 miles behind him, as he continued flying beyond Edmonton, Roger had that amazing experience of sighting from a plane that great wall of the snowcapped Canadian Rockies rising up before him. The sight was overwhelming. Suddenly, there they were. In the distance the snow draped mountains suddenly rose up on the horizon to greet him. He could scarcely believe what he was seeing. I've got to share this with the team.

On one of their predetermined frequencies, Roger attempted to reach the team with his ham radio transceiver. He was delighted to make radio contact with the team. All three of the team were there at Hank's place.

Roger attempted to describe what he was seeing. "This land through which we will pass on our train trip is awesome. I'm looking forward to the four of us experiencing this as we cross Canada on the train together.

"My first view of the Canadian Rockies is rising up before me. The grandeur is stunning. As I fly this small single engine plane toward these great mountains I am experiencing a deep sense of my smallness. I find myself repeating those words , O Lord, how majestic is Thy Name in all the earth."

He gave them the customary ham sign off. "Seventy-threes to all of you."

ii

Upon reaching Jasper, Roger parked the plane at the Jasper airport and checked in at his hotel. After supper, as he took a walk down the main street of Jasper village. He discovered an old building that had been transformed into an art gallery.

Roger was delighted to discover that the gallery was filled with an excellent display of local watercolors. Many were painted by a local watercolorist named Bill Webber. Roger studied the watercolors. These paintings look like the work of just the man I need to meet for some ideas of where to go painting.

Roger asked the attendant how to contact this man, Bill Webber.

"Bill Webber? He's one of our local artists. He's right over there. Let me introduce you." She called, "Bill Webber. Someone here to meet you."

When Roger introduced himself as Roger Renoir, Bill Webber's eyebrows went up ad he laughed, "Did you say Renoir? I'm delighted to meet a Renoir. Do you give Renoir autographs?"

"Sorry. Just the same name and a love of painting. Bill, I'm really impressed with your watercolors here in the gallery. I thought you might give me some suggestions of good areas for painting."

Roger explained that he was taking a break in a cross country flight to paint some watercolors in the Jasper area. He told Webber, "With the few days I have I could use some suggestions of spots for painting in the Jasper area,"

Webber replied, "Great to meet another watercolorist. If you are looking for some great areas for a watercolorist, you've found the right man. Now that I'm retired from the postal service I've been roaming all over this area.

"It so happens that I'm heading up into the high country tomorrow, for a few days, to do some watercolors. I'm leaving tomorrow morning. When my wife goes along, I paint and she reads. This time, I was planning to go by myself. I would be glad to have you go up with me tomorrow. This would help you make the most of your time here. I would be glad to take you up to one of my favorite areas."

"That would be great."

"It will be a four day trip. First, a day to get up into the high country.. Two days painting there. A day to back out to the truck and back to Jasper." "Your game for that. Sounds great to me."

"What's a watercolorist doing flying around in a plane?"

"I'm chauffeuring someone's plane back to Vancouver."

Webber said, "We will head up to a special location beyond Lake Malign. So, get yourself ready for an early pick up."

"That would be wonderful, Bill. Can you point out some place where I could rent some basic camping equipment?

"Yes, but that will not be necessary. I'm so well equipped I can provide all the camping equipment you will need. I'll bring you an empty back pack for your personal gear and your painting stuff. I have a good menu for painting. I'll bring the necessary food supplies. You can chip in on the cost of the food."

"That would be fantastic."

"Get yourself a good breakfast at your hotel. I'll come by with my old red truck for you about seven. Where are you staying?"

Roger told Bill he was at Mountain View Lodge.

iii

Late, the first night Roger's plane was parked there, the Jasper Airport's parking area was quietly visited by two men. After finding an inconspicuous place to park their rented car they made their way across the fields to the area where planes were parked. They were looking for a particular plane. When they located the plane, they used their tools to open the door. Upon gaining access, they climbed into the plane. They turned on small flashlights and began a careful search of the plane. They had no interest in the large locked special pack. They were interested in the personal baggage of the pilot. They searched all the side pockets and compartments used by a pilot for personal items.

When they returned to their car, one of the men said, "There is absolutely no smart phone in this plane. If he has it with him, he must carry it with him. We'll have to see where heads to go painting. Looks like we are going to do some camping."

CHAPTER 27

Lake Malign region, Alberta, Canada

"Remember the rainbows God made for the fallen world?
God did not have to make rainbows.
He could have just said it in black and white.
But it pleased God to make rainbows in the sky.
And it pleased the Holy Spirit to give certain people
gifts of drawing, imagining and making melody.
Find out why."
– Calvin Seerveld

Bill Webber picked up Roger at his hotel early the next morning, as planned, and they headed up into the Lake Malign region. When they came to the trail head for the high country, where Webber was heading, they parked Webber's old truck, buckled on their packs and started up the trail.

Then, as they got started, Webber looked back and pointed to another vehicle winding up the side of the canyon toward the same trail head. "Look. Another party is heading up this way. That's strange. I've been coming here for years and I almost never see anyone up here. It's too rugged for most hikers. That's part of the reason why I come up here. I usually have place to myself. I hope they know where they're going."

ii

The driver of the other vehicle that Bill had noticed took his time reaching the trail head. By the time he pulled into the parking area Roger and Bill were out of sight and on their way up the trail.

After waiting to make sure there were no spectators, a man dressed in clothes suitable for the mountains emerged from his truck. With the hood from his jacket pulled up close, his face was well concealed. He pulled on gloves and made his way to Bill Webber's truck. After he had examined the truck, he inserted a special devise and released the door lock. He climbed into the truck's back seat and turned on the manual switch for the small light over the back seats. Leaving the light turned on, he got out, reset the door lock, returned to his truck and headed out to the highway.

Shortly after he made his way back to the highway the driver, in his rearview mirror, saw another truck turn in to the trail head.

iii

Bill Weber's trail into the Lake Malign high country was a challenging hike for the two watercolorists. Finally, the tired hikers arrived at a special spot, along a small mountain stream, where Bill was accustomed to make camp the first night. They each set up their light one man back packing tents and Bill cooked his standard first night supper.

After supper Bill hoisted their packs up to hang between two trees, high and out of the way of any bears or raccoons. The men enjoyed the evening by their small campfire and spent the time getting better acquainted. When it was time to hit the sack Bill carefully extinguished their campfire. Then as they were preparing to settle down for the night, they spotted a campfire on another ridge.

Bill said, "That's a surprise. The challenge of the hike up here discourages most people from coming up this way. Seeing another camp fire here is strange. I never see anyone else up here. Well, tomorrow I can guarantee an early but delicious breakfast."

In the morning, Bill greeted Roger. "With a name like Renoir you must have inherited the painting secrets of your famous namesake, the great French impressionist, Pierre-Auguste-Renoir. Today you will learn some of the secrets of the mountain painter Bill Webber."

"That's why I'm here, Bill."

Bill explained, "One secret of the freshness and sparkle of my mountain scenes is that I start with a fresh mountain trout breakfast. Before painting the challenging scenes of the Canadian Rockies you must first have a fresh mountain trout, caught and cooked on the spot. Nothing gives my paintings that special mountain flavor like a couple of mountain trout for breakfast. I'll show you my special spot. Just to show you how optimistic I am, we'll take my cooking kit with us. We will cook our mountain trout right on the spot."

Bill led them to a fast flowing mountain stream. In a short while Bill's fly fishing skills had landed four beautiful trout. He built a small fire between some blackened rocks that Webber appeared to have used before. Soon they were enjoying the promised breakfast of freshly caught mountain trout.

Bill said, "One benefit of eating breakfast down here is less fish aroma around our camp to attract the black bears and other critters."

After breakfast they headed back to their camp. When they got there they just stood there completely amazed. Their camp site had been completely ransacked and trashed. Bill said, "In all my years in this country I have never had anything happen like this."

Roger's reaction, "Black bears?"

"No, these were two legged critters. See that print of a boot, unlike any of ours*. They were looking for something of value."

Roger was bewildered. "Who would do something like this?"

Bill said, "Not campers."

Roger first checked out his painting equipment. "Someone really rooted through my things but nothing seems to be missing. It's almost as if they were searching for something in particular. Even my fine pocket camera is still here. If searching for something of value, why did they leave behind my camera?"

"Roger, I have never had an experience like this. Enjoying the majesty of the Creator, and stealing don't run together."

Bill continued checking out his tent. "Look, Roger!" Bill held up a pair of jeans, "I left my cell phone in this pocket. I didn't want to chance wrecking my phone while fishing. But, look Roger. My phone is not in the pocket where I had left it. I found it lying here on the floor of my tent. Some character pulled my cell phone out of my pants pocket, checked it out and then left it."

"That looks like a top of the line phone, Bill."

"What impresses me is that the person rooting through my things, found this expensive phone in my personal things but didn't take it. For me that suggests he was looking for something, something in particular, perhaps even a particular smart phone."

"A particular phone?" Roger said, "Bill, you just turned on my lights. I think I know what has happened here."

"What do you mean, the lights went on?"

Roger said, "Bill, your suggestion that someone might have been looking for a particular phone was a wakeup call. I happen to have acquired a particular phone other than my own. It is, what you might call a hot phone. It belonged to someone who was involved in a serious crime. Whoever ransacked our camp may have been sent to find that phone. I happen to have that phone but I do not have it here with me."

"Are you telling me that you are holding on to some criminal's smart phone?" Bill laughed. "Do you go looking for trouble, Roger?"

"It's quite a story."

Roger told Webber how he had been taken prisoner by this gang of thieves at Bobcat Lake. "When the captured me they assumed I was an advance agent for the police. They decided that they had to move. There was a problem. What to do with me. Someone they called Mac, their expert shot, was ordered to eliminate me. He shot and everyone assumed that I was dead. They drove off to a new location. As you can see, the guy who never misses missed me."

"So how did you come to have this guy's smart phone?"

Roger continued his story. "When they hurried off, thinking I was dead, they left me all wired and tied up like an Egyptian mummy. I needed help to get out of there alive. Then I remembered how the gang's leader banged his smart phone down on a fallen tree. I wondered if he had left it behind. I rolled over to the area and found his phone. Since my mouth was partly taped shut, I used my one partly free hand to send a text message for help."

"So you believe that these guys think you could have that smart phone."

"These men now know that I'm the man they held prisoner on Bobcat. They may have the idea I might have that special phone.

Maybe, when they failed to find the phone among my things in Toronto, they figured I might have it with me. However, I left the phone with Emily, a member of our team back in Toronto."

Bill responded, "My wheels are turning Roger. To begin with, their following you here to search for that phone indicates that they had access to your flight plan. Following you here indicates that the addresses on that phone must be very crucial to someone. These days people are using phones addresses to detonate bombs

"Roger, let's take a look at that camp we saw last night."

When the two men reached the campsite whose fire they had seen the night before, they found the place deserted. Bill said, "Take a look at through these binoculars mounted on this tripod."

Roger carefully looked through the tripod mounted binoculars. "This rig is aimed right at our camp."

Bill asked, "Who knew the details of your trip, Roger? Who could have sent these guys to spy on you?"

Roger laughed, "Maybe your wife, Bill."

"No, not my wife. And since you're not married Roger, it can't be your wife either. Somehow these men gained access to your flight plan and knew of your planned stop in Jasper.'

As he looked around, Bill spotted a small leather case with a compass and a map. "I think I'll take these along as a souvenir. They'll think they lost these items somewhere".

On their way back to their camp Roger explained why he had grabbed the opportunity to chauffeur the plane to Vancouver. "I was desperate to do a disappearing act. The men who thought they had killed me at Bobcat Lake now knew that was I am still alive. I feared they would send a hit man to finish the job. So, when I heard that someone wanted to hire me to pilot their plane to Vancouver, I jumped at the chance to get out of Toronto fast."

Bill said, "It looks like God put me at the gallery, the other evening. I can help you with more than painting sites. I can help you dodge these guys."

"I'm open to all the help I can get, Bill."

Bill said, "There's more involved here than recovery of that smart phone. These men had to know your flight plan. Who could have given them your flight plan?"

Roger said, "As far as I know, the only other person who really knows my flight plan is Wilbur Linnberg. He runs a small private airfield, the Graf Zeppelin Airport near Toronto. He told me about the opportunity to deliver this plane to Vancouver. He recommended me for this flight. He helped me develop the flight plan. Wilbur loaned me his GPS. I've borrowed his maps."

"Roger, it sounds to me that someone is interested in more than that phone. Here they had you in their sights. Why didn't they just eliminate you? These guys are allowing you to complete your trip to Vancouver? They must have some particular reason for wanting to be sure you complete your flight to Vancouver.

"Tell me, Roger, what do you know about the people for whom you are chauffeuring the plane to Vancouver?

Roger said, "I eally nothing. I never met them. Wilbur made all the arrangements."

"Roger, we're here to paint. First, we need to get these guys off your trail. I know exactly how to do it. I have a plan."

"What's the plan?"

Bill said "As we break camp and head out for my special painting spot, we will do these guys the favor of leaving behind our well-marked topo map. However, this map we leave behind will be marked with a deliberately misleading route."

"How will this keep them off our trail?"

"Roger, the precious map we leave behind will not only lead them away from us but it will lead them into an area with very confusing terrain. Some years ago, I myself got confused and had a hard time getting out of there. Old timers around here call it the Canyon of No Return. And we have their compass. They will be like a lot of people, these days, men without a compass."

"Sounds great."

Bill said, "This should buy us time. We should have two good undisturbed days for painting before we head out to the truck again."

Roger and Bill broke camp quickly. They made their way to the special trail for which Bill was looking. Finally the two painters reached the high country that was Bill's destination. They suddenly broke into a clearing and stood at a breathtaking overlook. For a few moments the two painters just stood there. The marvelous view did all the talking.

"This is one of my secret painting hangouts, Roger. Welcome to Webber country. There's a special clearing down the way a bit, where we can set up our tents and make camp. I think that you'll find more than enough to challenge you along this ridge."

Roger just stood there taking in the vast view stretching out before him.

Bill said, "I hope you will feel it worth the wear and tear on your boots? This ridge has a lot of challenging sites. Let's get to work doing what we came here to do."

The painters were enjoying a beautiful morning. The air was clear. The mist had not yet risen in the mountains. Conditions were what painters look for. Roger and Bill spread out to locations that interested them. Each set himself to discover that particular area that would give him a compulsion to paint it.*

After about three hours they stopped for something to eat and drink. Then it was back to painting. Finally they called a halt for the day.

The two men took time to study each other's work. They were both interested in seeing what the other was doing and hearing some comment on their work. Hearing each other's comments helped them see further possibilities in their paintings.

The two men got an earlier start on their second day painting in Webber's high country.

Roger shared with Bill his feeling about the site. "It really has helped me to be here. I seem to have forgotten the danger that caused me to get out of Toronto in such a hurry."

On the morning of their fourth day they had to wind up their painting about noon in order to reach the truck in good time. After lunch they packed up their gear set off to hike back to the trail head. They arrived at the truck by early evening. Bill patted his old red truck on the fender, "Old Red! Ours is the only vehicle here. We appear to be the last ones out today."

After they loaded their gear in the back of the truck and got in, Bill turned the key. Nothing happened. He turned it again. Absolute silence. He turned to Roger with disbelief on his face. "Sorry about this Roger. That silence means my battery is, as Scrooge would say, dead as a door nail. Old Red's battery is dead."

"What could have happened?"

Bill said, "That's what I'm wondering. This battery is relatively new. We'll have to wait for help from whoever comes early tomorrow morning to give us a boost with my jumper cables. Looks like we put up our tents again. We'll have to spend the night here. With an early jump start, we should be back in town by supper tomorrow."

They set up their tents by the truck. Roger said, "I've got one small problem, Bill I don't mind another night up here but Old Red's dead battery is going to mean that I leave Jasper a day late. I was scheduled to fly out of Jasper tomorrow. This is going to make me arrive in Vancouver airport a day late."

Early the next morning a truck pulling a horse trailer arrived at the trail head. The driver quickly helped Bill jump start his truck.

With power restored, Bill checked out the truck to see what might have drained the battery. "There's the little culprit, Roger. Now that we have juice again you can see that little light shining over the back seat. It lighted up as soon as we had power. It has a manual switch. All those four days our truck was sitting here that little light drained the battery dead. I don't know how that light got turned on."

"I guess it got turned on by accident."

"No, Roger. When you come up here you get in the habit of checking such things. I made my routine check before we left. That light was not on. It is very clear to me that someone turned that light on and deliberately caused us to have a dead batter."

Roger was shocked. "Do you think it was those spies in in the other camp?"

"No, Roger, those guys had a different objective."

"You're suggesting, Bill, that those characters that raided our camp are not the only people interested in what we're doing. Someone else killed the battery?"

"Exactly."

When they arrived back in Jasper Bill drove Roger out to the Jasper airfield to check out his plane and to get the plane all fueled and set for a takeoff the next morning.

iv

As Roger and Bill drove off from the Jasper airport two men were seated in a truck near the airport. They waited until everyone except the guard stationed in the office had left for the night. In the darkness the men walked out to the area where Roger has parked his plane. They removed the engine's cover and went to work with some tools on the engine. They returned to their truck and drove away. By the light of day, only someone observing very carefully would have noticed the occasional drop of oil dripping from the plane.

CHAPTER 28

An Old Canadian Gold Rush Era Cabin
Canadian Rockies, Alberta

"Ther's gold and it's haunting and haunting,
It's luring me on as of old.
Yet it isn't the gold that I'm wanting,
So much as just finding the gold."
– Robert Service, Canada's Poet - 1898

Roger knew that when he took off from the Jasper airport that the terrain below would be rapidly changing. The graceful silver line of the train tracks below would have more curves and steeper grades. Roger would be flying over increasingly higher and more rugged terrain. Soon he would be looking down over the spectacular canyon of the North Thompson River. This canyon was so filled with powerful churning water that it had been necessary to run the East bound tracks on one side and west bound on the opposite side.

The canyon of the great North Thompson river, over which Roger would be flying, contained one of the most powerful cataracts in the world. Passengers on the great trains looked forward to seeing and photographing this swirling turbulence in the river. The powerful cataract had been called, by an early explorer, Hell's Gate.

At one time, great passenger trains were accustomed to stop briefly along the great cataract, so passengers could view and photograph the waters of the Hell's Gate cataract. The old viewing platform, from those days, though no longer used, was still standing.

The spectacular beauty and power of Hell's Gate's awesome churning white water was greatly increased by a nearby fast flowing tributary known as Treasure Creek. The name originated with the prospectors who had panned for gold along Treasure Creek during the Canada's nineteenth century gold rush.

A few miles upstream from the Hell's Gate, along Treasure Creek, a small stream of smoke could sometimes be seen rising through the trees. This smoke rising through the great lodge pole pines came from an old cabin. The cabin, built with hand hewn square logs, was a survivor of the Canadian gold rush of the 1850's. It had been built by the rugged men who, in those days panning for gold, worked Treasure creek. These days the smoke was coming now from a beautiful rebuilt stone fireplace in this old cabin.

The remote and isolated old cabin, sending up its plume of smoke, was now the summer retreat of a retired couple, Fred and Mary Christiansen. Fred had retired from the Royal Canadian Air force, where he had served as an airplane mechanic. Mary had been an elementary school teacher. In the early years of their retirement they had served overseas as Christian mission workers in East Africa. There Fred had put to good use his skill and know-how as an airplane mechanic. Now, in this chapter in their lives, they were enjoying their summers at this historic cabin.

The old cabin, with the surrounding acres of an ancient land claim, had been passed down through generations to Fred and Mary. Fred figured that the cabin has been built around 1855 by his great grandfather, a rugged man named Jack Patterson. Jack Patterson had stayed on after the gold rush days and was able to convert his claim into a settlement grant. Fred discovered that the property was an 1860 Crown land grant to Jack Patterson. The Crown Land Registry records confirmed that title to the property was passed down the line, first about 1905 to Fred's grandfather and then to Fred's father in 1960. Finally, in 2010 Fred Christiansen inherited the cabin.

Fred and Mary Christiansen prized this cabin built by those rugged nineteenth century gold prospectors. As they made the necessary repairs and improvements they were determined to preserve the original rugged character of the cabin. They wanted to preserve the work of those men who, with the tools of that day, squared the logs and fitted them together to create this rugged shelter.

One necessary step to make this remote cabin accessible was to develop a dirt trail to the cabin from the nearest settlement, the small community of Blue River. This enabled them to gradually bring in materials to repair the cabin and make improvements. They put on a new roof, and built an addition to the cabin. They added things like windows and screens.

As they made improvements, Fred and Mary stuck to their original commitment to keep the historic features of the cabin. They said, "If we're going to spend some time each year in an old gold mining era cabin let's keep it what it is, as far as possible."

There was, of course, no power line. They decided there would be no generator. They agreed that there would be no phone of any sort. They wanted to simply enjoy the cabin in its unspoiled surroundings. They chose to preserve the atmosphere of the mountains with no intrusion of modern media. Mary said, "Why come out here in the grandeur and magnificence of the Canadian Rockies and sit around watching TV?"

The difficulty of access helped maintain the atmosphere of this old gold miner's cabin. The journey to the cabin began with a train from their home in Vancouver. Certain runs of this train made a stop at Blue River. This settlement was their source of supplies and point of contact with the world beyond. They employed folks there to care for their horses and pack horses year round. Using their horses boarded at Blue River, Fred and Mary rode the ten miles tail to their cabin or, as Fred liked to say, back into history.

As Fred and Mary made improvements, they were careful to keep the basic nature of the old 1860 cabin. They developed a channel to bring water to the cabin. A small wood burning stove provided hot water for bathing. Unlike the gold mining days, the cabin now had glass windows with screens. Having no electricity or phone line helped them preserve the distinctive atmosphere of the cabin.

The only media gadget was a battery powered devise to play recorded music. They brought in a supply of batteries and a solar battery charger. For Fred and Mary, it was a fresh experience to hear, there in this rugged mountain setting, God's promise in Handel's Messiah, "Every valley shall be exalted!"

When visitors kidded them about using the old gold pans hanging on a wall, Mary had a ready answer. "When the prospectors left with their little bags of gold nuggets, they didn't take all the treasures from Treasure Creek. We have some gold pans but we're not here to pan for gold in Treasure Creek. Mary would laugh and tell them that each summer their living and loving Creator kept surprising them with treasures greater than gold.

About ten miles below the cabin, where Treasure Creek flowed into the North Thompson River, Canada's great transcontinental trains passed several times a week. This proved helpful for the Christiansens. To get some of the materials for their improvements they arranged for the train to drop off the materials, there below the cabin. The train made these drops at a point identified by the railway as kilometer 190, or simply K190. The pickup was not far from the old viewing platform, where the train used to stop for passengers to view the great Hell's Gate Cataract. The materials dropped by the train were then moved, in loads small enough to be hauled by their pack horses, up to the cabin.

The Christiansens liked to share the history of the cabin. They told the story of the men who set the old hand hewn timbers of the cabin in place. Those men were part of the North Thompson gold rush, of 1858. They were a rugged band of men and, despite their appearance, some departed rich, loaded with gold nuggets.

Fred liked to explain the mining process to their visitors. "The basic tool was the gold pan, like the pans hanging in the cabin. The pans were supplemented by the rockers and various forms of sluice boxes. The basic principle of separating the gold from the dirt was the fact that the gold was heavier than anything else."

One special joy of Fred and Mary at the cabin was to sit around an open camp fire and enjoy the night sounds peculiar to their rugged mountain setting, sounds like a hoot owl. They came to recognize also another sort of sound which was a feature of their location, the distant wail of great trains .

CHAPTER 29

Mt Carvel, British Columbia

"We regard God as an airman regards his parachute.
It's there for emergencies but he hopes
he'll never have to use it."
– C S Lewis

Due to Roger's delayed return from the painting
trip with Bill Webber, when he took off from the Jasper Airport early
the next morning, he was running a day late. He was excited about
the challenge ahead of him, a flight over the Canadian Rockies in this
single engine plane.

Roger had to laugh at the prominent Jasper airport sign that boasted
of the airport's elevation of 3,350 feet. In Nairobi, he regularly took
off from Wilson airport at 5,536 feet. However, the Jasper sign did
remind Roger that his starting elevation of well over three thousand
feet was a more critical matter here in the Canadian Rockies. Today's
flight was going to take him among many peaks of 5,000 feet. This
was an important consideration for a flight in single engine plane.

The basic flight plan was to follow in large measure the silver
tracks of the Canadian transcontinental train. That silver ribbon would
lead him through the lowest gaps in the awesome continental divide.
This route would help Roger cross the Rockies at the lowest possible
altitude.

Roger's consultants in Jasper strongly reminded him that for pilots,
mountains are great things to see and avoid. They advised him to keep
a distance from peaks to avoid dangerous down drafts. After conferring

with the officials in Jasper, Roger planned to make his crossing of the Rockies at about 8,500 feet. Jasper predicted great weather.

As he took off, Roger was remembering Wilbur's words, that this would be the flight of a life time. He would be making one of the most exciting flights in the world.

Roger's charts indicated where he would be crossing the Continental Divide today. The maps always indicate this with the dotted line. Yes, but where exactly is that Continental Divide? Roger laughed, I don't see any dotted line down there,

After crossing into British Columbia, Roger's view to the north gave him the wonderful sight of the spectacular 13,000 foot peak of Mt Robinson. He continued following the shining train tracks along the North Thompson River.

Suddenly Roger saw something moving down there on those silver tracks. It was amazing. He could see that the great transcontinental train, now equipped with three locomotives for the pull over the Rockies. The third engine had been added at Edmonton. Time for a snack. He found that the grand spectacle was sweetened by chewing some of Emily's peanut butter cookies. Thanks Emily. Wish you were here.

Roger was enjoying clear weather. He was realizing the extent to which his experience flying near the 17,000 feet snowcapped Mt Kenya in Africa prepared him for this single engine flight over the Canadian Rockies. In Africa, he had learned that in mountain country you maintain a higher altitude than you think necessary.

As he looked ahead to where the train made its way along the North Thompson River, Roger could see in the distance an area where the river was churning with white water. He checked his map. He was approaching the famous Hell's Gate cataract.

Roger turned his attention to altitude. I am at a considerably high altitude for this single engine plane. But even at this altitude, 8,000 feet, I am not very far from the high country over which I am flying. If I had an emergency over these peaks of five thousand feet, the distance from the plane to earth would vanish quickly.

The men at Jasper had impressed him with their counsel that in this high country there is less time to make a parachute jump. Here I am at about 8,000 feet but the area below me is close to 5,000 feet. Like they said, if I had an emergency I would have to leave the plane very quickly. .

ii

Roger was taking in the spectacular and rugged country below him while eating some more of Emily's cookies when suddenly the plane began to shake and vibrate. Then came a sound that Roger instantly recognized. "I know that sound, low oil. This engine is dying."

Suddenly there was the sickening sound of the engine starting to sputter off and on. I've got troubles. Serious trouble.

Roger remembered how in his emergency training in Kenya they kept saying, "Over high country your response time is short." His plane was losing altitude fast. As he scanned the mountains below him Roger saw that there would be no emergency landing.

The engine continued to make terrible sounds. Roger was talking to himself, "This engine's coughing itself to death."

Roger was doing some fast thinking. I was at about 8,000 feet. I'm losing speed and losing altitude fast. Most of those mountain ridges are close to five or six thousand. This plane is dropping fast. Not much time.

Roger quickly slipped his arms back again into the straps of the parachute pack and snapped the locks. Thinking of his cargo, he flipped the switch to dump unused fuel. He set the plane in a long glide.

Roger knew that his flight suit was well loaded with emergency items. Fast action was needed. Although he had been flying at an altitude of well over 8,000 feet, here in the mountains the ground, at many points, was not much more than three thousand feet below him. The window of time to parachute was shrinking fast.

As he prepared to step out of the plane he was glad that it was a high wing plane, and equipped with doors that would swing back for aerial photo work. He checked the straps of the parachute, popped open the door and stepped out.

When he was fully clear of the plane Roger pulled the rip cord. At first nothing seems to be working. Then it hit. There was that sudden jolt as his whole body was yanked upward. The rate of his falling had changed to the relatively slow movement that seemed like floating down over what was looking more and more like very rugged country.

He watched as the plane continue its silent glide toward the rugged area of the mountains in the distance. Then it vanished, out of sight. He was surprised. There was no sign of explosion or flames.

As he continued dropping rapidly toward the ground he was alarmed at the scene rushing to meet him. Nothing but sheet rock. Rocky and very rugged. My parachuting training and experience in Africa wasn't going to be of much help here.

"Lord, you can move mountains. This would be a good time to move one. How about a relatively soft spot when I hit the ground! Here I come."

iii

All that Roger saw rushing up to meet him was hard rock. This must be the worst place in the world to parachute. It's all just rock

"I need some help." Rocky cliffs were racing toward him.

Suddenly, Roger hit the ground, hard. He was down. Roger reached out and felt around him. He was stunned with the sudden realization that, he seemed to have landed, miraculously in a pocket of soft ground covered with tall grass.

Roger found he had no injuries except for some scrapes and bruises. He looked around. He saw his chute lines were caught on a tough old wind shaped pine. It appeared that as the wind swept him across the rocky cliff his chute caught on the strong branches of this rugged wind shaped mountain pine. When his parachute cords snagged on the pine the wind dropped him on this small shelf-like pocket on the face of the mountain.

Roger looked around, amazed. "It looks like someone reached out and caught me."

What a miracle. Someone simply reached out something like a first baseman's glove and caught me. It may be a children's song but it's literally true. He's got the whole world in His hands. He certainly reached out and caught me.

As Roger was lying there, still held in place by the parachute ropes, he looked out over the edge or the pocket like shelf where he had landed. It was like looking out from a box seat at a concert hall. Roger was amazed. Because my chute caught hold on this twisted rugged mountain pine I was kept from going on to land a couple miles below, on that mountain of rocky moraine down there.

Roger was awed as he kept looking down at the vast expanse of the rugged rock covered mountain. "If that pine had not reached out and snagged my parachute!" He just sat there for a few moments. "Thank you, Jesus!"

Then he laughed. Hank, would be saying "Why would God be so interested in reaching out and catching a guy like you?"

As he rubbed his bruises, Roger started talking to himself, "It was a hard hit, but I'm in one piece." He felt the ground under him. I must have hit the only soft spot on this whole mountain. He saw how his chute had swept along the rocky face of the mountain and his parachute cords had caught on the pine and prevented him from being swept across the jagged and rocky surface of the mountain.

After some effort Roger succeeded in disentangling the chute from the tree. He saw that he had landed on a very small earth filled mountainside pocket about the size of a tennis court. As he looked out over the sheer rocky cliffs above and below him he was unable to see any other spot like it. Roger marveled. Yes, it really does look like a first baseman reached out and caught me. He was amazed. No one's going to tell me that this was luck. My landing here was nothing less than a miracle.

Roger took stock of his condition. He was bruised but nothing serious. His left arm and leg were a bite banged up but working. Just a few scrapes and bruises.

The first priority was to get himself untangled from the chute. He unsnapped the chute straps. Finally he was on his feet.

The chute was whipping around in the wind. It was quit an effort to control it. He finally gathered the chute and secured it in order to prevent it from being caught in the wind. Roger found the knife in the pocket of his jump suit and got to work cutting the remaining cords of the parachute from the tree.

Roger was thinking how different his situation was from those old World War II movies. When those British agents parachuted into occupied France from low flying planes with temporarily silenced motors, upon landing, they hurried to bury their parachutes so the Nazis would not find them.

He laughed. No German troops are looking for me. I'd be glad if someone, anyone, were looking for me. If I am here very long, I'm going to need this parachute. I may need it for shelter. I might need it to attract any search planes.

Roger looked over the edge of his small mountain shelf. Below him he saw nothing but rugged rocky country. What would have happened if the chute had dropped him on that piles of rocky moraine. The terrain below him appeared impossible for travel. He began to realize the seriousness of his predicament.

Roger remembered his last view of the train tracks near the Hell's Gate cataract. He estimated he must be about ten or fifteen miles from those tracks but separated by impassable terrain. If no search and rescue party found him, attempting to reach those tracks might be his only hope of getting out of here.

He was thinking of the crashed plane. He had seen no flames or smoke, no indication from the area where the plane might have crashed. Could that ELT, that emergency landing transmitter, have survived the crash and be sending out a signal to help any rescue planes find me? Not likely. I have landed quite a few miles from where the plane crashed. If the ELT transmitter is working I need some way to attract any search planes to my location. I need to stretch out the parachute to help any planes spot me. A good fire giving off smoke might be helpful. I need to find stuff for a fire.

Roger was trying to calculate how far he might be from where the plane came down. That crash glide on which I set the plane might have brought her down five miles to the North of where I am. If some people do locate the wreck where would they look for a survivor? Would they ever spot me here, miles away. I need to make some smoke. In a pocket of his jump suit he found a lighter and soon had a fire going.

Roger got to thinking of that special delivery item in the plane. If the contents of that pack are really valuable whoever shipped it might launch a search to find the plane and recover their shipment.

Roger found himself thinking I may be here a while. I need to make some sort of shelter from part of the parachute. I need to stretch it out to help anyone looking for me to find me.

He found that an uprooted mountain pine had created a small hollow in the hillside. He attempted to fashion it into some sort of shelter. He got a fire going in front of this slight hollow. At this elevation, I don't suppose I need to think about bears or other creatures. He made a discovery in one of his pockets. Two energy bars. My first meal.

Time for prayer. Many thanks, Lord Jesus, for more than the energy bars. Many thanks for my good landing here. With the obstacles to getting off this mountain, what I really need is someone to find me.

A bit of irony struck Roger. I wanted to get away, to drop of sight. I've certainly succeeded in doing that. Right now, no one, no one in the world has the faintest idea where I am. I need to get making smoke.

CHAPTER 30

The Canadian Rockies, British Columbia

"Expect great things from God. Attempt great things for God."
– William Carey, 1891

Fred and Mary Christiansen really loved having breakfast out under the tall pines surrounding their historic prospector's cabin. They especially enjoyed the soothing sound of rushing water from Treasure Creek and an occasional bird call. This morning Mary was trying to coax a resident blue jay to come in for a snack. Suddenly Fred jumped out of his chair with such alarm that his chair toppled over. "Hear that Mary?"

"The airplane? Yes, Fed. It sounds sick."

Fred said "It's more than sick. That single engine plane is dying. I know the sound. That's definitely the sound of a single engine plane's dying." Fred rushed jumped on a table to see if he could see the plane.

"I see it. It's going down. There it goes. Out of sight. It's down. It looked like it was on a crash glide. I believe that the pilot may have had time to set the plane on a crash glide before parachuting. These mountains are an impossible place to parachute. In high country like this, when a pilot hits the silk, depending on his altitude, his survival is questionable."

"How good a glimpse did you get of the plane, Fred?"

"It looked like a four passenger single engine plane. I think it was very much like those planes I worked on in East Africa. It looked like the pilot had set his plane on a crash glide in preparation to parachute. As I saw the plane going down. I was making a mental image of its crash path.

"I'll get my topo, Mary. While it's fresh in my mind, I think I can draw on my map the bearing and path of the plane as it went down. I have a pretty good idea of where it probably crashed. From the few moments I saw of the plane's going down, I believe I can calculate the possible area of the crash."

Fred ran into the house to get his topographical map. He lined up the map on the table with actual compass bearings. He quickly drew a pencil line indicating his estimate of the total crash glide of the plane. He drew a circle to indicate the approximate spot where the plane probably crashed.

Fred then extended the line of the crash glide in the opposite direction from the possible crash site to show the path of the plane as it developed engine trouble. Knowing the area fairly well, Fed estimated the probable altitude of the plane over the mountains when the trouble began. He drew a second slightly larger circle. "

"What is the second circle, Fred?"

"This second and larger circle marks the last possible point, as I figure, where, at his altitude, this pilot still had enough altitude above this mountain terrain to have parachuted from the plane successfully. His possible survival depends on his altitude when the trouble began. This is the most important circle. This circle indicates the area in which any survivor, if he got out in time, would have had to parachute to survive."

Mary said, "You heard the plane going down, Fred. Do you think the pilot had enough altitude and time to parachute?"

"In Kenya, I worked on a lot of planes like the one I saw going down. I'm pretty sure that I know what happened out there. This pilot was hit with a dying engine. Low oil pressure."

May said, "Do you think he made it out of the plane?"

Fred said, "For a pilot, flying a single engine plane, at that altitude over this mountain county, survival was possible only if he was very experienced and recognized his predicament immediately. He had to act fast, very fast.

"In these rugged mountains, the key to his survival in a single engine plane like this, was his altitude when trouble struck. These mountains give the pilot very limited time to hit the silk.

"At his likely altitude, this pilot had to realize his problem instantly. He to take quick action to jump. He had to jump immediately. My seeing the plane in a probable crash glide suggests to me that he did jump. If he was able to parachute successfully, he probably hit the silk in the area that I have marked with the circle."

Mary said, "So, what are you thinking, Fred?"

"I believe that the pilot was able to parachute."

Mary said, "Are you're saying that there is good reason to look for a possible survivor?"

Fred said, "Yes. that's what I'm thinking."

"Fred, do you thinkvhe survived?"

Fred said, "Despite his low altitude over this rugged terrain, if he acted as fast as possible, he got out. I believe that we should look for a survivor. In these mountains, more than likely an injured survivor. We've travelled out there. We know the area. Hitting the silk over this rocky terrain will most likely mean serious injuries on landing. If we are going to find him that means we need to move quickly."

"Fred, don't you feel we should be notifying someone? You know, call in the troops?"

"In other circumstances Mary, yes. But this situation calls for immediate action. If there is a survivor, and if he is to be helped, we have to go immediately.

"We are here on the mountain. We know the area. We have to go now. Remember we have no phones here. We are ten miles by horse-back from Blue River. We have no way of knowing when a search by others might get under way. They would probably not call in search parties until they established that a plane went down. In this country such a wreck could be almost impossible to spot from the air. I know where to look for any possible survivor. If a survivor exists and he is to survive, we have to head out now."

Mary said, "In other words, without knowing if there is a survivor, to rescue any survivor we need to get moving now. OK. Let's get packing, Fred."

"I'll get the horses ready.

Mary said, "From previous trips in this area it looks like we will need to prepare for being out for four nights."

Fred agreed. "Yes Mary. If we find someone, depending on his condition, it may be a slow trip back. Let's get moving! By the way, Mary, you were wondering why we were out here in our cabin this year. Looks like we got our answer."

Fred got to work getting their horses ready. He prepared a third horse for a possible survivor. He felt that a trip like this called also for taking two pack horses, one for their camping gear and one for an injured person who might be unable to ride.

Mary went to work using their well tested trip list. Her trip list for the horses included hay, grain and treats. Her check list included feed and water buckets along with hay bags. She added basic emergency medical supplies for any serious injury. Their trip list for a three to five day trip had been used and tested many times.

By noon, Fred had the horses ready. Mary loaded their provisions, mountain camping gear, climbing ropes and other equipment on the pack horses. She hung special water bottles on their saddle pommels. The saddle bags were kept as light as possible. Mary packed snacks for situations in which they could not stop for a meal. She told Fred, "I'm thinking in terms of being out on the mountain four to five days."

Mary saw Fred getting ready the third horse. "You're a man of great expectations, Fred. The third horse says you really expect to find that bird that fell from his nest."

"When you pray, Mary, pray with great expectations. Let's go, "

Mary asked, "Fred, do you think some people will ask us why we didn't ride into Blue River to report the plane coming down?"

"Mary, this situation calls for immediate action. By actually seeing the plane as it went down, I have a pretty good idea of where the plane crashed. This has enabled me to calculate a where the pilot had to have hit the silk and possible landing area of a parachute. "Right now, as far as we know, no one else even knows that this plane went down. But we are not looking for a plane. There is no urgency to finding a wrecked plan. We are searching for a possible survivor who, in this rugged country, is more than likely to be seriously injured."

"Fred, I've got a description for this sort of trip. Finding a man on a mountain, without knowing if he exists, is like finding a diamond on a mountain side."

"It's not impossible, Mary. I worked on similar situations of single engine planes going down in Kenya. I put myself in the place of the pilot of this plane. An experienced pilot would know immediately that he had to get out of that plane, fast. At a probable altitude of, perhaps, only a three to four thousand feet above those mountains, he had to act fast. Very fast. He had to have set that plane in a crash glide and exited fast. We will start by heading toward my estimated location of the area where the pilot had to step out of that plane."

ii

The first day went very slowly. Fred and Mary spent a full day of working their way through very difficult mountain terrain, in order to approach the area where any parachuting survivor might have come down.

The rocky terrain with fallen trees was very difficult for the horses. By late afternoon of their first day, according to Fred's estimate, they had travelled about half the distance to the area of a possible landing by someone parachuting from the plane. They kept working their way through very difficult terrain. Finally, with both their horses and themselves tired and weary, they stopped to make camp for the night. Along with setting up camp they had to feed and care for their three horses and the two pack horses.

Mary laughed, "I feel like a mother robin looking for a bird that has fallen from his nest. We are attempting to find this bird in what must be some of the most rugged country in North America. We need some help, Fred. I mean real help. Help from up there."

While Mary prepared something to eat, Fred used the remaining daylight to study his topo and check out the terrain for the next day.

"Like you said, Mary, we need help and the possible survivor needs help. Let's look for that help we need. As they sat around their camp fire the two of them prayed, "Lord Jesus, if there is someone out there on this mountain, help us find this fallen bird."

iii

On Roger's second day on the mountain, he looked down over the sheer drop of the rugged rock hundreds of feet below him. He was stunned with the impossibilities of his situation. He threw anything that might burn on his fire.

Roger was wondering why stretch out the parachute or try to make smoke? I have no reason to believe anyone is looking for me? Although I'm a full day behind my flight plan, those men looking for my arrival in Vancouver won't be concerned about me. They will probably be just grumbling because the delivery did not arrive as scheduled.

Roger studied the cliff extending high above him. He saw a ledge more than a hundred feet above him. There is no way that I could climb up there. I should have kept Hank's two way ham radio in my flight clothes. It's not doing me any good in the wreck.

iv

In the morning of their second day, while the mist was still rising in the stand of trees where they had camped, Fred and Mary broke camp. They were now pushing well beyond established trails. With five horses, it was very slow going. Fred laughed, "Is this what they call bush whacking?"

They stopped to take a break and rest in a more open area along the top ridge of a cliff. Fred told Mary, "I figure that we have now entered the area of that circle I drew on the map as our target area for the parachute."

As they continued on, riding along the top of this cliff from which they could look off in the distance. Suddenly Mary called out. "Fred, hold up."

"What's the trouble, Mary?"

"Fred, it may be my imagination, but I think I smell smoke."

Fred called back, "Smoke? Up here, smoke can mean only one thing."

Fred and Mary immediately dismounted and secured the horses. Mary said, "When you want something badly sometimes your mind plays tricks on you."

Fred walked carefully along the drop off of the cliff. "It's not your imagination, Mary, I smell a trace of smoke too. It seems to be coming from below us. I'm going to get our big rope and lower myself down this cliff a bit."

"OK, if you see fallen bird. Flap your wings."

Fred began to slowly rappel down the face of the cliff. He moved down the cliff slowly and very cautiously. Mary waited with the horses.

Finally, Fred came to a ledge where he could rest his feet. Holding on to the rope, he leaned forward and looked below. There, below him, he saw a small shelf area on the mountain. Now, Fred could not only smell the smoke but he could now see traces of smoke rising through the trees on the small shelf below.

Then Fed saw it! Far below him on that small shelf of land Fred saw what they were hoping to see. He saw the white fabric of a parachute flapping in the wind. He was thrilled to see that the chute was stretched out between several small wind bent pines.

Fred yelled up the cliff to Mary, "I see something! I see a chute stretched out. Someone is down there. Someone tied down a parachute."

Then he saw the man! Fred was overwhelmed. His eyes filled with tears. On the small ledge below him, he saw the figure of a man, moving about.

Fred looked back up to Mary and gestured enthusiastically. With his hand he pointed below. Fred yelled up to Mary, "I see the bird that fell out of his nest. I see him. He's moving. He's moving."

Mary broke into tears.

Fred started calling, "Hello down there. Hello! Fallen Bird! Fallen Bird."

There was no answer. In the wind he could not be heard. Then he started a shower of small stone down the cliff. Fred pulled out the whistle that both he and Mary always wore in wilderness travel. Fred blew on it. Again he called.

Suddenly a figure below stepped out from the cliff and looked up. He started waving his arms. Fred heard the voice of the man calling, "Hello, up there. I'm here. I hear you!"

Fred lowered the end of his rope to the man below. When the rope reached the man, Fred called again, "Tie the rope around you well. Make a cradle to hold you!"

After the man had secured the rope arouind himself, Roger called, "Wait till I return to the top. We will help you up the cliff."

Fred worked his way back up to where Mary was waiting. After giving her a quick hug, Fred fastened their big rope to one of their horses. Then he yanked on the rope and yelled, "Ready!"

"Mary, keep your eye on the man below. Guide me as I work with the horse to help him work his way up the cliff to us."

Carefully and very slowly, with Mary's coaching, Fred led the horse slowly back from the cliff. The man below, helped by the horse pulled rope, carefully worked his way up over the jagged rocks of the cliff. Finally he reached the ledge where Mary was standing.

Mary greeted the rescued man with a big hug. She laughed, "Fallen bird you are back in your nest." She hugged him again and for a few moments they clung to each other.

Fred tied the horse and made his way back to the cliff edge. Fred embraced their rescued man, with the famous words, "Dr. Livingston, I presume."

Roger laughed and replied, "Yes, Roger Renoir Livingston."

Mary and Fred introduced themselves. Then Mary gave Roger another big hug. "Roger Renoir! We had no idea for whom we were looking. What a joy it is to find you!"

Roger reached out and held on to them. "Fred and Mary. Thank you. Thank you for coming to find me. I can't imagine where you came from. If you didn't have the horses I would think you came by helicopter. How did you know I was here? How did you get here? How did you find me? This is amazing!"

Fred said, "We are amazed as much as you. From our cabin, we saw your plane going down. We had no idea if there was a survivor of that plane. We just set out, hoping the pilot had been able to hit the silk."

"You simply saw the plane going down. You never saw my parachute? You mean that you just came out on this mountain looking for a possible survivor? Amazing. Someone above had to be involved in this one."

Fred said, "Definitely. We feel the same way, Roger."

Roger said, "Without you, I don't know how I would have gotten off this mountain. I don't know how I would have survived? Who would even know the plane was down, or where? Who would have known there was a survivor for whom to search? But the two of you looked for me and found me. Amazing."

Roger paused to wipe some tears. "I never experienced anything like this. I was in a situation from which there seemed no apparent escape. Then, out of the blue, Fred, you came rappelling down that mountain side cliff. You have no idea how wonderful it is to simply be found! You have to have been lost to know what it feels like to be found. Thank you! Thank you!

"How did you come to be on this mountain? What moved you to search for a possible survivor?"

Mary said, "Roger, you've been on this mountain since yesterday morning. You need something to eat and drink. Then you can tell us your story and we can tell you ours."

Mary handed Roger a plastic water jug and opened up her food pack.

Roger sat down on a fallen tree with his sandwich and water. He kept shaking his head in amazement. "When you saw my plane going down, what made you even suspect there might be a survivor? How could you be looking for a man that you did not even know existed?"

Mary smiled, "We didn't know. Our heavenly Father helped Fred calculate where any survivor would have had to make his jump. By God's loving kindness, Fred's calculations hit the spot."

Roger shook his head in amazement. "When my parachute was dropping me on the mountain things looked pretty black. I couldn't see how anyone would even know about the crash. When I failed to show up for my scheduled arrival in Vancouver, no one there would be thinking of looking for me. No one out there would be even looking for the plane or a survivor in these mountains. Things looked very impossible."

Mary laughed, "Roger, remember the song?" She began to sing. "Nothing, nothing, absolutely nothing, nothing is impossible for God"

"How did the two of you even happen to be out here in this rugged and uninhabited area? People don't just go riding on rugged mountain terrain like this."

Fred said, "Mary and I just happen to have a summer cabin in this area. It's a relic of the 1850's gold rush."

Mary said, "Yes, each summer we ask what are we doing up here? Why are we making this remote old cabin we inherited our summer home? Well, Roger, Fred and I got our answer today. You must be the reason why. We were out on our patio having a second cup of coffee, when Fred heard that screeching noise of your plane going down."

"Fred explained, "When I first heard the sickening sound your plane giving down I knew right away what was happening. I just happen to be a retired Royal Canadian Air force mechanic. I got just a quick glimpse of the plane in what appeared to be a crash glide. When I retired, I worked on single engine planes like your plane for a mission in East Africa."

"You worked on single engine planes in East Africa? I flew medical mission team flights out of Nairobi's Wilson airport for Mission Air in Kenya."

Fred laughed, "I may have been one of your neighbors at Wilson. When I heard that terrible sound of your plane going down, I knew immediately what was happening. As your plane was on its crash glide going down, I managed to get a quick glimpse of the plane's final moments. I figured the pilot might have set the plane on a crash glide.

"On the basis of what I saw, I was able to estimate both where the plane would crash and where the pilot have had to parachute. I got out my map and marked where the plane might crash hit, Then I figured where the pilot would have had to step out of the plane to survive. And here we are."

Roger was amazed. "Fred, your calculations were incredible."

Mary said, "It's all very impressive for us too. It all sounds pretty much like the story of Abraham. Abraham, went out, not knowing where he was going. Without even knowing if there was someone to look for, we set out. And, we did some praying. We just told God we're here. You will have to show us who we're looking for."

Roger said, "I wasn't very hopeful about anyone seeing my smoke signals Then, I saw some loose stones rattling down the cliff. I heard a whistle and then a voice. I looked up and there you were. I saw you, Fred!

"It was help from above in more ways than one. Who says that God doesn't answer prayer?"

Fred said, "We will camp here tonight and set out for the cabin in the morning. How do you feel about heading back in the morning, Roger? What sort of shape are you in?"

"I'm OK. Sore, but nothing serious."

Fred said, "You were very fortunate. Coming down on this mountain with a parachute could have been fatal. We brought an extra horse, with us. Do you think you are in shape to ride out with us?"

"You brought an extra horse? Wow! Talk about great expectations! "

"Well, like I told Mary, there's no point in riding out to find someone, unless you expect to find someone. I told Mary, If we expect to find someone, we need to take along an extra horse. So we brought along the horse. Are you up to a ride?

"I think I can handle riding out. I've got a lot of motivation to get out of here."

Mary said, "There's no phone at our cabin. When we get back to the cabin, we will take you to a place where you can reach the outside world. I imagine that you must be anxious to let people know you're alive and where you are."

"Well not exactly. It may sound strange, but as a matter of fact, I'm not in a hurry for everyone to know what happened or where I am."

CHAPTER 31

The Canadian Rockies, British Columbia

"You meant evil toward me, but God meant it for good."
– Joseph

As Roger and his new friends sat around their campfire, sipping hot chocolate, he continued regarding his rescuers with amazement. He said, "I'm still flabbergasted over how you found and rescued me."

Roger said, "The two of you were having breakfast out on your patio. You heard the sound of a single engine plane dying. And, Fred, for a few seconds you actually got a glimpse of my plane going down. You whipped out your topo map. You marked the crash glide and possible point of the crash. You estimated the altitude of the plane and extended a line backward to calculate where the pilot would have had to parachute. You figured where such a parachuter might have landed.

"Then you decided that anyone hitting the silk in these mountains would most likely need immediate help. So? So the two of you just took off to find a possible survivor. And you found me. Amazing."

As Roger sat there enjoying the company of his new friends, he said it again, "Amazing."

Fred laughed, "Yes, and with the surprising outcome of finding you, Roger, we ourselves are quite amazed. Want to see something even more amazing?" Fed stood and beckoned to Roger to go with him.

They walked a short distance from their fire and stood there in silence looking up, taking in the great magnitude of stars. Fred said, "This is another bonus of getting away from urban light pollution and living up here on the mountain." They stood there silently taking in the stars.

As they stood there Fred said, "I'm glad we went looking,Roger."

"Thank you, Fred. The three of us will always have a special relationship."

Fred said, "Earlier, you said that you were not in a hurry for everyone to know about the crash, that you survived or where you are. Is there something we should know?"

Roger nodded. "Yes, it's quite a story. I think you need to hear it."

Mary filled their cups again. "Fire away, Roger. A campfire always needs more wood and a good story."

Roger said, "When I was asked to fly this plane from Toronto to Vancouver, I had an urgent reason for taking the job. I needed to get away from Toronto as fast as possible. I was trying to get away from a man who had ordered me shot once and would finish the job if he could."

Mary said, "Wow, Roger, Sounds like you really do have a story."

Roger took them back to the events at Bobcat Lake, where he came upon the gang with the stolen radioactive material and how the leader had ordered him shot. "The shot fired to kill me ploughed into the mud against my ear. They thought they had killed me but the death shot had missed me."

Fred asked, "Why did you agree to fly the single engine plane to Vancouver?"

"I grabbed this opportunity to get out of Toronto in a hurry because this gang leader had learned both that I was alive and my identity. Flying this plane west was an opportunity to make a fast disappearance?"

After remaining silent for a few moments Fred said, "So you want to conceal the story of this crash because, as of now, no one knows where you are."

"Exactly. You folks have done more than rescue me from the plane crash. You have helped me vanish. In fact, during my stop for painting at Jasper, I discovered that the man pursuing me had men monitoring my trip. Now, since I fell out of the sky, your rescue has provided the gift of real isolation."

Fred was getting the picture. "So this terrible experience of the crash is serving a good purpose for you. As far as your pursuer goes, with this crash, you have just vanished from the earth. Through the crash you have escaped their surveillance."

"Exactly."

Mary said, "So, there's a big plus for you in this crash. If your plane's emergency landing transmitter didn't function, you've just vanished. And you want to keep it that way."

Fred laughed, "Roger, you're pulling an Amelia Earhart act. Back in 1937, when she set out to fly her Lockheed Electra across the Pacific, she just vanished. They are still trying to solve her disappearance. Now, your deadly enemy hasn't the foggiest idea where you are, whether you're dead or alive."

Mary said, "We will be happy to help you keep it that way for you Roger."

Fred asked, "Is there anything of special value that might be in the plane."

"I was hauling some special baggage. I was asked to deliver a special pack of some valuable electronic stuff to someone at the Vancouver airport."

Fred asked, "Anything else of value in that plane? Anything personal to retrieve?"

"My two way hand held ham transmitter might have survived the crash. With it I could reach my friends in Toronto without using the phone. There is also something of special value to me. My painting sketch book. At Jasper I painted several watercolors near Lake Malign. If those painting survived I would like to retrieve them."

Fred was curious. "How valuable was that pack you were to deliver in Vancouver?"

"I have no idea. They were paying me very generously to transport it."

Fred said, "Roger I have a proposition to put to you."

"Let's hear it Fred."

"As you can see, we are in very rugged country. It would be very difficult for anyone to return here. Would you be interested in going a bit farther to see if we can find the wreck? We could see if there is anything we can recover."

"Your calculations to find me worked well. If they prove as good for finding the wrecked plane it might be worth the effort."

Fred said, "The big question will be whether the plane went up in fire."

Roger said, "I did make an effort to dump the fuel to allow for a longer glide. So, it's possible the plane did not go up in flame. If that special pack survived could we haul it out?"

Fred said, "It depends on weight. Our pack horse might be able to handle it."

ii

The next morning, after a good breakfast, served up by Mary, they were on their way to check out Fred's estimate of where the plane might be found. After several hours they reached the area Fred had marked on his topo.

Fred took out his binoculars and scanned the area. Suddenly he called out, ;"I see the wreck. The plane did not go up in flames. One of the plane's wings is hanging in a tree. The engine has been torn off. The fuselage of the plane is in one piece. The challenge will be to get to it.

"It has been a very rough day. I suggest we rest the horses and camp right here. After a good night's rest, tomorrow we can tackle the job of getting to the plane and retrieving what we can."

The next morning, when they finally reached the wreck, Roger and Fred studied the wrecked plane. Any ELT devise had been removed. Fred said, "That means that, as of now, no one knows what happened to this plane or you."

Fred crawled into the body of the plane to examine the contents.. He began handing out Roger's painting equipment and paintings. Roger was especially glad to recover the hand held two way ham radio.

Fred was finally able to reach the large pack of technical equipment. He cut free the straps holding down the pack and dragged the pack out of the plane. After removing the locks, Fred opened the pack and began examining the contents.

Suddenly he stopped and stared in amazement. "Roger, Mary, come over here! You need to see this." Fred pointed to a series of dials in the pack. "Roger, have you any idea what you were hauling?"

"Not really, Fred. What in the world is it, Fred?"

"Roger, as I told you, I'm retired from the Canadian Royal Air force. I had quite a bit of training in handling explosives. I know what we have here. Look in here."

Roger looked in at the contents of the black pack. He saw a number of dials.

Fred said, "Roger, you were hauling a very powerful explosive device, a bomb! A very powerful bomb, a real block buster."

"Impossible, Fred!"

Fred continued to use his training in explosives to examine the explosive device. After some time he called Mary and Roger back. "I have disarmed this devise. This bomb is now no longer a danger.

"Roger, let me show you the timing mechanism. This bomb was set to explode on the day of your scheduled arrival in Vancouver."

Roger looked in amazement. "That was the day my engine failed.""

Fred said, "Roger, this bomb was set to explode as you were flying into Vancouver. You were recruited to be someone's kamikaze pilot. You were to fly this plane, like a World War II Japanese Kamikaze pilots, into Vancouver."

Roger stared at Fred, "If the bomb was set explode on that specific day, how is it that the bomb did not go off as scheduled, while I was still in the mountains?

"How is it I am still alive and talking to you about this bomb, Fred? How is it that this bomb did not explode blow me to pieces that day?

Fred said, "Good questions, Roger. And here's the answer. Let me show you a special feature of this bomb." Fred pointed to a particular devise in the pack. "This is your answer. This sophisticated bomb had a unique feature. The bomb was controlled by an altimeter."

Roger stared at Fred in amazement. "Altimeters go in planes, not bombs."

Fred said, "An altimeter was installed to control at what altitude the bomb would go off. This bomb was scheduled to go off on that scheduled day and time, but only as your plane dropped below a certain level. The bomb would explode only as you came in over Vancouver for a landing and dropped to a certain altitude. The bomb would detonate on the given day, but only when the plane descended to a preset altitude."

Roger was moved by his closeness to death. "At what altitude, Fred?"

Fred said, "The altimeter linked detonator was set to detonate on the set date as you brought the plane in over Vancouver. This bomb was to explode when you brought the plane in over Vancouver at one thousand feet."

Roger was staggered by what he was hearing.

Fed continued. "Do you see what kept it from exploding that day? At what altitude were you flying that day? From the start, when you took off in Jasper at what altitude did you take off?"

"I took off at just a few hundred feet above three thousand.. It is well known that the Jasper airport is located at an altitudes of a bit over three thousand. They have signs all over the place."

Fred continued, "You were a day behind schedule because that dead battery in the truck made you a day late in your schedule. As a result you were still in the mountains on the day scheduled for the bomb to explode. When you took off that day you were above three thousand feet."

Roger said, "But what prevented me from deciding to fly on and make up the lost time and arrive in Vancouver on the scheduled day?"

Fed said, "Roger, think a moment. When the plane started having engine trouble at what altitude were you?"

"About eight thousand feet, flying over elevations of around five thousand."

Fred explained, "Because of your one day delay you were still at five thousand feet the day set for the explosion. What is your guess of our altitude now at the crash site?"

"I supposed somewhere between five and six thousand feet."

Fred said, "My topo map indicates that our elevation where we are standing is about six thousand feet. That is why I was able to disarm his bomb."

Roger stared at Fred, "Fred that dead battery put me a day late and still in the mountains. That crazy engine failure caused me to crash while still above five or six thousand feet in the mountains. The failure of the engine kept me from continuing on and descending to one thousand feet for a landing in Vancouver."

Roger stopped. He had to hold on to part of the wrecked plane and just stand there. He was struggling to breathe for a few moments. Finally, he spoke. "I feel like someone had just kicked me in the stomach."

Fred said "You were protected from that diabolical plan by two events."

"Yes, Fred, that dead battery put me off schedule by one day. Then, in case I tried to make up that lost time and fly on to Vancouver on the scheduled day, an oil leak caused my engine to fail while still in this high altitude country. "

Fred said, "That engine failure came at a good time."

"Yes, it was almost as though someone wanted to make sure I didn't fly on to Vancouver that day."

Fred said, "Exactly, Roger. A little battery failure made you a day late. Your engine trouble prevented you from flying on to the lower altitude in Vancouver. Your engine trouble forced you to hit the silk while you were still at this higher altitude. It is almost as though your engine threw a temper tantrum to save you."

As he gasped what had saved him, Roger looked at Fred and Mary with amazement. I am really impressed with what it took to save me and your coming to find me."

As they prepared to head back to the cabin, Fred suggested that it would be a good idea to remove and scatter the explosive material from the bomb and take the rest of the device back with them.

Fred reasoned, "If the time comes to tell the police about this bomb they are going to want to see it."

After removing and scattering the explosive material they were able to load the devise on a pack horse. The journey back to the cabin brought them home to Fred and Mary's cabin just before dark.

As they enjoyed one of Mary's special suppers, Fred asked about the dead battery in Webber's truck. "You never did find out how your battery went dead, did you? That dead battery which delayed your flight by 24 hours. That dead battery also was a factor in keeping you from being in Vancouver at the set time for the explosion."

Mary asked, "What do you make of all this, Roger?"

"It's almost as if I had some unknown friend looking out for me."

CHAPTER 32

Old gold miners cabin, Canadian Rockies

"Be still and know that I am God…"
– Psalm 46

Roger found the aroma was very appetizing as he entered Mary's kitchen the next morning. Mary waved a pan loaded with trout. "The result of Fred's early morning fly fishing in Treasure Creek will soon be on your plate."

As they sat down to breakfast Fred said, "In most of Canada they call this an all-day breakfast. Here we call it the gold miner's breakfast."

Fred and Mary reached out and joined hands with him for their breakfast prayer. Fred led them in prayer. "Lord Jesus, we thank you for our new friend, Roger. Thank You that we could find him and bring him here."

Roger said, "Fred, when you were praying it seemed as though Jesus was right here at our table."

Fred laughed, "Of course. He was."

Roger said, "Fred, I have a question. "You told me that out here on the mountain you didn't have any sort of phone. Did you mean not any sort of phone at all? Not even a smart phone? And, when you said that you consulted with no one about a plane down before going out to look for any possible survivor, did you mean no one, absolutely no one?"

Fred smiled. "Look around. Do you see a phone?"

"OK. That means Mr. Dark Heart, who tried to use me as his kamikaze pilot, is facing some big questions. He hasn't a clue as to what happened to his plane or his bomb, Most of all he knows nothing about me? Great. Let's keep it that way for now."

Fred laughed, "Looks like there really are benefits to living here on the mountain. Roger, when that plane went down that man's plot failed. The plot to bomb Vancouver failed. The plot to kill Roger Renoir failed. He hasn't a clue to what happened to his plane. You saw the wreck in that ravine. No one will ever find that plane or the bomb. But best of all, Roger, he hasn't a clue where you are, Roger."

Roger held up his hand. "Wait a minute, Fred. This is all a new experience for me. I'm beginning to realize something. Now that this character, who has made two attempts on my life hasn't a clue whether I'm dead or alive, my situation has suddenly changed. I'm no longer just running. Now with your help, I am in a position to take some steps to change and reverse my situation. Many thanks, Fred and Mary."

After a moment of silence, Fred said, "Roger, up to now you have been running, but without the foggiest idea from whom? You have no idea of who it is from whom you are running. I gather that you have no idea of what he even looks like."

"Fred, I haven't the foggiest notion who he is or even what he looks like. I know nothing about the man. Struggling under that hood, at Bobcat Lake I never really saw the face of the man."

Fred said, "Roger, this might be the time to learn who he is, what he looks like."

That evening Roger showed his hand held two way radio rig to Fred. "My friend Hank and I are both ham radio operators. Since it seemed necessary to keep off phones, we set up a plan to communicate with our hand held two way ham radios. I thought I would try to make contact this evening."

Fred said, "Roger, let me offer one precaution. A serious attempt on your life has been foiled. This means you are in great danger. I suggest that you do not share any specific details of where you are or of what happened with even your friends. Tell them nothing specific about what happened to the plane, or where the plane is now, and especially where you are now."

"I trust my friends. What are you thinking Fred?"

"I'm thinking that while the ham radio call may bypass any phone tap it is also very essential that your friends have no specific knowledge, that they know none of the details of what happened, or where you are."

"You're thinking they might let something leak?"

"That's possible. Also you have no idea which of your contacts might be working with the bad guy. Take that man Wilbur, for example. You have no idea how he is involved or for whom he might be working."

"I think Wilbur is OK."

"I am thinking of something else. Your friends may be called in by the police and questioned. If your friends simply do not know where you are or what exactly happened, they can honestly say so. They must be able to tell anyone, that they simply do not know where you are, or what happened to you and the plane. Let your friends know you are OK, but for their own protection give them no specific information at this time."

"I get your point, Fred."

Soon Roger and Hank were in contact. Hank was greatly relieved to get the call. "The three of us have been getting together here at my place each evening at this time hoping to get a call from you. Where in the world are you, Roger? Where are you?"

Roger replied, "Let me put it this way. My flight has been interrupted. I think it best, at this time, that I say no more than that. With Mr. Dark Heart and others anxious to locate me, I think it is best to limit my report to that. Hank."

Hank said, "We have some further news for you. We followed up on your suggestion, that our phones might be monitored or tapped in some way. An electronics whiz friend of mine has confirmed that, as we suspected, all our phones are being hacked or monitored. However, something positive has come out of this. My friend has been able reverse this set up for our use. We are now able to pick up conversations by the enemy. You are no longer just running, Roger."

CHAPTER 33

Vancouver, British Columbia

"The best laid schemes o' Mice an' Men,
Gang aft agley,
An' lea'e us nought but grief an' pain,
For promis'd joy!"
– Robert Burns, To a Mouse, 1785

The day when Roger's bomb loaded plane was scheduled to make its descent for a landing and explode over Vancouver, two men, situated at a safe distance, were keeping the Vancouver airport under constant observation. They were there to witness the plane's descent and explosion over Vancouver and report to Toronto by phone on the effectiveness of the event.

When the scheduled arrival time for the plane had passed, the men continued anxiously watching, checking their watches and searching the sky. Nothing was happening. Finally the two hour time window had passed without sight of the plane. Nothing happened. There had been no sight of the plane.

They found themselves speculating over what could have happened. They were not looking forward to making their report to the professor.

ii

In Toronto the impostor and his men were filled with excitement as they waited at the warehouse for the phone call from Vancouver. The tables were loaded with food and beverages for the celebration. All they needed was the phone call that would confirm the success of the plan. .

As the men continued to wait, Hamu walked away from the men. He did not want the men to see his growing anxiety. He kept his eye on the clock. He was beginning to worry.

The men kept waiting and waiting. The two hour time window passed. Still no call from the Vancouver. Hamu kept checking his watch.

Finally, the phone rang. Hamu picked up the phone, pressed the speaker phone button so all could hear the expectant report. "Yes?"

The caller cleared his throat. He stammered, "We have to report that there has been no action. No action. Nothing to report from Vancouver."

"The plane?"

"No sight of the plane."

"Say that again."

"No sight of the plane."

Hamu was puzzled and alarmed. This could indicate all sorts of problems. He quickly took control of the situation. "Listen carefully, very carefully. Make no inquiries about the plane. Any inquiries may raise questions. Let me repeat. Make no inquiries. We do not want any sort of investigation. Get out of there."

Hamu cut off the call. He was stunned. What could have happened? Hamu ran through his mind the names of all those involved. Wilbur was working on the level with us. This man Renoir was eager to ferry the plane. The men who delivered the pack detected no problem.

Hamu was angry. That bomb was packed with power. It was cleverly designed with an altimeter to activate the detonator when the plane came below 1,000 feet. What could have gone wrong?

Hamu reviewed the entire plan. Apart from engine failure, there was no way that flight could have failed. There have been no reports of forced landings. Every detail was iron tight. There was no way this plan could have failed unless someone who knew about the plan intervened and somehow disrupted the plan. If that plane was kept from reaching Vancouver, it may have been the work of someone who knew the plan."

Hamu spoke to the men. "It appears that somehow our plane did not make it to Vancouver. There have been no reports of any plane down. As of now we do not know whether the plane crashed or whether it was diverted for engine trouble.

"The first question. Where is the plane? Whether the plane has landed somewhere or crashed we have to locate it. My first concern is to locate the plane and its contents. Our pilot was flying a single engine plane over mountains. Anything could have happened. If that plane crashed we do not want the wreck to be found with the bomb intact. We will not report the plane as down. The last thing I want is for officials to open up a search for that plane and locate it with that bomb?"

Hamu continued speaking to his men. "My second concern is the pilot. If the pilot is alive and now knows what was in that pack we have a problem. If he is alive and knows about the bomb he may tell his story?

"If this Renoir man is alive we've got to locate him. The man may now know too much? Renoir has caused us trouble from the start. It began when he stumbled on us at Bobcat Lake. Then we discovered that the man we thought Mac had eliminated was alive and painting near our warehouse. When we had him in our sights we should have eliminated him. Now, if he is alive, we have to keep him from going to the police.."

Hamu made his growing anger evident. As he spoke, he pounded his fist. "When we learned that this painter was also a pilot, and a very experienced single engine pilot, we came up with idea of eliminating him and using him as an unknowing kamikaze pilot to deliver our bomb for Vancouver. It was just too good a plan to pass up. Two birds with one stone. We made a mistake. If he is alive we need to locate him. And fast.

"I will have some men check with Wilbur. Wilbur may be able to make some discrete inquiries. He may learn of any unreported forced landings or crashes."

Daoud asked, "Are there any other steps to pursue?"

"Yes, definitely. As the French say, *Cherchez la femme*. Look for the woman. We obtained from Wilbur the names of the three closest associates of the pilot. Among these three friends with whom he flew, there are two women and one man. From what Wilbur has told us, if Renoir is alive, he will get in touch with touch with these fiends, back here in Toronto. If he is alive, they will know it. We will work on monitoring the phone taps.

"If the pilot died in a crash we have the problem of finding the plane. If the pilot survived he may have discovered the contents of our special package. If he discovered the bomb he is an even greater danger to us."

Daoud shared his concern. "If this man Renoir has survived a forced landing or crash what must be done?"

Hamu replied, "If Roger Renoir, is alive we must silence him. He cannot be allowed to go to the authorities with what he knows."

"Meanwhile, what do we do?"

"We have to find a way to implicate him in some crime. We have to make him appear to be part of some criminal gang. We have to make him fearful of arrest. We have to keep him running from the police as much as he is keeping his distance from us."

The professor instructed his men. "I want a phone tap put on all the phones of Renoir special friends. I want all of their calls monitored and recorded. Also, I want the apartment of his friends searched for my smart phone.

iii

After a break in their meeting, Hamu called the men together again, He asked for reports from each team on their preparations for Operation Toronto. One by one the leaders of the various teams reported.

The leader for team one reported. "As directed, we have arranged for five fender bender crashes to take place early that morning in several one way streets. We will be crashing stolen old cars to block nearby streets and delay police response."

Team number two spoke, "We will be waiting in the ambulance parked nearby. When the money truck has been stopped we will pull over next to it. It will look like our ambulance is there to aid the injured. We will be in position to move the cash quickly from the bank truck to our vehicle."

The next report came from team number three.. "In a particular large hotel underground parking garage, we, in uniforms of limousine drivers, will be waiting in two limousines for the arrival of the ambulance with the cash. When the ambulance arrives the cash we will move it to our limousines. The ambulance will return to traffic and be abandoned.

"Our men in the two limousines will repack the cash in two large suit cases for each vehicle. The limousines will then head into the hot zone, the area near where the money truck was stopped and Toronto train station. Since we will be headed toward the area of the robbery, we expect to be waved on by the police. We will continue to the Station's advance baggage check in. There these men with tickets for the August 18 run of the Canadian will go to the advance check window."

The leader continued. "Our men will ask for access to their previously checked baggage in order to make some changes. What they will really do is swop suitcases. Thy will move the tickets from the baggage checked before the robbery to the matching cases that hold the cash and avoid any future inspection."

Team number four made its report. "We have arranged for two large university student protest events. These demonstrations will happen on that that morning on key streets near the University campus. This will block traffic and police response."

Team number five made its report. "One of our men with contacts in the traffic control office will cause the traffic signal system in the area of the robbery to experience an area wide malfunction at the time of the robbery. Suddenly a large number of the traffic signals in the area will freeze on red. This will add to the confusion, and anger among the morning commuter traffic."

Team number six reported, "At the designated time, certain men will cause a giant traffic jam around the money truck. The vehicle immediately behind the bank truck, this painter Renoir's old Rover, will be used to crash into the back of the money truck and start blowing his horn. We will wait for the driver and guards, in exasperation, to violate their training and get out of the truck. At that moment, using pepper spray we will take them prisoners. The men dressed as ambulance crew will proceed to move the cash from the truck to the ambulance."

One of the men asked, "Why in the world are we attempting to pull off this robbery in the midst of the down town Toronto rush hour?"

Hamu explained, "We have inside information that this is a large shipment of unregistered cash. The cash being delivered is used cash that has been sorted and counted for select banks. The large amount of cash being delivered is unregistered. Since such unregistered previously circulated cash cannot be traced it is of great value to us."

Hamu stopped the reports, saying, "And with this amount of cash who can stop us?"

CHAPTER 34

Toronto

*"If you want to know what God thinks of money,
just look at the people he gave it to."*
– Dorothy Parker - History of the Rich

"What a view!" Sarah Weiss was looking out from the window of their Toronto hotel's twentieth floor room. "It's like being up on the roof of the world."

Albert said, "The morning rush hour traffic looks like a river of cars."

"The blowing of the horns seems awfully loud." Sara looked down from their window. "Come quickly Albert! Look down there. All that traffic, all of the cars, seem to have come to a halt. This major artery of Toronto traffic seems to have a blood clot."

They looked down in amazement, Albert said, "That expressway has become one big parking lot. Listen to those horns. A lot of angry commuters will be late for work." He laughed, "I'm laughing but I know it's not funny for the people in those cars."

Sarah said, "The morning rush isn't rushing."

Albert seized up the situation. "That traffic mess may be related to an electronic mix-up. As far as I can see, all the traffic lights are staying red."

"It's more than a traffic jam, Albert. See that big vehicle is in the middle of it all. It has a big number painted on the roof. It has small square windows on the side. It looks like a civilian tank. Another vehicle appears to have tail-gated that truck"

Albert got out his binoculars to study the scene. "Remember Roger Renoir's SUV. That vehicle that crashed into the big truck looks like Roger Renoir's car. I remember the special color. Yes, it is Roger's vehicle.

"Now, an ambulance has prevailed on drivers to allow it to move closer. Perhaps someone is injured?"

They continued watching. "Look Sarah. They're not moving people to that ambulance. They are moving large bags from the truck to the ambulance. Those bags look like the bags used in banks. Sarah, I think we are having an aerial view of an old fashioned highway robbery. A broad daylight robbery of a bank money truck."

"Albert, how could they be robbing that truck in broad daylight?"

"Sarah, we are witnessing a robbery in the midst of this traffic jam. There goes that ambulance with the money bags and lights flashing. They want it to look like they are taking an injured person to an emergency room."

Sarah took the binoculars. "The other cars are giving way to the ambulance. They drivers think they are helping the ambulance take someone to the hospital."

Albert said, "They're not moving injured. They're moving cash. Where are the police?"

Sarah answered, "I don't see a single officer. Not even a police car. The traffic jam has blocked off any emergency vehicles. Let's see what the TV can tell us."

A commentator was describing the situation. "We are receiving reports of utter chaos down town. In an incredibly bold rush hour robbery, men, protected by an incredibly huge traffic jab, are reported to have moved bags of cash from an armored money truck to another vehicle. Someone has phoned in a report that the getaway vehicle is an ambulance.

"The robbery took place in the midst of a record traffic jam in Toronto's commuter traffic. Traffic came to a stop during the rush hour through a wide spread failure of traffic lights. In the midst of the confusion, the crew of an armored money truck exited the security of their vehicle to deal with an annoying fender bender. When the guards stepped out of the truck they were attacked with pepper spray, disarmed and disabled with nylon ties. Bank officials said that when the guards stepped out to talk with the other driver they violated procedural rules.

"The robbers hauled bags of cash from the bank truck to their get-away vehicle, an ambulance. In this huge traffic jam, the thieves made a getaway as motorists gave way to the ambulance."

Albert switched to another channel. "Police now report that the vehicle that crashed into the bank truck was registered to an American by the name of Roger Renoir. Officers found a wallet in the vehicle containing Roger Renoir's New York State driver's license."

Albert said, "They're barking up the wrong tree. Roger could no more have been involved in this crime than the man in the moon." He turned to Sarah. "That license has to be a deliberate plant and that has my grey cells working. Why would the criminals want to implicate our friend Roger?"

ii

Later in the day of the big robbery in down town Toronto, Emily received a phone call from the Toronto police. She was asked to come immediately to be interviewed. Hank and Joan received similar calls.

They soon learned why they had been called in. An officer told the team, "We have learned that you folks are associates and co-workers of the American named Roger Renoir. Today, Mr. Renoir's vehicle was used to stop a bank truck and carry out a major robbery. Mr. Renoir's driver's license was found in this vehicle belonging to him.

"We would like to know the whereabouts of Mr. Renoir. We are asking you to share with us any information regarding where he is now. We would remind you that it is an offense to supply false information to authorities. Where is Roger Renoir?"

Hank said, "I have to tell you, sir, truthfully I do not know where he is."

Joan and Emily were asked the same question and each responded in the same way.

Out in the parking lot, Hank said, "This is crazy. They are telling us that the vehicle used for the fender bender to stop the armored truck was Roger's beat up Rover. The real question is why those characters would locate the repair shop, take Roger's old car that they had trashed at the Chinese restaurant and then deliberately used it for the fender bender to stop the armored truck"

Emily was puzzled. "Yes. They could have used any old car. Why would they go to the trouble to use Roger's old wreck? The police say they also found Roger's New York State driver's license in vehicle. Where could they have gotten his license?"

Hank said, "It evident that this gang was also interested in making life difficult for Roger. It looks like a deliberate effort to implicate Roger."

Joan said, "But Roger is nowhere around here. Why would they want to implicate Roger?"

Hank said, "There's something else about this action to incriminate Roger. I believe it identifies the robbers themselves. Their efforts to involve Roger indicate that these bank truck robbers are the same men stole that nuclear material. It looks like they want to eliminate Roger. Now it seems they want to keep him on the run, not only from them but also from the police. Perhaps they are afraid he might spill too much information to the police. They want to keep him running."

Joan said, "I see it now. They want to make him into a double fugitive. If he is keeping out of sight of the police he's less likely to be an informer. We need to share this with Roger tonight."

Emily said, "It really bothered me last night, that Roger would not tell even the three of us, where he was. Now I see the wisdom in his not giving us more information.

"There's something else you guys need to know. When Roger left for Jasper, at the last minute he realized that he had a souvenir from Bobcat Lake in his pocket. Roger handed it to me. It was that special smart phone the gang leader had left at Bobcat Lake.

"Yesterday some people raided my Toronto apartment. They wrecked the place looking for something. Today that phone is gone. It's the only item missing."

Hank was stunned. "The theft of the phone indicates that the phone is important to them. Their effort to recover that phone raises the possibility that there are key phone addresses on that phone. Such phones have been used to detonate bombs. This suggests that someone has weapons of destruction planted in key locations."

iii

Later that evening the team gathered at Hank's apartment to listen for a call from Roger. Hank said, "It is good Roger has the two way ham radio. My hi-tech friend has confirmed that, as we suspected might be the case, all of our phones have had been tapped. Someone has been listening to all our calls.

"However, we will be able to fight fire with fire. My friend has provided equipment that enables us to reverse the tap and exploit it to our advantage. Without our enemy knowing it we can now reverse listen in on our enemy. We can monitor what he is saying."

Joan asked, "Have you tested the setup, Hank?"

"You bet I have and it works. In fact, I have some amazing news. I actually heard this man, whoever he is, talking about plans to travel across Canada to Vancouver on the great trans Canadian train."

Joan and Emily laughing said in chorus, "Mr. Dark Heart on a train?"

"Yes, and this will set you back on your heels. This snake in the grass has actually booked the train out of Toronto on the very same date we are making our trip. He is booked for the August eighteenth run."

Joan's eyebrows arched, "The very same train we have booked for our trip?"

Hank laughed, "This calls for a celebration. The tide has turned. For the first time we know more about him than he does about Roger."

Joan said, "Yes, and Joan has to take Hank out to dinner."

"Great work, Hank." Emily said, "This may give us an opportunity to help Roger. Instead of just running he may be able to take some steps to turn things around.."

Hank said, "Yes, with this information, instead of running and hiding Roger may be able to go after this guy. This may open up the possibility of turning things around."

Hank pounded his fist. "I'm looking forward to sharing this news with Roger, if we can make contact with him this evening.

CHAPTER 35

An Old Canadian Gold Rush Era Cabin
The Canadian Rockies, Alberta

"Double, double toil and trouble;
Fire burn, and caldron bubble."
– The three witches - Macbeth, Shakespeare

The quiet and coolness of evening was falling over
the Christiansen's old miner's shack. A spectacular sunset was giving
a special red glow to the sky that was visible through a clearing. Fred
and Mary were out taking care of their horses, Mary was responding
to what she called the gift of the sky. She was singing softly the hymn
she sang that was part of her, "Day is dying in the west. Heaven is
touching earth with rest."

Fred stopped in his chores and called, "What got you singing, Mary?"

Mary sang her answer. "Heaven and earth are praising Thee, O
Lord Most High."

Roger was getting set to try to make a ham radio contact with
Hank. During the afternoon he had used Fred's solar battery charger
to charge his hand held rig. He sent out his CQ on a frequency previously planned. Soon he heard Hank's response, "You are coming in
loud and clear. How do you copy?"

Roger replied, "You are very clear. This is great. You have no idea
how good it is to connect with you"

Joan and Emily chimed in, "We're here too."

Hank said, "You were wise in keeping your location to yourself.
Today, we were all called in by the Chief Inspector. He asked each of
us individually where you might be. Thanks to your foresight in not

giving us your location, each of us could truthfully reply that we had no idea where you were."

Emily took the mic. "Don't get inflated ideas over it, but we've all missed you. Even I missed you."

Roger said, "What's going on in Toronto?"

Hank said, "Toronto is filled with talk about the big rush hour robbery. Some guys stopped an armored bank money truck. They pulled it off in the midst of the morning rush hour. In fact they used the congestion to aid them. It is reported that they hauled off bags of cash."

"Sounds very well planned."

Hank said, "Yes, and there is a reason why you need to know the details. Believe it or not, Roger, wherever you are, what happened here in Toronto affects you. That's why the police were asking us about you."

Roger "I'm thousands of miles away. How could I be connected with a Toronto robbery?"

"The TV report of the robbery says that evidence found at the scene implicates an American named Roger Renoir."

"Impossible."

"Brace yourself, Roger. The police say that the vehicle used to crash into and stop the armored bank money truck was an old Rover that belongs to an American named Roger Renoir."

Roger said, "They obviously used a stolen vehicle to crash into the bank truck. What's so significant about whose old beat up old Rover they used?"

"We believe they had a special reasons for using your Rover. It was deliberate. Remember, they learned your ID from those paintings. They know the painter that they took prisoner at the warehouse is also the witness they attempted to kill up at Bobcat Lake. They have good reason to try to implicate you. This use of your old Rover was deliberate. These men wanted to implicate you, by using your vehicle."

"But what did they hope to do by involving me."

"This is what we are thinking, Roger. It's obvious. Right now they have no idea what happened to their plane or their pilot. Not knowing what happened to Roger Renoir or their plane, they wanted to discredit and implicate you. They wanted to keep this Roger Renoir running not only from them but also keeping his distance from the police. So, they used this Rover to crash into that the bank's money truck to implicate Roger Renoir."

"But what could they hope to achieve through this??"

"Emily spoke up. "Roger, it looks to us that they want to keep you on the run. They may want to keep you from getting too friendly with the police."

Hank said, "Brace yourself. It gets worse. The police forensic unit searching the wreck discovered in the wrecked Rover a wallet with a New York State driver's license. The name? Roger Renoir. It's all over Toronto. The police want help in finding Roger Renoir."

"Let me get this straight." Roger paused in amazement. "You're saying that they want to keep Roger Renoir, not only on the run from them, but also on the run from the police. "

Hank continued. "Yes, and it gets worse. TV showed film of the police coming out of Roger Renoir's Toronto apartment. The police said that they found in Roger Renoir's place packets of cash still in bank wrappers like those used on the money truck."

Roger was stunned. After a few moments Roger responded, "So now, they are working to make me, Roger Renoir, a double fugitive. They want to keep this man, who appears to be running from them, also running from the police. They want to keep this man, Roger Renoir, from sharing whatever he knows with the police."

Hank responded. "Right on the nose. Until they can obliterate you, Roger, they want to keep you on the run from the police."

Roger said, "It makes me feel like a character in a movie. I was running from the bad guy to stay alive. Now I'm hiding from both the bad guys and the police. I can't go to the police for help. They would just throw me in jail. But, if the I wants to draw the snake in the grass out of his hole, I have to stay free."

After a moment of silence, Roger continued, "There is another reason for keeping my present location to myself."

Hank responded, "Another reason?"

"It's time to tell you what has happened since I left all of you at the Graf Zeppelin."

"Let me review my situation. First, the man who, through Wilbur, arranged for me to pilot this plane to Vancouver appears to be the man who had ordered me shot at Bobcat Lake. The men who took me prisoner at the warehouse suspected I was the man ordered shot at Bobcat Lake. Then, when they saw the signed paintings, this confirmed the fact that the painter at the warehouse, was the seized ono Bobcat Lake. Apparently, their leader was more determined than ever to destroy me."

"And how was he going to do that?" Emily asked.

He used Wilbur at the Graf s Zeppelin to persuade me to accept the job of flying their single engine plane to Vancouver. As you know I accepted the job of flying the plane to Vancouver to get away from Toronto.

What I have to tell you now is this. I was really hired to pilot a plane with a powerful bomb set to explode as I descended to land at Vancouver. I was, unknowingly, hired to function as a kamikaze pilot. It would be an unknowing suicide flight. Something like those World War II Japanese kamikaze pilots. It does not appear that Wilbur had any idea what was going on. Wilbur was very helpful in developing my flight plan.

"Since I am alive and talking to you, it is obvious that I never reached Vancouver. You've heard no report of a bomb in Vancouver. The fact that no one knows what happened to me or their plane or the bomb has improved my situation. Now, the man who concocted the scheme to blow me to pieces over Vancouver has no idea what happened to the plane or the bomb or me. He doesn't know and isn't going to know if I am dead or alive. He doesn't know and isn't going to know where the plane is or where the bomb is. All he knows is that his plane failed to reach Vancouver. That's all he knows and that's all he's going to know. I hope it is driving him crazy."

Hank spoke for the team, "Thank you for sharing your situation with us , Roger. We are grateful, however your escape took place, that you are alive and apparently secure.

"Thanks for this briefing. We look forward to hearing the details.

We have some news for you, some amazing news that may give us the possibility of turning this situation around. Although, like you, we still do not know who your enemy is, we now know where this Mr. Dark Heart is going to be for a few days."

"That sounds very interesting."

Hank continued, "As you know, we suspected that all our phones might be tapped. A high tech friend of mine confirmed that all of our phones were tapped. Someone was listening to all our calls. We're fortunate to have the resource of ham radio for this call.

"My friend did more than confirm the phone tap. He was able to bug the whole situation so that, without their knowing it, we can now also monitor them. As a result we have been listening in on the conversations of this snake in the grass."

Roger said, "Sounds great, Hank. What have you learned?"

Hank continued, "For one thing we know, as you suspected, that he is desperate to learn what happened to his plane and a special device. He is especially anxious to know whether you are dead or alive.

"More than that, we have picked up some terrific information about our mystery man, himself. We have learned that this man is planning to take the train from Toronto to Vancouver. More than that. We know when and on what train. This snake in the grass is planning to be on the August eighteenth train out of Toronto."

Roger said, "But that's the date of our team trip together. Does he know we will be on that train?"

"Not as far as we know. This character is, unknowingly we believe, going to be on the train we have booked for our trip."

Roger was silent for a few moments. He replied slowly. "This man who tried to blow my brains to pieces on Bobcat Lake, this man who tried to blow me out of the sky over Vancouver, this creature will be, unknowingly, on our August 18th train?"

Hank said, "Exactly. That's the situation."

"Unbelievable." Roger was silent for a few moments. Finally he said, "This could provide us with an opportunity to really turn around the situation. Let's think about what we could do to exploit this opportunity. We might be able to use this as an opportunity to draw this snake in the grass out of his hole. You have given me something to work on. I'll get back to you"

Roger gave his ham signed off. "Seven three."

ii

Since the Christiansen's cabin was in a later time zone, when Roger completed his ham radio call with Hank and the team, he sat down for supper with Fred and Mary..

Roger couldn't wait to share the news from Toronto with his hosts. "Fred, Mary there's a new development in Toronto that may open up a way to change my situation.

"My friends in Toronto shared with me that a hi-tech friend had enabled them to reverse the tap on their phones. Using this new set up, they have been monitoring this guy's conversations. They have been listening to confidential conversations."

Fred said, "Great, Roger. Anything that that might be helpful?"

"Yes. For the first time we finally have a lead on where he's going to be at a specific time and place."

Fred said, "That is a real turn around."

"Our team has learned that this man who twice tried to kill me will be a passenger on Canada's great transcontinental train. He's booked for the six day trip from Toronto to Vancouver."

Fred said, "Do you know when?"

"Yes. The exciting news is that we know when. He will be on the great train when it pulls out of Toronto Union Station at 8 am on the morning of August 18th."

Mary was puzzled. "Is there anything significant about the date?"

Roger smiled. "Mary, the August 18th train just happens to be the very same train on which our Mission Air team is booked for our special trip together across Canada. Finally, we know something specific about this character. At last we have the possibility of drawing this snake in the grass out of his hole."

Fred said, "Great. This could be an opportunity to turn things around?"

"We have to make use of this information. Fred. It's an opportunity to draw this snake out of his hole, identify him and do something to stop him in his tracks."

Fred said, "But how would you spot him on your train? You told me that you don't even know what he looks like."

"Yes, that's a major part of the problem, Fred. Yes, here I am hiding from this man at your cabin and I haven't the foggiest idea of who it is from whom I'm hiding. But if he is on our train this might give us an opportunity to turn things around."

Fred said, "You won't get far protecting yourself from him until you can identify the man."

"You're hitting the nail on the head, Fred. At the heart of all this, I still don't even know who gave the order to eliminate me. I don't know who pulled the trigger. I don't know who designed the bomb for my plane that was set to blow me out of the sky when I descended to 1,000 feet in Vancouver."

Fred said, "Vancouver? This guy knows that his bomb in the plane never got to Vancouver. Could he be transporting another bomb for Vancouver on the train?"

"That's a possibility, Fred. That makes it even more urgent that we do something with this information. We start this single fact. He will be on our train. The first challenge will be to identify this man of whom we know absolutely nothing. One man among 300 passengers. We need to identify this man. We have to exploit this opportunity."

Fred said, "Roger, Mary and I will do anything it takes to help."

Roger said, "Let's sleep on it. Tomorrow we'll find a way."

CHAPTER 36

Old Canadian Gold Rush Cabin

*"If I had an hour to solve a problem,
I'd spend 55 minutes thinking about the problem."
and 5 minutes thinking about solutions.*
– Albert Einstein, 1879 - 1955

In the morning, after a tasty breakfast, Roger decided to follow Mary's suggestion that he go exploring along Treasure Creek. She said, "A flowing creek is a good place to collect your thoughts, and enjoy just being you."

As he hiked along the rushing stream, Roger was surprised and impressed by the ingenuity still visible in the rusty remains of equipment used by the rugged prospectors a hundred and fifty years ago.

Finally, Roger came to a spot along the stream that got his watercolor wheels turning. He was soon painting a watercolor of the rushing stream. It was beginning to hit Roger that, after what he had experienced, getting back to painting was something he desperately needed. While painting he was conscious of feeling a bit like Roger Renoir again. Mary was right. Just being here along the stream, with the sun breaking through the trees and the sound of the flowing water, was good medicine.

As he worked on sharpening the details of perspective in his watercolor Roger smiled. Perspective. That's what you need, Roger. Perspective. You need to step back and regain some perspective on your life. What are you doing here at the cabin? How long are you going to keep hiding from this man who, twice now, has attempted to kill you? Isn't it time to get your life back on track?

Suddenly Roger knew what he needed to do. He packed up his painting gear and headed back to the cabin. As he returned to the cabin he called out to Fred and Mary. "Eureka! Fred, Mary, I found it?"

Fred said, "What did you find? A gold nugget?"

"No, in the midst of all I've been experiencing, I've I found the need for renewed purpose,"

Mary said, "What do you mean by renewed purpose?"

"Fred, Mary, I've decided to stop running. I'm going to stop running. I'm going to take the initiatives amd turn this situation around."

Mary said. "Good. What turned on the lights?"

"Fred, Mary, knowing that this character will be on the August 18th train has given me a kick in the pants. Knowing that this character will be on our train demands that I do something.

"Now, I have a place to start. Now, for the first time, I know exactly where this snake in the grass will be. Beginning Tuesday, August eighteenth, and for the six days following, this man will be on that great transcontinental train."

Roger paused for a moment and then continued. "I'm going to stop running. Starting today, the man being hunted, the fugitive, is going to be the hunter."

Fred reached out, gave Roger a hug and said, "Great. Where do you propose to start'?"

"I don't know. Looks like we have to develop a plan."

Mary said, "Did you say we? Roger, now that you are including a woman, let this woman remind you that ideas, like eggs, need warmth to hatch. Let's start with some coffee and freshly baked cinnamon rolls"

As they sat down together Fred said, "What do you see as your first objective?"

Roger said, "First I want to simply to identify the man. Fred, this information about his being on our train opens up a great opportunity to isolate and identify the man."

"I agree. But Roger, there's one small problem. In high travel months, like August, this great transcontinental train boasts three hundred passengers. Also, remember that this character was tapping the phones of your friends. He probably knows your team will be on that train. You may not have a picture of him but you can be sure this character has your team in his sights. And that means, dollars to doughnuts, this man will be wearing some sort of disguise, maybe one of those notoriously realistic life masks and a wig."

"Fred, it looks like we need some way to provoke him, to draw him out, to make him show his colors in spite of himself."

"Roger, it's going to take something special to rattle such a hardened man. What sort of a situation on a luxurious train would provoke a visible reaction out of this well-organized bomb builder?

Roger smiled, "I know a moment that, not too long ago, scared the living day lights out of me?"

"Was it when that bullet hit the ground an inch from your head?"

"No. Fred, remember when you called me over to the wrecked plane to show me what you found in that big black pack? You showed me that bomb I had been hauling in m my plane all that time. I was stunned."

Fred said, "Yes. I remember. Was that the moment that knocked you out of your pants?"

Roger said, "No, it hit a bit later. It was when you showed me the altimeter devise. It had been set to trigger that huge bomb the moment I came in at a certain altitude. When it hit me how close I came to being blown to pieces, I almost blacked out."

"Yes. I remember. You practically stopped breathing. I thought you might faint."

"I thought my heart stopped beating. It scared the pants off me. It hit me between the eyes. If the engine had not failed while I was still at five thousand feet, if the failing engine had not prevented me from continuing my flight and dropping down to one thousand in Vancouver, I would not be here talking about it. I was stunned at how close I was to being blown to pieces."

"Yes, I remember seeing your reaction. I thought you were going to pass out."

"Fred, is there some way that we could create a moment of truth like that for this bomb buildering character? Could we find a way to set up some sort of an encounter that would produce a visible reaction like that in this man? He must be a rather hardened man. How could we scare the living daylights out of him in such a way that his ID, regardless of any disguise, would be obvious?"

Fred said, "It would take a real threat to spook a hardened bomb builder like this man."

Suddenly Roger held up his hand and just stared at Fred. "Fred, a light just went on. Speaking of his bomb, I just remembered that we brought back his deactivated bomb pack from the wreck, in case we needed evidence, Could we use his own devise to give him the same scare the sight of his bomb gave me? This man hasn't the foggiest notion what happened to the plane, his bomb or me. What if he suddenly found himself staring at his own bomb, about to go off? We still have his bomb."

"Good thinking, Roger. You're suggesting we find a way to confront him with his own bomb, the bomb he designed and whose power he knows, to shake him out of his shoes. Roger, your grey matter is finally working."

Mary said, "See, my cinnamon rolls are finally going to work."

Roger said, "All he knows is that the plane with the bomb never reached Vancouver. He hasn't the foggiest idea what happened to his plane, to me or to his powerful bomb.

"Fred, what if this clever man, the man who designed this bomb rigged with an altimeter to go off below 1,000 feet, suddenly found himself suddenly face to face with his own invention, ticking away at a location that was obviously well below one thousand feet!"

"Roger, when I discovered his bomb in the wreck out there in the mountains, we were well still well above five thousand feet. This was the only reason that I was able to disable his bomb. We were at a high altitude.

"That bomb has a tamper proof feature. It was rigged to detonate if anyone attempted to change the settings at a low altitude. This would prevent anyone, even the designer, from turning off the detonator, at a low altitude. If we used his bomb we would have to confront him with his bomb ticking away some place close to 1,000 feet."

Roger said, "In a few days, at eight o'clock on the morning of August eighteenth, this man will be boarding the Canadian, in Toronto. That's well below three thousand feet. Toronto's almost at sea level, about 250 feet.

Fred agreed. "To confront him with his own bomb on the train sounds great, but moving his bomb from the Rockies to the train in Toronto appears impossible."

Mary laughed, "Impossible? Did I hear you use that word, impossible? Remember that children's song. Nothing, absolutely nothing, nothing is impossible for God."

Fred agreed, "Yes, Mary, nothing is impossible with God, but our getting this man's bomb to the train in Toronto would be a challenge."

Suddenly Mary held up her hand. "Listen! Do you hear what I hear?"

Fred laughed, "Yes, your favorite sound, Mary, the lumber train whistle."

Fred turned to Roger. "Mary keeps wondering why the engineer on that locomotive has to sounds his train whistle out there where there are no people."

Mary said, "Yes, the bears aren't going to listen to it."

Roger asked, "Where does this whistle come from, Fred?"

"It's the whistle of a lumber train that cuts through this region. It hauls out freight cars of local lumber to make connection, down where the major freight and passenger trains run, down there in North Thompson River canyon below us."

Roger said, "Mary, you've got my wheels turning. Are you telling me that this local lumber train connects with the major cross country trains on the main line down in the canyon below us? Are you telling me that our great transcontinental passenger train will pass along the North Thompson canyon on those tracks in the canyon below us?"

Mary said, "Yes, the transcontinental trains pass through the North Thompson River canyon, just a few miles below us several times a week."

"You mean our team's train, the train leaving Toronto on Tuesday August 18th, the train on which our enemy is travelling, in a few days, will pass down there on the tracks along the canyon below us?"

Fred said, "Yes. As I recall the schedule, those trains reaches Jasper on the fourth day and continues across these mountains on the morning of the fifth and sixth days.

"Fred, are you telling me that the August 18th train, the train on which my friends and this dangerous man are booked, will be rolling along down there on the afternoon of Saturday, August the twenty-second?"

Roger laughed, "That snake in the grass on board Canada's greatest train is going to pass, down there in the canyon, not too far from where we're sitting right now."

Roger pounded his fist, "Then, all we have to do is get that great train to make an unscheduled stop. With our team on board, one of our team could activate an emergency stop?"

Fred replied. "It's not quiet that easy, Roger. An emergency stop would never last long enough to accomplish what we want to see happen. To create a situation in which there would be some sort of confrontation with this man, we would need a real stop, a stop for a couple of hours. We would have to create some sort of problem that forced the train to come to a total halt down there in the canyon below us, along the North Thompson River."

"Fred, could he escape from the train down there? Could he flag down a motorist and get away?"

"No, not a chance. Down there along the North Thompson, there are no roads. Only cliffs. There is barely room for the tracks. Mary and I know the area. We've gone fishing down there. That canyon is isolated."

Roger was puzzled. "How could we stop such a great train for a couple of hours?"

Fred said, "Stopping a huge train like that is no simple thing. Three powerful locomotives of over 3,000 horses each power that great train over these mountains. Stopping the Canadian would be a really major operation. The first questions, however, is not whether it can be done but whether stopping such a train is justified?"

Roger repeated Fred's concern. "You're saying that the real question is whether there a valid reason for taking such action? You are saying that stopping this train can be justified only if we are stopping a greater evil. Certainly, stopping this enemy of Canada constitute such a valid cause"

Fred said, "Yes, the first question is whether stopping this great train justified? We need to ask why we would we be stopping this train? First, to identify and possibly stop a man who has committed serious crimes and threatened the life of Roger. But there is also the urgent need to prevent additional crime. This man's plan to bomb Vancouver with Roger's flight has failed. Now, there is the possibility that he plans to bring a replacement for the Vancouver bomb on board. Is stopping this great train to stop this still unidentified man justified?" The answer is definitely, yes!

Fred paused for a moment. Then he said, "The next question is this. Can it be done safely?"

Roger said, "What would be your major concerns, Fred?"

"We would have to create some sort of emergency that, without causing any damage to the train or passengers, would force the great train to stop. We would want to stop the train in a situation in which officials would encourage the passengers to disembark and stretch their legs while some obstacle on the track is cleared."

Mary said, "Get your wheels are turning, Fred? Not far from here, down on the North Thompson we have the perfect place to do something like that. K190 would be the perfect place to stop that train."

"K190? What are you talking about, Mary?" Roger asked.

Mary said, "Its old railroad language, Roger. K190 means Kilometer 190. Years ago, as the big passenger trains passed through down there in the canyon, they made a twenty minute stop at K190, so passengers could disembark and photograph one of the little known wonders of North America, the roaring cataract down there. It's called Hell's Gate."

"Where did it get the name, Hell's Gate?"

Mary said, "In school we learned that the name Hell's Gate came from the journals of the famous early explorer of this region, Simon Fraser. Back in 1808, when he was exploring the area, Fraser compared this powerful cataract to hell. Fraser said the cataract was, like hell, a place of no return. In his journal he wrote, "Surely these are the gates of Hell." Since then the cataract has been called Hell's Gate."

Roger asked, "Have the two of you ever been down there?"

Mary said, "Fred and I have camped down there on a fishing trips. It's a very rugged and dangerous place. There are no roads in the canyon. The only way to see the great cataract is by train or horseback. The old observation platform is still standing but these days the trains just slows down. Roger, if you want to confront this man, Hell's Gate would be the perfect place."

Fred said, "I have to agree with Mary. It would be just the place to do what we want to do."

Fred started envisioning how the great train could be stopped. "I can see the scene. While the train is stopped for some obstruction on the track, passengers grab the opportunity to get off the train to view the great cataract and take pictures.

"The man we're looking for joins the passengers getting off the train. Suddenly he spots and recognizes his bomb pack. When he examines it, he discovers that this powerful bomb he designed is ticking away toward explosion. He recalls that the settings cannot be changed without detonation. The terror in his face is very visible. Mary is right. K190 is just the place to confront this character. Roger, let me show you K190 and Hell's Gate on my topo."

Fred and Roger studied Fred's map. Fred commented, "Some say that this is possibly the most powerful and spectacular cataract in

North America. At Hell's Gate cataract the North Thompson River boils through a rock lined narrows that extends for several soccer fields in length. There are no roads. A few trails of First Nation fishermen. Only train passengers get to see this powerful cataract. The old viewing platform is still standing. They say, like Hell itself, there are no roads out of Hell's Gate."

Roger asked, "How could we safely stop a great train like that down there, Fred?"

"We would have to bring the train to a stop for a couple hours. To do this we would create some problem on the track, something that might take a couple hours for a work crew to correct. When the conductor encouraged passengers to exit and view the cataract, hopefully the bomb's designer would also exit. We could arrange that once off the train he could find himself face to face with his lost bomb. When he found himself face to face with the bomb, ticking toward explosion, we would expect to see an immediate reaction."

Roger asked, "But, Fred, how do you envision bringing to a complete stop such a great train like this with its three engines and 300 passengers."

"From our fishing trips down there we are aware of a high area that extends along the track. We could prepare to drop a couple big lodge pole pines from this area high above the tracks to the tracks below. This would force the train to stop. A work crew from Kamloops would have to come to clear the track. That would take several hours."

Mary spoke up. "Enough talk. Let's just pack up and ride down there tomorrow. It's rugged but beautiful country. We could ride down to the ford, cross the ford and ride on downstream along the West bound tracks to the K190. We would head back up here to the cabin the next day."

Roger said, "Since it's such rugged country, let's make it more than a visit. Let's take along the bomb pack and everything we would need. Fred, if you could get the bomb re-programmed tonight, we could take that bomb pack with us and go. Let's take what we need to get things set. Then, if we decide to follow this plan, everything would be in place?"

Fred said, "Since the explosives were removed the bomb pack will be relatively light. When we get down there I can replace the weight of the explosives with sand. We can also take a small chain saw and the cables and tools needed to prepare the tree drop."

ii

The next morning Fred and Mary got set to make the journey on horseback, along with two pack horses. They prepared to head down the trail down to the North Thompson ford some distance upstream from the cataract. They loaded the original bomb pack and mechanism, minus explosives, on one pack horse. Fred added the tools and things needed to prepare a way to drop trees on the track. Their camping gear and supplies went on the other pack horse.

By noon they reached the ford on the North Thompson some distance upstream from Hell's Gate cataract and the old observation deck at K190.

While Mary was breaking out lunch Fred said, "I won't be able to fish at the cataract. I'll see what I can catch for supper here at the ford." Fred headed for a special pool below the ford with his fly fishing gear. He returned to their resting spot, with several large trout. He said, "We'll pack these away for supper."

After the break for lunch they continued down along the North Thompson. Before long they came to the place where the tracks for the West bound trains began running along the river. Their trail now ran along the tracks and headed down stream toward K190 and Hell's Gate Cataract. They began to hear the thunder of the cataract, As they got closer the air was filled with the spray. Suddenly they were there and overwhelmed by the roar and thunder of the cataract. After their rough journey they were all glad to have finally reached K190. They secured the horses and went out on the old viewing platform.

To be heard with the constant roar of the cataract, Roger spoke loudly to Fred and Mary, "I've never experienced anything like this,"

Mary said, "The power of our Creator God in this roaring cataract should renew our trust in the sufficiency of His power to deal with all the needs we bring to Him."

Fred said, "Let's get to work." They repacked the bomb was with sand to represent the weight of the original explosives. Fred installed new batteries and checked the settings on the devise so that the bomb devise would be ready for the irreversible turning on. After the bomb pack was well concealed in a tool shed, they mounted their horses and worked their way up the mountain side to an area overlooking the track. Fred said, "I've got to find the place from which to drop the trees so they to crash down on the right spot across the tracks."

"What do you mean by the right spot," Roger asked.

Fred replied, "When we drop trees down this cliff and on to the track, the first consideration is to avoid a crash. That means making sure that the engineer of those three powerful engines sees the trees falling. He needs to see well in advance, from at least two kilometers away, that there is something falling down the mountain side. He will need to have as much time as possible to stop that great train in time. He will need to stop the train just a bit past the viewing platform at K190. We want the three engines to stop far enough beyond the old viewing platform so that the passenger cars are stopped as close to the viewing platform as possible. When the train stops we want to make it possible for many passengers to disembark to view the Hell's Gate Cataract. We want the passenger cars to be as near as possible to the viewing platform. That will determine where we want the trees to hit the track."

Roger nodded, "That makes sense. What else are you considering, Fred?"

Fred explained, "We have to make an intelligent estimate of how long it will take the engineer to stop a train like this. This passenger train will require less distance to stop than a freight train, but it will still require a good warning of an obstacle on the tracks. Also, the slight down grade will make it harder to stop. When we actually drop the big lodge pole pines we have to time the actual falling of the trees in such a way that the engineer will actually see the avalanche of falling debris two kilometers or more ahead."

Fred finally found the spot where he could drop the trees and also see about two kilometers down the tracks he said, "This looks like the best spot. There is a reasonably clear pathway down the mountain side for three big lodge pole pines to tumble down to the tracks. From here we will be able to hear and see the approaching train. We want to time the drop onto the tracks so that the train can make a safe stop.

Fred looked for a group of several lodge pole pines that could be prepared to fall crashing down on the mountainside to the tracks. He then set to work on preparing the trees. They had to be cut and rigged in such a way that when the anchor cable was released all three pre-cut trees would go crashing down the steep rocky cliff. When these cables were all in place, Fred went to work cutting a forester's notch in each tree. The cables would support and hold each tree in place until the time came for dropping the trees. They were cut with a notch that would cause each tree to fall forward and crash to the tracks. As they fell they would take a lot of other smaller trees and rocks down the mountain with them

Fred said, "These trees will create a major obstacle. It will probably take the work crew an hour to get here. When the work crew arrives from Kamloops they will face a couple hours work."

When they returned to the viewing platform and looked upstream they saw a fishing platforms. Fred explained that this was used by First Nations Canadians. Fred pointed out the two heavy cables that were stretched across the raging waters of the cataract. He explained, "Those cables are used by the local First Nations fishermen to cross he cataract, but only if they really need to cross over."

Roger said, "All the gold in Fort Knox would not get me out on those cables across the cataract."

Fred said, "Yes, those cables are definitely something to stay away from. I have been told that they have a special safety harness that they wear and which attaches to one of the cables when it becomes necessary to cross the cataract. Those large gear mechanisms are for putting tension on the cable. They look pretty rusty to me."

Fred said, "Before we start back up to the cabin, I want to review how we will go about operation big pine on the day we stop the train. We have to leave the cabin, with enough time to us get here a good hour before the train reaches K190.

"Today, we will leave the big the bomb pack in that old railroad tool shed. On that day the train is expected, we will draw the pack out from the tool shed and position it on the walk way to the observation platform. I will check the batteries and look to see that the clock and detonator mechanism are working properly.

"When we have finally arrived at the area high above the tracks, where we prepared the lodge pole pines, we will sit by the cable release and wait for the train. When we hear the train we will be ready. As soon as the train appears around the bend, in that moment when the engineer can see what is happening, we will drop the trees. In this way the engineer will see the falling trees in time to stop the train safely.

Roger looked at Fred, "I am impressed. This should really stop the train and provide for our special plan."

Fred said, "When these trees tumble down the mountainside they will take a lot of rocks and smaller trees with them. The train should be stopped for quite a while."

Roger had a concern. "Stopping of the transcontinental train is going to affect many other trains. I assume that the train's engineers will make contact with the traffic control officials and the work crews?"

Fred nodded. "We have to keep in mind why we are doing this. We are seeking to identify and stop a man devising violent attacks on the people of this nation. Let's hope for the right outcome."

Mary said, "No apologies. Here is a chance to identify and stop this man. If he could plant a bomb for Vancouver in your plane, Roger, who knows what he will have stashed on this great train headed for Vancouver".

CHAPTER 37

Toronto

"No man means all he says,
and yet very few say all they mean,
for words are slippery and thought is viscous."
– Henry Adams, 1838 - 1918

It was late in the evening and Hamu was rather puzzled to hear his doorbell ring. He was surprised to see his lieutenants Nibal and Daoud standing there with a third man.

Daoud introduced the stranger. "Professor Fouad, this is Joe. He is the man who set up our phone tap on the phones of Roger Renoir and his friends."

Nibal said, "We are here tonight because we believe it is urgent that Jo share with you a major problem with our phones."

"Speak up! What's the problem, Jo?"

Joe said, "I wanted to inform you, professor, about this as soon as possible. I have discovered that both your cell phones and land lines are being tapped. Someone has modified your phone taps on the phones of Roger Renoir's friends. Your phone taps are being tapped in reverse. The people whose calls you were monitoring are now listening to your calls."

Hamu was shocked. "Are you telling me that the friends of Renoir, have been listening to all my calls?"

"Unfortunately, yes."

Hamu said, "This is a very serious matter, very serieous. Since our plane never reached Vancouver, I've been arranging a special trip to

Vancouver by train. And you are telling me that these characters may be aware of all my plans?"

Joe said, "It is quite likely that they know any plans discussed by phone."

Hamu was stunned. "This is a disaster. I'm glad you came tonight. I must take steps to cancel and change everything."

Nibal spoke up, "Well not really. Jo has suggested that there is a way you could use this situation to your advantage."

Hamu laughed. "To my advantage? How in the world could such a disaster work to my advantage? All my plans will have to be cancelled and rescheduled."

Nibal said, "Not necessarily."

Hamu looked at Nibal intently. "What do you mean by not necessarily?"

Nibal laughed. "Professor, by their spying on your affairs, the friends of Mr. Renoir will have developed an ailment we call vulnerability. They are vulnerable."

Hamu said, "Vulnerable? What do you mean they are vulnerable? Vulnerable to what?"

Nibal laughed, "Professor, Joe has called to our attention that by all this listening they have not only picked up information. They have come to regard everything they hear as factual information. These listeners have come to accept what they hear as fact. They believe whatever they hear."

Nibal laughed again. "These listeners are now very vulnerable."

Hamu said. "This is no laughing matter. I'm the one who is vulnerable, vulnerable to their listening to my plans. You say they are vulnerable? Vulnerable to what?"

Nibal said, "They are vulnerable to deception. They have made themselves very vulnerable to the virus of misinformation."

"How can such a mess work to my advantage?"

Nibal said, "Their listening to your phones has made them vulnerable to taking everything they hear as fact. You can now say over your phone whatever you want them to believe. They are going to swallow anything and everything you feed them."

Hamu was not convinced. "So what do I feed them?"

"Misinformation. Their listening has made them gullible. You can take advantage of this by supplying them with misinformation."

Hamu pounded his fist. "Where do I begin?"

Joe explained, "As you and your men talk on the phone, supply these gullible listeners with whatever you want them to hear and believe. Use your talk on the phone to supply them with misinformation! Their listening gives you a golden opportunity to mislead them in any way you wish. Their phone can serve as a ring in their nose. You can lead them in any way you wish."

Hamu said, "What about the plans for my trip to Vancouver?"

Nibal said, "Continue with your plans for the trip. Simply let them hear you telling various people that you are cancelling your August eighteenth train trip. Speak about problems that have forced you to change your plans. Their snooping has made them very vulnerable to misinformation."

Hamu said, "Misinformation! I like that term. Misinformation."

Joe added, "You can easily mislead these friends of Renoir in Toronto. Let them hear that you will not be on their train. Give them a false sense of security."

Nibal said, "Yes, go on with your trip as planned. They will assume that you will not be on their train. They will no longer be on the lookout for you. However, wear some protective disguise, a life mask and wig."

"Jo cautioned, "Yes, even though they will not be looking for you on the train, we strongly urge you to use your skills in disguise."

After his men had left, Hamu was amused. Misinformation. And they think they are telling me how to use misinformation. This impostor is the biggest piece of misinformation they will ever see. Confusing the friends of Roger Renoir with misleading information will be interesting. I like the idea.

ii

Hank was putting in his scheduled time to monitor the reverse phone tap when he realized that he was hearing a different message.. He could scarcely believe what he was hearing. The conversations indicated a drastic change in plans of their Mr. Darkheart. From what he was hearing the whole situation was changing. Roger's pursuer had cancelled his plan to travel West on the August 18th train.

Hank quickly contacted the others. "That snake in the grass, as Roger calls him, will not be on our August 18th train with us, after all. I picked up several conversations of men talking about the fact that their leader has postponed his trip west. That looks like the end of any plan to draw that snake out of his hole on the train."

Joan and Emily were disappointed to lose this opportunity for Roger to identify the man. They both admitted that they were also a bit relieved. Joan said, "Now we can just go ahead and enjoy our trip together as we originally planned."

That evening, in their secure ham radio contact, Hank briefed Roger on the big change in the plans of the gang leader. "We have picked up several conversations that indicate our target has changed his plans. He will not be travelling on the August eighteenth train, after all. We heard him talking about his making the trip sometime in September. We are sorry the plan to identify him has to be cancelled. However, now we will be able to relax and enjoy our trip together."

Roger replied, "I'm glad to get this information now. This means some big changes in plans at this end? My friends and I had worked out a plan to stop the big train. We will put those plans on hold.

"I am planning to meet all of you and board the train in Winnipeg. Since the police are looking for me, I will board the train as Tom Murphy. See you in Winnipeg." Roger signed off, "Seven-three."

When Roger joined Fred and Mary by their fireplace he faced them silently for a few moments. His friends looked up, wondering what Roger had heard through the ham radio call.

Finally, Roger unloaded the news. "Hank has filled me in with some news that means a big change in our plans and preparation at the Hell's Gate cataract. Through the phone tap Hank and has learned that the leader of this gang is not going to be on the train leaving Toronto on August eighteenth. Now, after all our efforts to set up things to stop the train at at K190, it looks like our preparations to stop the train will not be needed. Hank picked up several conversations in which the professor was talking about having changed his plans."

Fred and Mary were stunned. Mary said, "You mean, after all our preparations, their big shot, this man they call the Professor, is not going to be on the train pulling out of Toronto on August 18th?"

Fred nodded thoughtfully, "What are we going to do with all our preparations. We left the bomb pack, ready to go, down there in a tool shed. Everything is set to drop those lodge pole pines on the track. Everything is ready to go at Hell's Gate?"

Roger said, "I suggest that we keep everything at K190 on hold. Let's just keep everything in place. Hank thinks that the man may be on a September train. Let's just let everything stand as it is."

Fred agreed, "No problem, Roger. We may be able to use our preparations at Hell's Gate at a later date."

Mary wasn't satisfied. "OK, but remember that characters like this are notorious for changing their mind. If he changes his mind once, he may change it again. What if this character is playing games with us? What if he decides to go as planned, on August 18th?" Characters like this often change their minds."

Roger replied, "Mary, if this character decides to turn around and go August eighteenth after all, operation lodge pole pines will go ahead as planned."

Mary wasn't satisfied. "Roger. This leads to another question. What if all this information through the phone tap is pure baloney? What if this character is on the train afteral? What if, there on the train, you suddenly learn that he is among those 300 passengers after all? What then?"

Mary continued to express her concern. "What if you who are on the train suddenly discover that this man you want to stop is somewhere on the train? What if you have good reason to believe that he has another bomb for Vancouver and all of you on your train? Suppose you desperately need us to stop the train and help you stop this character? What are you going to do?

"How in the world would you let us know, up at our old cabin? If you were on the train and this man and the train needed to be stopped? How in the world would you get the message to us, up here at the cabin? How would you let us know, in time to stop this great train and its three locomotives? How would you spot this man among 300 passengers?:

Roger responded, "That's a tough question, Mary. Yes, though unlikely, it is possible that we, on the train, might discover that this character was actually on the train after all. How could we contact you to activate operation lodge pole pines?

"Yes, with all four of us on the train, if we discovered somehow, that the man was on board, even though we had no idea how to identify him, what would we do to reach you?

"To reach the two of you, in time before the train would reach Hell's Gate, we would have to reach you fast, very fast. How could we possibly reach you to activate the plan in time to stop the train?

"You have no phone at the cabin. It would seem impossible to reach you."

Mary cleared her throat. "Did I hear you use that word impossible, Roger?"

"Sorry, Mary. I stand corrected." Roger asked his question again. "If the train were only one day from Hell's Gate, how could we get a message to you up here at the cabin?"

Fred replied, "The only one way to in reach us in such an emergency would be through our friends, the train police, stationed in Blue River.

"You would have to call the officers at Blue River and ask them to deliver an emergency message to us at the cabin. You would ask the officers to send someone on horseback out to our cabin to deliver to us a very urgent message. That would take about an hour. Keep in mind that the trip on horseback from the cabin to K190 and Hell's Gate would take at three to four hours."

Fred continued, "Here is a message that would suggest urgency and keep things private. Give them this special message. Things have changed with the professor. The professor has taken a turn for the worse. Come as soon as possible. Use the key word professor. "

Roger repeated the message. "Things have changed with the professor. The professor has taken a turn for the worse. Come as soon as possible."

"Yes, we would need to hear reference to the professor. The title professor needs to be there. That is what they call their leader, the professor. That's the key word. The word professor will confirm that the message is reliable."

Roger said, "We're unlikely for us to need such a plan, but I feel better knowing that we have this possible way of reaching you."

CHAPTER 38
"Toronto Union Station

"What lies behind us and what lies ahead of us
are tiny matters compared to what lives within us."
– Henry Thoreau, Walden Pond 1845

The three team members in Toronto, Emily, Hank and Joan, made a trip together to Toronto's Union Station. In consideration of Roger's being in another part of the country, some changes in their bookings for the trip were necessary. They had informed the police that they had no idea where Roger might be. They needed to make some corresponding changes in the reservations for their trip west.

Their first step, consistent with Roger's location being unknown, was to cancel his booking for the trip west on August eighteenth. Emily made a new reservation for a man named Tom Murphy. She spoke of this man as a western ranch hand, who would board the train in Winnipeg. Emily arranged for this man, Tom Murphy, to board the train as it pulled into Winnipeg on the evening of the train's the second day out of Toronto.

The team had mixed feeling about the fact that their unknown enemy, the man they called Mr. Dark Heart, had changed his plans and would not be on the train leaving Toronto on the 18th. They had hoped to use his presence on the same train as an opportunity to identity Roger's pursuer. However, they were greatly relieved to feel that now they could relax and simply enjoy this trip as originally planned. In view of the situation they decided to skip the time in Jasper and do some things together in Vancouver.

While there in Toronto's Union Station, Emily noticed again the sign for Advance Baggage Check-in for First Class passengers. Emily was curious and went over to that window for more information about this Advance Baggage Check-in.

She learned that First Class passengers on the trans-Canada trip could deposit baggage in advance as early as a month ahead. The date of deposit would appear stamped on the baggage tag. This would guarantee the baggage being accepted on the train. Such baggage would receive special handling and be locked up separately from other baggage until requested.

Just then, four men in business suits, brushed past her on their way to the Advance Baggage Check-in. They were inquiring about some Advance Check-in baggage. Emily heard the agent call out, "Oh, your last access was August tenth!"

Emily was thinking, "That date, August tenth, rings a bell for me." She asked Joan. "Does August tenth say anything to you? Why would I remember that date?"

"Emily, everyone in Toronto knows that date. August 10th was the day we were all watching the news of Toronto big money truck robbery on tv. Why do you ask?"

"When those men were asking for access to their advance check in baggage. I heard the attendant call out that August tenth was the date of their last access to the baggage."

Joan laughed, "Maybe they checked in those millions of dollars from the big robbery that day. Maybe they each needed a fresh packet of hundred dollar bills."

ii

The time had come for Roger to leave his retreat at the cabin with Fred and Mary. He had to be on his way to join the team at Winnipeg. The first part of his trip to Winnipeg was this ride, with Fred and Mary, down the trail from their cabin to Blue River. At Blue River he would catch a train to Jasper. From there he would take a train to Winnipeg. It was hard to be leaving these very special friends.

The days at the cabin with Fred and Mary had been a wonderful time of recovery for Roger. The protection of this isolated cabin had helped him gain new perspective on his situation. He felt ready now to attempt to turn things around. He was prepared to stop running and take the initiative in dealing with his pursuer. Although the plan to confront his enemy at Hell's gate, Operation Lodge Pole Pines, was now on hold, Roger knew that Fred and Mary were ready to help him identify and overcome this dangerous man.

Nevertheless, Roger was feeling the pressure of being a double fugitive. He had to keep his deadly enemy wondering what happened to him. At the same time, after being implicated in the big Toronto robbery, he had to keep out of sight from the police.

This ride out to Blue River was Roger's first venture from the cabin in his changed appearance. He had grown a beard, facial camouflage, as he called it. He had let his hair grow. Mary had found some well-worn clothes like western cattle ranches wore. She felt that her prize contribution to his new image was a pair of really well-worn boots that fit him perfectly. She said that the hat she located for him looked like it was rooted on him. Her final touch was a well-worn leather vest.

Fred paid Roger a great compliment. With a laugh, Fred said, "Tom Murphy, once you looked like you had been weeks out on the range. Now you smell like it too."

Roger said, "Fred, we had a great plan to stop the train and confront that snake in the grass with his bomb. We'll have to come up with a new plan."

Fred laughed, "With that costume you may pull him in with a lasso?"

"Fred and Mary, through these days with the two of you, I feel I've had my life handed to me again. It makes me wonder what the Creator wants me to do with this life.

"Men, like my enemy have been recruiting and brain washing young men to exploit them and use them in their drive for power. The Arab Spring has not stopped the world wide epidemic of recruiting young men and women to kill people they don't even know. This world needs people reaching out to this generation with the great alternative to darkness and hatred. This world is getting smaller every day. There is a desperate worldwide need, for young men and women to spread an epidemic of love, to share the great alternative of the life the Creator offers us all in Jesus."

Fred said, "We're with you on that."

Roger said, "Remember old President Nixon's hatchet Chuck Colson. He has to be one of the great men of the past century. When Chuck Colson ran into Jesus, Colson became a new and different person. He discovered the alternative to politics of greed and ambition. When he got out of jail, Colson was not satisfied to simply get out of jail. He wanted to bring the presence of Jesus to men in prison. He formed Prison Fellowship to turn around the lives of men. Through Colson thousands of imprisoned men are finding a new way."

"Well, what are you thinking, Roger?"

"When you guys picked this fallen bird, as Mary calls me, off the mountain side it wasn't my first rescue. God had intervened in my life a couple of other times. First, back in Africa. He provided a way to escape when we were held in life threatening captivity. Then in the north woods of Ontario, he made sure a bullet missed my head by a hair. Here in British Columbia, a bomb in my plane was programmed to blow me out of the sky. But through divine intervention, I was saved when engine failure forced me to leave the plane by parachute.

Fred said, "Wondering what God has in mind, eh?"

"Yes. Since He sent you folks to pick me off the mountain, Fred, I've been thinking that my goal should be something more than simply seeing men like Mr. Dark Heart captured and marched off in handcuffs. The Creator must have in mind a plan for a man like that snake in the grass to become a new and different person."

As Roger rode along with Fred and Mary, on their way out to Blue River, the days, since Fred and Mary found him on the mountain side, seemed to have gone by too quickly. These two wonderful people were a special gift.

The days at the cabin had been a much needed time to examine his life. Roger was thinking of God's wonderful provision that Fred, due to his military experience and training, had the expertise to defuse that bomb in the wrecked plane. Fred had come up with a great plan to stop the train and confront his foe.

As they waited for Roger's train for Jasper, Fred said, "You look like the real thing with your clothes. If I were a detective looking to see if you were genuine, I would check out the boots. You can't fake the wear on a pair of boots."

When Roger's train arrived, along with her farewell hug Mary laughed. "You look a lot better than when we found you on the mountain, Roger."

As Roger boarded the train at Blue River he called to Fred and Mary, "Keep those big lodge pole pines on hold. We might need them."

iii

After the rather short run from Blue River, Roger got off the train at Jasper to catch a train East to Winnipeg. In Winnipeg he would join his Lunatic Loonies friends for the long planned trip together on the great train.

As Roger was checking out the famous historic locomotive on display by the Jasper station, Roger was thinking, while I'm here in Jasper, I have to catch up with Bill Webber. When he turned around there, to his amazement, Bill was walking up to greet him.

Webber laughed as he saw how the western clothes had changed Roger's appearance. "I believe I know you, but I'm not quite sure. What's your name?"

Roger laughed, "Tom Murphy."

Webber took in the mustache. "Look at those boots. You even smell western."

Roger said, "I hope that's a complement. How did you know I was coming to Jasper?"

Webber said, "You asked your friend Hank in Toronto to keep me up to date on developments. Hank simply told me your flight had been interrupted. Then he sent me this rather puzzling message. He told me to check passengers arriving in Jasper today."

"Bill, a lot has happened since our days painting and my flight out of Jasper. Let's go somewhere and get something to eat. I have to bring you up to date."

The two watercolorists went off to a favorite restaurant of Webber's. Roger shared the story of his engine trouble, his having to parachute from his plane and the how, after his parachuting, Fred and Mary rescued him on the mountain and took him to their cabin. He explained how engine trouble had interrupted a plot to use him as a kamikaze suicide pilot.

Webber said "You had quite a close call."

"Yes, Bill. Then we learned that the guy who was behind all this might be on the very same train we had booked for our team reunion.

Roger explained the plan to stop the train and trap his enemy and how that was now on hold."

"So, what is happening now?"

"Yesterday morning, August 18th, the team left Toronto, as planned. I am to meet them in Winnipeg tomorrow evening. And then we are on our way to Vancouver, without the bad guy."

Weber said, "Are you sure that he will not be on that train? Sometimes men like this are very clever at confusing their opponents."

"The team heard several conversations about his change in plans. Apparently he is not going to be on our train."

Bill said, "I think it is time to share something about myself."

"Fire away, Bill."

"Roger, I had thought it best not to share this with my new painting friend. Your friend, Bill Webber, is not really the retired postal employee he said he was. He is a retired officer of the RCMP with whom he maintains special contacts."

"That's quite a change of identity.

"Roger, if you should encounter this man or any of his people on this train, you will need all the help you can get. I would like to be on this train with you."

"When I saw the jam you were in, I figured I could be of more help keeping my full identity out of the picture. Then as I learned more about your situation from Hank, and that you had become a double fugitive, on the run from both your deadly enemy and the police, I saw that you needed some anonymous back up.

"This is what I have done. I have cleared up this question of any involvement by you in the Toronto robbery. Out of concern for you and without giving any specific reason, I have arranged to be appointed the special plain clothes officer and agent for this train from Winnipeg to Vancouver. I have also enlisted some friends, retired officers like himself, to be on board, just in case any problems arise. I simply asked them to keep their eyes open and be available if needed."

"You are a real friend, Bill. You are certainly taking our situation seriously,"

"You may be in very serious danger."

PART FOUR

THE TRAIN

CHAPTER 39

"There are no ordinary people.
You have never talked to a mere mortal."
– C. S. Lewis

Joan was laughing as they made their way through the crowd of Toronto's Union Station. She was filled with the excitement as she spoke to Emily. "It looks like half of Toronto is here to see us off."

They were looking for the Pre-boarding Lounge for the trans-Canada train's First Class passengers. Finally, Joan spotted it. "Look. There's the sign. Pre-boarding Lounge. First Class passengers. I've been looking forward to this trip, ever since we came up with this idea back in Nairobi. August eighteen has finally arrived."

Emily said, "Back in Nairobi, none of us had any idea of how much the four of us would need such a getaway."

Joan agreed, "Yes. When I heard that this deadly enemy was going to be on our train I had mixed feelings. I wanted to help Roger draw this snake in the grass out of his hole. But I wasn't too happy about it. Then, when I learned this character would not be on our train, after all, I was certainly relieved. Now, I'm just looking forward to a wonderful trip together."

Emily laughed, "Yes, and now I won't have to be going around like a detective in sun glasses, scanning faces for people who might be part of his gang."

"Are you sure you have turned off those detective eyes. Emily?

Emily looked around, smiling. "I don't see many suspicious looking characters right now."

Joan smiled. "Emily, look at all the practice you could get here. See that father with his teen age son over there. It looks like it's just the two of them are on this train together. I don't see the mother anywhere."

Emily said, "Yes, it does looks like a father and son trip. They are from New Zealand."

"How can you tell?"

Emily gestured toward the boy's carry on item. "See that big flag sticker with the four stars on the boy's carry-on baggage. That's the Southern Cross of the New Zealand flag."

"Good detective work, Emily. The boy looks totally preoccupied with his smart phone."

After a few minutes Emily said, "Joan, check out that hi-tech teen-ager again." The New Zealander is comparing some electronic devise with a new friend. They look like they had known each other for years."

Emily studied the parents with the other boy. "The other hi-tech boy appear to be British."

"How can you tell, Sherlock?"

"Check out the mother's green tote bag. See the name Harrods, Harrods at Knightsbridge London, the world famous store. They're British."

"I'm impressed with your Sherlock Holmes eyes, Emily."

Emily laughed. "The boys seem to be really hitting it off together. This will make the days on the train a fun time for them. Joan, although that dangerous character will not be on our train, I still enjoy studying the faces of the people on our train."

Joan said, "Good. I'm sure that Hercule Poirot would want you to keep those grey cells working. By the way, we need to keep on the lookout for Albert and Sarah Weiss. It will be fun having them on our train. Some people think he's Einstein."

"It's more than looks, Joan. His mind works like Einstein. If I had a problem I would want him on my side. And I like his German accent."

Emily and Joan enjoyed picking up the nearby conversation of two ladies. One was saying, "I'm well prepared for this trip. I've brought along Agatha Christie's mystery, Murder on the Orient Express."

The heard her friend reply, "Do you think someone is going to get murdered on this train?"

Emily and Joan spotted a man sitting at a table, enjoying a cup of coffee with his paper. He looked like he might be close to six feet and in his mid-thirties.

Joan zeroed in on his clothing. "Take a look at that jacket. Looks like a genuine Harris Tweed. He looks like a product of Scotland. What do you say, Sherlock?"

Emily said, "The tweed look like the real thing. Definitely a real Scotsman. We can call him Mr. Tweed."

As they continued to roam around the boarding lounge, Emily focused on a man with an unusual black leather hat. "Joan, take a look at Mr. Black Hat, over there. Now he really looks suspicious"

Joan nodded in approval. "Yes, Sherlock. You better keep your eye on him."

ii

As he sat there in the crowded Pre-boarding Lounge in his black leather hat, Hamu was field testing his disguise, his life mask and wig.

The assurance that Renoir's friends would not be expecting to see him on the train was encouraging. However, he had no idea how much they might know about his appearance. He was taking no chances. He had decided to wear this special life mask and wig. He planned to present himself, in chance encounters, as a business man from Jordan.

Mr. Black Hat was confident that on this trip he would succeed in getting the cash from the big robbery out of Toronto. This cash would finance his war against the West. He smiled as he thought of his next meeting with Vashti. Such large amounts of cash might have another use.

To Hamu's surprise his special agent Daoud, one of the dining room managers on the train, joined him at his table.

"As you saw me sitting here, Daoud, how did I look?"

Daoud switched to Egyptian Arabic, "Professor, your appearance is very convincing. The life mask is excellent. No one would suspect that you were wearing a mask. You look just like the person you plan to say that you are, a Middle East business man from Jordon. That excellent natural wig also helps. Everything looks good."

iii

Not far from Hamu, the two teenage hi-tech
enthusiasts were discovering that between them they had quite a treasure of hi-tech gadgets.

Bill, who lived in London, asked Henry, whose home was in
Auckland, New Zealand, "Do you have any idea of the distance
between our homes?"

Henry checked on his smart phone. "My home in Auckland, New
Zealand and your home in London, UK are 11,387 miles apart."

Bill said, "Our homes are half way around the world from each
other, Wow."

The boys passed two men, very intent in their conversation.

When they had moved a little farther away, Bill, sheltering his
mouth with his hand said, "Did you hear those two men babbling away?"

Henry said, "Yes, I was wondering what language they were
speaking."

"That was Egyptian Arabic, Henry."

"How do you know it's Arabic and Egyptian Arabic, Bill?"

"It's a fringe benefits of my father working overseas. When my
father was assigned to the British Embassy in Cairo, I went to school
there. I picked up quite a bit of Arabic, or, as some Egyptians would
say, Coptic Arabic."

"You mean you understand Arabic? Cool!"

"When I had to learn it I didn't think it was so cool."

"Is Egyptian Arabic different?"

"When the Muslims armies invaded Egypt, around 800, they forced
Arabic and the Muslim religion on the Egyptians. Egyptians have their
own version of Arabic. In Cairo my teacher told us the full story. Prior
to the Muslim invasion, Egypt was had many Jews and Christians in
Alexandra, the city built up by the Romans."

"In New Zealand you never hear much about places like Egypt".".

"Guess who in Cairo really taught me the most about Egypt."

"No idea."

I really learned about Egypt from a great Sunday School teacher
in Cairo."

"You learned something in Sunday school?"

"Yes, it happens more than people realize. My Sunday School teacher explained that around 300 AD there were many Greek speaking Jews in Egypt. They translated the ancient Hebrew Scriptures, or the Old Testament of the Bible, into Greek. It's called the Septuagint, because seventy men produced it."

"Bill, did you catch what those guys were saying in Arabic?"

"Something about the baggage car. The guy in the black hat was asking if someone named Mac was going to have the baggage car job on the train. The other man was saying, "Yes, Mac will be looking after your precious baggage in the baggage car."

As they moved along Bill said. "It looks like there will be quite a few guys speaking Arabic on board. That guy in the tweed suit was reading an Arabic newspaper."

Henry said, "Do you think they could be part of some Arab gang?"

CHAPTER 40

Toronto Union Station

"Oh what a tangled web we weave,
when first we practice to deceive!"
– Sir Walter Scott, 1820

After Daoud left him waiting with the passengers for the call to board the train, the man in the black hat was focused on the lounge TV. He was amused to hear a reporter, grilling a Toronto police official. The newsman was expressing the public outrage over the failure of the police to recover the cash stolen in the great Toronto's rush hour robbery.

The newsman was demanding, "What you are doing to recover that cash? What are you doing to keep those millions from going to finance attacks across Canada?"

"The officer replied, "Proper steps are being taken. Not one dollar of that cash is going to leave Toronto. We have established an iron ring around this city."

The reporter said, "Really? The only money recovered, so far, was the bundle found in the apartment of that American. What have you done to get that American man, Renoir?"

The officer being grilled said, "We will soon have the American suspect in our net. I assure you, an iron ring surrounds Toronto. That morning rush hour robbery cash is going nowhere."

As he sat there in his disguise, Hamu was amused with the boast of an iron ring around Toronto. With the steps taken to secure the loot in pre-checked baggage, he was not very worried about that iron ring.

Hamu enjoyed reviewing the steps taken to conceal the cash. A week before the Toronto robbery his men deposited four large pieces of baggage in the Advance Baggage Check-in at Toronto Union Station. Those pieces of baggage were stamped as having been received on that date. With their Advance Check-in date, a date prior to the robbery, these pieces of baggage would be passed over during any inspection. All we had to do was to transfer the cash to those pre-checked bags, or switch the tags. It was as simple as that.

He was pleased with the skill with which his men had carried out the excellent transfer of the cash. When they arrived at Union Station with the four suit cases of cash taken from the money truck, they presented their Advance Baggage Check-in ticket stubs and asked to have access to their previously checked baggage. While two men kept the attendant busy with questions, the other men were switching the dated tags from the pre-checked baggage to the bags filled with cash from the robbery. These bags were then returned to pre-checked baggage.

Hamu was confident that even if their train should be stopped for inspection, the baggage dated as checked in before the robbery would be passed over.

ii

Suddenly the announcement came for all passengers to proceed to the boarding platform and their assigned accommodations.

When everyone was onboard, imperceptibly, smoothly, and silently the great train began to move. It was only as they looked out their windows that the passengers realized that the train was moving. You could hear many completely surprised, persons calling out, "Look, we're moving."

As the train began to get up speed, the exciting realization spread. Passengers were saying, "We're moving. Look out there. We're moving."

The passengers were sharing this sudden awareness of the tremendous power moving this great train. It was the beginning of a series of experiences beyond their expectation that the passengers would share together. Two great engines, with their tremendous horsepower, were turning a hodgepodge of individuals from around the world into a community of fellow travelers. As the train, with its consist of over thirty passenger cars, began to gain speed, passengers heard the attendants swinging shut heavy doors.

One mother was telling her son, "This train is longer than the Empire State Building lying on its side. Imagine two engines pulling something the length of the Empire State building?"

The attendant, Lars, stopped by Hank's compartment. Lars shared more information about the Canadian. He explained, "This train's consist begins with two powerful diesel-electric locomotives, each with 3,200 horse power. To cross the continental divide in British Columbia, a third engine will be added in Edmonton. With these three engines this train will pass through the mountains of the continental divide at about 3000 feet."

Hank was impressed. "That totals about ten thousand hp."

Lars rattled off the types of coaches and sleeping cars. He described the dome observation cars and dining cars. "In our 32 cars we move 365 people and a crew of 43."

Emily and Joan met with Hank in the special lounge car at the end of the train. It was called the bullet car for its rounded shape, at the tail end of the train. It was a great place to visit together. The three of them were looking forward to their arrival in Winnipeg at the end of their second day, when Roger, travelling as Tom Murphy, would joint them.

iii

About a half hour out Toronto, passengers were surprised to suddenly feel the train slow down and finally come to a complete stop. A voice came over the sound system.. "The train is being stopped for a brief police inspection. Be assured that the train will soon be on its way."

Passengers could see that the train had been stopped in a very isolated area. Police vehicles surrounded the train and a small army of officers was boarding the train.

Further instructions came over the speakers. "This train is making a brief stop at the request of the Toronto police. We are asking all passengers to return to their assigned accommodations. Officers are boarding this train to carry out a necessary search. Pleases cooperate with the officers. This stop and search operation should take no more than an hour. The baggage of all on board will be inspected. The officers would not be here if there was not good reason for searching this train."

Many of the officers were heavily armed. Several men and women officers were assigned to each section of the train. They went through the baggage in all the compartments. Since on this train people keep their baggage with them in their compartments such an inspection took time.

The search apparently failed to find anything for which the officers were looking. There was one note of consolation in the final statement of the officers. "The agents found that one passenger had an extremely valuable painting which had recently been taken from a major Toronto Gallery."

iv

Hamu's confidence that any search would find nothing was confirmed. As planned, the pre-checked baggage in the baggage car, with tags dated prior to the great robbery, enjoyed immunity from the search.

When the train was on its way, Hamu met with his men in his compartment. He was furious. His men were surprised by his anger over the fact that this train was stopped for the search.

Their leader demanded, "Why was this particular train picked out for inspection? Yes, nothing was found. But I have a question. Of all trains out of Toronto today, how is it that this train was stopped for a search?"

One of the men said, "But nothing was found, professor."

Hamu said, "Yes, but only because we had taken special precautions. Yes, we still have the cash but only because we concealed it through the Advance Baggage Check-in."

Daoud said, "We are glad your wisdom devised such precautions, Professor."

Hamu said"Yes, but I have this question. They say that 50 trains a day move over 5,000 passengers in and out of Toronto every day. This train, this trans-Canada train, was known to be filled largely with tourists. The inspection of this train was not merely by chance. Officials had to have had some reason for hitting this train. Why was this train searched?"

The men were silent.

Hamu continued, "I'll tell you why. It was the work of a mole. Someone that knew of our plans to be on this train must have given the police reason to check this train."

Daoud asked, "What makes you so certain it was a mole?"

"Informing the police to stop this train had to be done by someone who had access to our most private decisions. If the police were advised to stop this train, it had to be by someone who knew what we were doing. ."

Finally Daoud spoke up. "But there remains one question. If this informer knew you would be on this train, and with you most certainly the cash, how is it that this person appears to have known nothing about where, due to your advance planning, the cash was actually concealed?"

Hamu nodded silently for a few moments. His anger cooled. "Interesting. Good thinking, Daoud. \Yes, it does appear that this informer's knowledge was limited. He knew of our plan to be on this train but he did not know of our earlier arrangement to conceal our treasure on this train. Interesting. The mole may be someone who came on the scene more recently."

CHAPTER 41

On board the Canadian, Sudbury, Ontario

"All the world's a stage
And all the men and women merely players."
– Shakespeare

While the great train with 300 passengers on board, was pulling out of Toronto, about two hundred miles to the north, in Sudbury, two future passengers were involved in a wedding. Local observers were wondering why the couple selected mid-morning for this event. This wedding had been planned for morning so that the couple could begin their wedding trip on board the great transcontinental train out of Toronto. After its early departure from Toronto, the train, was scheduled to make a stop at Sudbury about midday.

The small crowd of friends posing as wedding guests knew that the couple were really just playing the part. They had been married some years before. On this occasion they were posing as bride and groom to provide an explanation for their considerable baggage. A number of packages made to appear as wedding gifts held yellow pigs, the plastic shelled lead storage containers for radioactive material. Some pieces of baggage marked repeatedly as fragile contained well disguised components of an explosive device.

This wedding event was planned as cover to move the radio-active material stolen from the power station, as well as components of a sophisticated explosive device. Taking these items on board at Sudbury was planned to avoid inspection by police in the Toronto.

The wedding crowd gathered by the couple's considerable baggage to give the newlyweds a sendoff. When the train rolled into the Sudbury station their friends would be there to help the couple board with their considerable baggage. Sudbury had been selected for boarding the train because it was near where the stolen radio-active material had been concealed. Also the Sudbury police had no detectors for radio-active substance.

ii

The morning after the Sudbury stop, as the train rolled west, passengers were enjoying an excellent breakfast in the beautiful décor of the dining car. The train was now passing through the great forests and spruce bogs of northern Ontario. The passengers at breakfast were enjoying an exciting view of the great north woods through the wide dining car windows by their tables. An attendant pointed to the fact of few roads. He reminded people that there was really no way of viewing this country that surpassed travelling through the region by train.

At the far end of one of the dining car, a man in his mid-thirties was standing by the dinning car's beautiful etched glass entrance partition. The dining car manager, in the process of seating a couple at their table, held up his finger as a gesture to wait. The man standing at the entrance waved his hand as if to say, "OK, I'm in no rush." He seemed to enjoy just taking in all the activity and the splendor of the great train's dining car.

The passengers seated at their tables were enjoying breakfast with the constantly unrolling panorama of the northern forests and lakes. If these travelers, busy eating and conversing, looked up and took in this man waiting, they might have assumed that he was a business man quite accustomed to the luxury of train dining cars. Actually, in his native Egypt, Hamu had never experienced anything that came near the luxury of this train's dining car. As he waited to be seated, he was enjoying the atmosphere and the aroma of the train's dining car. He had only one problem. As an Egyptian, he was bracing himself for what these people called coffee.

This morning on this trip west, Hamu would be meeting the couple who had boarded at Sudbury. These Two Viper agents had never really never met real professor Fouad face to face. Hamu decided that it would be just as well if they continued to have no idea of how he really looked. In his meetings with them, he was being cautious. He was continuing to wear his wig and face mask.

There was another consideration in concealing his real appearance from the agents he would meet on this trip. If any of these agents should be taken into custody and were interrogated, they would be incapable of giving any clues to his appearance. He decided to use his facial life mask and wig in dealing with the agents he would meet on the train.

There was another reason for using the disguise on the train. He had no idea how much Roger Renoir's friends on this train knew about his appearance. To be on the safe side, he had decided to cover up his white hair and his white facial hair with a natural hair wig and his made to order latex life mask.

Finally, Hamu received the signal from the dining car manager, to come to a table. As he came to take his place at the table, Hamu brought his hand to his temple, exposing the tattoo on his wrist and saluted his agent, Daoud. Their eyes met for an instant, and the manager nodded. In reply, Daoud raised his hand in a light hearted salute that exposed his tattoo.

Hamu eased himself into his chair and was soon busy talking with the couple seated at this table. They told him all about their wedding in Sudbury and how they had boarded the train with much baggage. They were on their way west with a honeymoon stop in Jasper.

As Hamu picked up the menu, he managed to expose the small tattoo of two vipers on his wrist.

"The woman and her husband turned slightly to look at each other. They nodded and slowly positioned their hands in a way to expose the two vipers tattoo on their wrists.

After they had shared breakfast and visited together Hamu placed on the table his dining car seating card which showed his compartment. The young lady commented, "Oh you are in compartment "F". We are just a bit further at C."

Hamu said, "Perhaps you will join me in Compartment F for some good coffee later this morning."

The couple seemed very agreeable to a visit.

CHAPTER 42
Winnipeg station

*"A young man who wishes to remain a sound atheist
cannot be too careful of his reading."*
– C S Lewis - 1953

It was late afternoon and, in Winnipeg's historic station. A large crowd was waiting for the arrival of the great trans-continental train from Toronto. For the travelers this would be the end of their second day out of Toronto.

Among those waiting by for the great train by Winnipeg's pre-boarding lounge, were two men in well-worn western clothes. Their outdoor working clothes distinguished them from most city people around them. Their western boots and wide six inch brimmed Stetson hats reinforced the impression that these men had just come off the range.

Despite the news that Roger's enemy had cancelled his plans to be on this train, Roger and his painting friend, Bill Webber were being very cautious. Roger's cancelled reservation had been booked for a Tom Murphy in Winnipeg. With input from Hank, Emily had made a reservation was for Roger's painting friend, Bill Webber, to board the train as Bill Hunter.

As passengers began to pour off the train, Roger kept scanning the faces of the crowd for his team. When Roger spotted his friends he waved to get their attention. Finally the team spotted Roger and hurried to greet him.

Webber laughed. "You did a good job with your costume, Roger. Even your best friends weren't sure it was you."

As they exchanged hugs and greeting, Emily said, "This calls for a real one." She delivered her version of a real hug on Roger. Finally, Emily said, "I'm back to earth now. Roger, you didn't fool me for a minute. I was just being patient and waiting for Hank and Joan to recognize you."

Roger introduced Bill Webber. "I want you to meet a real water-colorist and very real friend, Bill Webber. During our trip you need to get used to calling him Bill Hunter. That's his ID for this trip. Bill was very helpful to me during my painting stop in Jasper. As Bill learned more about our concerns, he insisted on coming along with us as we head west. Bill has made our cause, his cause."

Bill said, "I'm be glad to be with you on this trip as backup.""

Hank said, "Welcome to the Lunatic Loonies, Bill. We're anxious to hear your full story, Roger. During those calls back and forth by Ham radio you never gave us the full story of where you were or why you were there."

Joan said, "Yes, Roger. You're going to have to bring us up to date. A lot has happened for all of us since you took off from Graf Zeppelin Airport."

Just then Albert and Sarah Weiss joined them. "Greetings, friends. Who are these western friends?" When Sarah Weiss realized the stranger was Roger, she was amused. "I think you have some stories to tell us, Tom Murphy."

Joan said, "Yes, but the stories are all too long to hear without food. Emily and I have already arranged for the dining car staff to set up a special table for us as soon as the train gets rolling again."

Roger and Bill got settled in their compartments. By the time the train was on its way again, the special table Joan had ordered in the dining car was available to the team.

The team had a lot of catching up to do. During their dinner together the team brought Roger up to date concerning things at the Toronto end.

Roger told them the story of his flight from Jasper. His friends were shocked to learn the details of how Roger parachuted from the plane. They were all impressed with his account of his parachute landing and rescue by Fred and Mary."

Emily said, "What were you thinking, when you saw Fred rappelled down, to you, out of nowhere, on that rope? It sounds, in more ways than one. like a gift from above."

Hank was amazed that this couple, the Christiansens, the only people living anywhere near the crash, saw Roger's plane going down and set out to find any possible survivor. When Hank heard how Fred calculated where any parachuter might have landed, Hank said, "Don't try to tell me that our Maker isn't personally concerned for his people. There's no other explanation of a story like yours, Roger."

Roger said, "There are a few more significant details. He went on to tell them how they found the wreckage of the plane and the powerful bomb they found on board. Roger described the events that worked to foil the plan to use him as a Kamikaze. He told them how the truck's dead battery put him a day behind schedules. He explained how the engine's failure, through loss of oil, prevented him from going on to destruction in Vancouver. This prevented him from dropping to the elevation where the bomb was designed to explode.

The team was stunned. Hank said, "In other words several events intervened to save you. A dead battery and a failed engine combined to literally save your life."

Roger explained that they later learned that the bomb explosion was controlled by an altimeter devise. "The bomb was programmed to explode as I brought the plane below one thousand feet to land in Vancouver.

'After taking off from Jasper at an altitude of 3,350 feet the failure of my engine in the mountains prevented flying on to descend to one thousand feet and destruction. I was never permitted to fly below five thousand feet. It was almost as though someone, who knew what was going on worked to preserve my life.".

Emily stared at him with tears flowing.

Albert Weiss took off his glasses, wiped his eyes and said, "Wunderbar! Wunderbar!"

Joan said, "This team has been preserved through some amazing events"

The team came to the conclusion that in view of the events they had come through they would post pone the planned camping side trip in Jasper. They decided to look forward to a special time together in Vancouver.

Albert and Sarah Weiss particularly enjoyed getting to know Bill Webber. Albert liked the story of Bill's scheme to leave a misleading map to the Canyon of No-return. Albert laughed and laughed. "Maybe they are still trying to get out of that canyon using your map."

Bill laughed. "Yes, and they have no compass."

Weiss said, "No compass? That is at the heart of many problems today. What is lacking today? Many men and women lack an inner compass to give direction for their lives. They will never find what they are looking for in life without the real Compass." Weiss pointed upward. "Like the North Star, He is our compass."

Roger said, "We figured that the men who rooted through our camp might have been looking for that special smart phone that I found at Bobcat Lake."

Hank replied, "You need to know that Emily's place was broken into and ransacked. The bad guys have that smart phone now!"

Roger was concerned. "You mean Mr. Dark Heart has that smart phone again?"

Hank said, "Yes, and I never got to edit out the addresses."

Emily tied the evens together. "You never got to Vancouver on the day the bomb was set to explode because your flight had been delayed by a dead truck battery. On that day you might have flown on to a lower altitude where the bomb would explode, you were kept in the mountains above 5,000 feet by an engine failure. Roger, it looks to me that you have a special unseen friend."

Roger said, "There is something else you need to know. We thought this man might be on this train with another explosive device for Vancouver."

Roger explained the plan and the arrangements to stop the train. However, from Hank's ham radio call, we learned that Mr. Dark Heart had cancelled his plan to be on this train, Fred and I came up with a great plan to spot and identify this man. We had the idea that we would confront the man with his own bomb ticking away."

Hank asked, "How did you plan to confront him?"

"Fred and I planned to stop the train by causing a landslide to go tumbling down on the tracks. In fact, we prepared trees cut and ready to be dropped down the mountain side to stop the train. We had the idea that when the train was stopped and passengers were allowed off the train, that our opponent would also leave the train with the passengers.

"We planned that he would spot the bomb pack that had been concealed in my plane. Curious, he would open the pack. Suddenly, the man who built that bomb and knew its power would find himself facing death from his own bomb.

He would see his timing devise clicking down toward explosion. He would know he was below 1,000 feet and the settings could not be changed. We were confident that his very visible reaction to the bomb would confirm his identity. Also, if he had brought on board the train an even more powerful bomb bomb, which this bomb would trigger, his reaction could be even more fearful."

Hank replied, "But surely you got our message before you left the cabin to meet us. You heard that this man cancelled his plan to be on this train."

"Yes, we got your message. Before I set out to meet you at Winnipeg, Fred and I put our plan on hold. I told Fred and Mary that this man we were looking for was not going to be on this train. We put all of our preparations on hold."

Hank asked. "But what if we learn that our Mr. Dark Heart deliberately misled us? What if we discover that he is on this train and with a second bomb for Vancouver? What if we want to activate your plan and stop this train? What then?"

Roger said, "There is no way to quickly contact Fred and Mary. No means of communication. No phone. In their old cabin Fred and Mary are living in the days of the Canadian gold rush.

CHAPTER 43
Winnipeg

"Surely what a man does when he is taken off his guard
Is the best evidence for what sort of man he is..."
– C S Lewis

During the train's stop in Winnipeg, as directed by Hamu, baggage containing a portion of the radio-active materials taken on board at Sudbury was being delivered to agents already in place in Winnipeg, Hamu then retreated to the isolation of his compartment. As he looked out over the down town area of this mid-Canadian city, the professor, as he was called, enjoyed taking stock of his efforts. I have placed the bomb in this key city. After I exist the train in Kamloops this train will roll on to deliver and explode the devise on board to Vancouver.

The bombs will be visible signs our power. Meanwhile our soft war, the less visible campaign, will continue to undermine this nation. We will support efforts like those working to suppress the voice of the Christians. We will create confusion in government. Through our support of groups like the Citizens Freedom Society, in both Canada and the United States, we will make the forgotten foundations increasingly forgotten.

Hamu checked his watch. The train would be in Winnipeg for another hour. He decided it was time to call Vashti. It was time to let her know that she must meet him in Kamloops. She has to get used to cooperating with me.

It is essential that Vashti plays her part convincingly. She must be seen as a wife whose husband was injured as a result of Israeli bombs.

Her support is essential as this impostor plays the part of her husband. We will not talk about the alternative. She must see that she really has no alternative.

He was reviewing his contacts with the woman. That first meeting went reasonably well. I delivered the message she feared most, confirmation that Fouad died during that bombing raid by the Israelis. She heard me tell her that I had witnessed the bombing that resulted in her husband's death. She seemed to accept me as someone who was interested in looking after her interests.

This woman, Vashti, is a shrewd woman. When I told her that she must play the part of the wife with a wounded husband, she seemed to understand the serious problem for me if she did not cooperate. She did not raise the question of what would happen if she did not support my impersonation of her husband. I think she knew that she would have to be removed from the scene.

Hamu flipped open the professor's wallet and looked at the professor's picture of his wife. She is a very attractive Egyptian woman. Who knows? Perhaps as she recovers from her husband's death she may want to continue this role playing. At some point she may want to do more than simply play the part of the wife of a man no longer living. She may want to take the place of the wife I lost also to western made weapons.

ii

When the phone rang, Vashti was startled to hear the voice of the impostor. If only this were Fouad calling.

"Vashti. This is the impostor, your surrogate husband, calling." He laughed. "I am on my way west again. I'm calling from Winnipeg. How are you feeling?"

"How am I feeling? How would expect me to be feeling? On your visit, you informed me that I was a widow, a woman whose husband was killed by an Israeli bomb.

"Then, you dropped a bomb on me. You explained that, for your protection and to end the pursuit of Interpol, you had exploited the strong resemblance between you and my dear Fouad. To end being a fugitive pursued by Interpol and Jewish Mossad agents. the world was told that it was you, Hamu, who had died and that the professor, Fouad, survived with injuries. Then you took on my dear husband's identity. You are impersonating Fouad. You escaped from Gaza and came to Canada on my dear husband Fouad's passport. How am I feeling? I'll tell you how I am feeling.

"You informed me that this woman, the woman who had just learned that her husband was blown to pieces by an Israeli bomb, had to help you. You insisted that I tell the world and live the lie that Fouad was only injured. You demanded that I support your impersonation of Fouad. You insisted that I tell the world that my dear husband is this man recovering in Toronto. How am I feeling? I'll tell you how I am feeling.

"Without putting it in words, you made it very clear that I had no option. I saw that if I wanted to go on living, there was no alternative. You made it clear that, for you to continue your escape from the endless pursuit of international police, I had to support the idea that the man people saw recovering from his injury was Fouad. How am I feeling? I'll tell you how I am feeling.

"This widow is expected to carry on this performance, to go around acting as though my dear husband was only injured by that Israeli bomb in Gaza City. And now you have the nerve to call and ask, how am I feeling? I'll tell you how I feel, I have had my fill of this whole charade."

"Vashti, I am calling to let you know that I am on the West bound transcontinental train. We are stopped at the Winnipeg.

"Vashti, I realize that I left you with a very difficult task. When I brought you the news of your husband's death, I couldn't soften the news. I realize that I made a very difficult request of you, a woman just told her husband had been killed. I asked you to go on acting as though your husband were alive, to make possible my impersonation of the professor."

Vashti let the phone be silent for a few moments. Then she replied. "When you demanded that I back up for your impersonation of my husband, you made it very clear that I had no choice. I have attempted to do what you demanded. I have answered the questions of friends as you directed. I have been living a lie. But you are not Fouad. You may look like him. You may carry his passport. But no one can step in the shoes of my Fouad!"

"Vashti, as I told you, I am on the West Bound Canadian. I am calling from Winnipeg where we are stopped to take on passengers. I am calling to inform you that I am going only as far as Kamloops. I will arrive in Kamloops in three days, Sunday evening, August 22."

"So, you are getting off at Kamloops? Why are you telling me?"

"My work for Two Vipers requires that I leave the train in Kamloops. I am asking you to meet me in Kamloops. It may be helpful for you to meet me at some distance from friends and associates. I am asking you to purchase a ticket on the East bound train leaving Vancouver early in the morning of Sunday the 22nd and arriving in Kamloops that evening. My West bound train will pull into Kamloops about two hours before your East bound train."

Vashti was startled and wondering what this man might be up to. "Why should I travel to Kamloops? If it is necessary for you to talk with me you can contact me, as you did the last time, here in Vancouver"

"Vashti, it is absolutely necessary for you to meet me in Kamloops. This is due to urgent matters that I cannot share on the phone. I have made reservations for each of us at the Royal Mountaineer Hotel. A room has been reserved for you, adjacent to my own."

"Did I hear you say that you have reserved a room for me? That sounds very improper. I am mourning my husband's death and you tell me that you have reserved a room for me? Who do you think you are? Has walking around with my husband's passport gone to your head? You may impersonate him but you are not Fouad."

"Vashti, it is necessary for you come to Kamloops. This is not an option?"

"Give me one reason why I should I travel to Kamloops to meet you? I have done all that I could do to meet your demands here in the university community. I have been living the lie. I told our associates that Fouad was in Toronto, recovering from injuries. I have provided the lies you demanded."

"I appreciate that, Vashti."

"Can you think of anything more difficult for a woman who loved her husband and lost him than pretending she is not a widow? Can you imagine what that takes? I have been dealing with the report you gave me that my dear Fouad was killed by Israeli bombs, I have been attempting to live the lie that my dear Fouad is alive. It is tearing me apart.

"This is as far as I go. I am certainly not going to rendezvous with you in Kamloops."

Hamu was not used to being talked to in this way, especially by a woman. Doesn't this woman have any sense at all? "Vashti, you must come to Kamloops! It is absolutely necessary!"

"And I suppose it is absolutely necessary that I take a room there adjacent to your own? No way!"

Hamu was furious, being talked to in this way by a woman. He was struggling to control himself. He was boiling.

He replied in blunt language. "As I told you, I cannot allow anyone to undermine my identity as the professor. Your role in maintaining the idea that Fouad survived the bomb, is crucial. This meeting in Kamloops is vital." His anger was growing.

"If you want to speak with me you will have to do so in Vancouver. I have no desire to travel to Kamloops. Why should I journey to meet you in Kamloops? Why don't you stay on your train to Vancouver?"

Hamu was not used to any one telling him what to do. He was repeating to himself her stubborn words. Her refusal to cooperate triggered his anger. He yelled into his phone, "Why don't I stay on the train to Vancouver? Why? I'll tell you why! Because neither this train nor the people on it are ever going to arrive in Vancouver."

He shouted, "No one now on this train is ever going to reach Vancouver alive! They'll be blown to pieces!"

Hamu stopped! As soon as the words were out of his mouth he put his hand to his mouth. He stopped himself. What am I doing? That was the wrong thing to say. I've just blown away a major secret.

Hamu quickly changed his tone. "Vashti, disregard what I said. Of course the train is going to get to Vancouver." He attempted to laugh. I was just blowing off steam."

He forced himself to laugh. "Pardon my wild language. I was trying to get across to you that it is absolutely necessary for you to meet me in Kamloops. Also, it may be easier for you to appear as someone whose husband is recovering from injuries if we meet some distance from your home."

Vashti remained silent. She said to herself, I know what I heard. This man said something he never intended to say. He exploded and yelled at me in anger. He said that that no one on this train will make it to Vancouver. He was furious with anger when he let loose that's storm of words. Boiling with anger, he let it slip. This man plans to destroy that train and everyone on it. I learned long ago that anger brings out what a person is really thinking.

Vashti quickly reviewed what she had heard.. He let it out. He has a bomb on that train. He is going to blow that train to pieces with all its passengers. No one on this train will reach Vancouver. It is a terrible thought. This man, in his anger, has just exploded with his plan to destroy that train. That's why he plans to exit the train in Kamloops?

Vashti pressed her finger on her phone and ended the call. The call was ended but her anguish and fear was boiling. This man is filled with evil. He is out of control. Someone has to inform the authorities. This man's madness has to be stopped.

iii

After hanging up, Vashti's face was drawn into an intense frown. She held her head in her hands. She was struggling with the terrible revelation that had been dumped on her. In an explosion of anger, this man has let it out that he is actually planning to destroy that train and all its passengers. . His plan to exit from the train at Kamloops, the last stop before Vancouver, confirms in actual planning what his outburst reveals.

His effort to get me to go to Kamloops carries the same message. He has just let out that he has a powerful explosive device on that train. This man is getting off at Kamloops for one reason, for his own life. With his demand that I meet him in Kamloops was he assuming he could take me with him? Adjacent rooms reserved? Does he have the illusion that I might be attracted to such a man?

I may be the only person who knows what he intends to do? He must be stopped. But how? If only Fouad were here.

I have to get this information to the right people and fast. That train must be stopped. Who is going to listen to a woman crying out that a great train with three hundred people is about to be blown to pieces? If only I knew someone on that train. i need some help. Vashti picked up the phone to call her most trusted friend.

iv

Hamu returned to his compartment very unhappy.
Hamu you have made a terrible blunder with your big mouth. This
woman knows everything. Fortunately she is a woman. Who is going
to listen to some excited woman? No one will take her seriously.

After leaving Winnipeg the train continued on its way to Edmonton.
There another of Hamu's agents proceeded to exit with some of the
radioactive material brought on board the train by the agents posing
as newlyweds in Sudbury.

After allowing time for new passengers to board the train in
Edmonton, a third diesel electric locomotive was added to the train.
The additional third locomotive was coupled to the front of the lead
engine. The third locomotive was added to power the train for the
climb through the Canadian Rockies to Jasper and on to Kamloops
and Vancouver.

The train soon began making good use of the added power of the
third engine as it headed into the mountains and across the continental
divide to Jasper.

CHAPTER 44

Jasper, British Columbia

"Readers are advised to remember that the devil is a liar."
– C. S. Lewis

As the great transcontinental train continued on from Edmonton, the great consist of over thirty cars was now powered by three diesel-electric locomotives to cross the challenge of Canadian continental divide. Now, as the train made its way toward Jasper, the passengers were enjoying the spectacular grandeur of the largest National Park in the Canadian Rockies. People stayed by their windows. Some were hoping to spot mountain goats or mountain sheep at salt licks. Shortly before reaching Jasper the train passed through a 735 foot tunnel.

The train's fourth day out of Toronto ended with an overnight stop in Jasper, so that the passengers would be passing through the spectacular scenery of the mountains by day. On this trip, rather than spending the night, as usual, in local Jasper hotels, the passengers would be staying in their accommodations on the train. For many passengers, staying in their compartments on the train for the overnight Jasper stop was very appealing. There was no need to move baggage to hotels. The passengers could visit the shops and other points of interest in Jasper and return to spend the night on board the train.

One passenger, leaving the train to see the Jasper sights, was a man noted by some of his fellow travelers for his Irish tweed clothing. When this man, sometimes referred to as Mr. Tweed, joined the passengers leaving the train, he headed for a fast food restaurant. He bought a takeout meal and took it to an outdoor table that was a good distance from other customers. He looked around to make sure other passengers were some distance from him and took out his smart phone. The man referred to as Mr. Tweed closed his eyes for a few moments and then made a phone call.

That same evening, two train travel days west of Mr. Tweed at his table in Jasper, on the coastal side of the Canadian Rockies, in Vancouver, sitting out at a table in her back patio, Vashti was enjoying the last hours of the evening, She smiled as she thought of many special times here on this patio with her husband, Fouad. Vashti was remembering that day when, here on the patio, they had received that letter inviting Fouad to return as a guest lecturer back in Cairo, that journey from which he never returned.

As Vashti looked off toward the spectacular sunset that was deepening over Vancouver, she was deeply aware of how much she was missing her husband, Fouad. Thinking of Fouad, she silently called to mind that Scripture defining marriage which her Canadian friends often quoted. Vashti was fond of that description of the Creator's wonderful purpose in marriage. She had been told that this description of marriage was repeated three times in the Scriptures. Vashti softly mouthed the words to herself. "For this reason a man shall leave his father and mother, and shall cleave to his wife, and the two shall become one flesh." Then she was saying half aloud to herself, "One, yes, very much one."

As she was running those words through her mind Vashti was thinking how God had shown His loving purpose for them, in the wonderful life she and Fouad had enjoyed in their marriage, since coming to Vancouver. The memory of the life they enjoyed together was very meaningful to her in her loneliness.

It was now two days since the imposter's terrible outburst, in that call from Winnipeg. That train must be in the area of Jasper. Vashti was still in turmoil over that call. She continued to struggle with the burden of knowing what she had learned in that call.

She had gone to work immediately to make this deadly danger known to the railroad police. She had described this man who was impersonating her late husband. She explained that this man had a powerful bomb on board the great train as it continued on toward Vancouver. She got absolutely nowhere. The way no one took her warning seriously was very upsetting.

Vashti had assumed all she would have to do was to warn the railroad authorities of this great danger. She expected them to take immediate steps to prevent this catastrophe. Nothing of the sort happened. She was repeatedly told that her information was insufficient for action. No one with the power to act was inclined to take her warning seriously.

After repeatedly unsuccessful efforts, Vashti was getting more desperate. She was feeling the pain of being alone with this burden. She found herself prayerfully saying aloud, "If only Fouad were here. Fouad would find a way or make a way."

Vashti picked up an old copy of their Egyptian newspaper. She read again the report of the Israeli attack on Gaza City. She shook her head as she read again the gruesome details of a direct hit by an Israeli bomb on that guest house where Fouad was staying. The account told how rescue workers had moved the injured and unconscious professor from the ruins of the guest house to a vehicle for transport to Cairo for medical care.

That report of injury had given her hope. It had all been so misleading. She now realized that this confusion was related to Hamu's plot to take on the identity of his look alike, Fouad. They made it look like it was Hamu who had been killed by the bomb. The confusing report that Fouad was only injured was made so that Hamu could begin his impersonation of Professor Fouad.

Vashti read the article again. "The physician gave his report on his examination of the professor to a man named Rachti. He was to drive the injured Professor to Cairo for medical care." "Rachti," she exclaimed aloud. She hadn't caught that name before. Rachti drove Fouad to Cairo! We knew Rachti and his wife well. If only I had some way to reach them. They would tell me more about what happened."

Vashti buried her face in her hands and wept. If only the Savior could visit me as he did those grieving women long ago."

Suddenly the phone on the patio table rang. She picked up the phone. "Hello."

"Vashti! It's Fouad."

"Fouad? Who do you think you are? You may be impersonating my husband, but don't you think for a moment you can start calling yourself by his name when you talk to me. I will not tolerate your calling yourself Fouad." She cut off the call.

The phone rang again. She debated whether to answer. With anger she picked up the receiver. "This has got to stop."

"Vashti." Then, with words and a voice she had not heard for so long, the voice said, "Vashti, my greatest blessing. This is your husband. This is Fouad."

"Fouad!" She broke down in tears. "Is it true? Is it really you?"

"Yes, and I have much to tell you. But first, are you alone? Can I speak to you freely knowing no one else could hear us?"

"Oh, Fouad! Yes, I am sitting here alone out on our patio. I have been praying ever since you left, that somehow, as our Christian friends put it, God would be holding you in the hollow of His hand. Where are you?"

"Vashti, I am back in Canada. I am not very far from you. I am traveling on the great Canadian transcontinental train. The train has stopped here in Jasper. I'm calling you from Jasper. I am seated at a picnic table in Jasper. I am only two days from Vancouver. I will be with you in Vancouver, in two days."

"Oh, Fouad! It is impossible to tell you what it means to hear your voice. I have to tell you, Fouad, a deceitful man, a man looking like your twin brother, came here to see me. He said he came from Cairo to tell me that you had died of your injuries in Cairo. But it was a lie. You are alive. You are alive. Praise God for His goodness!"

"Vashti, I regret deeply that you heard nothing from me until now. Complete secrecy that I had survived a plot to kill me was necessary. It was required to preserve both my life and yours. My silence was also necessary to protect those who risked their lives to save me."

"Fouad, hearing nothing was terrible. Then to be given the lie that you had died! But that is all gone with the joy of hearing your voice."

"Vashti, I could not call you before this. The concern was not only for my own security and the safety of those helping me. It was also for you. You were in a very difficult situation. If you knew I was alive and it leaked out the consequences would have been disastrous. For your own protection and the safety of myself and my helpers I had to just disappear and allow those who planned my death think they had succeeded. Those who carried out the elaborate plot to kill me had to go on believing they had been successful."

"Fouad. How wonderful to hear your voice!"

"Vashti, you were right in your concern about my trip to Cairo. There was more than hostility. I landed in the midst of a plot to get rid of me."

"What were they planning to do?"

"When the Two Vipers leader in Gaza City learned how closely Hamu and I resembled each other, Hamu got the idea of using our very close similarity in appearance to help him escape the endless pursuit of international police.

"The idea was to lure me back to Cairo. That was the purpose of the letter we received. When they got me to visit Gaza City, the plan was to arrange for my death. They would use my body to convince Interpol that it was not the visiting professor, Fouad, but Hamu who had died."

"Their plan was to have me killed during an especially provoked Israeli air attack. An explosion planted in the guest house and detonated during the Israeli attack would make it appear that an Israeli bomb had killed me. The plan was to use my look alike body to convince the police that it was their notorious fugitive, Hamu, who had died in the Israeli attack. They promoted the idea that the visiting professor was only wounded. This way Hamu could then take over my ID."

Vashti said, "So, the fears of my woman's intuition were well founded."

"Yes, very much so, Vashti. It all started with that letter inviting me to give the lectures in Cairo. It was a death letter. It was part of their cunning to lure me back to Cairo. After the lectures I would be invited to Gaza City."

"Yes, I worried about your going to Gaza City.

"To encourage me to visit Gaza City they arranged for our old friend Rachti to drive me to Gaza. But even while we were driving to Gaza City, their scheme was in process."

"While Rachti was driving you from Cairo?"

"Yes. The plan was for them to provoke an Israeli attack that night by a vicious rocket on Israel that very afternoon, While Rachti was driving me to Gaza, we heard he report of the rocket attack taking place. They were confident that the Israelis would retaliate that night. They did. They launched a terrible bombing attack."

"And the reason for provoking the Israelis?"

"Cover for my murder. During the anticipated Israeli bombing attack they planned to kill me by exploding a bomb planted in the guest house where I was sleeping. The heart of the scheme was to use the Israelis bombing raid as a smoke screen for my murder by their explosive device. They even used seized Israeli type explosives to destroy me, in the guest house. It was planned as the perfect crime. Who was going to investigate the Israelis?"

"So, the Israeli attack was cover for the bomb in the guest house?"

"Yes. Their cunning included a further deception. When my look alike body was recovered it was to be clothed to look like Hamu and be identified as the body of their leader, Hamu. They led everyone, officials and international police to see this as the death of Hamu.

Vashti said, But how did they keep people thinking that you, Professor Fouad survived?"

Fouad said, "To represent me, the supposedly injured professor, they used a dummy seated in Rachti's car. The dummy was dressed like me in western clothing and wrapped in bandages. People were told that this bandaged person in the car was the injured professor. This dummy was to represent me as injured but still alive."

"How did they come up with such a scheme?"

"Over the years, Hamu, and I had unknowingly come to look increasingly very much like each other. Someone gave Hamu a photo of me to show him how much Hamu and I had come to resemble each other. The two of us, in addition to our very similar facial features, had developed white hair and white beards. We looked like identical twin brothers. Hamu came up with the idea to exploit this striking identical appearance to help him escape the pursuit of Interpol."

"And what happened to the dummy that represented you?"

Fouad said, "The dummy in car that represented the injured professor being driven back to Cairo for medical help. The car contained all my personal things. All my personal things were essential to enable Hamu to present himself as the professor. Hamu, was going to assume my identity. He planned to use my passport and ticket home to escape the police in the Middle East and gain entrance to Canada.

"Hamu concealed himself at my visiting professor's apartment in Cairo. When Rachti arrived at the apartment with the dummy and all my personal things, my wallet, personal papers, my rings and other personal items, the dummy disappeared and Hamu took over my identity. A day later, the impersonator, dressed in my clothing and using my passport, flew from Cairo to London and then on to Toronto."

Vashti said, "And then this man, the man who arranged for your death, thinking he had succeeded, had the nerve to come here to visit me. The man behind this plot to kill you came here and told me how sorry he was to inform me that my husband had died of Israeli inflicted injuries."

Vashti held her head in her hands.

Fouad said, "Vashti, it was necessary to let the deceiver go on thinking he had succeeded. The impostor was not lying in one regard. As this man who looked like me was telling you that your husband was dead, he actually believed that I was dead.

"He believed that the body pulled out of the bombed building was my body. It was absolutely necessary for my survival and those risking their lives help me that this plotter go on believing, for the present, that it was indeed my body they had dragged out of the ruins and used to convince the police that Hamu was dead.'

Vashti responded. "So, while this man, Hamu, was deceiving the police he himself was being deceived by you and your friends. Amazing. Fouad, as our Christian friends here would put it, God, in his great love held you in the hollow of His hand."

Vashti paused and wiped her eyes. "He kept you in His hiding place." After a moment, when she could speak again she asked, "How, Fouad? How did He do it?"

Fouad said, "How? Vashti, the answer is through some of his people, some brave and loving friends. They put love and friendship above self. It's a story in itself. I'll have to tell you when we get together. As of now, the impostor has no idea that I am alive. For now we must keep it that way."

Fouad paused in his phone call for a moment. Then he said, "We had to keep you in the dark, for another reason."

"There was another reason why you delayed calling me?"

"Yes, Vashti There was another reason why I could not let even you know I was alive. My impersonator finally realized he had made the incredible mistake of forgetting that the professor had a wife. With that realization, a problem suddenly hit the impostor. If this woman tells people that her husband died, it will be impossible for me to be concealed by impersonating the man.

"Vashti, the fact that the victim, had a wife became a real problem for the impersonator. If he was going to impersonate me, you, the dead man's wife, would have to convince folks that she was not a widow. She had to be persuaded to tell people that her husband was alive and undergoing recovery.

"It hit Hamu that this widow would have to cooperate. And for here to cooperate she will have to realize there was no alternative. You realized this and responded very wisely."

"Fouad, this man made it clear that I had no choice but to cooperate. Although he never expressed it in words I was made to realize that if I did not support his impersonation, I might have to be silenced."

"Vashti, you were given an almost impossible assignment. This was another reason why it was necessary that I delayed letting you know I was alive. This role playing would have been even more difficulty if you knew the full story."

"What a terrible death plot. Fouad. What gave this man such a dark heart?"

"Vashti, Hamu's bitter hatred of the West goes back to his father's bitter hatred of our Egyptian ruler, Sadat, who, after the six day war made peace with Israel. I have learned that, as a boy, Hamu actually saw his own father captured as one of the officers who shot down the Egyptian ruler Sadat. Later in battles with Israel, Hamu's wife was killed, as he would say, by weapons from the West."

Vashti said, "Your story of his early years helps me see, to some extent, the source of Hamu's anger here in Canada. But, Fouad, I sense there is also something missing in this man's story. It appears that there is something in his story that he never experienced. It looks like this man never experienced what we have experienced in our lives, since coming here, that special gift of unconditional love.

"Fouad, there's something else I have to tell you. This is something hard to explain over the phone. However, it cannot wait until you reach Vancouver. Just two days ago I learned that this man, the impostor, this man who still assumes his murder plot went as he planned, this man who thinks you are dead, is on your train."

Fouad was stunned for a moment. He said "Vashti, this is a matter of great concern for us. We had been expecting this man on our train. Then we learned that he had cancelled the plan to be on our train. This is very important for us. He is on our train? How do you know he is on our train?"

"Fouad, this man carrying your Canadian passport called me two days ago from Winnipeg, where the train had stopped. Both of you, the murder planner and you, his supposed victim, are on the very same train."

Fouad said, "Vashti, this is very critical information for us on the train. You say he called you from Winnipeg? Vashti, why would he let you, know that he was on the train?"

" He insisted that my meeting him in Kamloops was a necessary part of my acting as though my husband were alive."

"What did you say?"

"I said I was not meeting him in Kamloops.

"The more I refused to join him in Kamloops, the more his anger increased. Finally, he exploded in anger. He said that he was not asking me to meet him in Kamloops. He was directing me to meet him in Kamloops. He said that he had made reservations for me of us at the Royal Mountain hotel. A room had been reserved for me adjacent to his room.

"I told him that I was mourning my husband's death. Reserving a room for me was very improper,"

"On the phone I could feel his anger growing. Again he said that I had to meet him in Kamloops. When I refused again, he yelled that was not an option."

"I told him one more time that I was not going to meet him in Kamloops.

"That did it. He exploded in anger. It was like fireworks going off. He yelled at me, 'You want to know why can't I stay on the train to Vancouver? I'll tell you why! This train is never going to reach Vancouver. No one on this train is going to reach Vancouver! He paused. Then he roared at me. As this train pulls into Vancouver, everyone on this train will be blown to pieces!

"Then he stopped. He stopped cold. It was hitting him what he had done. He had revealed his entire evil plan. There was a moment of absolute silence. Then just as quickly he changed his tone. He laughed loudly and said that he was sorry. He told me that the train was going to Vancouver but that I must meet him at Kamloops.

"I was knocked for a loop. I was stunned. I knew what I had heard. In that burst of anger, this man had let fly something he never intended to say. I discovered long ago that truth rides on anger. When he exploded and shouted, in burning anger, that no one on this train was ever going to make it to Vancouver, I realized that he was clearly yelling the truth. It was his uncontrollable anger that triggered the explosive revelation that everyone would be blown to pieces.

"He, of course, quickly changed his tone. He immediately tried to cover up what had slipped out. I was no fool. I knew how anger brings out what a person is really thinking.

"I ended the call. I just sat here shocked by what I had heard. This character is set to destroy the great train with all its passengers."

Fouad was silent for a moment. He was stunned with what his wife was telling him. Vashti's revelation confirmed the fact that, despite all the talk to the contrary, the impersonator was on the train and travelling with a deadly bomb.

"Fouad replied, "Vashti, you have just given to all of us on this train, a terrible warning. We have been traveling with deliberately given misinformation. We had come to believe that he was not on this great train."

Vashti said, "Now that I know you are on the same train, it is all the more frightening. His plan to leave the train at Kamloops, that last stop before Vancouver, confirms the fact that he is planning to destroy this train at Vancouver."

"What have you done to inform railroad officials?"

"I immediately called the Vancouver train police. I told them about this terrible man and his plan to destroy the train. They asked for his name. I said that I didn't know by what name he travelled. Then they wanted to know where I got this information. When I said that I heard it from his own lips, they asked again for his name. I had to admit that I did not know his real name. When I told them he was impersonating my husband there was a long silence. I could hear two people talking about me off line. Then they began to treat me with condescension. I began to sense that they thought I was mentally confused."

"Then what? What was their response?"

"The more I talked the worse it got. Finally, this officer told me to call them when I had more specific information."

"Vashti, it is understandable that hearing something like this over the phone would sound unbelievable to those men. When I hang up here in Jasper I will go immediately to the Jasper office of the train police.

Fouad said, "I will insist that the police investigate this matter. This train must not leave Jasper until this man and his bomb are located. I have to end our call now. I must hurry. I have much to do. Love. Much love."

After she hung up Vashti sat there enjoying the afterglow of the thrilling call. Those lonely hurting days are past. Fouad is alive. Thank you, God, for such a miraculous gift? You are alive. You live with us."

As she thought of her prayers for Fouad, it suddenly hit Vashti that what matters is not the strength with which we pray so much as the great love and power of the one to whom we pray.

Vashti enjoyed looking back on the wonderful life changing call from Fouad. What a contrast to that earlier call of hatred and anger from the man who had purposed to destroy her Fouad.

Vashti found herself praying, "I pray that as you changed our lives and cast out such hatred in us, that you will turn around and change this angry man who plotted to kill Fouad. I pray that the same power that thwarted and overcame this evil plan to kill Fouad will overcome the evil plan of this man to destroy this train. Open his eyes and turn him from the darkness of hatred to a life filled with the knowledge of your unconditional love."

In Jasper, after Fouad closed the call with Vashti, he remained sitting there at his Jasper picnic table. He was stunned by what his wife had just told him. This man is prepared to leave the train in Kamloops. He will abandon 300 passengers and crew to total destruction in Vancouver. What a deadly enemy.

Fouad found himself repeating that word enemy. Enemy? That's what he is, an enemy. Then he laughed. The word enemy reminded him how their Christian friends often repeated those words of Jesus, love your enemies. love those who hate you. He found himself saying aloud, "Enemies? Even enemies like this one?"

Is God telling me to forgive an enemy like Hamu? This man ordered my death, simply to use my look alike body to convince international police that he was dead. It is only by using some special people that my Creator God kept me alive. This enemy took steps to get rid of me and to steal my identity. It sounds like he was thinking of stealing my wife. And I could overcome something like that?

Vashti says, he is on our train. Despite my unsuccessful efforts to find him on the train, Vashti informs me that the man is on the train and with a powerful bomb.

Fouad sat at his Jasper picnic table for a while. I've followed this cunning schemer and impostor from Cairo to Toronto. Now, Mr. Tweed, you have another job to do. Somehow, you must persuade the people here in Jasper to stop this train.

CHAPTER 45

Jasper

"We shall fight on the beaches,
we shall fight on the landing grounds,
we shall fight in the fields and in the streets,
we shall fight in the hills;we shall never surrender."
– Winston Churchill, 1940

While many of the great train's passengers were still out on the town in Jasper, the man many referred to as Mr. Tweed was making his way to the Jasper railway station office. With anxiety he hurriedly entered the station office and approached the young officer on duty..

The officer on duty said, "What can we do for you, sir?"

"I'm a passenger on the trans-Canada train leaving Jasper in the morning. I'm here to inform you of a serious danger that threatens the train and its passengers."

"May I see your passenger's ticket confirmation, sir?"

The passenger handed the officer his train ID.

"Mr. Hughes, good to have you on board. What can we do for you?"

"I want to report a serious danger that threatens our train and everyone on board."

The officer frowned and looked intently at the passenger facing him. "A danger? You wish to report that some danger may threaten our train?"

"Not may threaten. Threatens. You and those in charge need to know that a very serious danger threatens the passenger travelling on our train. A man with a concealed and very powerful explosive device is travelling on our train. This bomb is designed to explode and destroy the train and its passengers, as the train enters Vancouver."

The eyebrows of the young man at the desk arched. "Are you telling me that you think someone has a bomb on board our train? Would you please repeat that, sir?"

"Yes. That's why I am standing here. I have come to inform you, and those in charge, that there is a man traveling on the big train with an explosive device. This device is on board to destroy this train along with many passengers."

The attendant turned and looked for help from his superior, the officer in charge. Turning back to the passenger the attendant said, "A bomb on board? That's a rather serious matter, if true."

The passenger pressed his lips together for a moment and then replied, "What do you mean, if true? Why do you think I am standing here?"

For a few moments, the attendant simply stared at the passenger.

The man bringing the warning pounded his fist on the counter. "This situation is, as they say, a clear and present danger. To prevent a great catastrophe, preventive steps must be taken immediately. There is a passenger on board with a bomb. He must be found and apprehended before this train leaves Jasper."

The young attendant said, "Sir, that's very hard to believe."

The passenger said, "Of course, That's why I am standing here. You must get this warning to your superiors, fast."

The senior officer moved closer to hear what was going on. Finally, he took control of the situation. "I hear you talking of someone traveling on our train with some sort of explosives."

The man in tweeds said, "He's not travelling with fireworks. Many passengers could die. Your railway police must deal with this situation before the train pulls out of Jasper."

The officer said, "Please identify this man. Here is the list of all passengers on board. Please identify this person? Point out this person's name?"

The visitor shook his head. "A list of passengers is not going to help. Do you think that such a person would be travelling under his actual name? No, of course not. Anyone about to commit such a crime has to be travelling, under a fictitious identity. To find and identify this man, armed officers will have to search the train."

The evening visitor to the railway office looked very intently at the two officers. He was wondering how to help them realize the gravity of the situation? Finally, he said, "The situation demands immediate action. Israel's Mossad men are looking for this man. He is widely sought by international police. He will be taking every possible means to conceal his identity on this train.

"Ever since this train pulled out of Toronto, four days ago, I have been searching the train to determine if this man is on board. I am very familiar with his appearance. The fact that even I have not spotted him does not mean he is not on the train. It may simply indicates that he is very well disguised."

The officer in charge said, "Sir, if you, someone who apparently knows the man, after four days of looking for him on the train, have not seen him, what makes you so sure that he is really on our train?"

The passenger was silent for a moment. "Good question. How am I so sure this man is even on the train? I'll have to tell you.

"About an hour ago, I spoke on the phone with someone in Vancouver who confirmed that this man is on our train. My contact in Vancouver actually talked by phone with this bomb builder two days ago, while the train was stopped in Winnipeg. During that phone call, this man boasted how his powerful bomb would blow this train off the track as it pulled into Vancouver. Furthermore, I learned something else that confirms the plan to destroy the train as it approaches Vancouver. This man with the bomb is scheduled to leave the train at Kamloops, the last stop before Vancouver."

The officer shook his head. "Sir, this information is all third hand. You say that someone in Winnipeg spoke to someone in Vancouver who told you, someone here in Jasper, that there is a man on board with a bomb. For something like this we cannot rely on second or third hand reports. We can't stop this train on hearsay. We need to see some hard evidence before we do something like stopping a great transcontinental train like this with 300 passengers.

"We need something specific. For example, something like a picture or a passport. We have to know of whom we are talking. That raises a good question. Is it possible that this man you're talking about carry a passport? Something like that would be helpful. You say you know this man. Do you know if he carries a passport?"

The passenger smiled and said, "As a matter of fact, I do know." Yes, he very definitely carries a passport. He carries a Canadian passport."

The officer said, "Great. Now we're getting somewhere. You say that this man carries a passport. I don't know how you could know this, but it might help if we had the name on that passport."

To their surprise, the train agents heard the passenger reporting the danger give a quick to reply. The man in tweeds said, "No problem. Yes, he carries a passport. I am very familiar with the passport this man carries. The name on his passport is Fouad. He used this Canadian passport to enter Canada. He is using this passport to impersonate a Professor Fouad. This man with the bomb is not Professor Fouad. He is not the person indicated on the passport."

The officer stared at the passenger. "I'm really confused. You came here, to the railroad office, insisting that we locate a man with a bomb on our train. You tell me that you know he carries a Canadian passport. Not only that. You happen to know the name on his passport, Fouad. Now, you tell us that the person with the passport is not the man whose picture is on the passport. How could this man whose picture is on the passport have come to hold a false passport?"

The passenger in tweeds smiled. "How could he come to carry this false passport? Simple. The way anyone does. He stole it. He is able to gets away with this stolen passport because he looks exactly like the picture on the passport. With this passport he is able to impersonate a Professor Fouad. But he is not the real Professor Fouad."

The railroad officer was silent for a few moments. Finally he asked, "How do you know that he is not the person identified on the passport? How do you know he is not Professor Fouad?"

Their visitor in tweeds smiled, "Because I happen to be the real Professor Fouad."

For a moment there was a dead silence. Fouad saw the look on the faces behind the counter. He was getting no further with these agents of the railroad than Vashti was with the Vancouver agents.

The lead officer closed his eyes for a moment and then opened them. "Mr. Hughes or Professor Fouad, or whoever you are. Your story is getting more confusing all the time.

"You claim there is a dangerous man on this train who is set to destroy our train. You say that you have no idea under what name he may be travelling. Then you tell us he carries a passport. You say the name on the passport is Professor Fouad. but he is not Professor Fouad. You say that you ae professor Fouad.

The officer was silent for a moment. Finally he said, "Our railroad officials here in Jasper would have a hard time swallowing your story.

"Mr. Hughes, or Professor Hughes, or whoever you are, you say that there is a man on this train who is planning to destroy this trains. But your information is rather confusing.

"We have asked you to identify this man that you are talking about. Describe the man. Give us his name? You tell us that you have no idea under what name he is travelling or what he may look like. You suggest he may be travelling with some sort of disguise. Then you tell us that he carries a passport. You even give us the name on the passport, Fouad. But then you tell that is really a stolen passport. Finally, you say that you are that Professor Fouad.

"Mr. Hughes, you have us completely confused, You have come with a serious charge. You claim that a passenger has brought powerful explosives on this train. Yet, you have given us no clear information to go on. We cannot stop a great train like this with three hundred international passengers to go on a wild goose hunt.

The office said, "Sir, we cannot stop this train of three hundred people on the unsubstantiated word of one passenger who says that there might be a bomb on this train. If there were such a bomb on board, we would stop the train."

Fouad interrupted, "If there were such a bomb? What do you mean, if there were? There is a bomb on board this train. This train and all its passengers are in serious danger. Your train management must stop this train and get the people off until this man and his bomb are removed. You must act now."

The officer turned to his associate, raised his eyebrows and shook his head. Both looked at each other and rolled their eyes

Finally the lead officer said, "Sir, we get all sorts of wild stories on this train. To launch an investigation of the train, such as you request, we have to have more definite information. There are three hundred people on this train. We have to know for whom and for what we are looking. We need names and specific information."

"Mr. Hughes, I will walk back with you to the train. I will inform the attendants about your complaint. If you have further information, inform your attendants, they will contact us."

The officer came around the counter. The officer took hold of this man they considered s rather confused and escorted him back to the train.

At the train the officers spoke to two attendants. "This is Mr. Hughes. He is concerned that someone on this train may have some sort of explosive device on board. We told M. Hughes that if he has any further specific information he is to share with attendants like yourselves and through you the conductor."

ii

_____

Fouad found that the two train attendants seemed more interested his story than the men in the office. One attendant introduced himself, "I'm Lars. You're saying that there might be some dangerous explosive on board the train?"

"I didn't say there might be. There is someone is on this train with a powerful explosive device. This man and his bomb need to be located fast."

The other attendant said, "We will be glad to help you get to the bottom of your concern. Who is this man you say has an explosive device?"

"I have no idea what name he is using. I can't describe him because he may be wearing a disguise of some sort."

The attendant, Lars, said, "We will be glad to help you. May I see your voucher, sir?" He examined the card and said, "We will be glad to escort you to your compartment, Mr. Hughes." One of them immediately took him by the arm and led the way.

As they passed along to another railway car, Fouad was uneasy with the way he was being led to the next car. They stopped at a compartment F.

Fouad said, "This is not my compartment. My compartment is farther down."

"Yes, we know. There is someone here that may help you with your concern." They knocked.

When the door swung open, Fouad found himself confronting several attendants in train uniform.

The attendant escorting Fouad said, "This is Mr. Hughes. We were told by the Jasper officers that he has the idea that someone has a bomb on board the train."

Fouad realized that he must be standing in Hamu's command center on the train. It was a good thing that they regarded him as a bit mixed up. Then he realized something. These men are new recruits. They never knew me. Great! My life depends on keeping things that way. If Hamu discovers who I am, I'm a dead man.

Fouad was growing concerned that they might see that he was wearing a life mask. Was it too much to hope that they would not spot the mask? That would be fatal. But they have no reason to look for a mask. You never see what you are not looking for. These men have no reasons to think I am anything more than a mixed up tourist.

One of the men took charge of the situation. "Mr. Hughes, the men say that you are worried that someone on this train might have a bomb. Where did you get such an idea?"

Fouad saw the question as an opportunity. "Where did I hear such talk? Same place everyone did. Didn't you hear about it? That guy who came on board in Winnipeg was talking about a bomb. He kept going on about bombs. It made me nervous. So, I was telling the men in the Jasper office what I heard."

Fouad was amazed how they seemed to swallow his story. Some laughed. He kept silent. These young guys had swallowed the line about the dining car loud mouth.

Their leader stood there silently for a moment and then said, "Mr. Hughes, we can't have you going up and down this train upsetting passengers with bomb talk. We'd like you to share this concern with one of our more informed officers. We often use the isolation of the baggage car to meet with people like yourself. I'll ask these two attendants to escort you there.

"Take Mr. Hughes to the baggage car. Put him under the care of Macintosh and ask Mac to take care of him until the professor can talk with him." Fouad saw the man winking to the others.

The two men led Fouad to the baggage car. The men instructed the man in baggage, Macintosh, to keep the passenger there until he heard from the professor. Suddenly, as they sat him down and bound his hands together with nylon tie and fastened him to a pipe Fouad realized that he was a prisoner.

After the men left, Fouad look around. The man they called Mac seemed to be ignoring him. Fouad realized that he needed to escape in some way. I can't sit here waiting for Hamu to discover that the man he thought he killed, the man he is impersonating, is alive. If he discovers that I am alive, I won't be alive long. I've got to get out of here both for the survival of the passengers on this train and my own survival. I promised Vashti I'd do something to get this train stopped. He looked at the ropes and nylon holding him. I've got to find a way to save this train. It looks like I'm going to need some help.

CHAPTER 46

Blue River, British Columbia

"…let us run with endurance the race that is set before us…"
– Hebrews

Now that they had sent Roger on his way to meet his team, Fred and Mary were getting back into their regular routine at the cabin. They were enjoying the beautiful crisp August morning for their weekly ride down the trail to Blue River for supplies.

When they completed their shopping and were ready to ride back to the cabin they loaded their purchases in the side pockets of their pack horse. Finally, before beginning the ride back to their cabin, they decided to go across the main street to chat with their friends in the local police office.

As they entered the office, their officer friend was in the midst of a conversation on the police radio. With a hand over the mic he turned away to greet them, "I'm talking with the Jasper office. I'll be with you soon." Since the officer had the call on speaker phone, they overheard both sides of the conversation.

Their friend in the Blue River office was laughing over something that happened at the Jasper office the night before. The local Blue River officer was enjoying the call. "You say this guy came into your office there in Jasper and tried to convince you that someone on the train was actually planning to blow up the train?"

The Jasper officer replied, "Yes, this guy kept insisting that there was a dangerous man with a bomb on this train, someone who called himself the professor but who wasn't really the professor. He kept saying that this man, the so-called professor, was set to blow the train off the tracks as she rolled into Vancouver."

The Blue River officer asked, "Was he off his rocker or drinking?"

The Jasper officer laughed, "Good question. We noticed that he was wearing some fine Scottish tweeds. My co-worker, Jim, was convinced that he was loaded with Scotch. Scottish Tweed on the outside and Scotch on the inside."

The officer in the Jasper office went on, "What convinced us that he was really unhinged was his confusion about who he, himself, was. His ticket showed his name was Hughes but he said that was not his real name. This guy was really mixed up.'"

Fred and Mary listened carefully as the Jasper officer continued. "I asked him once more to tell us who has the bomb. Wait till you hear this. Our man in the Scottish Tweed said that the man with the bomb was called professor but he was not really the professor. Finally, this character said, "I am really the professor."

The Blue River officer asked, "What did you wind up doing?

"We politely ushered him back to his train."

As they were listening, Fred and Mary stared at each other in amazement.

Fred said softly, "Mary, did you hear what I heard?"

"Yes, I heard that someone on the train was trying to tell them that there was a man on the train with a bomb."

"Mary, did you hear what that person was called?"

"Yes, Fred, I heard it loud and clear. This man in Jasper said that the man on board with a bomb called himself the professor."

Fred looked intently at his wife. "Mary, without realizing it, this man who was making the complaint in Jasper was telling us, though our officer friend here in Blue River, that the man called the professor is definitely on board the train. The man who had everyone believing he had cancelled his trip is on the big train, is actually on the train, after all."

Mary said, "Yes, and, as suspected might be the case, with a bomb."

"Mary, do you remember where we last heard someone called the professor?"

"I sure do, Fred. It was when Roger told us to forget stopping the train at K190. Roger said that man who poses as the professor, was not going to be on the train."

"Mary, through our officer friend here in Blue River, we are being told that the man who twice planned to kill Roger, the man they call the professor, is really on that great transcontinental train, after all. Despite his fake phone calls, that snake in the grass is really on the big train."

Mary said, "That man wasn't getting much help from those men at the Jasper office. Is there still something we can do with this knowledge that this man called the professor is on the train after-all, and with a bomb?"

Fred nodded. "Even though Roger and his team are on the train, it is not likely that they will hear what we are hearing loud and clear, that the professor is on the train."

Mary said, "Those phone calls that Roger's friends heard on their phone tap in Toronto were given to mislead them. It sounds like the man who tried to kill Roger with the bomb on the Vancouver plane is on the train, and, as suspected, with a bomb for Vancouver. Fred, we have to do something and fast."

Fred said, "Mary, I've heard enough. That man in Jasper, with this message that there is a bomb reported on board the train, is informing us. Now, we have even greater urgency to drop those pines and stop that train at K190. Operation lodge pole pines is no longer just a scheme to draw that viper out of his hole. We have to stop the train and block the use of that bomb. From what we heard from Jasper, if we don't stop this man no one else is going to."

"But Fred. The train is ready to head out of Jasper. Do we have enough time?"

Their officer friend came out to greet them, "Sorry I got tied up on the radio phone."

Fred said, "That's Ok. We've got to be on our way. We're thinking of riding down to the old viewing platform at Hells' Gate to see the big train go by today. Do you think we could get there in time to see the big train come through? When would we have to reach Hell's Gate to get there before the big train rolls through?"

The officer replied, "Well, it's now close to nine am. The men in Jasper said the big train would pull out of Jasper in about an hour. Wait a minute. They may be delayed with a partial crew change in Jasper. The Silver Lady should reach us here in Blue River about twelve noon. The big train might leave here about one. I'd say she should reach

Hell's Gate cataract about three-thirty. That gives you a bit over six hours. Think you can make that Fred?"

"We'll give it a try. Thanks for the schedule details."

When they got back to the cabin Fred and Mary quickly saddled up two fresh horses. Mary asked, "Can we do it, Fred? Can we reach K190 before the train?"

Fred checked his watch. "We'll have to push our horses. "We've used over a half hour getting back to our cabin, We're now down to having about five and a half hours.

As they rode off, Fred said, "We have to get there in time to re-set the bomb pack, install a fresh battery and wire the bomb pack in place. We have to make our way up to the pre-cut lodge pole pines up on the mountain side. Our real challenge is to drop the trees at the precise moment the train comes into sight so the engineer sees the debris crashing down the mountain."

As they made their way down the trail, Mary asked, "How many engines do they have on that big train?"

"Now, in the mountains, the train will be running with three diesel electric locomotives, each with 3,000 horses."

Mary laughed, "Nine thousand diesel fed horses against our two real hay fed horses. Those diesel fed horses haven't a chance."

CHAPTER 47

On board the Canadian train west of Jasper

"If you're alive, there's a purpose for your life."
– Rick Warren

The great train, making its way toward the continental divide in the Canadian Rockies, was climbing through breathtaking scenery. No longer burdened with the concern about Roger's enemy being on this train, Roger and Albert Weiss, were enjoying a good conversation in the train's Park Car Lounge. This very last car on the train was also called the Bullet car because of its rounded streamlined shape suggested a bullet. The comfortable seating and snacks being served by the attendants made this a good place to visit.

Roger was telling Professor Weis more about his experience flying west. "When this bad guy learned I was also a pilot, this character contacted Wilbur Linnberg, who operates the Graf Zeppelin airport. He used Wilbur, as his agent, to persuade me to fly his plane to Vancouver. His goal was to explode the bomb as it came into Vancouver. He would get rid of me at the same time. I had no idea that I was flying as this man's kamikaze pilot."

Weiss said, "The special events that brought you through your flight alive are amazing."

Roger said, "Yes. I had some surprising help from above. The sudden failure of the plane's engine came at just the right time to keep me from continuing on to a lower altitude for landing, when the bomb was set to explode."

"Do you think your enemy has any idea what happened to you or and the plane and his powerful bomb? Does he even know you if you're dead or alive?"

Roger said, "Not as far as I know and I want to keep him from knowing."

Weiss said, "Do you have any idea as what he looks like?"

Roger said, "No, not a clue. That is why we were so interested in learning that he would be on this train. We had a plan to draw this snake out of his hole and identify him."

"Wunderbar! What was your plan?"

Roger said, "We planned to stop the train by dropping trees down the mountain side to the tracks where the train would be approaching the great cataract called Hell's Gate. We will reach that area later today. Our plan was that as this man exited from the stopped train he would suddenly stumble upon his big bomb pack. The device would appear to be ticking away. We figured his reaction would be very visible and would make his identity obvious. However, when we learned that he had cancelled his plans to be on this train, we put that plan on hold. We had to cancel Operation Lodge Pole Pines plan."

ii

As the train worked its way through the majestic Rockies, there were two passengers who, after they checked out the scenery with a look or two, pursued other interests. The two teens on board, Bill and Henry, were thoroughly absorbed in their high tech interests. Their latest achievement was to intercept the phone messages sent by various individuals on the train. They were quite pleased with their accomplishment.

Bill, the youth from Britain, called out to his friend from New Zealand. "Henry! Listen to this stuff. We're picking up stuff in a language I know. These guys are talking in Arabic. I told you I had to learn Arabic when we lived in Egypt. Listen to this stuff." "What are they saying?"

"These characters are talking about money."

"What's so unusual about that, Bill? Everyone talks about money. That's all some people think about."

"Henry. These guys on board are talking the way bank robbers in movies talk money. Remember when the police stopped our train just out of Toronto? Someone said they were searching the train for money from Toronto's big bank truck robbery. They didn't find any. Well, it sounds like these guys are talking about the money those officers never found. It sounds like there must be suitcases of cash hidden somewhere on this train."

"This sounds serious. What should we do about it?"

"Henry, we've got to tell someone about this. Let's find our friend, that waitress, Barbara. She'll know what to do."

When the boys found Barbara, Bill asked her, "Barbara, did you ever see one of those big train robbery movies?"

Barbara laughed, "If you guys are planning to pull off one on this train, cut me in."

"Barbara, this is not funny. With our equipment, we heard men talking about what they will be doing with the large amounts of actual cash on this train."

Barbara said, "People usually are tight lipped about their money. Why do you guys think these men would speak so openly?"

"Perhaps they assumed no one on this train could understand them. They were speaking Egyptian Arabic, which I happen to know, they probably felt pretty secure."

"How is it you know Arabic, Bill?"

"No problem. When my Dad worked at the British Embassy in Cairo I went to school in Cairo. I had to learn Egyptian Arabic."

Barbara listened as Bill played the Arabic recording with Bill's translations. Then she waved her hand to stop. She said, "Enough. This is very serious. We've got to get this to the right person. I think I know that person. We've got to locate Roger Renoir. I last saw him in the Bullet Car lounge, talking with that that man who looks like Albert Einstein.. Bring your stuff."

When Barbara brought the boys into the Bullet lounges, she apologized, "I'm sorry to interrupt your visit but we have something very important to share with you. When you hear it, I think you will agree that it is very important."

Roger called out, "No problem, Barbara. Please join us."

Barbara introduced the boys. "Bill and Henry, the two boys referred to by passengers as the two hi-tech boys, picked up some conversation between individuals on this train that I think you men should hear."

Roger said, "We're all ears."

Barbara explained, "The boys intercepted some serious conversation between men on this train. The men were speaking in Arabic."

Roger laughed, "Neither of us know Arabic. "

"No problem. It so happens that William, is fluent in Arabic. When his family lived in Cairo William learned Arabic in school. He has taped parts of this conversation in Arabic and inserted his translation. You will hear the actual conversation in Arabic and William's immediate translation."

Roger said, "OK, let's hear it."

The boys played the actual recording and Roger and Professor Weis listened. The two men could scarcely believe what they were hearing.

Roger and Weiss were stunned by what they were hearing. When they had come on board, Roger and the team relaxed because they believed that their enemy would not be on the train. These recording with translation gave overwhelming evidence that men from the big Toronto robbery were definitely on the train. One of the speakers was definitely the man in charge. Obviously the information in those previously intercepted phone calls about cancelling the plans to be on this train intercepted back in Toronto was planted to mislead them.

Roger and Professor Weis looked at each other and nodded. They were struck by undeniable evidence that large amounts of cash from the big Toronto robbery were on board. Furthermore, they were convinced that if the cash was on board, the man in charge would have to be on board."

Roger pounded his fist. If only they had kept operation lode pole pines active. Too bad they had put it on hold. There was no way he could reach Bill and Mary from this train. Even if he could reach them there seemed too little time to activate the plan.

Roger remembered how that flood of officers had searched through the train and found nothing. Now, thesec two boys discovered evidence that the cash the officers failed to find was on this train. The loot from the big Toronto rush hour robbery was definitely on this train. Roger was puzzled. If all this money is on this train, the leader, the man called the professor, has to be on the train. The problem is that we haven't a clue to what he looks like. More than likely he is disguised? If only we had not cancelled our plan to stop the train at Hell's Gate.

Roger spoke to the boys, "What you have shared with us is very serious. Thank you? Yes, it sure does sound like robbers in a movie, but this is not a movie. This is a very real life situation. These men are very dangerous. They will kill to preserve that cash. For your own safety, keep all of this to yourselves."

Roger took the hand of each of the boys looked at him intently. "You have performed a real service with this information. Mention this to no one else."

Roger turned to Barbara, "Many thanks for bringing this to our attention. Tell no one else about your having this information. These men are ruthless. It is very important that these men do not know that they have been over heard and translated. If they discovered that you know what you know, you would be in great danger."

iii

After Barbara and the boys left, Roger and Weis just sat there for a moment looking at each other.

Finally Roger spoke. "We face a very challenging situation. We were cleverly misled. That talk about the professor taking a later train was a planned deception. If all that cash is on board, their leader, the professor, has to be on board."

Weiss nodded. "Yes, the cash is not likely to be on this train without the man."

Weiss continued thinking for a moment or so silently. Then he said, "Roger, too bad you cancelled that Operation Lodge Pole Pines. You were all set to draw the snake out of his hole. Is there any way that you and your friends, Fred and Mary could reactivate that plan you were telling me about?"

"We don't have that option, Albert. It's too late to do anything. This train is headed into that area in the mountains. Time is limited. Although the cabin of my friends is only few hours from K190 and Hell's Gate, the area where we planned to stop the train, there is no way to reach them. The problem is that they have no phone in their old gold miner's cabin. If we got the message to them, there would not be time for them, on horseback, to reach the Hell's Gate area and stop the train."

Weiss pressed his lips together and nodded his head. Finally, he said, "If anything is to be done it looks like it will have to be done by those of us on this train."

Roger laughed, "Get your grey cells working, Albert."

Weiss laughed, "What do you mean by get them working? Roger, when you are a professor of geophysics your grey cells never stop working."

"What are your grey cells telling you, Albert?"

"We need to connect the dots, Roger. Let's re-examine the information you have."

"OK, Albert. Let's review what we know and connect the dots. Dot number one. If the police out of Toronto searched this train, they must have very good reasons to search this train. The police had a tip. So, although a hundred officers searched and found nothing the cash could still be on the train."

Albert nodded.

Roger continued. "Dot number two. Two sharp teenage hackers, one of whom speaks Arabic, came to us with the report that some Arabic speaking men on this train were talking about cash, about the large amounts of actual cash on this train. Our young friends confirm that, despite the failure of the police search, there is an enormous amount of cash on this train."

"And where does that lead us, Roger?"

"That leads us to dot number three. If the cash is on the train my deadly enemy, the professor, has to be on this train. But remember that the enemy has known all along that my friends, were booked on this train. Since he took the precaution to mislead the team whom he knows would be on this train we can assume that he is taking other precautions. He is most likely very well disguised."

Albert nodded. "So, to find the man we are looking for is going to be difficult."

Roger said, "Albert, too bad that Geiger counter Sarah says you brought along does not detect paper money."

Albert held up a finger. "Wait, there is dot number four. There's some more helpful information we have, dot number four. You were telling me that the big Toronto cash robbery was carried out by the same gang of men who tried to execute you on Bobcat Lake. Roger, those very same men, not long ago, were handling nuclear material for their bombs. I think that information may be dot number four."

"How can that help us find the man on this train?"

"Roger, dot number four is very important. Knowing that the man with the stolen cash is the same man who was stashing stolen nuclear material at Bobcat Lake is crucial. This means the hands, the shoes and clothing, the shoes of those that stashed the money were stashing nuclear material and designing dirty bombs with radioactive material. Both crimes were carried out by the same men."

Roger said, "OK, but how does that help us locate the man?"

Albert smiled. "Individuals working with radioactive materials invariably carry invisible traces of these substances of which they are not aware. Traces of nuclear material cling to and remain unknown on those who handle it. It is more than likely that anyone working with such materials continues to carry traces of those materials. And this leads us to dot number five."

"What's number five, Albert?"

"My geiger counter, Roger. You said it was too bad that geiger does not detect money. Nevertheless, the Geiger counter may help us find the man with the cash. How? These men with the cash are probably loaded with nuclear traces. Since those who handled the cash also handled nuclear material my advanced Geiger can lead us to the man and the money."

Roger said, "Where's the Geiger?"

CHAPTER 48

Crossing the Canadian Rockies by train.

"When it is dark enough you can see the stars."
– Ralph Waldo Emerson, 1890

As he worked his way from car to car, Roger was finding the task of going through the cars with Albert's geiger devise quite a challenge. To appear as casual as possible he had hung part of Albert's devise over his shoulder like a camera. He concealed the earphones which would give him the click-click radiation signal under his western hat. He tried, as much as possible, to make the wand with the sensor appear more like a cane.

He had to laugh at what he was doing. Trying to locate cash with a geiger counter. But Albert had a point. The men with the cash had also handled nuclear material.

As Roger walked along in the third car, he suddenly began to hear an occasional click in his earpiece. The indicator on the hand wand held was blinking. Someone who handled radioactive material must have passed through this car not too long ago. He moved more slowly along the corridor of this sleeping car.

Suddenly, Roger began to hear more rapid clicking on his ear phones. The light on the wand was sending signals. He continued moving very slowly. He was looking at his gage in amazement. This area is loaded. The clicking was quite intense.

He was stopped opposite a compartment labelled F. There was no question that someone who had handled radioactive materials passed here. Roger decided that he needed to get out of there fast. These guys are on board after all. I have to let the others know that we've been misled.

Roger was about to turn off the geiger and get moving when, suddenly, the door of compartment F swung open. Roger found himself facing a man in the uniforms of a train attendant. He appeared to be of Middle East origin.

The man., seemed as startled as Roger. Then the attendant focused on the wand Roger was holding in his hand. He asked, "What is the devise making that click, click sound?"

Roger replied quickly, "Oh, it's one of those detectors used to find lost things."

The attendant said, "Metal detector? I've used one of those. That looks like something else."

Roger turned to leave.

"Just a minute." The door had opened wider and another voice called out from the compartment. "I'd like to see that devise." Suddenly, from behind the man at the door, another man, stepped forward. He also wore a train crew uniform.

Roger thought this man looked like one of the dining car managers. Roger found himself staring into the business end of semi-automatic pistol. It appeared to be nothing to argue with, a Beretta with a suppressor.

The man waved his weapon. "I think you better step inside here."

The men pulled him into the compartment. Roger heard the compartment door close behind him. He was immediately relieved of Weiss' equipment.

Roger felt like kicking himself. I really blew this one. What a mess. You were right, Albert. It was like you figured. The people involved with the money had also been handling, nuclear material. Your gadget led me right to them. Yes, and right into their hands.

Roger tried talking his way out of this one. "I'm sorry to have bothered you. I was checking out this gadget for a friend of mine."

The men continued to examine the devise. He realized now that the man with the revolver was one of the dining room managers. He seemed to be in charge. He took the devise over to a large piece of baggage. It immediately gave a high intensity signal.

He turned off the devise and looked at Roger. "What is a ranch hand, if you are a ranch hand, doing on this train with a geiger counter?"

Roger tried a laugh, "Oh, these gadgets find all sorts of things. You never know what you'll find with one these gadgets."

"Well, you've found a lot of trouble."

The man with the Beretta turned to his companions. "Call Scarface in baggage. Tell him we're going to bring him another visitor. It's another man for him to hold until the Professor decides what to do with them."

Roger's arms were pulled behind him and fastened with nylon ties. The men splashed liquor on him. Roger believed they were preparing for any chance run in with passengers. They wanted to give the impression they were helping an intoxicated passenger. In this way they set out for the baggage car.

At the baggage car Roger's s captors gave a special knock. The leader called through the door, "Scarface, Daoud here." Roger heard a key unlock the door.

When the door opened and the two men led Roger through the doorway, he was dumbfounded. He was face to face with the Henderson's cabin man Macintosh.

It was the man who had visited him at the cabin, the Macintosh he had met with Emily in Toronto. The situation seemed to confirm his suspicion that this was the Mac who fired that shot that missed on Bobcat Lake.

Daoud, said, "We found this guy using a geiger counter. That sort of devise could be used to trace the stuff like we took on board at Sudbury. Hold him here in baggage with that crazy man in tweeds until the Professor decides what to do with them." He laughed. "We're not too far from the big Red Squirrel Spiral Tunnel. The professor may want us to drop them there."

After the men fastened Roger to the bench, alongside the other prisoner, Daoud said, "We will get back to you after we talk to the professor."

Roger saw that Macintosh did not appear very happy to receive another prisoner. Despite my efforts to change my appearance this man, Mac, must know who I am. However, the man is still giving no sign of knowing me. The men called him Scarface. He has to be the man called Mac who was ordered to shoot me at Bobcat Lake. This man, despite his long relationship with then, has been deceiving the Hendersons.

Roger was getting more concerned. It does not look like they intend to let me walk out of here.

ii
_____

In his compartment, Hamu was finally enjoying what he regarded as real coffee. The dining car had offered a special for internationals, Turkish coffee. Hamu had ordered a large carafe of the brew brought to his compartment. As he sipped his coffee, he was thinking that all he needed was a hookah, a water pipe, and he would think he was back in Cairo.

The coffee made Hamu think of the cost to living as an impostor. You're not, of course, the person whose ID you assume. You're no longer you. You are captive to your new identity but that's not really who you are.

Hamu was reviewing how he got where he was. When those Israeli bombs hit Rafah and our explosive devise destroyed the guest house, really two men died. First, Fouad, the man whose body they recovered from the guest house ruins. Another man also died that day. As that battered corpse of the professor was identified as my body, as I, Hamu, was pronounced dead, in a way, this man Hamu also died that day.

It was the perfect crime. Both the media and the international police, viewed that mangled corpse as the broken body of Hamu. As the word went out that the professor had survived with injuries I was able, with the aid of his passport, to step into his shoes and appear as the professor. Through our very close resemblance, I was able to take his passport and present myself to customs as the professor. But I'm not the professor and never will be. I'm also no longer Hamu.

Hamu stirred his Turkish coffee. This man will never be returning to a Cairo coffee house. As that famous novel put it, you can't go home again.

Hamu took another sip of his Turkish coffee. He was musing. When I came to Canada using his passport it seemed so easy. I assumed that I would just step into being the Professor. But the impostor can't really become that person.

Hamu continued to review his life thus far as an impostor. I have a really much tougher job than an actor when he takes on a certain identity to make a film. When viewers watch an actor fill a part, they may say, for example, the actor really resembles Churchill. They know he is not Churchill. When I take on the ID of someone like the professor I have to have them thinking I am the professor. But I know I'm not.

Perhaps those who believe in a personal Creator God have a point. Only a Creator who is himself a person, making persons in his own image, could make a persons. Novelists can't make persons. Imposters can't make persons. I'm impersonating Fouad, but I'm still Hamu.

Hamu noticed that the great train seemed to be moving more slowly. The train must be on a steeper grade. We may be approaching the Continental divide. He was impressed with the rugged country the train was going through. Someone had explained to him the great challenge to keep the gradient of the tracks from being too steep. He had heard how the engineers, in certain locations, had lengthened the climb to make the gradient more gradual. It was for this reason that one of the great tunnels, the Red Squirrel Spiral tunnel had been created. The goal was to keep the maximum gradient as close to 2 % as possible.

Suddenly a special knock sounded on his door. He recognized the knock. "Come in." Daoud, his agent serving as dining car manager, stepped in.

"What's going on?"

"Professor, since we took prisoner that man in tweeds who was telling people there was a bomb on board, we have had to take another prisoner."

"Another prisoner? Are you out of your mind? What are you doing? We can't be taking prisoners on a train,"

"We discovered this man outside our compartment with a geiger counter seeking to detect radioactive materials. He had discovered traces of nuclear material, such as we brought on board at Sudbury. Here's his devise." He handed Hamu the gadget.

Hamu looked at the devise. "Yes, it appears to be a geiger counter. After they failed to locate the Toronto cash, the police must have put him on this train.

"Daoud, we have a problem. If they are looking for traces of nuclear material they may believe that if they find nuclear material on this train they will find us, and if they find us they will find the money."

"What do you want us to do with these men? Macintosh is holding them in the baggage car, the man in tweeds, the one who was telling everyone there was a bomb on board and this man who had the geiger."

Hamu said, "Two birds in one trap. We will have to dispose of both of them. We have no other option. I have heard talk about the big tunnel coming up. The great tunnel they call the Red Squirrel Spiral Tunnel, is coming up soon. That may be the best opportunity to dispose of these men. Direct Macintosh to put each of the men in heavy bags to be tossed off the train in the tunnel. When we are near the tunnel send two men to help Macintosh toss this excess baggage."

CHAPTER 49

Crossing the Canadian Rockies by train.

*"And thus I clothe my naked villainy…
And seem a saint, when most I play the devil."*
– Richard III, Shakespeare

The men who had delivered the captive Roger to Macintosh in the baggage car told Macintosh that the professor wanted to talk with him about the prisoners. After making sure the two men were secure, Macintosh went with the men.

For the first time, the two prisoners found themselves alone in the baggage car. The man in tweeds spoke softly, "It's time I introduce myself to you, Roger Renoir."

"You know my name?"

"Of course, Roger. And more than your name. In fact I know all about your previous imprisonment."

Roger was stunned! "You mean that you know of my being held at Bobcat Lake up North?"

"No, I was referring to your more recent captivity in the old Toronto warehouse."

"Only my closest friends know of that. Just who are you?"

"As you were painting your watercolor by that old warehouse, the men working in the area gave you a rough time. They slit your tires, the two back two tires."

Roger was puzzled. How could this stranger know all this? He stared at the man.

"You are wondering how I could know these thing. Here are a few more. While a prisoner there, you were tied up and blindfolded in a second floor room."

"Yes."

"The Two Vipers men were holding you there until they learned from their leader, the professor, what to do with you. You were really concerned. One of the men said that you were the same man they held prisoner up North at Bobcat Lake. You were thinking that they might come back with orders to finish the job.

"While you were sitting there, tied and blindfolded, you heard someone come into your makeshift prison. Suddenly you could feel some of your nylon ties and ropes being cut. Nothing was said. Then, this persons placed the knife handle in the one hand that was free, your right hand."

"Only the person who actually placed the knife in my right hand could know that."

"Yes, and after leaving the knife in your hand this person left. You were then able to remove the blindfold and complete the task of cutting yourself free. You crawled through a window and out on an old rusty fire escape. Then, dropping to the ground, you made your escape in your Rover. CAA had replaced the tires. You took off to meet Emily."

"Roger looked with amazement at the man. "Only one person would know those details, the person who cut me free and put the knife in my right hand. I am quite sure that I might have died there, that day, if you had not freed me."

"Roger, it was not a case of whether you might have died. It was a case of when."

"I was in an impossible situation. You saved my life."

"In such tough situations you realize that God can use even you if you make yourself available to Him."

"I thank you. I thank the Savior who sent you. Just who are you?"

"Roger, let me tell you something else that no one knows. You were painting in Jasper with a man named Bill Webber, who, I happen to know, is also on this train. You were up pretty high in the mountains painting watercolor landscapes."

"Right. One of the greatest painting days of my life. Do you know everything?"

"Three days later, when you headed back to Bill Webber's old red truck you had a problem. Bill's truck battery was dead."

"You know that, too?"

"In the morning someone gave you a jump to start the truck. Then, as you restored power, the little light over the back jump seat came on. The battery went dead because someone had turned on that manually operated light over the back jump seat. With that light on during the days you were up there painting, the battery died. I'm sure that you found that very upsetting."

"Yes. That dead battery put me a full day behind my flight schedule. And that meant…" Roger paused amazed.

Roger said, "Yes, and that lost day kept me from flying on to Vancouver on the scheduled day, which I've learned was the day when the bomb in my plane was programmed to explode when I came in to below 1,000 feet. I was saved by that dead battery. Amazing. Because of that prank, I was still high in the mountains on the day the bomb on board was programmed to explode."

The man in tweed said, "The next day when took off from Jasper you had further problems."

"Problems? That's an understatement. While I was at still flying at about eight thousand feet and over mountains of five thousand feet, my engine died. I landed by parachute on the mountain.

"A couple named Fred and Mary Christiansen rescued me. When we found the wreck, Fred discovered a powerful bomb in the plane. Fred discovered that the bomb was controlled by an altimeter devise to detonate the moment, after the set date, when I flew below one thousand feet. Fortunately, I was still flying at about eight thousand feet when the engine failed. That engine failure forced me to abandon the plane while still in the mountains. That oil failure also saved my life."

"Let me explain Roger. While you were up there painting, my technical adviser and I examined the settings on that big black pack in your plane parked in Jasper. The settings on the bomb were locked in a way that my friend could not modify at that altitude. We knew we had to keep you from dropping to 1,000 feet on the day that bomb was set to go off."

"You saw the settings on the bomb pack at Jasper Airport?"

"Exactly. To make sure you did not get ambitious to make up time and fly to Vancouver and your destruction, my mechanic friend saw to it that your plane's engine would develop trouble. When my friend tinkered with your plane's oil system he intended to cause a forced landing shortly after takeoff. Sorry you had to parachute in the mountains."

Roger was dumbfounded! "Who are you?"

"Telling you who I am will requires more than simply giving you my name. If I can do it with my hands fastened as they are I will show you who I really am."

Roger's fellow prisoner reached up and grabbed his face with both hands. Despite the fact his hands were fastened he had enough freedom to reach his face. He pulled and proceeded to peel off, part way, what appeared to be the very skin of his face. It was an incredibly well made life mask. As the mask came off he revealed under the face mask a tan face with a white mustache and a well-trimmed white beard.

"Perhaps you will recall our meetings, first in Heathrow airport and then our visit with Emily after my last lecture in Cairo. Remember this song. Let me sing it again for you. And he shall come, He shall come to us like the rain, like the spring rain, watering the earth. He kept his promise."

Roger was stunned. For a moment he found himself just staring at the man.

Finally Roger spoke, "I know you! Of course I know you. It's you, the professor. You are the Egyptian professor I met that day in Heathrow Airport. You were returning from Vancouver to lecture in Cairo. And then in Cairo, on our forced trip home, Emily and I attended your last lecture in Cairo. What a great lecture. You're Professor Fouad. That white beard and mustache are unmistakable?

"Exactly. Yes, I'm the man."

"And then, a few days later, when we boarded a British Air flight for London you were on that flight and across the aisle from me. You seemed very preoccupied."

"No, Roger. The man on the London flight was not the man you met in Heathrow. That was not the man you heard lecture in Cairo. The man on the flight to London was my look alike, my impersonator. Yes, he looked like me but he was not me."

"That man on the plane looked exactly like you. Wait, I made a sketch of the man on the plane. I recall his unusually shaped ears. Turn your face. Yes, I see it now. His ears were very different. Otherwise he was a carbon copy of you. Who in the world was this man who looked so much like you?"

"The man you saw on the plane in Cairo was my impersonator. He is the man who now holds us captive. He may come here to see his prisoners at any time. Let me pull my life mask back in place."

With his life mask back in place, Fouad continued, "Roger, the man you saw on the plane, who looks like an identical twin, was my double. The resemblance is so close that this man, a fugitive from international police and Mossad, came up with the idea of killing me and making it look like it was he who had died. His associates convinced everyone that the broken body destroyed by that explosive in Gaza was his body. He used that body to convince Interpol that their fugitive, the notorious Hamu, was dead.

"When you saw him on the flight to London, this man, thinking he had killed me, was impersonating me and using my passport to flee Egypt for Canada. Roger, as you can see that plot failed. With the help of friends I was able to escape his death plot, while letting him go on thinking he had succeeded. You and I have this common bond. Both of us, so far, have both escaped his efforts to kill us."

Roger said, "When I was taken prisoner, comments by the men indicated that the man in charge is with us on this train."

"Yes, I also learned only today that not only is he on the train but that he has on board a powerful devise with which he is planning to destroy this train in Vancouver. Quiet. I hear someone coming."

CHAPTER 50

Crossing the Canadian Rockies by train.

"Surprised by joy"
– C S Lewis

The two prisoners in the baggage car discontinued their conversation with the return of their keeper, the man called Mac. Roger was upset by being held prisoner by this man who may have fired that murderous shot at Bobcat Lake. Roger just stared at him.

This man, Mac, the trusted care taker for years for the Hendersons up north, the man who visited him so cordially at the cabin, all this time, was working with this hateful gang. It was obvious now. This has to be the man called Mac who fired that shot to kill me at Bobcat Lake. And all along he has been working with Mr. Dark heart.

The two men faced each other for a moment. Roger saw that the man was feeling more awkward than he. Their guard seemed embarrassed to be their guard..

Finally Roger spoke. "When you visited me at the cabin, I wondered if you were with them, whether you were Mac, the man ordered to shoot me. I never saw the shooter and I suppose you never got a good look at me, the victim, lying there on the ground."

Still no comment from their guard.

Roger went on. "When you arrived at the cabin that evening and introduced yourself as Mac, you seemed so friendly. I couldn't believe you were one of them and the same Mac who got the order to take care of me. The Toronto police assured me that you could not be the man named Mac who had been ordered to shoot and kill me.

"When we met you at the Toronto station I was puzzled. I thought it very strange that you would be working on our train going west. Now I find that, as I suspected, you are associated with this hate filled man who now holds us captive.

The man remained silent

Roger said, "At Bobcat everyone was saying what a great shot you were, you never miss. Mac, I have one question. I have to know. Was it a miss or did you shoot to miss?"

Silence.

Roger repeated his question. "Was it a miss or did you shoot to miss?"

Macintosh looked at Roger and after a few moments of silence he repeated the question. "Did I miss or did I shoot to miss?"

Roger said, "Yes, I'd like to know. It was my life. I deserve an answer."

Mac said, "Let me answer your question." Mac slid open the side door of the baggage car. They were passing a small village and the train was going more slowly. Mac picked up his rifle and pointed to a sign. He spoke again. "See that light bulb." He fired. The bulb was scattered. "You're asking me whether I missed or shot to miss. Does that answer your question? Yes, I am the man called Mac who was ordered to shoot you."

Macintosh continued, "If you knew me you would know the answer to that question. I accepted the order to shoot you, as I did, because it had to appear that you were dead. Was it a miss or did I shoot to miss? Of course, I shot to miss.

"When suddenly I had this order to shoot you, I did some fast thinking. If they saw that I was not completely with them I was in trouble. In working for the Two Vipers I had gotten into more than I bargained for. Did I miss or shoot to miss? Yes, I deliberately shot to miss while trying to make it look good for me and bad for you."

Roger just looked at the man in silence.

Mac paused for a moment and then went on, "It is a great joy for me to learn that you are the man I shot to miss and that I did miss. Ever since that day that shot has been a terrible burden for me."

Roger was puzzled. "Why? You shot to miss and missed."

Mackintosh looked at them silently. Finally, he spoke. "The next day the news was everywhere that an officer on duty had been shot in cold blood on Bobcat Lake. According to the news, I had not missed.

"The press told exactly where his body was found. They described the fatal wound. They gave his name and described his family. It hurt deeply. I had been so sure I had missed that prisoner. That my shot had killed the man tore my heart and has grieved me, until today.

"And now, today." Mackintosh paused. He continued, "And now today, I learn that I did miss. I am meeting the man I aimed to miss and missed. You are alive?"

Again after a pause, with deep feeling Macintosh continued, "What a joy! Since that day I have been burdened that I killed the man I tried to save that day.

"Your capture by these men is tragic but it brings joy to see the man I was ordered to shoot, alive, It is a great joy for me to know that when I shot to miss I did miss. I am sorry that you have been taken prisoner by these men but I thank God that you are alive."

Roger just looked at the man. "Somehow, Mac, I think I always knew that shot was the shot of a sharp shooter. It came so close. I am grateful for your expertise. It never occurred to me that the man shooting was on the spot too. Thank you. Thank you for life."

For a moment the two men just looked at one another. Then Macintosh with tears in his eyes, embraced Roger.

Mac said, "I can't tell you how much it means to me to meet you, alive. I'm relieved to learn that my shot did what it was supposed to do, keep you alive. I accepted the order to shoot you because I knew that I could carry out the order in a way to protect you and make me look like I was with them. I was protecting not only you. I was also protecting myself by appearing to be working with these men. By the way, did I hurt your ear?"

"No, it was close but I was not hurt. I must admit that at first I was not sure if I was dead or alive."

Macintosh turned to the man in tweeds, "And why have they brought you here?"

The man in tweeds replied, "It's a long story. To simply things let me say that if your leader knew who I really am he would be ordering you to fire another shot. I also am a person who was ordered killed and whom he believes is dead."

Macintosh looked at them for a few moments. Then he spoke rapidly, "I have in mind a way for you to escape, but we have to act fast. The two of you have to do a disappearing act and fast. Somehow or other we have to get the two of you off this train. And it has to be done in a way that will gives me cover and does not suggest that I helped you.

"What are they ordering you to do about us?

"The professor, told me to get you ready for dumping. On a train the only way to dispose of bodies on a train is by dumping them from the train.

"We are coming soon to the great Red Spider Spiral Tunnel. I have orders to give you shots to knock you out and get you ready to be dropped in the tunnel. In about an hour, our train will be rolling along for quite a few minutes in the darkness of this great tunnel. Two men will come to swing out your bodies in bags from the side doors of the baggage car. This tunnel is in a desolate mountain area. No people at all. If anyone found your bodies, at best, they would find only a few bones mixed with bones of animals.

"Notice how they are involving me. They want to involve me in these things to bind me to them. When you are implicated in a murder you have no place to go."

"The professor is coming to check out the two of you. He wants you both to be blindfolded. After he checks you out, I am to get you ready for the drop in the tunnel."

Just them someone pounded on the door. "Scarface! Open up."

"Coming!" Mac laughed. "I let them call me Scarface. It keeps them scared of me, I told them I got it in knife fight. When inspection is over be ready to move and fast."

CHAPTER 51

On board the train in the Canadian Rockies

"God cannot be restricted.
Like the author of a novel,
God is entirely in charge of the plot."
– Dinesh D'Souza

Macintosh told his prisoners, "Brace yourselves. The professor is coming. He is very upset that his men took the two of you prisoners. He is coming to check out the two of you before he disposes of you."

Roger said, "How much time do we have, Mac?"

Macintosh said, "Very little. After he checks out the out the two of you, I am supposed to give you knockout shots and get you ready in bags, so your bodies can be dumped off the train in the big tunnel coming up.

"Red Spider Spiral Tunnel is coming up in about an hour. It's no ordinary train tunnel. This tunnel makes a long cut through the mountain. As it loops through solid rock, the wide spiral of the tunnel reduces the grade. Our train will be in the darkness of the great tunnel for quite a few minutes. The professor has ordered me to give you knock out shots and to pack your bodies in two big bags. Then two of his men will come here to swing your bodies out the side door as we pass through the tunnel.

"I was ordered to load each of you in one of the large canvass bags used here in the baggage car. While the train is passing through the tunnel, two men will come here to swing each of these bags into the tunnel. They figure that no one will ever find your bodies in this tunnel."

Roger said, "But first the leader is coming to see us?"

Macintosh said, "Yes. I have been ordered to blindfold you." The professor wants to be sure that no one can later identify him. It may also increases his sense of power over you."

Roger said, "Is there any window of opportunity for us to escape?"

"After he visits you, we will have about an hour. I see one possible escape. I'm working on an idea."

Roger said, "Mac, the professor has no idea what happened to the pilot of his bomb loaded plane. I need, if possible to keep it that way. It is important that this man they call the professor does not discover who we really are. When you blind fold us for his visit, try to also conceal as much of our faces as possible"

"Fouad said, "Yes, cover as much of our faces as possible with the blindfold. We are both men he failed to kill previously."

Shortly after Macintosh got their blindfolds in place, Roger and Fouad heard a knock on the baggage car door. They heard Macintosh opened the door and greet their captor and the men with him.

The prisoners heard their captor laughingly say. "So these are the special guests." The sound of that voice resonated with a strong impact on Roger. Roger was hearing again the voice that had twice ordered his death.

The blindfolded prisoners heard the strong voice of their captor. "Which is the one who was looking for the cash from Toronto robbery with a geiger counter?"

The prisoners assumed Macintosh pointed to Roger. Their captor addressed Roger, "So you are the man who came snooping with a geiger counter. They say you use the name Murphy."

He laughed. "Tell me Murphy, what did your fellow police expect you to find? A hundred officers searched this train above Toronto for the cash from the Toronto robbery. They found nothing. What made them think you would find what they didn't find?"

Their captor laughed again. "And with a geiger counter? Did they think the seized cash was all in coins? Hamu turned to Macintosh and laughed.. "This man was hunting for paper money with a geiger counter."

Roger kept silent.

Hamu turned to his other prisoner. "And you, you there in the tweeds. You're the one called Hughes, the crazy man who has been telling people there was a bomb on board? Well, since you're not going to be around much longer, let me tell you that there is a bomb on this train, a big one. Too bad you won't be around when it blasts this train off the tracks."

Hamu looked at his captives in silence for a few moments. "I am really sorry but you have made it necessary for me to dispose of the two of you. And we have to make sure you disappear."

Their captor paused. "Sorry, but I have to send the two of you on your way to the world beyond this."

Hamu shrugged his shoulders. "This train is on its way to Hell's Gate. I don't know if you are on your way to heaven or hell. I don't think any of us really know what lies beyond this life. I know I don't. I guess none of us know." He laughed, "But you will soon know."

Hamu was silent for a moment. "I may not know your ultimate destinations, heaven or hell, but there's something I do know. Your bodies are going to have a more fantastic tomb than the pharaohs of Egypt. Something greater than the pyramids of Egypt."

Hamu laughed. "Your resting place, in a little over an hour, will be in the famous Red Spiral Tunnel, deep in the heart of the great Canadian Rocky Mountains."

Fouad spoke. "Some final words?"

Hamu laughed, "Last words? Sure. We can't deny a man his last words. Right, Macintosh? OK, let's hear them, Mr. Hughes or whoever you are."

"You said that you didn't really know where any of us will be after this life. Let me tell you that we know, both of us know where we will be. We are going to be with the One who made us."

Hamu laughed, "Don't feed me that stuff. When you're dead, you're dead." He laughed again, "Ever been to or seen those pictures of Pompeii? The skeletons of the people of Pompeii, buried in volcanic ash by the eruption of Mount Vesuvius are still there. Hamu laughed again. "When you're dead you're dead. Someone would have to come back from the dead to tell me otherwise."

Fouad said, "Exactly. And that's what it's all about. Someone did come back to tell us otherwise. His name is Jesus, the One who created all of us and these mountains. Jesus died our death. He came back from the dead with the great invitation. He's alive and he invites us to receive Him and his gift of eternal life."

"The two of you have a little over an hour. Next you will be trying to tell me that there are aliens on Mars?"

Roger replied. "The question is not whether there is life on Mars. What matters most is that this is the visited planet. Jesus, the Creator, really came. When Jesus came it was Creator God who came. He's extending to you the great invitation."

Fouad spoke. "We don't know how much time we have. We have accepted the great invitation. Do you know where you are heading?"

"Where am I heading? Good question." Hamu laughed, "This train is heading down the North Thompson River to that great cataract called Hell's Gate. Hamu said, "That's where I'm heading. Hell's Gate."

Hamu remained silent for a moment. Finally he spoke. "Soon this train will be entering the great Red Spiral Spiral Tunnel. That's where you're heading." This old tunnel will be your grave."

Hamu laughed, "I don't know if you will meet God, your maker. I am pretty sure some hungry bears in the tunnel will soon be chewing on your bones."

"Macintosh, give them the needle. Get them bagged, zipped up and ready for the tunnel toss. I will send two men to give them the big toss."

ii

As soon as their captor and his men were gone, Macintosh locked and bolted the baggage car door. He quickly removed the blind folds from Roger and Fouad cut their nylon ties. "We have to work fast, very fast."

Macintosh opened two large shipping boxes that contained clothing. "We must work fast. We have about forty-five minutes at best. We have to make a convincing dummy figure for each bag. Find whatever material you can to fashion together for each bag, something that will feel and weigh like a body. We have to convince the men who come to swing these bags into the tunnel that one of you is tied up in each bags."

Shoes were placed in the bottom of the bags. Trousers and jackets were packed with clothing. Macintosh added some weight items. Each stuffed figure was quickly inserted feet first into each of the two large bags.

When they had done their best to simulate the weight of each man's body they dragged the two canvass bags to the baggage car's open door. As Macintosh was looking at the bags he grimaced. "We need something more."

Suddenly Macintosh pointed. "Look. A canister of animal blood being shipped somewhere. Just what we need." Macintosh broke the seals on the canister. "They can replace this shipment, but we can't replace the two of you.

"This should be very convincing." He splashed blood on the dummies in each bag and tossed the shipping canister out the side door.

"Now to get the two of you out of sight." Macintosh flung open a large storage cabinet. He pulled out material stored there. "Quickly, fold yourselves up as small as you can in this cabinet." Once they were positioned, Mac piled things on top of them. I think there are enough cracks to give you air. Macintosh stacked a number of boxes and several suitcases against the cabinet. He tossed the empty suitcases and other loose items out the baggage car's open side door. "The tunnel is coming up fast."

The voice of the train master came over the sound system. "Approaching the great Red Spiral Tunnel. Expect several minutes of darkness."

Macintosh called to the men in the cabinet. "We're ready for the bag jossers."

Suddenly the train was in the total darkness of travelling through the great tunnel. The two men sent to toss the bodies came knocking on the baggage car door. Macintosh admitted them and pointed to the two bags with his flashlight.

The two men positioned themselves for swinging the huge bags through the open side door. One asked, "Is that blood? I thought you were just going to knock them out with a shot. The bags look bloody. What happened?"

"They put up a fight. I had to use my knife."

The man laughed, "Like the time you got your scar fighting that bear."

The men picked up the first bag. One said, "These guys are heavier than I expected."

"Yes, I added some stuff. I thought some more weight would give the bags momentum when you give them the toss."

The men lifted the first bag. One called out, "On the count of three. One, two, three." The first bag went flying through the doorway. One called out again, "One, two three." The second bag went flying. With the second toss and the men left.

ii

As soon as the two men were gone, Macintosh locked the baggage car door. He quickly opened the door of the cabinet and pulled out Roger and Fouad..

Fouad said, "Mac, thank you for the risks you took to preserve our lives."

Roger said, "Yes, thank you Mac. For me, this is the second time that you've been there to stand between me and those who wanted to see me dead."

Macintosh spoke quickly, "You're not out of the woods yet. To survive, we must work to get you out of here and off this train. Keeping you out of sight on this train will not be easy. Now that you are supposed to be lying in the tunnel it will be necessary to get you off this train as soon as possible. I have an idea on how to do that. Come with me, quickly."

Macintosh led them through the doorway at the front end of the baggage car. "This covered passageway between the baggage car and the third locomotive takes you to a storage area at the back of the third locomotive. Roger and Fouad stepped into a small chamber in the back of the third locomotive.

Mac told them, "The locomotive engineer and his assistant are up front in the control center of the first of the three locomotives. They operate the three locomotives from the lead locomotive. It is very unlikely that anyone will come back to this passageway in the third locomotive. However, if you hear anyone coming, the two of you must conceal yourselves in this small empty storage closet.

"The number one priority is for the two of you to keep out of sight. For my survival now, as well as yours, we must maintain the idea that the bears are gnawing on your bones back there in the tunnel. You must be seen by no one."

"We get the message," Fouad said, Macintosh explained intently what had to be done. "We have to get you off this train, as soon as possible. Fortunately, there is an opportunity coming up for you to get you off this train. When we approach the great Hells Gate cataract, the train will go through what they call a photo opt slowdown. The train will be slowing to almost a walk for passengers to view and photograph this great spectacle of the churning water of the great cataract. This slowdown will last a few minutes.

"When this slowdown happens, you must drop from the train on the side away from the cataract. Roll down off the track area into the drainage ditch along the track. Conceal yourselves in whatever brush or high grass you find, until the train picks up speed again and is out of sight."

Macintosh explained, "You will hear the conductor announcing the great Hell's Gate cataract. As the train slows down you must drop from the train. For the three of us to stay alive you must vanish from this train. The Hell's Gate slowdown is a readymade chance to escape. Jump, roll out of sight and lie still until the train resumes speed and passes on. Keep lying where you have landed until the train picks up speed and is gone."

"We hear you." Roger said. "That leaves us in a remote part of the Rockies. No roads. No people. How do we get out of this area?"

Macintosh said, "Once the train is out of sight, your best bet is to hike back upstream until you come to a bridge across the North Thompson River. Cross that bridge to the other side of the river where the East bound train runs. Hike back down stream to other side of Hell's Gate cataract where the eastbound train will also slow down for photos.

"Then run alongside, the East bound train. Grab the hand bars and swing up onto the boarding platform of the East bound train. Explain your predicament to the chief conductor."

Fouad said, "But it's not enough for us to escape. What about the bomb designed to destroy this train and its passengers at Vancouver?"

"That's number two on my list. First, I have to get the two of you off this train. If you are found to be alive they will not shoot to miss. I too will be a target.

Macintosh continued his briefing. "In about an hour, you will feel the train really slowing down. You will hear the train master announcing that the train is slowing down for passengers to take in the great Hell's Gate Cataract. When you hear that the train is slowing move quickly from this compartment out onto the back walkway of this locomotive. Using the two white painted safety railings step down to the lowest step and get set to jump. Jump out as far as you can. Jump past the railroad ties and gravel. Aim for the drainage ditch. When you land go flat, face down. Lie still. Keep as low as you can. We do not want any passengers to see you. Everyone should be looking toward the cataract."

"And our next step?" Roger asked.

Macintosh said, "After you find a bridge and cross over to the other side of the North Thompson River wait for the East bound train. Then when the next east bound train slows down to enable passengers to observe Hell's Gate Cataract, you will be able to board the slow moving train that is heading east."

Fouad asked again, "But what about the threat of this man's new bomb?"

"Once you are on board the east bound train tell them your story. Insist that they contact Edmonton. Insist that they order a search of the west bound train at Kamloops. When this train reaches Kamloops I will also notify the train police where you are. I will also insist that train police search the train for the bomb."

Fouad asked, "Will they take us seriously?"

Macintosh said, "New passengers do not board a train in the midst of these mountains. I think that the fact you dropped from the East bound train will give you credibility. Tell them your story. Tell them that there is a powerful explosive device on the westbound train. The bomb has been designed to destroy train and passengers when approaching Vancouver. Stress that this train must not leave Kamloops until the bomb has been located and defused. Time is limited. Tell them that we believe the bomb is set to explode as the train enters Vancouver."

Roger said, "Meanwhile we will be pretty much on our own."

Macintosh laughed, "Better on your own at Hell's Gate than in those bags at Red Spiral Tunnel."

Roger asked again, "What if we fail to board an East bound train? What if we are stuck there?"

Macintosh smiled and shook his head. "Roger. I worked for Emily's family for quite a few years. Do you really think Emily Henderson is going to let you just disappear?"

CHAPTER 52

Hell's Gate, North Thompson River-

"Let us run with endurance
– Letter to the Hebrews, AD 65

Fred and Mary were discovering that the intense and desperate race to reach K190 and Hell's Gate, before the great diesel powered train, was a very different sort of race. In this race, as Fred and Mary kept pushing their horses, a major difficulty was that they had no way to gauge how they were doing. Unlike horse races like the Kentucky Derby, the couple on horseback and the engineer in the locomotive cab were never insight of each other.

There was another difference. Only the contestants on horseback were aware of how crucial it was that they prevailed. As Fred and Mary raced to reach Hell's Gate before the train, they did so with the urgency of knowing that the lives of many people depended on getting to K190 in time. The engineer in the cab of the lead locomotive had no idea of being in a race in which the outcome mattered so intensely.

Only the couple racing on horseback realized what was at stake. It was a race to preserve the threatened lives of the three hundreds passengers and crew. The engineer in the front cab, operating the three diesel electric locomotives, hadn't a clue that the lives of 300 passengers were at risk. The information driving that the couple on horseback was, of course, not available to the engineer. While the couple kept pushing their horses, the engineer in the cab of the lead locomotive had no idea that he was involved in a such a desperate race.

Fred and Mary's push to arrive at Hell's Gate in time to stop the train had become much more urgent. Originally, stopping this train was a scheme to spot and bring out into the open this man who had twice tried twice to kill Roger. Now more was at stake. This man was on the train with a powerful bomb. They had good reason to believe that he was set to destroy the train and as it approached Vancouver, The lives of 300 passengers was at stake.

The race was now a race for life. Fred and Mary had to reach Kilometer 190 before the train. Fred was determined to drop those lodge pole pines he had pre-cut and stop this train. Fred told Mary that he was going to stop those three diesels in their tracks.

Though the trail from their cabin to Hell's Gate on the North Thompson was downhill and familiar to Fred and Mary, it was extremely difficult for their horses. The trail was very steep and frequently obstructed by fallen trees. It was hard going for the horses. Fred and Mary pressed their horses as much as possible but this rugged trail was very difficult and dangerous.

Fred said, "We're in a very unusual race, Mary. Its two horses with eight hoofs hitting the ground versus three diesel locomotives, each with eight power driven wheels hitting the rails."

Mary laughed, "Those diesel fed horses haven't a chance against these real hay fed horses. They will need all that diesel fed horsepower."

As they continued, pressing their horses as much as possible, Fred was thinking all that they needed now was for one of the horses to step into some one's bear trap. They had finally made it down to the North Thompson. They had crossed the ford that enabled them to reach the side of the river and the west bound tracks. Suddenly trouble hit them. Mary's horse went lame.

Mary quickly slipped off her horse. She hugged and tied her horse to a tree. After giving her horse some feed in a nose bag, Mary grabbed Fred's waiting hand as he swung her up behind him. Fortunately, their trail now followed a level path along the river. This was a big help as they pressed on, riding double.

They finally reached the point in the canyon where their trail and the railroad tracks now ran side by side. Soon they were moving alongside the powerful North Thompson River. As the North Thompson began to pound through an increasingly rocky narrows it was becoming filled with powerful churning white water.

When they were reached K190 and the boiling white cascade of Hell's Gate. Fred pounded the air. They arrived at their destination with no train in sight. "We made it. We're here." Heavy mist and the thundering sound of the cataract filled the air.

Fred turned to give Mary a hug.

With a few tears in her eyes, Mary said, "We did it."

Everything seemed the same. Fred checked out the fishing platforms and the two cables of the First Nation fishermen. There was no sign of recent fishing activity. The famous old viewing platform, built in the days when the train stopped for viewing the Hell's Gate Cataract, seemed in good shape.

Fred checked his watch. "I figure that we have about forty minutes till the estimated time for the train to reach Hell's Gate. We need every one of those minutes. Let's get to work."

They hurried to the tool shed where they had stashed the now powerless bomb. Fred dragged out the bomb pack. He installed a new battery and activated the mechanism. He set the timer for detonation about two hours after the anticipated arrival of the train. The settings were locked in. The bomb was designed so that no change in the settings could be made at this altitude without triggering the bomb.

With the detonator lights clicking away, Fred and Mary tugged the heavy bomb pack out on to the observation platform. The sand that Fred had inserted duplicated the weight of the explosives removed. They positioned the big black pack holding the bomb in a conspicuous place on the approach to the old observation platform. Fred wired it in place.

Frank swung Mary up on his horse to ride behind him again. They headed for the spot high above the tracks where the great lodge pole pines Fred had cut were held in place by cables. Their exhausted horse carried them up to the spot where Fred and Roger had prepared to drop the trees to the tracks bellow.

Fred found the three great lodge pole pines he had pre-cut still held in place by the cables and ready to be released to go tumbling down the mountain to the tracks. Fred checked his watch again. "Close. Looks like we still have about ten minutes to go."

Suddenly then they heard the sound for which they were waiting, the distant sound of the train's whistle. It was approaching the bend and would soon come into sight. The train was now just moments away from coming into view as it made the turn on to the straight away.

Fred stayed focused intently up the track. The plan to stop the great train safely was contingent on Fred's being there to drop the great pre-cut pines at the right moment. Fred's had calculated that it was essential for the engineer to spot the trees crashing down to the tracks, as soon as he pulled onto the straight away. For the safety of everyone involved Fred was very concerned that the engineer have sufficient time to stop the train without crashing into the stuff on the tracks.

Suddenly they heard, louder now, the wail of the train whistle again. The train was going to come into view quickly.

Mary was happy to hear that sound. "I know why he's blowing that whistle today. He's saying, 'You won. You won.'"

Mary prayed aloud, "Lord Jesus, let these big pines do their job. Stop this train and stop this hate filled man. Like a locomotive on a turn table, turn this man around."

As they looked down the track, Fred kept focused on the spot where the train would come into view as it came around the bend. His hand was on the cable release.

Talking aloud to himself Fred said, "We must drop the trees as soon as the train makes that turn and comes into sight. I want the engineer to see these trees tumbling down to the track. He has to have all the time we can give him to bring that consist of thirty cars to a safe stop. He will have not much more than two kilometers to stop the train at Hells Gate. On this slight downgrade he will need every inch to stop that train safely."

Fred and Mary, along with Roger, had figured that, since it would take several hours for a work crew to come and clear the track, the passengers would be encouraged to step off the train and view the Hell's Gate Cataract from the viewing platform. As the passengers went to view the cataract it would be natural for the man who was their target to go also.

The plan was that as the man who was their target went out on the viewing area he would suddenly see and recognize his bomb pack. When he examined the pack he would find his bomb made for the plane ticking away, there in a location obviously well below its 1,000 foot altitude set for explosion.

They hoped that the man's immediate reaction, regardless of any disguise, would reveal his identity. It was their expectation that, since he had designed the bomb, he would know its great power. Also, as he discovered that it about to explode, he would know that, at this altitude, it's settings could not be changed. His reaction would be obvious.

From what they heard in the office at Blue River, Fred and Mary realized that now the situation would be even more threatening to this designer of bombs. They now knew that the man had with him on this train another and probably even more powerful bomb. This designer of both bombs, would realize instantly that the explosion of the bomb in the bomb pack designed for Roger's flight, would trigger the deadly bomb on the train. He would see his life threatened.

Suddenly Fred saw what he waiting to see. About two kilometers down the track, the lead locomotive with its lights blazing had come around the bend and into sight.

Fred immediately released the cables restraining the huge pre-cut lodge pole pines.

For a moment the tree's seemed to just stand there tottering. Fred stood aside with clenched fists. He was anxious. Did I cut far enough? Then the cut trees started to fall. With a great force the huge trees toppled over and came down, crashing through the trees below them. They took more and more small trees with them as they rolled down the rocks with a great crashing roar. Much material came crashing on to the track below.

Fred turned to Mary. She was in tears. He gave her a big hug and prayed, "Lord Jesus, long ago you once said that Hell's Gate, the real Hell's Gate and all the forces of evil in this world would not prevail against or withstand your power and purpose. Lord, we need to see your power and purpose working here today."

CHAPTER 53

On board Train
Hell's Gate Cataract on the North Thompson

"Grow old along with me! The best is yet to be,
the last of life, for which the first was made.
Our times are in his hand who saith,
A whole I planned, youth shows but half;
Trust God: See all, nor be afraid!"
– Rabbi Been Ezra – Robert Browning, 1869

The three powerful locomotives, each with 3200 horsepower, had pulled the train's great consist of thirty passenger cars across the Canadian Rockies Continental Divide. Now, after crossing of the challenge of the great continental divide at three thousand feet, the train was beginning to make its way down through the spectacular scenery of the western slope of the Canadian Rockies.

On the downward slope, the wide swing of the great Red Spiral Tunnel was helping to reduce the degree of downward passage. The great tunnel had been designed to reduce the down grade of west bound trains and the upgrade of the east bound trains. After the tunnel the train continued descending as it made its way along the narrow and rocky canyon of the North Thompson River.

In the air-conditioned cab of the lead locomotive, with all the controls at his fingertips, engineer Bill Hoover was preparing to take his train around a major curve and onto the straight away that would take the train along North Thompson. He looked forward to this run along the churning white water of the great Hell's Gate Cataract. As the train rolled along, this second generation engineer had his eyes on the silver rails before him. Bill Hover loved his job.

Suddenly, as the train rounded the big bend and came onto the straight away, Hoover's eyes blinked in disbelief. About two kilometer ahead an avalanche of trees and rocks was cascading down the mountainside above the track.

The experienced engineer reacted instinctively. He knew right away that at his present speed on this slight down grade, he had barely the time needed to bring his train to a stop in time. He immediately hit the train's air brakes. He then took the necessary steps to switch the power of the three locomotives to generate power for the supplementary braking system.

By this swift action the motors of each diesel electric locomotive were instantly transformed into powerful generators. The three powerful locomotives were now converting their traction power into additional breaking power. The power that enabled the train to cross the continental divide was now providing additional braking power to supplement the train's air breaking system.

With the shrill squealing sound of metal on metal, the great train kept braking until it thundered to a halt. The lead engine came to a stop only a couple car lengths short crashing into the huge pile of trees, rocks and forest debris piled up across the tracks. The engineer's quick action had brought the great train to a safe stop.

Hoover pounded his fists in victory. He pulled out his trainman's blue handkerchief to wipe his face, took a big breath and closed his eyes to say, "Thank You, God!"

Engineer Hover shared a high five with his assistant engineer. If his lead engine had plowed into the fallen logs and rocks it would most certainly have derailed and torn up track. He was saying, "Talk about timing. It was a good thing that I saw that stuff coming down the mountain when I did."

ii

Among the passengers, as the train was approaching the North Thompson there was growing anticipation for viewing the great Hell's Gate cataract. Passengers were at their windows with cameras at ready. The train was filled with excitement. Those fortunate to have seats in domed observation cars were filled with expectation.

No one seemed to realize that the train was not just slowing down. Everyone seemed to assume that the braking was applied to give them more time to view the Hell's Gate cataract. As the train kept braking severely, passengers were filled with excitement.

Then, suddenly with a hard jolt, all of the cars of the great train came to a sudden and complete stop. Some passengers in the dining car almost slid off their seats. Some plates flew off the tables and a few glasses tipped over. Passengers in the dining car struggled to keep their plates and cups from sliding off their tables.

The impossible had happened. Something had stopped the great train. The huge three powerful engines that had just crossed the Continental divide at 3,000 feet had suddenly brought the great train to a complete stop.

One passenger called out, "Wow! Did we hit a rock?" A joker replied, "No, we hit an iceberg?" Another voice called out, "If this were the Titanic I would be troubled."

Someone called out, "Remember, we are out West where all those stage coach robberies took place. Now we have train robbers. This train is about to be robbed. Hide your valuables."

Someone shouted back, "You've been watching too many old train robbery movies." Then a quiet voice volunteered, "The tracks are probably buried by an avalanche."

An answer came back. "You're crazy. This is August. It's too early for a snow.

iii

While his assistant was on the phone explaining the situation to the Conductor, Engineer Hoover was in contact with the Edmonton train control center.

"Hoover, here. I am stopped with lead locomotive 3434 at kilometer 190. We have an avalanche of fallen trees and rocks across the tracks. I was able to stop the lead engine a good car lengths from the debris. All passenger cars are safely lined along Hell's Gate Cataract."

In response to questions, Hoover said, "No derailment. No, apparent damage to the track. Fortunately, I saw the avalanche falling as I turned onto the straightway. This gave me time to stop before hitting this small mountain of fallen trees and rocks."

The supervisor from Edmonton said, "Good work Hoover! We appreciate your bringing your three hundred passengers to safe stop. And no damage to the locomotive. Great! No injury to passengers and crew. Great! Thank you, Bill."

After some further inquiries Hoover said, "It looks like a job for our heavy duty work crew out of Kamloops. They will need a heavy duty crane for the lodge pole pines and rock. They may need to check alignment of the track."

The supervisor said, "Thanks for your alert response. The work car from Kamloops should reach you in a couple hours. It sounds like three to four hours of intense work."

iv

The voice of the lead conductor addressed the passengers over the sound system. "As you are aware, our train has come to an unscheduled stop. There is no cause for alarm." He gave a short of laugh. "You will not need life jackets. Our crew was able to avoid the iceberg."

He continued. "Our excellent engineer stopped the train in time to avoid crashing into the material that had fallen on the track. We are waiting for a work crew from Kamloops to remove the debris on the tracks. We expect to be stopped here for about four hours. Relax. Take pictures. Enjoy getting to know your fellow passengers. All snack bars and dining room cars will be open."

The conductor continued. "You have the good fortune to be stopped by one of the world's most spectacular sights, another eighth wonder of the world, the Hell's Gate Cataract. Usually we just slow down here. Take advantage of this unusual opportunity. Exit the train and view this great sight.

"There are some precautions to observe. Stay by your train. You will see, a bit upstream, the fishing platforms of the local First Nation fishermen. You will also see two cables installed across the cataract by the fishermen for crossing the cataract. This area is used exclusively by the fishermen and dangerous. This area is closed."

V

In their perch on the mountainside high above the tracks, when the train finally thundered and shuddered to a loud earth shaking stop, Fred let out a long and powerful sigh. "He was able to stop in time. Wow that was close."

Fred continued watching the activity by the great train below them. Then, wishing that he could speak to Roger on the train far below, Fred called out, "Roger, we did our part. We hope you guys realize what's been happening. Your train did not just stop. Roger. Operation lodge pole pines has been activated. Get on the job, down there."

Mary said, "Do you think they will get the message? Fred, is it going to hit Roger why we activated the plan? Roger, we stopped your train because that snake in the grass is on the train?"

Fred said, "Mary, when Roger sees how the train has been stopped, it will hit him, right between the eyes, that only we, only we, Fred and Mary, could have carried out operation lodge pole pines to stop this train."

Mary called out, "Roger, if this train has been stopped, as planned, it means one thing. Despite all the talk you heard, the man we're looking for is on this train. Do your stuff."

Mary turned to Fred. "This whole scheme has really gotten bigger. First, it was a just a plan to draw this snake in the grass out of his hole. Now we have a bigger job. Yes, now, we have to find both the man and his bomb."

Mary said, "Fred, I'd like to see us do more than that. It would be great if we could do more than simply identify the man and find his bomb."

Fred said, "What is my creative wife thinking now?"

"I'd like to see this man, running with hatred, stopped, derailed in his tracks, turned around and made into a new and different person."

Fred laughed. "Mary, what you're looking for would take something like those huge turntables they use to turn locomotives around and put them on a different track. Maybe that's what we need here. It takes something great to turn a person around."

CHAPTER 54

Hell's Gate cataract on the North Thompson

"Never be afraid to trust an unknown future to a known God."
– Corrie ten Boom

As the train continued its gradual descent down the canyon of the North Thompson River, Roger and Fouad stayed hidden in storage area of third locomotive, as Macintosh had advised. They kept the door of their hiding place open to monitor where the train was taking them.

They were trusting in the escape plan Macintosh had given them. They kept waiting for the conductor's announcement that the train was approaching the great natural attraction, Hell's Gate Cataract. They were waiting for the time when the train would be slowing to give passengers opportunity to view and photograph the great cataract. They kept waiting for the slowdown and the opportunity to make their jump and escape from the train.

The two men were set to jump from the train on the side away from the cataract. They planned to lie flat, wherever they landed, until the train resumed speed and moved on. They would hike upstream to the next bridge. They would cross over the North Thompson River and hike back down on the other side of the river to Hell's Gate cataract. There they would wait for the next east bound train. As it slowed down for its passengers. to view the cataract they would board the train and ask for emergency service.

Suddenly, at last, they felt the train slowing. Roger said, "Looks like this is it."

The two men moved quickly from their hiding place. They held on to the white hand rails of the locomotive as they moved down to the lowest step. They could hear the roar of the cataract.

Roger said, "I think this is as slow as it is going to get. On three let's go." Roger and Fouad jumped out from the train, as far as possible. They hit the ground on the side away from the where the passengers were viewing the cataract. Roger and Fouad remained in the drainage ditch where they had landed.

The two men continued lying there, motionless, as the train continued its slowdown. Their plan was to remain lying flat in the drainage ditch until the train picked up speed again and moved out of sight. They continued lying there in the drainage ditch, just a few feet from the tracks, waiting for the train to resume speed.

As they continued lying there, in the ditch along the tracks, Roger said "The train is continuing to slow down. It is scarcely moving. Maybe we jumped too soon."

Suddenly they were overwhelmed with the loud, ear piercing, sound of wheels, just a few feet from their ears, scraping and screeching, steel on steel. Then, giving off an ear-splitting squeal and a loud thundering sound like an explosion, with a final powerful shudder, the great train came to a complete stop. It all happened right in front of their faces.

They had been expecting the train to resume speed so that they could complete their escape. Now, with the surprise of the train thundering to a complete stop, the two men were puzzled and just looked at each other. Speaking together, they both said, "What's going on?"

In few minutes, the answer to their quandary came over the train's sound system. "This is your conductor speaking. Our train has made an unscheduled stop. There is no cause for alarm." They heard his attempt at a joke. "We have not hit an iceberg. You will not need life jackets. Here at the spectacular Hell's Gate Cataract, where we are stopped you, will need only your cameras."

After a short pause, the voice continued, "A small avalanche of trees and rocks has tumbled down the mountain side on to the tracks and we have been forced to stop. There has been no damage to the train. A work crew from Kamloops will soon arrive to remove this debris from the tracks. In a few hours we should be on our way."

The conductor continued, "Meanwhile, since we will be stopped here for a few hours, relax, take pictures. Enjoy this opportunity to exit the train. Go out on the Hell's Gate Cataract observation platform.

The train's snack bars and the dining cars will be open. Get to know your fellow travelers. Three blasts of the train whistle will call you to board when we are ready to continue.

"While the delay is unfortunate it also provides a rare opportunity. You could not have been stopped at a more spectacular scenic spot. You are stopped at Hell's Gate Cataract, a spectacular sight which, with no roads in the area, is visible only from this train."

After another pause, the conductor continued. "If you did not know better, you would suspect someone stopped the train deliberately, so you could enjoy this amazing natural wonder."

Roger turned to Fouad. "Did you hear that? He said that you might suspect someone stopped this train deliberately? Fouad, I just got a wakeup call. That must be exactly what has happened. It just hit me. Someone really did stop this train deliberately. And I know who. Some dear friends have put in action a plan we had developed together. It had been cancelled but they re-activated the plan."

"Roger, did your head hit a rock? Are you saying that someone, here literally in the middle of nowhere, deliberately dropped trees down the mountain and stopped this train?"

"Exactly, Fouad. And it was not just someone. Two wonderful people I know dropped the precut trees and stopped this particular train here at the Hell's Gate Cataract, exactly as we planned. Our train being stopped, here at the Hell's Gate, was not due to some chance mountain avalanche of trees and rocks. Every detail of this stop is exactly as planned."

"Roger, the conductor just told us an avalanche of trees stopped the train."

"Fouad, it look like this is an accident of nature but I am telling you that this avalanche was deliberately planned and triggered by people following a definite plan. My friends must have received some critical information that caused them to activate the plan."

Fouad looked startled at Roger. "Are you cracking up, Roger? We are in as remote and uninhabited and inaccessible area of the Canadian Rockies as you could find. There are no people in this area for miles. We've been told that this chance avalanche of trees and rocks coming down the mountain to stop our train was simply an act of nature. Roger, these things just happen."

"Let me explain, Fouad. When you and your helper sabotaged my plane by causing my engine failure you saved my life. When my plane went down among five thousand foot mountains you prevented me from descending to 1,000 feet in Vancouver where the bomb on board was rigged to blow me to pieces. By forcing me to parachute from my plane at 5,000 feet you saved my life.

"But saving Roger Renoir took more. I parachuted into really rugged mountain country but help was on the way. God put it into the heart and mind of two people who saw my plane going down to look for anyone who might have survived. After two days searching in that very rugged country, this amazing couple, Fred and Mary Christiansen, found me and took me to their remote mountain cabin."

Fouad said, "Sounds great but what has that to do with our situation now?"

Roger continued, "While I was recovering and hiding out from the man who had planned my death over Vancouver, I made ham radio contact with friends in Toronto. I learned that this unknown man was going to be on this train which rolled out of Toronto on August 18. Possibly with a bomb. With the knowledge where this man would be, I saw this as an opportunity to draw this snake in the grass out of his hole and identify him."

"Roger, I know what he looks like. I've been looking for him on this train without success since we left Toronto, five days ago. How were you going to spot him?"

Roger said, "We had deactivated and brought out his unexploded bombpac from the wrecked plane as possible evidence. That bomb pack gave us the idea for a plan to make this man show his colors.

"We planned to use the deactivated bomb rescued from the wrecked plane to get the attention of this man who had planned to kill me. We realized that at Hell's Gate this train would pass only a few miles below the cabin. We figured that, if the train was stopped for a couple hours by something on the track at the great cataract, the passengers would leave the train to view the Hell's Gate cataract. Hopefully this man would join them. We planned to use his bomb pack, recovered from the plane, as a trap. We would place it some place so that he would be confronted with this bomb, the bomb from the plane. He would find it ticking away toward explosion. We figured that when he realized that that this was his bomb, and that it was about to explode, his reaction would make his identify obvious."

"Quite an ambitious plan."

Roger said, "Yes. However, after making all the arrangements, we heard through our phone tap, that he had cancelled his plan to be on our train. So, we cancelled our plans to stop the train. And now? Now, here we are with the big train stopped as originally planned. Although we cancelled the plan, the train appears to have been stopped exactly where planned and exactly in the way we planned."

Fouad asked, "Who could have activated the plan?"

Roger said, "There's only one possible explanation of this train being stopped. Fred and Mary. Somehow, they must have learned, that the man was on the train, after all. They must also have learned, as we did, that he has on board a new bomb designed to destroy this train in Vancouver.

"Only these two people knew enough to have acted to reactivate our plan to stop the train. They must be hoping that we on board realize what was happening and do our part as planned."

Fouad said, "Now, with the train stopped, what is your plan?"

"Our targeted man has no idea what happened to me or his plane and his kamikaze bomb. When, during this stop, he comes upon his old bomb pack and finds it ticking away toward explosion, his reaction should make his identity obvious. Once we have identified the man, we will identify him for the train police.

Suddenly they heard the conductor's voice. "Use this unexpected opportunity to view this great natural wonder. We estimate that it will take about two hours for the work crew coming up from Kamloops to get here. Then about two more hours to clear the track sufficiently for us to proceed."

The train master continued, "A word of caution. Farther upstream you will see the fishing platforms built by local First Nation fishermen. You will see two steel cables spanning the ravine. They were installed by the fishermen. Their equipment is dangerous. The area is strictly off limits. You are directed to keep some distance from the fishing platforms."

Fouad said, "If your friends, Fred and Mary, learned that the professor was on board, they must have learned, as I learned from Vashti, that he is on board with a very powerful bomb designed to destroy and blow this train off the tracks in Vancouver. Your plan to draw this snake in the grass out of his hole is now even more urgent."

CHAPTER 55
Hell's Gate on North Thompson River

*"Is there a purpose to our lives,
or are we cosmic accidents
emerging from the slime?"*
– Chuck Colson, How Now Shall We Live?

When the train was slowing down and they made their jump from the train, Roger and Fouad were focused on escaping from the train with their lives. With their realization that the great train had been brought to stop at the Hell's Gate cataract by Fred and Mary, Roger and Fouad found their focus suddenly turned around. Still lying in the ditch where they had landed, they listened as the conductor encouraged passengers to step off the train. and go out on the viewing platform and to view the great cataract.

Roger was pleased with what he was hearing. He explained the plan more fully to Fouad. "This is exactly the situation we wanted to create. We thought that, with a stop of a couple hours, the passengers would wander off the train. We hoped that our target man would leave the train with the other passengers and then spot a very familiar pack, the bomb pack he had designed for the plane.

Roger explained to Fouad the thinking behind the plan to stop the great train. "We figured our man would be very surprised and curious when he spotted this very familiar looking bomb pack. We're expecting that he would feel he had to examine this pack.

He hadn't had a clue to what happened to the plane or me, the pilot, or his bomb pack. All he could know was that his bomb loaded plane never reached Vancouver. In our plan to stop the train, we hoped that when he saw the familiar bomb pack from the plane, he would feel compelled to check it out. His actions would identify the man..

Roger continued briefing Fouad. "We figured that when Hamu opened the pack and saw his own devise ticking away toward explosion, his face and actions would immediately confirm his identity. He will immediately see that the bomb is ticking away toward explosion. Also, as the designer of this devise, he will know that any attempt to change the settings, below 1,000 feet, will cause instant explosion. He would be very much aware that, at this point, he was well below 1,000 feet. It would hit him that he cannot stop what was about to happen. At the same time, he would realize immediately that this bomb was going to trigger the explosion of the even more deadly bomb in his compartment."

Fouad said, "Roger, as you think of this man who planned to kill both of us, you have no idea what he looks like. I, as his double, am very aware what he looks like. It was because we so closely resembled each other that he planned my murder so he could have my death regarded as his death. I have been looking for him on this train since we left Toronto and I have not been able to spot him. He has to be wearing some sort of disguise or mask. This makes your plan to identify him by his reaction to discovering his own bomb pack clicking away to explosion, a great plan.

"Roger, let me show you, again, what your mystery man will looks like." Fouad removed his wig and slowly pulled off his life mask. He ran his fingers through his white beard and his white hair. "Ah, that feels good. Roger, this is what your enemy looks like."

"So, Fouad, when I finally see this man without any disguise I can expect him to have the white hair and the white facial hair, just as I am seeing in you?"

"Yes. Roger, I'm preparing to return to being with Vashti. This life mask is off permanently. Sooner or later this man, the impostor, is going to have to deal with the fact that I am alive. Perhaps, that will happen on this train. I boarded this train to return to Vashti in Vancouver. I called from Jasper to let her known I am alive and on my way home. This mask is off for good.

"The impostor is going to have to know, sooner or later, that Fouad is alive. His impersonation of me must come to an end."

Roger said, "Let's get out there and see if he is drawn to the bomb pack."

Roger and Fouad slipped out from below the train and joined the passengers moving out on the viewing platform. As they mingled with the crowd, Roger kept searching the area above the track for the two people he knew had to be up there. Finally, he spotted his friends, with their horse, high on the mountain. There, partly concealed behind brush, Fred and Mary were watching the scene below.

"See them up there?" Roger gestured to their hiding place.

Fouad kept looking. "That older couple with the horse? They stopped this train? I'm impressed."

"They are watching to see us do our part down here."

Fouad said, "If you succeed in spotting him today what do you hope to do?"

Roger said, "The original plan was simply to see and identify the man who ordered me shot and loaded my plane with that bomb. I needed to know from whom I was running. Now, with the bomb the situation has changed. The next step will be to inform the police.

"Now, knowing about the bomb on board, the situation is drastically changed. Now, once we spot the mam, we must seek his arrest and deactivate the bomb on board this train. Also, we now know that the cash stolen in the Toronto robbery is on board somewhere. We want to locate and deactivate the bomb. We want to retrieve the cash. Then we want to help the police bring his campaign against the west to an end."

Fouad said, "We've seen some of his men. Do we have sufficient manpower on board to handle this?"

"God seems to have anticipated our needs. Fouad, it so happens that my painting friend, Bill Webber, is really a retired officer of the RCMP. He insisted in joining us on this train incognito. He has some plain clothes officers with him. These experienced men are equipped to take control of the situation as the need arises."

ii

With the train stopped, Hamu was getting anxious. From his compartment he was watching, with growing concern, the people pouring off the train to view the Hell's Gate cataract. He was more than disturbed by this unexpected stop. He was anxious to see the train moving again and reach Kamloops. He wanted to get off this train with his men. Some were directed, as soon as they reached Kamloops, to retrieve that valuable pre-boarding checked baggage that contained the cash from the Toronto robbery.

Dropping those two men in the tunnel made him more anxious to reach Kamloops and get off this train. He felt well protected by his disguise but the impostor was getting increasingly anxious to reach Kamloops and leave this train.

Hamu had seen the Spiral tunnel as a quick solution to a problem. Dumping the bodies in the tunnel was an expedient way to dispose of those trouble makers. Now, with the train stopped, people will be asking questions.

Hamu was very concerned, now with the train stopped, that people would be asking about the man with the Geiger counter. It will be the same with the man in tweeds who was babbling about a bomb on board. Friends will be asking about him.

While the train was rolling along people would assume that a person was somewhere on the train. Few would bothered to ask questions. How can you get lost on a train? But now, with the train stopped, there will be questions.

Hamu watched the passengers moving off the train. I don't like this situation at all. If I could leave the train now, I would grab the prechecked baggage holding the cash and take off. I would reset the timer and leave my bomb with its clock running. The problem is that we're in the middle of nowhere. We are only a half day's travel from Kamloops but there is no way out of this place. He looked toward the cataract. Hamu laughed. Hell's Gate. Yes, like they say, there is no escape from Hell.

Hamu decided to leave his compartment, mingle with the crowd, and learn what was going on. He was interested in hearing what people might be saying. He took a quick look in his mirror to check his disguise. He adjusted his wig and life mask, stepped down the steps of the car and mingled with people heading toward the viewing platform.

Once he had his feet on solid ground, Hamu stopped to take in the spectacular soaring mountains surrounding him, Many of the peaks appeared to be covered with great sheets of rock. He had heard that the mountains here appeared to just go straight up. In whatever direction he looked he faced great expanses of sheer rock in the surrounding mountains.

Hamu had an interesting thought. What if the men I ordered dropped in the tunnel were right in their last words? What if, as they claimed, there really was a Creator, a person who, like a great conductor, was directing and controlling the forces of nature that shaped these mountains? What if someone was behind the earthquakes and glaciers?

Hamu was impressed with the amazing forces that it took to shape the towering mountains and the vast expanse of rock all around him. What, if, as those men I dropped in the big tunnel suggested, someone, using earthquakes and glaciers really made these mountains? What if, as they believed, this really is the visited planet? He laughed. They should know by now.

Hamu continued scanning the area. Yes, he saw that, as the train master had pointed out, there are clearly no roads around here. No roads except this railroad. The only way in or out of here is by this train. With the train stopped my options are limited.

Hamu saw the tracks for the East bound train on the other side of the churning waters of the gorge. I don't see any bridge. That means there is no way over there unless you can walk on water. I don't see any anything going across Hell's Gate except those cables the conductor says local fishermen strung across the ravine between their fishing platforms.

Hamu saw the small mountain of trees and rocks that had stopped the train. That work crew from Kamloops will have quite a job. But they might provide a way out of here. Possibly when the work crew comes I can slip the foreman a bundle of cash to take me with them back to Kamloops. Most people will do anything for cash. He continued to move out toward the observation platform with the crowd.

iii

As Albert and Sarah Weiss exited from the train they were looking for Roger and getting anxious. When they met with the team, Albert asked, "Have you seen Roger? I loaned him my geiger counter. He was going to check for any radioactive material on the train."

Hank said, "Radioactive material on the train?"

"Yes, Hank. Despite the failure of all those police to find the cash from the Toronto robbery on our train, Roger and I believed that that cash might be on this train."

Hank said, "And Roger went off looking for cash with a geiger?"

Weiss said, "Yes, does sound crazy. Here's the connection. While a prisoner of this gang on the Toronto waterfront, Roger, by listening to their conversation, learned that the radioactive material thieves and the men staging the Toronto rush hour robbery were the same gang."

Hank laughed, "But why look for cash with a geiger?"

Albert smiled. "Easy answer. Roger and I figured that since the Toronto money thieves also handled stolen radioactive materials, they might be leaving traces on the train. So Roger took off through the train with my geiger. Have you seen Roger? Any idea where Roger might be?"

Joan laughed, "Look in the dome observation cars. That's the closest to a plane."

Emily felt it was time to brief the Weiss couple about why the train was being stopped. "Albert and Sarah, there's something we have to share with you about this train being stopped."

Sarah said, "We're all ears."

"Our train was not stopped by some unexpected natural avalanche. The trees and rocks rolling down on the tracks to force our train to stop here at Hell's Gate was a planned happening. Stopping this train was planned by Roger and his friends, Fred and Mary Christiansen. They had planned and prepared to stop this train at this exact location, here at Kilometer 190, here at Hell's Gate Cataract."

Weiss shook his head. "This is a scenic spot, but why stop a train here?"

Emily continued, "We had learned by a phone tap that this unknown man who twice tried to kill Roger would be on board this train. Roger and his friends planned to stop the train here to create a situation in which they hoped to identify the man and turn things around.

"They planned to stop the train and identify the man as they saw his reaction to being confronted with one of his own bombs, ticking away. They thought the man's reaction would make his identify obvious."

Weiss said, "But why then is this coming as such a surprise today?"

Emily said, "We ran into a problem. Later, after all our planning, from our phone taps we learned that this man would not be on the train as planned. So, Fred and Mary left things in place but cancelled the action to stop the train.

"Now, although the plan was cancelled, much to our surprise, this train has been stopped anyway. We are stopped here at very spot planned and by an avalanche of mountain debris, as planned. There can be only one explanation. Fred and Mary learned that this man is on the train, after all."

Hank said, "Only Fred and Mary could have possibly carried out this plan. But why? Perhaps these older friends, Fred and Mary were confused and stopped the train anyway?"

Weis said, "Confused? No, this well planned and executed stopping of the train was not carried out by confused persons. There is, of course, a far more likely explanation."

Hank asked, "What could be more likely than they were confused?"

Weiss tapped his head. "Roger told me about Fred and Mary. They are very sharp people. Fred and his wife Mary were clever and searched for any possible survivor of the Roger's plane crash. Fred, calculated where any survivor might have parachuted. Fred and Mary found Roger. This excellent team, created through God's' gift of marriage, located the wrecked plane and found the undetonated bomb."

Weiss stopped and laughed. "They are not absent minded professors. No, if that team stopped this train they were not confused. The more likely explanation is that these two very sharp people somehow discovered that, in spite of his attempts to confuse people, this character was on the train. No one had to tell them what to do. They took action."

Hank said, "You mean they just acted on a hunch he was on the train?"

Weis said, "No, no, not at all. Fred and Mary are not the kind of people who act on wishful thinking. They acted on information. They learned the man was on the train. They knew this train had to be stopped. They knew that they were the only people who could do it. They acted."

Weis took off his glasses and waved them for emphasis. "I see three key facts.

"Number one. Since Fred and Mary act on reliable sources of knowledge, their stopping the train indicates this man you are looking for is definitely on this train.

"Number two. Supports that conclusion. Earlier today, Roger and I learned that two young hi-tech boys on board intercepted calls on board. Some men were talking about large amounts of money this train. If the money is on this train it confirms that the key man must be on the train. "

"Number three. Now with the train stopped we still do not know where Roger is with my geiger. Roger is not the sort of person to get lost on a train. Roger's disappearance can mean only one thing. He has run into the trouble maker. His opponent is on this train. We need to see the plan Fred and Mary activated succeed. We must locate this man. We must locate Roger."

iv

From their position behind the tool shed Roger and Fouad continued to watch the passengers going out on the observation platform.

Roger said, "The passengers headed out to the platform to view the cataract are showing no interest in the pack. With the man who designed and packed his bomb in that pack it will be very different. He has no idea why the flight never reached Vancouver. He is still wondering what happened to the plane and its bomb. He does not know if I am dead or alive. So, if he spots that special pack in which he packed he bomb he will have to check it out. He will be very curious. When he sees the timer running toward explosions time, there's going to be a reaction. He will realize immediately that his life is in great danger. He will, know that any attempt to change the settings below 1,000 feet will trigger instant explosion. He will be very much aware that he is well below 1,000 feet here at Hell's Gate."

Fouad said, "He told Vashti that the bomb he brought on board would destroy the train. I believe we will see the reaction of a man greatly terrorized."

Suddenly, from their concealment Roger spotted a man stopping to stare at the bomb pack. Roger put his hand on Fouad and silently nodded toward the pack, "A fish is nibbling at our bait."

The man continued to stare at the big pack. He was wearing a black leather hat pulled down over bushy black hair. He was wearing a suit suitable for someone in the business world.

The man appeared to be very curious. As he moved closer to the pack he put his hand to his chin. He was obviously greatly puzzled. He pulled the pack open. His mouth opened. He stopped frozen in disbelief.

Touching his own face and hair to indicate the man was disguised. Fouad mouthed the words, "Mask and wig."

The man moved closer to examine big black pack. Fouad said softly, "Our snake has come out of his hole."

V

Hamu was stunned by what he was seeing. Can this be the plane's bomb pack? Is this my bomb for Vancouver, the bomb from the plane? That's what it is. How did it get here?

How could it have wound up here? There must have been a crash. Some Canadian first nation men must have pulled the bomb pack from the wreck and parked it here.

Hamu moved a bit closer. It is definitely the bomb pack from the plane. The locks are missing. He pulled open the pack. He was amazed. Yes, it was the bomb he had designed for the Vancouver flight. He saw that the pack still contained the special altimeter devise he had installed to explode the devise below one thousand feet.

Suddenly, he saw the little red count down lights are flashing. Somehow he must have accidentally activated the system. This devise is programmed to explode below 1,000 feet. We're well below 1,000 feet here in the North Thompson Canyon. The little red numbers are clicking away. This little monster is set to explode.

Suddenly, Hamu remembered, to his dismay, a feature he had built into this monster. He put his hands to his face. I designed this devise with a systems lock. Any attempt to alter the settings below 1,000 feet will trigger an immediate explosion. Once turned on, any attempt to change the settings will trigger explosion. This thing is moving toward blast off and there's no way I can stop it.

Suddenly another problem hit him. The explosion of this devise will certainly detonate that even more deadly monster I have brought on the train. There's no way to stop this. I've got to get moving and fast.

Hamu was growing more terrified. He was feeling claustrophobic in his wig and facial life mask. "I can't think with this stupid mask." He tore off his hat and wig and pulled off his facial mask and said, "Hamu will deal with this as Hamu. Hamu will survive."

Hamu looked desperately around him. Obviously no roads. No bridge. I have limited time. When this devise from the plane explodes that monster I brought on board will detonate. Everyone here will be buried alive. I'm getting out of here.

As he scanned the area Hamu saw another elevated platform a short distance up stream. That must be the fishermen's platforms. Then he spotted the great cables stretched across Hell's Gate cataract. Those are the fishermen's cables, the cables the conductor talked about. Great. Hamu there's your way over Hell's Gate. You're getting out of here, fast.

Hamu started running toward the fishing platform and the cables. Although running was difficult with his prosthetic devise he was moving fast.

vi

When Roger saw the man rip off his life mask, he saw that, the man's white hair and white beard and facial features were, as Fouad had said, identical to Fouad's.

Roger told Fouad. "I'm seeing for the first time the face of the man from whom I've been running."

Roger was shocked by what he saw in the man's eyes. He saw an intensity of the fear he had never seen before. Roger saw something else in the man's eyes, a strong determination to survive.

Roger turned to Fouad. As he looked from the face of his friend to study the now exposed face of his enemy, he was shocked with the complete similarity. He could see now the origin of Hamu's plan to destroy Fouad and lead the police to believe that it was Hamu who died.

Roger focused again on Hamu. The intensity of the mam's face showed a realization of the greatness of the danger facing him. He could see the man's realization that the bomb in the bomb pack from the plane would detonate the more deadly bomb on the train?

Roger spoke softly to Fouad, "He must be dealing with the fact that that he designed the bomb so that no one could alter the settings."

Fouad said, "Yes, and it must be hitting him that this bomb's explosions could also detonate the larger and more deadly bomb in his compartment. He's staring at death."

They saw the man's eyes were searching in every direction for a way out of his situation. They saw the man looking back up stream. Suddenly he was moving. With a face filled with desperation he was on the move, pushing people out of his way. This man was determined to survive.

Fouad said, "He isn't letting his prosthetic devise slow him down."

Since he had thrown his disguise aside, they could see in Hamu's face and his desperation and frantic drive to survive. He kept pushing people out of his way. The man was running to escape certain death.

As they watched this man's desperate efforts to escape what appeared to be certain death, Roger and Fouad were both experiencing something new. They were seeing for the first time this desperate man as a person like themselves.

CHAPTER 56

Hell's Gate Cataract on the North Thompson

"Prayer is an acknowledgement
of your dependence on God
and His direction of your life."
– Elizabeth George - 1999

After Hamu had ripped off his wig and face mask, Roger and Fouad suddenly saw in his wide open eyes the desperation of the man staring at the bomb pack. They could see that his face was frozen by fear. After his eyes locked on the little flashing red lights in the devise, the designer of the bomb knew that his powerful creation was moving toward an unstoppable explosion. The open fear filling his face exceeded anything Roger had envisioned seeing.

Suddenly, Roger and Fouad saw that the man was on the move. Now, with his wig and face mask ripped off, they could see the man's determination. Their man was on the move and shoving people out of his way. Roger and Fouad set out after him. They were amazed at the force with which Hamu was making his way through the crowd. Where could he be going? With so many passengers out to observe the cataract Roger and Fouad had trouble keeping the man in sight.

As they pushed after their man Roger called to Fouad. "He looks like your twin brother. Where does he think he's going?

Fouad said, "From what Vashti told me his bomb on the train could destroy the train and its passengers. Fear, especially of the more powerful bomb on board, must be driving him."

"Is he crazy enough, Fouad, to thinks he can escape the impact of the explosion by crossing Hell's Gate cataract on those fishermen's cables? Those cables are in no condition to be used. Someone left them sagging.

Roger and Fouad continued to push through the crowd of passengers as they followed after the man running from the bomb pack. The goal of the man was clearly to reach the two great cables the fishermen had stretched across the cataract.

When they realized this was his goal their pursuit was becoming more urgent. Their purpose was changing. Now, they were no longer simply trying to capture the man. They were racing now to stop the desperate man from the fatal mistake of attempting to cross the raging cataract on those old sagging rusty cables. From what Roger and Fouad could see, those sagging cables lacked the tension required for a successful crossing. Hamu kept running. It was increasingly clear that Hamu saw the two cables stretching across the Thompson River's great cataract as his only way to escape the coming disaster.

The cables stretched across the raging cataract from one fishing platform to the platform on the other side looked about an inch in thickness. The cables were swaying in the wind. It appeared to be quite some time since these cables were last used by the fishermen.

Fouad called to Roger, "Those fishermen may have deliberately left the cables slack to discourage anyone from risking their life by going out on them."

The distance across the raging water appeared to be about the width of a playing field. The lower cables, apparently for the feet, at midpoint sagged to not much more than about twenty feet above the raging white water. The parallel upper cable for the hands was about five feet above the lower cable.

As they got closer, Roger and Fouad could see that on the fishermen's platform there was some sort of gear cranking devise, apparently used to maintain the required tension of the cables. It appeared well rusted. A sign warned, "Access limited to members of the First Nation Fishermen's Association. All cable users are required to wear a safety vest attached to the upper cable."

ii

Roger and Fouad saw Hamu was climbing up the
ladder to the fishermen's platform. Their fugitive, quickly and without
hesitation, grabbed hold of the upper cable over the cataract and
stepped out onto the lower cable. The desperate man immediately
began working his way out on the cables. He was sliding each foot
along the lower foot cable and walking each hand along the upper
cable. The vigorous working, hand over hand on the upper cable,
showed the intensity of a man fleeing for his life.

As they watched Hamu work his way out on the cables, Roger and
Fouad saw a man driven by one thing, survival.

The large crowd out on the Hell's Gate observation platform was
turning to watch. At first, some people appeared to be wondering if all
this was part of a show arranged by the train operators to keep them
entertained. For a while the crowd seemed to be excited by the possibility of seeing a daredevil cross Hell's Gate on the cables. The crowd
soon became silent with fear as they began to see the great danger faced
by this man, whoever he was, moving inch by inch across the cataract.

For a few moments Roger and Fouad also stood on the fishermen's
platform, watching this desperate man making his way, inch by inch.
The lower swaying wet cable was at times, perhaps, no more than
twenty feet above the powerful churning water.

Fouad turned to Roger. "Are you feeling what I'm feeling?"

"Yes, I'm praying that he makes it."

"Same here, Roger."

As the spectators continued to watch the desperate situation of the
man out on the cables, the crowd became silent. It was beginning to
sink in that this was not some stunt. They began to realize that they
were seeing a fear driven man fighting for his life. As the passengers
watched in silence, it seemed that they were waiting to see when he
would drop into the churning waves of Hell's Gate.

Roger and Fouad, stood on the fishing platform by the big rusty
gear mechanism used to tighten the cables. They watched, with
increasing fear, the efforts of the man..

Roger said, "Does he really think he can make it across Hell's
Gate on those slippery and swinging wet old fishermen's cables? Wait

till he reaches that low point of the cable sag. "He's not going to get much farther."

Since Hamu had ripped off his mask, Roger was watching the man not as a persistent enemy but now simply as a desperate person. As Roger focused on the man struggling out on the cables, he was stunned to realize what he was feeling. Hatred for the man who had twice developed plans to kill him just wasn't there. As he saw the man's white hair blowing across his wet face, Roger was surprised to realize that he was simply praying for the man to survive.

Suddenly, for a moment, the desperate fugitive turned to look back. For the first time Hamu was looking at the two men pursuing him. He stared, for a moment with his eyes opened wide in shock. What he saw was impossible. Suddenly, he was looking at the pilot he had sent to his death on that bomb loaded plane. He's alive? He must have made a forced landing. That's how the big bomb pack got here.

Then, the man working his way, hand over hand on the cables, focused on the white hair of a man on the fishing platform. Hamu's own likeness was standing there. Impossible. Hamu was telling himself that man standing there couldn't possibly be standing there. That man was killed when the Gaza City guest house was blown to pieces. He's dead. I've been using his passport. I'm working with his widow. It has to be his ghost? Hamu continued staring.

Then their eyes met. Hamu was shocked. It was Fouad. The impostor's white brows arched and his mouth open in amazement. It's Fouad. It really is Fouad. He was staring at the man whose murder he had arranged. It can' be. Fouad was cremated. His ashes were scattered in Gaza City. Hamu kept looking. But it is Fouad. The dead man is alive.

Hamu quickly turned to continue his efforts to cross the cable. The cables, now farther out over the cataract, had sagged lower under Hamu's weight. With the increasing sway of the cables the physical challenge of maintaining his hold on the cables was increasing.

Hamu's fear of the explosion was now being replaced by the threat of the powerful churning white water of Hell's Gate, a few feet now below him. Now that he was farther out over the raging waters. Hamu was finding that, with his weight, the slack cables were swinging closer to the raging cataract. The wet rusty cables out here were becoming increasingly hard to grasp and hold. Even more difficult was keeping his feet on the lower cable. This was especially the case for his left foot. With the prosthetic devise there was no feeling.

As he glanced back, Hamu could see, in the anxiety of the faces of the men on the fishermen's platform.

Now, as he pressed on, Hamu's weight on the slack cables was bringing him down closer to the powerful churning and swirling water of the cataract. The powerful churning waves of the cataract seemed anxious to swallow the man on the swaying cables.

iii

As the men on the fishermen's platform watched the man out on the sagging and swinging cables, suddenly, with a loud crashing sound, the rusty gear devise that maintains the tension on the lower cable gave way. The lower cable lost more tension. As people saw the cable sag and drop closer to the churning water, you could hear groans of dismay from the spectator passengers.

The immediate result of the cable going slack was disastrous. As the cable under his feet lost more of its tension, Hamu's feet immediately lost contact with the cable. With his feet no longer in touch with the cable, suddenly Hamu was hanging from the upper cable by his hands. He was dangling helplessly.

Fouad moved quickly. He grabbed the handle of the cranking devise and attempted to crank in the slack of the lower cable. The mechanism was frozen in rust. Fouad was unable to get the lower cable's rusty cranking devise working. It kept resisting all is his efforts to free up the gears. Then Fouad spotted a heavy wrench lying nearby. Using this tool to pound and loosen up the devise, he finally succeeded in breaking free the mechanism. He began turning the large cranking devise. The gears were turning. Soon he saw tension was returning to the cable.

Hamu saw the lower cable beginning to recover tension. He looked back toward the platform. He saw the man whose ashes were supposed to have been scattered in Gaza City working the crank. He had trouble believing what he was seeing. There was the man whose death he had planned as the perfect crime back in Gaza City. Now, that man was trying desperately to save Hamu's life, by working like mad to restore the cable's tension. Hamu, swinging just a few feet above the churning waves of Hell's Gate, watched Fouad's efforts. As Fouad looked out to see the extent of recovery their eyes met. Neither could believe what was happening. For both of them it was an incredible moment. Fouad later said that he could feel a great power present in that moment.

Slowly the cable began to pull taunt again. Although the lower cable was now within reach of his feet, Hamu was unable to get his feet to rest on the lower cable again. He was still hanging simply by his hands swinging over the churning water. He needed help, fast.

Roger had been waiting for Fouad to restore tension to the cable. When suitable tension appeared to be restored, Roger moved out on the cables. Sliding his feet on the lower cable and moving carefully, hand over hand on the upper cable, Roger slowly worked his way out toward the desperate man. Roger continued walking his hands along the upper cable. He was soon drenched with the wind driven spray of the cataract. With Fouad working to maintain the increased tension, Roger continued moving out further on the cables. Carefully he moved his feet along the lower cable while inching his hands on the upper cable.

Suddenly one of Roger's feet slipped from the lower cable. He was almost in the same predicament as the fugitive, Hamu, hanging out there from the upper cable by his hands. Fouad quickly jammed his big wrench into the cranking devise to lock the cable in place and hurried out on the cable to help Roger.

When Fouad reached Roger, holding on with one hand, Fouad was able to reach down with his other hand, grab Roger's wet clothing and pull Roger's leg back so that his foot rested on the lower cable.

While Fouad worked his way back to the gear box to maintain cable tension, Roger resumed moving along the cables again. Roger continued his effort to reach the helpless man hanging on with his remaining strength, swinging from the upper cable

Roger saw that this man hanging by his hands could not last much longer. He moved out on the cables as fast as possible.

Roger was aware of a very natural response to the situation. He found that he was praying for the man out there. "Lord Jesus, help this man hang on. Give new strength to his hands. Help me get to him in time." Roger continued his own very careful movement out on the cables. It was a slow inch by inch careful process. Finally he was next to the desperate man swinging from the cable on which he still hung on for life.

With both of them struggling to survive out there their eyes met! It was not the eyes of a long term murderous foe and his intended victim. It was simply man to man.

Then Roger saw the heart of the problem. Hamu could not move his left leg, the leg with the prosthesis, back on the now tightened cable.

Roger continued moving closer to this man holding on to the wet cable and swinging above the raging cataract. One slip of either a hand or a foot and he would be gone.

Inch by inch Roger moved toward the struggling man. Suddenly he had made it. Then, locking his left hand on the upper cable, Roger lowered himself as far as he could and reaching out was able to reach out and grab the clothing of the leg that was swinging wildly. He pulled this leg with the artificial foot toward him. Then, with a tremendous effort on his part and with a matching effort by the fugitive, Roger swung the leg with the prosthetic devise back on the cable. This gave Hamu sufficient leverage to restore his other foot to the cable.

The look of desperation became a look of amazement. Their eyes met for a moment as they exchanged the smile of victory. For both of them It was a we did it moment!

Roger, still concerned with getting back to safety himself, looked at the man who had ordered his death on Bobcat. He looked into the eyes of the man who had loaded his plane with a bomb that was to detonate and kill him as the pilot. They stood for a moment face to face. Hamu freed one hand from the cable briefly and brought his hand up for a quick salute.

In the midst of the roaring thunder of Hell's Gate, Roger returned the gesture.

Breathing heavily Hamu turned to look back through the mist and over the churning water toward Fouad, now back on the fishing platform. Hamu looked back toward the man whose death he had planned so carefully. They faced each other for a moment. Their eyes met. The men nodded to each other. Once again Hamu made the gesture of a quick salute

Then Hamu turned and faced Roger for a moment. With the thundering roar of the cataract it was impossible to say anything. For a moment the two men stood there face to face on the swinging cables.

Hamu, with his white hair blowing in the wind, faced Roger. Speech was impossible. He nodded slowly. Then, the fleeing impostor turned and continued his desperate journey on the cables swaying above the waters of Hell's Gate.

Roger retreated to join Fouad on the platform. Together they watched the man they had rescued continue his precarious journey on the wet and slippery cables swaying in the wind. Finally, the man was completely across Hells Gate. Roger and Fouad watched the fugitive finally step off on the fishing platform on the other side.

The fleeing man turned and looked back for a moment. Then the man vanished in the brush along the stream that flowed into the cataract at that point.

As they watched the figure disappear on the other side, Roger spoke softly to Fouad. "We are seeing something very real here."

Fouad turned to Roger. "Yes, something has happened here today. Something real. Something real has taken place. We have experienced the power of something greater than the hatred of men."

Roger spoke. "We saw something here today you seldom get to see?" Roger spoke softly to Fouad. "Something very real happened here today. Yes, we saw something new and different here today?"

What was it?" Fouad asked.

"We are seeing something greater than the hatred of men. Unconditional love, the same love with which God loved us in the Savior."

CHAPTER 57

Gold rush country, British Columbia

"There's gold in them thar hills."
– Mark Twain, 1895

As they turned away from watching Hamu vanish into the brush on the other side of the cataract, Roger and Fouad were glad to find that they had been joined by Bill Webber and his undercover officers.

Webber embraced Roger and Fouad. "I'm sure grateful to see both of you back on terra firma. That was a power filled happening out there over the waters of Hell's Gate. We saw a very different sort of power at work today. There was obviously someone else out there with all three of you. There was an invisible presence with you on those cables."

After he had introduced the officers that he had brought along with him, Webber said, "Roger, you really did draw the snake out of his hole. Your bad guy has been clearly identified. It should be only a short while until we track him down.

"I have called for additional officers to be sent up from Kamloops. My director should arrive with our explosives expert and some other men, shortly by helicopter. Other officers will arrive on the special work train coming from Kamloops."

Roger said, "I'm sure glad that you decided to travel with us, Bill. We had no idea that things would develop as they have."

Webber said, "Roger, we have some urgent concerns. Our first priority is to locate the very dangerous bomb reported to be on the train. We need to locate and remove, as quickly as possible, whatever explosive devise he brought on board. The team, on its way, will include men especially skilled in dealing with explosive devises. Our expert in defusing bombs should arrive shortly by helicopter. We have to locate and remove the devise before the train can start moving again. Any information that might help us will be appreciated.

"Then there is the need to locate the large amounts of stolen cash that may be on board. Dr. Weiss put us in touch with the teenage boys who picked up the conversation in Arabic about large amounts of cash on this train. We need to locate quickly any such cash.

"And then a third area of concern. It appears this man was not on this train alone. While we are here in this isolated area we need to identify individuals on the train who were working with him."

Roger told his friend, "Find Macintosh, the man in the baggage car. He was captive to working with them. He's the man who saved our lives. Macintosh knows everything. Macintosh can identify other men on board who are working with this man. Macintosh will know the location of the bomb and the location of any cash on board." Roger laughed. "Yes, get Macintosh, Scarface Macintosh, to help you."

Webber said, "We also have men who will work on tracking down the fugitive. I saw that this man was moving with difficulty. He won't be able to go too far in this country. We should be able to track him down shortly."

"Thanks for being with us Bill. We all really appreciate your back up on the train."

When Albert and Sarah Weiss made their way to the fishing platform, Albert embraced Roger, "I am glad to see you in one piece, Roger. I was worried about you and my Geiger." Albert laughed. "Of course more about you than the Geiger. By the way where is it?"

Roger said, "Albert, your Geiger worked great, in fact so much so that it lead me right into trouble. Your gadget helped me make contact with the lead man. Webber's men should help you find it."

Roger introduced Fouad to Albert and Sarah. "Fouad was that unknown person who intervened several times to foil and Hamu's efforts. I would not be standing here today without the help of this man."

Albert grabbed hold of Fouad and said, "Wunderbar. We call men like you the salt of the earth."

Emily and Joan with Hank joined them. Emily stood still for a moment and just looked at Roger. With tears really flowing, she wrapped her arms around Roger. They held each other for a few moments.

Emily stepped back and said, "This was quite a day for rescue operations. We saw you two men saving your deadly enemy. We were holding our breath. It was quite a relief when you made it back to that fishing platform."

Emily said, "Roger, I have a question. Something very important to me. It's about Macintosh. He has been the custodian of our family's cabin for years. Now, he has been working on this train. What have you learned about our Macintosh? What's the story with Macintosh? Is he a good guy or a bad guy?"

Roger smiled, "Well my suspicions were not that far off the beam. When Fouad and I were taken prisoner on the train, we suddenly found that we were being kept prisoner in the baggage car and under the watchful eye of Macintosh."

Emil gasped."Macintosh was working with them?"

Roger said "Yes, but fortunately with greater purpose. He was looking for a way to safely break away from them. By working with them on the train, Macintosh was in a position to help us. We discovered that he wanted to be free of this gang as much as we.

"By the time Macintosh realized the kind of organization for which he was working he was trapped. He wanted to get free from his involvement but he had to be careful. He realized that they would never allow him to go free. When we, as prisoners, were put under his supervision we learned that he wanted to get away from them as much as we did."

Emily insisted, "I need to know. Was he was that man called Mac who was ordered to eliminate you? Was Macintosh the Mac who fired that shot to kill you on Bobcat lake?"

Roger said, "Brace yourself, Emily. Yes, it was your man Macintosh who fired that shot as ordered on Bobcat Lake. When we were taken prisoner on the train, Fouad and I were placed under his care, I asked him, "Did you shoot to miss or did you miss?" I was quite moved when he said to me, 'I shot to miss.' "

Emily was in tears. "He shot to miss?"

"Yes. Macintosh fired that shot deliberately to miss. It was an act of great courage as well as marksmanship. He had to keep up appearances. If he didn't carry out the order they would suspect his loyalty and possibly shoot him. Macintosh obeyed the order to shoot me because he knew that he alone could satisfy the order in such a way as to keep me alive. He obeyed that order to keep them from directing someone else to carrying out that command and execute me. That shot by Mac was aimed to save both himself and me."

Emily said, "Wonderful."

Roger continued the explanation. "But there was more involved. To mislead this gang and make it appear that their prisoner was killed, the police gave a press release that reported that one of their officers had been shot and killed at Bobcat that day. Since Mac never saw clearly who I was, all this time he has been burdened by believing that his careful shot to miss had killed the captive officer. When we were taken prisoner on the train. Mac was as glad to learn that I was that man he shot to miss and that his shot to miss had missed."

Hank asked, "Roger, how did you and Fouad escaped alive from this train?"

"Once again, Macintosh, came to our rescue. Scarface Macintosh, as they called him, was our guard in the baggage car. Since it is pretty hard to hold prisoners on a train and even more difficult to conceal bodies very long, they developed a plan to dump our bodies from the train. "

Joan said, "Hurry up Roger. Tell us what happened."

"Macintosh was directed to give us knock out drops and put each of our bodies in a large shipping bags. A great tunnel was coming up shortly. The plan was that, as the train was passing through the darkness of that long tunnel, two of Hamu's men were to heave the two bags containing our bodies out the side door of baggage. They figured that the grizzly bears would soon make our bodies disappear."

Joan said, "How did you escape?"

"Macintosh saved us. At great risk for himself. Macintosh helped us fill the bags in a way to make each bag look and feel like it contained one of our bodies. He hid us in a closet. When two men came to swing each bag through the side door of the baggage car we weren't in the bags, thanks to Macintosh."

Emily was in tears. "Roger, I've known Macintosh most of my life. You can't imagine what this story means to me. He is the Mac we have always known. He risked his life to save you. First with the shot to miss. Then to save you, along with Fouad, from the death toss. He saved you twice."

Hank interrupted, "Good thing Roger. Tough guys like you would have given those grizzlies indigestion."

Joan asked, "But what has happened to the man that caused all these problems? Where is the man the two of you saved over Hell's Gate, the man we saw finally make it across over Hell's Gate?"

Fouad smiled, "Good question."

ii

Once his feet landed firmly on the other side of the Hell's Gate, Hamu turned and looked back across the powerfully raging cataract. He peered through the spray and mist and saw the cables swaying just a few beet above of the deadly roaring white water. Did I come through that? This must be what they call a miracle?

As he looked back through the spray and mist Hamu saw the men on the other side. They appeared to see him. He turned and moved quickly behind nearby rocks and brush to get out of sight.

Concealed now by the brush Hamu looked back again at the distant figures on the fishing platform. As he looked across the roaring water and saw the men on the other side he considered what it took to bring him to where he was standing. He was thunderstruck. Those two men, both of them men that I took steps to kill, knowing who I was, acted to save me from certain death. They not only saved my life but risked their own lives to do it. They risked their lives to save this man. Amazing.

Suddenly, Hamu remembered something that happened the day following the symposium back in Toronto. It was a Sunday. A man from the university in Vancouver, taken in by his impersonation of Fouad, thinking he was Fouad, invited him to go to church with him. Hamu remember the strange words he saw painted on the wall of that church. Words he remember because at the time he thought they were crazy.

That day, Hamu saw on the church wall, the words, "Greater love has no one than this, that a man should lay down his life for another." Today, two men, men I ordered killed, came out of nowhere. They put their lives on the line for me. They knew who I was and they saved my life. That's what it was, that greater love.

From his hiding place Hamu watched what was happening on the other side. He saw some men. They were moving around like officers.

Those officers mean that a search party will soon be organized. Fortunately for me there is no nearby bridge. That will delay the search party. When they locate a bridge to get over here they are going to do everything they can to find me. I've got to get going and discover a way to fool that search party. I did not cross Hell's Gate to wind up in a prison cell. He headed up the ravine carved by a stream flowing in to Hell's Gate. He passed a sign indicating that the stream was called Treasure Creek.

Hamu followed a trail that ran upstream along what he found to be a powerful stream flowing into the North Thompson at Hell's Gate. As he followed the stream he saw old rusted ruins of the Canadian gold rush. He saw remnants of old sluice box devises used to wash the gravel and discover the heavier gold. There were remnants of old cabins.

Hamu began to realize how his efforts out on the cables had completely exhausted him. He was at the end of the rope as far as his energy went. He needed a spot where he could both rest and avoid discovery by the search party that was sure to come after him. Then he found the place he needed. The area where he had stopped along the stream appeared to have been the site of considerable gold mining years ago. There were pieces of old sluice boxes and rusty equipment in the water.

Suddenly he heard something. Hamu recognized the unmistakable sound of a search party. How could they have gotten across Hell's Gate so soon? They must have the help of a helicopter.

Hamu ran up the trail a short distance and then back tracked to a point here he could slide carefully down into the water among some of the old ruins of the gold mining days. He recalled old movie scenes where the fugitive hid under water using a reed for breathing. Hamu grabbed and tested a couple reeds. He heard the voices of the search party. It sounded like three or four men. Great! They do not seem to have search dogs.

Hamu heard the searchers coming closer. Hamu submerged himself in the water in a pool where bushes had grown along some old ruins of the gold rush days. He was able to hold himself under water in this sheltered spot in the stream and use the reed for air. After waiting a reasonable time he finally raised his head to look around. From his place in the water he saw the party moving upstream.

His pursuers appeared to be group of four men. They were heavily armed. He could see that they were professionals. They seemed to go about the job of pursuing him in a very organized manner. From what he could see and hear, these men appeared to have a well thought out plan. They were determined to find their man. They were handicapped by not having dogs

Although the water was very cold, Hamu decided to stay concealed in the water waiting to see what the pursuers would do. If they do not find any more signs of my passage they will be coming back down stream. Finally they were coming back down the trail. Hamu quickly went under water again. He waited a reasonable amount of time and then carefully raised his head to the surface. He saw the pursuing men working their way back down toward the train tracks.

After the pursuers had passed down stream Hamu prepared to get out of the stream. As he moved around in the water, Hamu felt some objects in the water beneath him. They seemed very heavy and difficult to move. The two objects seemed to be connected with some sort of wire. He was curious. The objects were very heavy. With some difficulty he pulled one up and examined what he had found. It appeared to be made of old green glass. It was embossed with an eagle. A wire of some sort was fastened below the ring at the top connected them together. He was curious what he had found. He brought the two heavy flasks up onto the stream's bank.

As he sat there soaking wet and cold, Hamu was quite pleased that he had managed to give the search party the slip. He looked at the two heavy items he had pulled out of the stream. I know what they are. These things are old whisky flasks. Must be something very old and Canadian. Maybe from the days of what they call the gold rush. What in the world could make them so heavy?

Then suddenly the sun broke through on the flasks. There was the answer. The two old whisky flasks were packed solid with gold nuggets. No wonder they're so heavy. Men probably died to accumulate this treasure. If I can hang them over my shoulder they're going with me.

Hamu sat there, reviewing what he had come through and his present situation. It was obvious now that the explosion of the bombs from which he fled never took place. The officers perusing him must have found and disarmed his newest explosive device in his compartment. By now, they will probably have recovered the cash from the Toronto robbery.

Hamu began to take stock of things. Two men worked and risked their lives to save me from waters of Hell's Gate. There were also two prisoners on the train, those two I interviewed with the blindfolds on them.. By some means, could those two with the blindfold have escaped? Could they be the men who came out on the cables to save me? I'll have to find out if they're the same two men. They talked of life beyond this life. If what those men believed is true, if there really is life beyond this life, they certainly saved me from more than the Hell's Gate cataract.

Hamu was considering his situation. I'm alive. My life has been given back to me. But who am I? Interpol is convinced that the man Hamu died in that Israeli air raid in Gaza City. As far as they are concerned Hamu is dead. My days impersonating Professor Fouad are over. The professor is alive. I can't go on as the professor. This impersonator needs to become someone else. He paused in his thinking of the men who saved him. Then something hit him. Yes, perhaps a new and different person.

Hamu knew that going up this stream offered no escape possibilities. In these mountains, like the train manager said, there are no settlements, no roads, and no people. The only way in or out of these mountains is the train.

Then he recalled one of the announcements. The conductor had informed the passengers that they might get to see the East bound train slow down on the opposite side for its passengers to view the great cataract. Hamu was now on the side of the East bound trains. He decided that the East bound train was going to become his escape route. He would head back down to the East bound tracks and stay out of sight near the tracks. When that east bound train slowed down for passengers to view the Hell's Gate cataract, he would swing up on board. He could tell the conductor that he got separated from a hunting party.

After he had carefully worked his way back to the area where the east bound train would slow down for Hell's Gate, Hamu looked for a way to concealed himself as he waited for the East bound train.

As Hamu huddled in his hiding place, waiting for the East bound Canadian, he saw in his mind's eye again Fouad who saved the day by restoring tension to that lower cable. . That was Fouad. How in the world did he escape with his life from Gaza City?

From all the reports the perfect crime was moving along perfectly. Since his death was seen as the work of Israeli bombs there was no investigation. The perfect crime ran well except for one thing. The murdered man is still very much alive. Rachti reported everything was going as planned. At every step Rachti and everyone else was under the surveillance of others. How could Fouad have been blown to pieces and still be here at Hell's Gate. He was here to make sure I didn't fall into Hell's Gate. He pulled me out of the jaws of death.

Hamu had another question in his mind. If he survived my murder plot and got his passport replaced and returned here to Canada, how is it that his wife did not know he was alive? When I told her that Fouad had died, she showed no signs of knowing he was alive.

That suggests Fouad had returned to Canada only recently. Having known all the inner workings of Two Vipers what has he been doing? I had been looking for a mole betraying inside secrets of our work. Could the professor have been my annoying undercover agent?

That gives me another puzzle. How did that man, Roger Renoir, escaped the shooting on Bobcat Lake? And how did he escaped being blown to pieces on that plane? And how did those two men avoid being fed to the bears in the great tunnel? And then how did they wind up here at Hell's Gate to save my life?

Hamu examined the two old green flask crammed with gold nuggets. Hamu looked at the treasure in his hand and laughed. He thought of those suitcases of cash left back on the train. I left all that Canadian cash from the Toronto robbery back there on that train. Now I am holding the treasure of a gold miner of more than a century ago. They say, you can't take it with you. This gold miner obviously didn't. But I'm taking these two flasks with me.

Hamu arranged the heavy whisky flasks so they hung on each side under his jacket. This stuff is heavy. He recalled learning in school that a cubic inch of gold weighs about twelve ounces. No one runs anywhere with a large amount of gold. Weighted down with the two bottles, hung over his shoulders, Hamu said to himself, "If I want to get out of here this is all I can carry." He headed back down toward the tracks. He planned to conceal himself in some brush near the tracks as he waited for the East bound train..

After waiting in his hiding place for several hours, he finally heard the whistle that had to be the East bound train. When it came into sight. Hamu watched the East bound train as it slowed down to almost a walk for passengers to view the great Hell's Gate cataract. Then, doing the best he could with his prosthetic, Hamu ran along the slow moving east bound train. As he got moving about the same speed as the train, Hamu grabbed a hand rail and swung up on the train.

Hamu was relieved that the crew of the East bound train had heard only of the avalanche that had stopped the West bound train. They gave no sign that they had been informed to look for any fugitive. They were amazed and anxious to hear how it happened that they were picking up this isolated man in the middle of nowhere. He explained his predicament to the conductor and others as planned. He told them that he had been out hunting with friends. He explained his horse had been injured and that he had to put down the horse. He told them that the others had pressed on but he, with no horse, had to take the train and head out to Jasper.

As he rode along on the train, Hamu found himself reviewing what had been taking place in his life as the impostor. He was pondering his experiences posing as the Professor.

I cannot go back to being that person known as Hamu. Hamu died back in Gaza City. That is well established with Interpol and the media. I'm now out of business as an impersonator of Professor Fouad. Professor Fouad is alive and he is returning to Vancouver. What lies ahead for me?

He recalled how he had gone along with that invitation to go to the church service in Toronto. A song sung that morning had stayed with him as an impersonator. "Be a new and different person." At the time he had disliked the song. Now, he was thinking, that sort of describes what I need to be doing.

That song says, "Be a new and different person." Those men who saved me were a new and different sort. Maybe after I shave off this beard I can set out to be a new and different person.

iii

Shortly after all Hamu's escape across the cataract on the cables, the work crew from Kamloops arrived. When the crew had removed the debris and checked out the track, engineer Bill

Hoover, gave three strong blasts on the train's whistle to call everyone back to the train.

Fred and Mary declined the invitation to ride out on the train. "No, we have to go back and get that wonderful horse we left by the ford and walk her back up to the cabin.

Emily said, "You have all the details about our get together in Vancouver. We will be looking for you at our celebration in Vancouver. It won't be complete without you. In fact it wouldn't even be happening without you."

The reunited team and their friends were soon gathered in the dining car of the train for the journey on to Vancouver. Hank was telling Fouad, "I 'm looking forward to meeting this special lady behind the scene, your wife Vashti."

Roger said, "Fouad, we wish we could meet the friends that saved your life in Gaza City. While that murder plot appeared to be a perfect crime, those dear friends managed to pull the rug out from under that scheme. I want to hear how they did it. We would all love to meet them.

CHAPTER 58

Vancouver, British Columbia

"Never was so much owed by so many to so few,"
– Winston Churchill - 1940

After seeing the fugitive disappear on the other side of the churning Hell's Gate cataract, the two officers Bill Webber had brought with him on the train concentrated on what they could do until reinforcements arrived with the work crew from Kamloops.

Following Roger's suggestion the officers contacted Macintosh. With his aid they recovered the cash from the great August Toronto robbery that had been concealed as pre-checked baggage.

When the police explosive experts arrived, they finally located and deactivated the powerful explosive device on board. It had been concealed as part of the baggage taken on board at Sudbury by a couple posing as newlyweds.

After the work crew had cleared away the debris and checked the alignment of the track, the engineer gave his three blasts to indicate that the train was ready to resume its journey. As word spread about the deadly power of the bomb that had been on board since Sudbury, it was a rather subdued body of passengers that continued their spectacular journey. That evening, in the luxurious accommodations and the dining cars, conversation was rather subdued.

After all that they had witnessed at K190, the passengers were greatly relieved to stop for the night in Kamloops. After their overnight stop in Kamloops, the passengers were able to enjoy the spectacular mountain scenery of the trip's last day and their final arrival in spectacular Vancouver.

The morning after their arrival in Vancouver, the four members of the team and all those involved in the events at Hell's Gate, were involved in extensive interviews with both rail and provincial officers.

When Fred and Mary Christiansen told their full story to the authorities, both rail and provincial officials thanked them for their courageous service. The officials assured them that the mountain avalanche that stopped the train would be officially reported as an act of nature.

At the end of their long morning with the authoirities, the four members of the team and several of their friends were able to sit down together for lunch. Their primary concern was to plan a special dinner celebration the following evening. They wanted to get together with all those who had shared in the things they had just come through.

Joan said, "We need to get together while everyone is still here in Vancouver.

Emily agreed. "Yes. We were not alone in all these happenings. It will be great to celebrate with all those who were used to help us prevail in all these events."

Emily paused. Then, gripping the hands of those next to her, she said, "We prevailed. The enemy did not prevail. I like that word prevail. After our experience at Hell's Gate, the word prevail reminds me of that great promise of Jesus. Jesus promised, 'The gates of hell shall not prevail against you. That's what Jesus promised."

Joan said, "Yes, and you Fouad, you are one of the reasons the forces set against us did not prevail. Fouad, we've been hearing about your wonderful wife, Vashti. We want both you at this celebration."

Fouad smiled, "Yes, Vashti and I will enjoy being with you. However, to really learn how I survived the perfect crime you need to meet two special people from Gaza City, our dear friends, Rachti ad Tala."

Hank said, "If only we could bring Rachti and Tala here to Vancouver?"

Fouad said "That won't be necessary. They are living quietly and privately here in Vancouver. I brought them here from Gaza City because their lives back in Gaza City might be in danger when it became known that I was still alive. I brought them here for their own safety. To appreciate how God provided for all of us, you have to hear their story. They have quite a story."

Emily and Joan nodded. Emily said, "Professor Fouad. Please invite Rachti and Tala to share in this special occasion as our guests. We can't wait to hear their story."

Roger said, "Another special couple, Fred and Mary Christianson, made our get together possible. They rescued this parachuter. They gave me a hiding place. They not only developed the plan to stop the train and draw the snake out of his hole. When they learned what was happening they took action. Realizing that a powerful bomb was on the train, they made the decision to activate the plan to stop the train. They successfully stopped the great train at Hell's Gate. They saved many lives by putting the plan into action. Fred and Mary will be coming in to Vancouver by train."

Joan said, "Also Albert and Sarah Weiss."

"Roger agreed. "Albert was the first among us on the train to put things together and conclude that Mr. Dark Heart was on the train."

Emily said, "Yes, and Barbara. Our waitress from Graf Zeppelin days took two teenage boy seriously. She brought them to Roger and Albert. They gave us the first sign that the cash from the great Toronto Rush Hour Robbery was on our train."

Hank said, "I believe those two hi-tech teenagers could be with us. Barbara said that their families will be here in Vancouver for a few days."

Roger said, "I talked with my fellow watercolorist, Bill Webber. He will be with us. Bill is a lot more than a watercolorist."

"There's one more very special person," Emily said. "My family's long term caretaker at Bobcat Lake, Macintosh. I'll make sure Macintosh joins us. At great risk to himself, he repeatedly put himself on the line for us."

Roger added. "Yes, Scarface Macintosh, the man who aimed to miss. Fouad and I would not be here planning this celebration had it not been for Mac's intervention."

Wow, what a party" Hank said. "I hope the food is as great as the company."

ii

That evening on their floating hotel in Vancouver harbor, the mission flight team came together to enjoy a wonderful celebration with their circle of new friends. They were all enjoying the presence of the various persons who had shared in making such an evening possible. As they sat at table together everyone enjoyed the unique bond among those present.

Roger spoke to those around the tables, "When the four of us, Joan, Hank, Emily and I, planned, back in Nairobi, a transcontinental train trip together, we never anticipated that it would wind up with an evening like this, with so many wonderful new friends.

"Our special new friend, Professor Fouad, wants to speak to us."

Fouad rose to speak. "I want first to present to you my wonderful wife Vashti who, behind the scene, was constantly involved and in prayer for us."

Those present around the table gave Vashti a strong welcoming applause.

Fouad continued, "Vashti and I have two special guests to present to you. However, first I need to make sure that all of realize where this journey we experienced together began.

"This ordeal we have been through began when Hamu, the leader of the Two Viper Brotherhood in Gaza City, discovered the remarkable similarity in appearance between me, this Professor Fouad, and himself. Some said you would need finger prints to tell us apart.

"Hamu was amazed when he saw a recent picture of me. He was stunned with our likeness. Then his wheels started turning. Hamu came up with the idea of arranging my death and making my death look like his death. He planned to use the similarity in our appearances, to escape his life as a fugitive from international police. With the death of Fouad, Hamu planned to escape further pursuit by international police. Hamu would take Fouad's passport and escape to Canada.

Mr. Dark Heart, as some of you called him, planned the perfect crime to kill me, have the body recognized as Fouad's. He would them impersonate me, Fouad. It seemed the perfect scheme to escape further pursuit by Interpol and Israel's famous Mossad.

"There was one problem. This man, his look alike Fouad, was no longer in Cairo. I was on the faculty here in Vancouver, 6,000 miles from the Middle East and Gaza City. He had to find a way to draw me back to Cairo and the Middle East.

"The plot began when I received a very flattering letter of invitation to be a guest lecturer at my university back in Cairo. Actually it was a death letter. It was the first part of the plot to lure me back in Cairo and Gaza City.

I was to be wiped out while visiting Gaza City. Then, impersonating me and using my passport and ticket, Hamu would fly to Toronto and take over the leadership of Two Vipers in Canada.

"Who says women don't have special intuition. Vashti was suspicious. Over Vashti's worries, I accepted the invitation to be a guest lecturer in Cairo.

"Following my lectures in Cairo, while I was being driven to Gaza City, rockets were being fired from Gaza City into Israel to provoke a retaliatory attack that night. The plan was that, during the certain to come Israeli retaliatory bombing air attack that night, the guest house in which I was sleeping would be blown up with explosives that resembled an Israeli bomb. It would appear to be death through an Israeli bombing. There would be no investigation. My murder was set to be the perfect crime.

"But God intervened. Who says God is not at work in our world today? Two people conspired, at great personal risk, to undermine this perfect crime. Please welcome Rachti and his wife, Tala. I owe my life to these dear friends."

iii

Following enthusiastic applause, Rachti began their story. "From the very start of the murder plot, Hamu needed me. He needed someone like me to drive Fouad, after the Cairo lectures, to Gaza City. Why? He knew that Fouad would trust me. My wife, Tala, and I had grown up in and gone to school in Cairo with Fouad and Vashti. When I was dragged into the plot, I was told that I had no choice. Any failure would be paid for with both our lives.

"So, while in Cairo lecturing, Fouad was invited to Gaza City to meet old associates of the Two Viper movement. To remove any reservations about going to Gaza City, Fouad was told that his old friend, Rachti, would chauffeur him from Cairo to Gaza City."

Rachti said, "I had no choice but to drive Fouad to his death. At the same time I was frantically trying to come up with a counter plot of my own. It was a challenge. I had to not only find a way to foil the plot but to do so without Hamu, the master plotter, knowing. If I failed both Tala and I would die. Hamu had to go on thinking that his murder scheme was working?"

Emily spoke up, "You had a really impossible task."

Rachti said, "That's an understatement. While we were driving from Cairo to Gaza City another part of the murder plot was already in progress. Fouad and I heard the news as we drove along. Powerful rockets were being fired from Gaza City against the Israelis. This was being done to provoke a sure retaliation bombing attack on Gaza City that night. To provoke an Israeli retaliation attack that night was an essential part of the plot. The anticipated bombing attack was needed to cover up the explosion of the bombs planted in the guest house to kill Fouad."

Rachti continued his account. "It was a fast moving plot. What could be done in so little time? It seemed impossible. I needed a lot of help.

"As soon as I had delivered Fouad to the sham reception dinner, I took off to activate my counter plot. I hurried home to spell out to Tala, what we had to do. I'll let her tell her part."

Tala rose to continue the story. She was in a beautiful traditional Egyptian dress and very pleased to be part of the occasion.

Tala told her story as she experienced it. "As soon as he arrived home, Rachti told me flat out that we faced a life or death situation. Rachti explained to me the scheme to kill Fouad with explosives during the provoked Israeli air raid. I was in shock. I couldn't believe that my husband, even to save our lives, had agreed to work with others to bring about the death of our dear friend, Fouad."

Rachti added his description. "I told Tala that we had to act fast. We had to go immediately to the guest house and draw Fouad out of his assigned quarters, which were loaded with Israeli type explosives. In a few hours, during the Israeli raid, Hamu's men would detonate the bomb where Fouad was sleeping."

"To prevent Fouad's death, the first task for Tala and myself was to draw the professor out of the guest house for a brief visit to our home. We had to get him to our home before the Israeli bombing began."

Tala resumed her account. "Yes. And once we got him there we needed a plan to keep him really hidden in our home. His only chance to survive this plot was for Fouad to really disappear from life on this planet. I was concerned. Where could we be sure to conceal him from neighbors or others who came to call?"

Rachti said, "I reminded Tala of a recent carpentry job in our home and how she had said that the room seemed smaller. It was smaller but I had never told her why. Now, I told her what I had done. I told her I had constructed a hiding place.

"I reminded Tala how some Christian friends had shown us the movie about the Dutch woman, Corrie Ten Boom. The film told how the Dutch Ten Boom family hid Jews fleeing from the Nazis? I reminded her that the Ten Booms had constructed a special concealed small space behind a linen closet. It was called the hiding place. This Christian Ten Boom family, at great risk, hid Jews from Hitler's Gestapo in that narrow hiding place behind a false wall."

Tala remembered the movie. She had been impressed how the Ten Boom family concealed Jews fleeing Hitler."

Rachti said, "I told her how I had thought of all the hatred and killing swirling around us in the Middle East. Millions fleeing for their lives. I thought we might need such a hiding place someday."

Tala said "Yes, and I asked Rachti if he had built a hiding place behind a false wall behind the linen closet in our house?'

Rachti said, "I told Tala that God put it into my head to build such a hiding place for His people in our home. These days, in our part of the world, people who live with an obedience to a higher voice than the ruling power sometimes need a hiding place. When we came to know Jesus we became very definitely a minority like the Ten Booms under the Nazis."

Tala interrupted. "When he told me about this hiding place, I wasn't very surprised. It sounded just like Rachti."

Rachti continued, "When Tala and I discovered the meaning of faith in Jesus, I found that I didn't just believe in God. Anyone can say that. Even the devil believes in God. I came to realize that Jesus had a special purpose for my life. I felt that God Himself was telling me to build a secret hiding place in our home."

Tala said," I told him, you never told me, your wife a thing about this. Why didn't you tell me?' "

Rachti said, "There was a reason I didn't tell Tala. I realized that if a hiding place was really needed, the very existence of such a hiding place had to be something that was not even talked about in our home. I decided that I would tell Tala about the hiding place only when it was time for that secret little room to become just that, a hiding place."

Tala added, "We remembered the song they sang that night when they showed us the movie. We sang it together. You are my hiding place. You always fill my heart with songs of deliverance. Whenever I am afraid, I will trust in You, I will trust in You. And that's exactly what we did."

Rachti continued, "To save Fouad meant we had to get Fouad out of that death trap, the guest house, as soon as darkness came. We had to not only bring Fouad to our home. We had to keep him there, like a prisoner, in our hiding place. He could not have the option of going outside of our home."

"Tala had to serve him more than tea. I gave her a small bottle of some powerful knock-out drops from a pharmacist friend. I told Tala to mix a spoonful of this in the tea she served Fouad. Be very sure you don't get a drop of it in your tea or mine'."

Tala laughed. "I said, Rachti, You want me to drug our guest?"

Fouad said, "I told Tala that if our friend, had any notion of what was going on that he would want to fight back. We are going to give him some help to sleep through this time of danger. I also prepared a written note for Fouad to read when he woke up. It said, 'Fouad, you have to disappear and lie low. As far anyone in Gaza City is concerned, you are dead."

Tala continued the story. "We drove quickly to the guest house. When Fouad opened door, we greeted him. Surprise! We have come to invite you to our home for tea. Fouad was delighted to come to our home. As we visited the knockout drug acted quickly. Within a short time, Fouad spoke of feeling very sleepy. Before we knew it Fouad had fallen into a deep sleep."

Rachti continued, "Quickly, we stretched him out on a blanket and moved our friend to the hiding place behind our linen closet and the false wall. There we made Fouad comfortable. I removed his very familiar outer western clothing. I eased off his wedding ring and his university ring from our sleeping friend. We gathered the professor's wallet and personal effects in a bag. I had to take his gold pocket watch and chain. I also removed even the special tortoise shell glasses for which he was known.

"I was hoping that Fouad would forgive me for what I was doing. I was doing this to save his life and ours as well. I took Fouad's ostrich leather brief case, which many had seen at the reception. Also I took along the Professor's very different western shoes. I left some more typical Arab clothing for my drugged friend.

"After we eased him on to a small bed, knowing Fouad would not take all this easily, we fastened handcuffs that were linked by a chain to the bed. I told Tala that our friend would be furious. Be braced for it. Fouad has to stay here until I return. He cannot be allowed to leave this home. It's a matter of life and death, for all three of us."

"I left a letter for the professor. I explained the details of the plot. The murderers had to believe that they had succeeded in killing Fouad. As long as they thought he was dead, he would be safe. He had to remain concealed in our home. I stressed with Tala that keeping Fouad hidden was a matter of life or death for all of us. Under no circumstance could he even think of leaving this house. No one must know that he is alive. Not even his wife, Vashti. . And no one did know."

Roger spoke up. "I have a question, Rachti. When you removed him from the guest house, where in the world were you going to get a body to take his place? You couldn't go out and use just any body. The substitute body had to resemble the professor."

Rachti smiled. "Those words, God provides, are not to be taken lightly. God does provide and he provided for us. It so happened that my good mortician friend, Iben, with whom I shared this counter plot, came up with the answer.

"Iben had the answer. Miraculously, Iben was able to provide a body that could take the place of Fouad's. Iben had been holding for some time in his storage facility an unidentified body from a previous Israeli bombing raid. His efforts to identify the body had failed."

Hank had a question. "But a key part was the unusually close similarity of the two men in appearance. How could this poor man's body fill that need?"

Rachti said, "Good question. I had asked Iben the same question. My friend Iben said there was no problem. He assured me that he had the means to make this man's bearded body resemble that of Fouad. He had the means to make sure that this body would have white hair and white facial hair. He assured me that, after the bombing, when the men saw this battered body in Fouad's western clothing, surrounded with Fouad's personal things, those involved in the plot will see what they expected to see, the bloody broken body of the Professor. When they see that battered body in western clothing they are not going to want to look too long.

Rachti said, "Before I left the house, I gave Tala some strongly worded directions. I told her that Fouad, had to be made to realize that his being concealed was essential for both his and our survival.

Rachti left a note for Fouad. "I had known you, Fouad, for many years. I knew that you, Fouad, would not take such an attack lying down. We had to keep you, Fouad, the man who was supposed to be dead, out of sight."

Rachti continued his story. "Now we come to the critical part of this counter plot. I drove off quickly to the garage of my mortician's friend. Iben took me to his work room to inspect his handiwork. When Iben unzipped the body bag and showed me what he had done. I was amazed. The hair on the dead body had been bleached white as well as facial hair, the beard and mustache. He had even stained the skin to a darker tan to resemble both Fouad and Hamu. For a moment I thought it was your body, Fouad.

"Then, I had a question. I reminded Iben, that this body had been held for some time. Would the men who would recover the battered body expect to see more open wounds and blood on such a newly battered body? Iben told me that he had handled many such severely injured bodies as a mortician. He had the same concern and had taken care of that. He assured me that when this body was hit by the explosion there would appear to be much blood on the body of the victim of the bombing. Iben was confident that the men who would be there with me to recover this body would see it as a recently killed person.

Rachti continued his account of that night. "We dressed the body Iben had prepared in Fouad's clothing. We added personal things like his wedding ring and his university ring and his distinctive glasses. Then we quickly loaded the body, now dressed like Fouad, into my vehicle and headed for the guest house. We hoped most residents would be far from their windows and hunkered down in the most protected places for the anticipated Israeli strike. It was crucial that we could do what we were doing without being seen.

"Our arrival at the guest house was the most dangerous part of this plan. Quickly, we supported the body in Fouad's clothing between us and made as though we were assisting a drunken man to the guest house. Once we were inside we placed the body in the room assigned to Fouad. Sorry Fouad. We had to make use of some of your very personal possessions, your wallet, glasses, and your special ostrich leather brief case. Yes, we put even your rings on this body. Sorry, but it was necessary. Then we got out of there as fast as they could.

"I drove Iben quickly back to his place of business. My work in setting up the substitute look alike body was completed. I went immediately to carry out my assigned task as a participant in the murder plot. I drove quickly to the location where, according to the assassination plan, I was to await the Israeli bombing. You have heard the things that followed when the body was found.

"Tala and I are delighted to share in this occasion. Thank you for bringing us here to share in this wonderful evening together."

CHAPTER 59

Vancouver, British Columbia

"God loves you just the way you are,
but He refuses to leave you that way.
He wants you to be just like Jesus. "
– Max Lucado

After hearing the amazing story told by Rachti and Tala, everyone was enjoying getting to know them, along with Vashti over their desert and after dinner coffee. Some were also talking about the man who came close to carrying out the perfect crime. He seemed to have disappeared after his escape across Hell's Gate. A renewed search for the fugitive in the Hell's Gate area found no traces of the man. Some were all wondering whether he managed to escape by boarding the east bound train.

Roger with a short laugh said, "It would be great to hear from you, Hamu. You're the one person missing this evening."

Fred Christianson shook his head. "It's almost as though he had a helicopter parked on the other side of Hell's Gate. He just seemed to vanish. Mary and I, of course, know that area along Treasure Stream. It is a very rough and barren rocky area. Really, no place to hide. Yet once he took off up Treasure Stream he seemed to just vanish."

Bill Webber agreed. "My friends among the officers would like to know what has happened to him. They couldn't find a trace of the man. They figure that when the East bound train slowed down for Hell's Gate he may have managed to board the East bound. They haven't a clue as to what happened to the man."

ii

As they were visiting around the table, Roger was envisioning those moments out on the cables again. He shared with Emily some of his memory y of those moments out on Hell's Gate Cataract.

Roger said, "I can still see his eyes, out on the cable, as we struggled face to face. Hamu knew that he did not have much time. He was hanging on there in desperation, swinging on that rusty cable. He was kicking wildly, trying to find the lower cable. We were being soaked and freezing in the cold spray of the cataract. He was as close as you can get to losing it all. And he knew it. I could see it in his eyes.

"In the midst of this hopeless situation, the man turned and looked back toward his double, toward Fouad working on those rusty gears to restore tension. The two men, with their masks now discarded, looked like twin brothers facing each other. In that moment their conflict was a thing of the past."

Emily asked Roger, "Now having gone through those moments out there over Hell's Gate Cataract together, how do you feel about the man who was out there on the cables? How do you feel about this deadly enemy now?"

Roger was silent for a few moments and then replied. "It was a rare, one time only, experience, sharing with another man, face to face, such a deadly situation. Hamu was facing imminent death. The end could come any moment, and he knew it. Although this was, of course, the first time we had ever stood face to face, we each knew clearly who the other was. The immediate challenge overshadowed everything. When our eyes met, our past involvement was just that, a thing of the past. The present danger was all that mattered and, without any discussion, Fouad and I were going to save this man..

"You ask me how I feel about him. A good question. In those moments out on the cables, the past was past. In the harsh reality of that moment what mattered was different, very different. We were just men struggling to survive and determined to save the man in danger. We had a different feeling about the man. He had a different attitude toward us. We were three men struggling to stay alive."

Roger paused for a moment. "In our desperate Hell's Gate struggle, out there on the cables, when Fouad joined us, it was just the three of us. We were in it together. It was all very different from my experiences back in Kenya.. Those events seem to have prepared me for that challenge out on the cables."

"What experiences prepared you?" Fouad asked.

On my very first morning back in Kenya, while painting in Nairobi Game Park I found myself looking into the end of a revolver. I was angry. Those characters were interrupting my painting. God was gracious and sent my old friends, the park guards, just in time.

"On our first mission flight back in Kenya we wound up as prisoners of some terrorists who were holding the four of us for ransom. In Africa, people held for ransom are seldom ever seen again. There was no visible way to escape. Then came a soft knock. The door was unlocked by two Kenyan friends. They didn't have visible wings but they were clearly special messengers of the One who is really in charge of life on this planet. At great personal risk, they rescued us.

"Here in Canada, only some weeks ago, I was ordered shot by this man who was out on the cable. The man ordered to do away with me happened, just happened to be both a man whose life was directed by Christ and an expert shot and. The shooter aimed to miss and missed.

"You know the later events, Fouad. I was a prisoner in that Toronto warehouse, facing certain death and you, Fouad, came and set me free.

"I was flying with a plane rigged with a bomb set to destroy me when it exploded over Vancouver. On the way my plane's developed a fatal engine problem that forced me to parachute. The engine dying kept me from flying to the lower altitude where the bomb on board would have exploded. Someone, a person in obedience to the Creator of life had sabotaged my plane to preserve my life.

Then in the train's baggage car, where the two of us were to be bagged and thrown from the train like garbage, a servant of Christ just happened to be there to arrange a way for us to escape with our lives.

Fouad said, "Roger, It looks like the two of us had some similar intervention in our lives. When Rachti and Tala, back at their house, worked together to protect me from the plot to kill me, I sensed how their efforts were directed by the One who gave me this life."

Emily said, "Keep in mind that the man, who was fleeing on the cable has had his life handed to him again. He's no longer the impostor. He's just himself. This man who tried to take the lives of the two of you has had his life suddenly handed back to him. How? By Someone using as His agents the very men he was determined to destroy. I wonder what that Someone is saying to him."

iii

Just then the head waiter came to the table with a phone. "Phone call for Professor Fouad and Vashti, with speaker phone requested.

Fouad took the phone. A strong voice called out, "Professor Fouad? Vashti?"

Vashti and everyone around the table was hearing the call with speaker phone on. Fouad replied, "Yes, Fouad and Vashti here. Who is calling?"

A voice came over the phone, "My contacts told me that you are having a special dinner to celebrate your successful journey past Hell's Gate."

"Yes, who is this calling, please?"

"The other man of those three who survived out over Hell's Gate. This is the man whose life you saved out on those cables. You came out on that cable along with the Roger Renoir. I am calling to express my thankfulness for your saving me at great risk to yourself. Your courageous kindness saved me from Hell's Gate. And not just from the cataract. I mean from hell's gate. You saved a man who deserved hell..

"I plotted to take your life and use our unusual similarity in appearance to impersonate you. I am calling to apologize. I want also to apologize to you, Vashti, and express my regret for plotting to take the life of your husband."

"Fouad replied. "We are pleased to accept you apology."

Vashti added, "Yes, we are grateful you survived for a new day in your life."

"Having had my own life given back to me, I have to say that I am grateful that the perfect crime I planned failed. I ask you who saved my life to accept my thankfulness to you. Also I want to express my thankfulness to that One the two of you serve, who preserved both your lives from my schemes and then gave you the heart to rescue me from Hell's Gate."

"What will you do now?"

"A good question. As you know, I used what they thought was my body, to make it appear to my pursuers that I, Hamu, was dead. I might as well let things stand that way.

"Assuming that you had died, I became your impostor. Now, thanks to you and the one who kept you alive, I, the would be murderer, am alive.

"This calls for some sort of a complete turnaround in my life. You are alive. I can now no longer impersonate you. I will have to find a new ID. I have sent your passport back to front desk where you are celebrating."

Vashti spoke, "We have discovered that our Creator has a great purpose for everyone to whom he gives life. That means that in his love for you, he has protected you, with loving purpose. Become new and different person."

"Thank you, Vashti. I am glad the Professor is back and that you, Vashti, have him back."

"Fouad, Roger, in some way we are all survivors. Like the two of you, I have been given a second chance, the possibility of a new life. If I become a new and different sort of person, I will need a new name.

""Let me talk to Roger Renoir, the other man who risked death to rescue me."

iv

Roger took the phone, "Roger Renoir here."

"This is the man you last saw out over Hell's Gate. I am calling, Roger, to thank you for your courage and kindness. Without hesitation you risked your life to save me. What I experienced out there on the cables spoke to me. I am calling to express my gratitude for your putting everything on the line to save someone like myself. You not only saved my life. You gave me a new sense of the meaning of my own life.

"What you men did is strong evidence for me that this must be, as you put it when you were my prisoners, the visited planet. The rescue that I experienced by the two of you, both men I tried to destroy, had to begin with Someone."

Roger replied, "Thank you for your call. We are glad that you survived Hell's Gate. Both Fouad and I also, both of us, have been given our lives again. We are both interested in doing something more with our lives. We are both praying for something new in your life. Be a new and different person."

"Your giving me a second chance has had a wonderful impact in the life of this man, a man without a country, now a man without a name."

The caller continued, "Your action when you men saved me from Hell's Gate has had a great impact on me. As I was hiding from the search party that came after me I had some time to take stock of things. I was comparing what I dished out for you men and what you dished out for me. I sought to destroy your lives. When I was in great danger, when I was at the end of my rope, you risked your lives, both of you, to save me.

"At Hell's Gate more than a raging river threatened me. It was more than a violent cataract. For me it was hells gate until I experienced your effort to save me.

"When the two of you, both men whose lives I had sought to destroy, saved me from the raging cataract called Hell's Gate, you also saved me from more than certain physical death. You saved me from the very gates of hell itself."

Roger replied. "Thank you for your call Hamu. Fouad and I were both saying that these events have also caused us to examine our lives. May God show you the wonderful purpose the Creator has for your life."

Their caller said, "Roger, signal your head waiter there to bring you a package that was left for you."

Roger called the waiter. "Do you have a package for us?"

The waiter wheeled in a package on a dining room cart.

Hamu's voice called out, "Open the package."

Roger put down the phone to move the small package to their table.. "This is really very heavy for such a small package. What is it, a piece of railroad track?" When he opened the package he found he was holding an old blue glass whisky flask. It seemed to be filled with gravel.

Hamu's voice called out, "Carefully dump out the contents on a napkin!"

Roger spread a napkin and pried out the cork from the flask. He shook the flask so that the contents spilled out. The eyes of around the table stared in amazement at a small mountain of beautiful solid gold nuggets.

Hamu continued. "When I was hiding from the search party I hid in a deep pool of water in Treasure Stream. There under some old ruins of the gold rush days my hands discovered this old whisky flask. It seems unlikely that mid nineteenth century miner will be returning for his treasure. The gold nugget collection is for the two of you. Half of them are for you, Fouad and Vashti. The other half is for you Roger. If you should be so fortunate as to persuade Emily to marry you, you may want to fashion your wedding rings from some of these nuggets."

Roger and Emily's eyes met. Emily laughed, "I think he is trying to encourage you, Roger."

Then the speaker continued, "In the other bag you will find something else."

Roger shook the other bag out over the table. Suddenly a smart phone fell out.

Roger was stunned.

Hank spoke up, "It's his smart phone. It's the one you left with Emily, the phone that was stolen from her apartment."

Hamu continued. "Yes, it's that phone on which I entered addresses for the bombs in key cities. It was the phone I planned to use to trigger explosives. Yes, this is the phone which you found at Bobcat Lake. It probably saved your life at Bobcat Lake. You must have used it to call in the RCMP helicopter, there on Bobcat Lake."

Roger answered, "We suspected that this phone might hold the phone addresses that would enable you to detonate bombs!"

Hamu said, "You figured correctly. This phone did hold key addresses for detonators of bombs already in place. I have erased those entries."

Roger looked toward Hank in amazement.

Hamu continued, "I surrender this phone to let you know that something new has come into my life. Something happened in my life when you and Fouad saw me hanging desperately over Hell's Gate. The two of you knew very well that it was I who tried to kill you. But when you saw me hanging helpless over Hell's Gate you acted to save my life.

Roger looked across to Fouad and replied, "We just did what we do, Hamu!"

"Exactly. That's the point. You did what people like you do!"

"We didn't think twice."

The voice on the phone said, "That's the point, No, you didn't have to. Putting your lives on the line, you saved me from immediate death. What you did struck me with the reality of who you are. Without even thinking about it, you made real to me the fact that the One who directs your lives is real."

"Wonderful"

The caller said, "I remembered your words, what were to be your last words, when I had you at my mercy and blindfolded in the baggage compartment. Remember what you said, Roger?"

"No, not exactly."

You said, "He's alive and he's died your death. He's extending to you the great invitation."

"Yes, I remember now. Yes, the great invitation."

"Well, I want you to know, I'm checking out that great invitation."

CHAPTER 60

The Ngong Hills, Nairobi, Kenya

"I will lift up my eyes to the hills
from whence cometh my help."
– Psalm 121

Shortly after their banquet in Vancouver the four members of mission air team were delighted to receive some especially good news. The gang that had held them captive for ransom had finally been tracked down. The entire self-appointed Kenyan branch of the movement had been convicted of several crimes in Nairobi Game Park. They were then extradited to Ethiopia, where they were also charged with prior crimes.

Word came from Bill Williams, their mission director at Wilson Airport in Nairobi, informing the team of the capture and arrest of the gang that had held them prisoner. Williams informed the team, that with these arrests the Mission Air team could now return safely to Kenya. Mission Air was asking them to return for the remainder of their planned term of service. The threat to them had had been removed. Mission Air was asking the team to return to Nairobi, where they are urgently needed.

When the team in Vancouver learned that it would now be possible for them to return for the remainder of their planned service with Mission Air they were delighted. They immediately made arrangements to return.

Upon their return to Wilson, the team was immediately assigned to make another flight to the Yida refugee camp.

Following their return from their first flight to Yida, Roger and Emily got clearance from Bill for a private flight with one of the planes. They picked up their plane and headed out from Wilson Airport. As they flew over the Ngong Hills, a kiss seemed in order.

Emily said, "That was certainly an improvement over the last time I got an airborne kiss."

Roger explained, "This plane has auto pilot."